KU-021-065

THE SLAP

Christos Tsiolkas is the author of three previous novels: *Loaded* (filmed as *Head-On*), *The Jesus Man* and *Dead Europe,* which won the 2006 *Age* Fiction Prize and the 2006 Melbourne Best Writing Award. *The Slap* won the Commonwealth Writers' Prize 2009, was longlisted for the Man Booker Prize 2010, and was shortlisted for the 2009 Miles Franklin Literary Award and the ALS Gold Medal. Christos Tsiolkas is also a playwright, essayist and screen-writer. He lives in Melbourne.

ALSO BY CHRISTOS TSIOLKAS

Loaded

The Jesus Man

Dead Europe

'Brilliant, beautiful, shockingly lucid and real, this is a novel as big as life built from small, secret, closely observed beats of the human heart. A cool, calm, irresistible masterpiece.' Chris Cleave

'Nothing short of a tour de force. Tsiolkas puts a microscope to family life and presents us with a vision both of unflinching honesty and great tenderness. The luminosity of his prose and the brilliance of his characterisation render the ordinary quite extraordinary.' Colm Toíbín

'Now and again a book comes along that defines a summer. This year that book is *The Slap*, the writing has shades of Martin Amis, Nick Hornby and Anne Tyler... The ideal summer read; escapist, funny and clever.' *Daily Telegraph*, 'Book of the Summer'

'Nothing less than a modern masterpiece' *The Times*

'A genuinely important, edgy, urgent book. The novel keeps readers constantly on their toes, pushing boundaries, questioning lazy assumptions, provoking, and above all, smuggling in unease under the guileful blanket of a gripping read.' Neel Mukherjee, *Sunday Telegraph*

'Riveting from beginning to end. Tsiolkas's real talent is for exploring the inner lives of his eight primary characters... And each of these characters is a sharp observer of those around him or her, so many more lives are illuminated as well. The novel's forward energy is unexpectedly overwhelming.' *Guardian*

'A tremendously vital book in every sense. Completed at a gallop, it fairly crackles along, juiced up with novelistic license and peeled-eyeball candour, the characters driven by their appetites into a thrilling, vital approximation of what it is to be alive.' *Sunday Times*

'This ingenious and passionate book is a wonderful dissection of suburban Australian living, tackling issues of race, class and gender... Tsiolkas writes with a refreshing lack of sentimentality. A beautifully structured and executed examination of the complexity of modern living.' *Independent on Sunday*

'Dazzling' *Independent*

'Tsiolkas is a hard-edged, powerful writer, but glowing at the heart of all the anger among these feuding families are sparks of understanding, resignation and even love... leaving us exhausted but gasping with admiration.' Brigitte Weeks, *Washington Post*

'A layered, briskly paced story about complex people. Think Tom Wolfe meets Philip Roth.' *Los Angeles Times*

'*The Slap* is a strikingly tender book... it claws into you with its freshness and truth.' *Sydney Morning Herald*

'One of the most astute chroniclers and critics of our age and culture. Tsiolkas is a passionate, poetic, political polemicist, but his critiques take the form of enthralling stories that are peopled with characters that bounce off the page and turn up at your local gym, in the backyard pool, down at the shops or around the barbecue on a Sunday afternoon... A clever, elegantly structured novel.' *The Advertiser*

'Christos Tsiolkas's novel bursts out of one reckless act and rackets away into a dense maze of consequences. Like all Tsiolkas' work it is wildly energetic and fearless, thrillingly about our lives now.' Helen Garner, *Independent Weekly*

'Tsiolkas writes about carnality, relationships, and dark emotions with a stomach-punching brutality... *The Slap* promises to provoke controversy.' *Sydney Sun Herald*

'Sprawling, affecting and often wildly comic... Mandatory bedside table reading. It's a perfect social document... More importantly, it's also a hell of a read.' *The Australian*

'*The Slap* is provocative and profane, throbbing with sex, drugs and loud music, and ultimately, despite its ferocity, exultantly life-affirming.' *Adelaide Review*

CHRISTOS TSIOLKAS

THE SLAP

Atlantic Books
London

First published in 2008 in Australia by Allen & Unwin Publishers, 83
Alexander Street, Crows Nest NSW 2065, Australia.

First published in Great Britain in 2010 in trade paperback and hardcover
limited edition by Tuskar Rock Press, in association with Atlantic Books.

This paperback edition published in Great Britain in 2011 by Atlantic Books.

Copyright © Christos Tsiolkas 2008

The moral right of Christos Tsiolkas to be identified as the author
of this work has been asserted by him in accordance with the Copyright,
Designs and Patents Act of 1988.

All rights reserved. No part of this publication may be reproduced,
stored in a retrieval system or transmitted in any form or by any means,
electronic, mechanical, photocopying, recording or otherwise, without
the prior permission of both the copyright owner and the above
publisher of this book.

This novel is entirely a work of fiction. The names, characters and
incidents portrayed in it are the work of the author's imagination and
not to be construed as real. Any resemblance to actual persons, living
or dead, events or localities, is entirely coincidental.

1 3 5 7 9 10 8 6 4 2

A CIP catalogue record for this book is available from the British Library.

Paperback ISBN: 978 1 84887 356 8

TV tie-in ISBN: 978 0 85789 652 0

Printed and bound by CPI Group (UK) Ltd, Croydon, CR0 4YY

Atlantic Books
An Imprint of Atlantic Books Ltd
Ormond House
26–27 Boswell Street
London WC1N 3JZ

www.atlantic-books.co.uk

For Jane Palfreyman, who is *sui generis*

HECTOR

His eyes still shut, a dream dissolving and already impossible to recall, Hector's hand sluggishly reached across the bed. Good. Aish was up. He let out a victorious fart, burying his face deep into the pillow to escape the clammy methane stink. I don't want to sleep in a boy's locker room, Aisha would always complain on the rare, inadvertent moments when he forgot himself in front of her. Through the years he had learned to rein his body in, to allow himself to only let go in solitude; farting and pissing in the shower, burping alone in the car, not washing or brushing his teeth all weekend when she was away at conferences. It was not that his wife was a prude, she just seemed to barely tolerate the smells and expressions of the male body. He himself would have no problem falling asleep in a girl's locker room, surrounded by the moist, heady fragrance of sweet young cunt. Afloat, still half-entrapped in sleep's tender clutch, he twisted onto his back and shifted the sheet off his body. Sweet young cunt. He'd spoken out loud.

Connie.

At the thought of her, sleep surrendered its grip on him. Aish would think him a pervert if she had overheard him. But he was definitely not that. He simply loved women. Young, old, those just starting to blossom and those beginning to fade. And sheepishly, almost embarrassed at his own vanity, he knew that women loved him. Women *loved* him.

Get up, Hector, he said to himself. Time for the routine.

The routine was a series of exercises that he executed without fail every morning. At most, it never lasted more than twenty minutes. Occasionally, if he woke with a headache or hangover, or with a combination of both, or simply with an ennui that seemed to issue from deep within what he could only assume to be his soul, he managed to complete it all in under ten minutes. It was not strict adherence to the routine that mattered but simply ensuring its completion—even when he was sick, he would force himself to do it. He would rise, grab a pair of track-pants, throw on the T-shirt he'd worn the previous day, and then perform a series of nine stretches, each of which he would hold to a count of thirty. Then he would lie on the rug in the bedroom and perform one hundred and fifty sit-ups, and fifty push-ups. He'd finish with a final set of three stretches. Then he'd go to the kitchen and switch on the coffee percolator before walking to the milk bar at the end of the street to buy the newspaper and a packet of cigarettes. Back home, he would pour himself a coffee, walk out onto the back verandah, light a smoke, turn to the sports pages, and begin to read. In that moment, with the newspaper spread before him, the whiff of bitter coffee in his nostrils, the first hit of sharp tobacco smoke, whatever the miseries, petty bullshits, stresses and anxieties of the day before or the day ahead, none of it mattered. In that moment, and if only in that moment, he was happy.

Hector had discovered from childhood that the only way to challenge the inert, suffocating joy of sleep was to barrel right through it, to force open his eyes and jump straight out of the bed. But for once, he lay back on his pillow and allowed the sounds of his family to gently bring him to complete wakefulness. Aisha had the kitchen stereo turned to an FM classical music station, and Beethoven's Ninth Symphony was flooding the house. From the lounge room, he could hear the electronic squeaks and tinny reverb of a computer game. He lay still for a moment, then threw back the sheet and looked down at his naked body. He raised his right foot and watched it crash back on the bed. Today's the day, Hector, he told himself, today's the day. He leapt out of bed and put on a pair of red Y-fronts, pulled a singlet over his head, took a long, loud piss in the ensuite, and stormed into the kitchen. Aisha was breaking eggs over a frying pan and he kissed her neck. The kitchen smelt of coffee. He switched off the radio in mid-crescendo.

'Hey, I was listening to that.'

Hector flicked through a nest of CDs stacked clumsily next to the CD player. He pulled a disc out of its case and put it into the machine. He pushed through the numbers till he found the track he wanted, then smiled as the first confident notes of Louis Armstrong's trumpet began to sound. He kissed his wife's neck again.

'It's got to be Satchmo today,' he whispered to her. 'It's got to be "West End Blues".'

He performed his exercises slowly, counting up to thirty in slow, measured breaths. Between each set he swayed to the slow-building sensual progression of the jazz music. He made sure that with every sit-up he felt the tightening of the muscles in his belly, and with every push-up, he was conscious of the pull of the muscles on his triceps and pecs. He wanted to be alert to his body today. He wanted to know that it was alive, strong and prepared.

On finishing, he wiped the sweat from his brow, picked his shirt off the floor where he had flung it the night before, and slipped his feet into his sandals.

'Want anything from the shop?'

Aisha laughed at him. 'You look like a bum.'

She would never leave the house without make-up or proper clothes on. Not that she used much make-up; she had no need to—it was one of the things that very early on had attracted him to her. He had never been fond of girls who wore thickly applied foundation, powder and lipstick. He thought it was sluttish, and even though he was aware of the ridiculous conservatism of his response, he could not bring himself to admire a heavily painted woman, no matter how objectively beautiful she might be. Aisha didn't need the assistance of make-up. Her dark skin was supple, unblemished, and her large, deep-set, obliquely sloping eyes shone in her long, lean, sculptured face.

Hector looked down at his slippers, and smiled. 'So can this bum get you anything from the shop?'

She shook her head. 'Nah. But you're going to the markets this morning, aren't you?'

'I said I would, didn't I?'

She glanced up at the kitchen clock. 'You better hurry.'

He said nothing to her, irritated by her comment. He didn't want to hurry this morning. He wanted to take it slow and easy.

He picked up the Saturday paper and threw a ten-dollar note on the counter. Mr Ling had already reached for the gold packet of Peter Jackson Super Milds but Hector stopped him.

'No, not today. Today I want a packet of Peter Styuvesant Reds. The soft pack. Make it two packs.' Hector took back the ten-dollar note and placed a twenty on the counter.

'You change smoke?'

'My last day, Mr Ling. This is going to be my last day of smoking.'

'Very good.' The old man was smiling at him. 'I smoke three a day only. One in morning, one after dinner and one when I finish in shop.'

'I wish I could do that.' But the last five years had been a carousel of stopping and then starting again, promising himself that he could smoke five a day, why not, five a day would not do much damage; but he could not stop himself rushing through to the end of the pack. Every time. He envied the old Chinese guy. He'd love to be able to smoke three, four, five a day. But he couldn't. Cigarettes were like a malignant lover to him. He would find the resolve, soak his pack under the tap and chuck it in the bin, determined to never smoke again. He had tried cold turkey, hypnotism, patches, gum; maybe, for a few days, a week, once even a month, he could resist all temptations. But then he would sneak a cigarette at work or at the pub or after a dinner, and immediately he would fall back into the arms of his spurned lover. And her revenge was exacting. He would be back to worshipping her, not able to get through the morning without her. She was irresistible. Then one Sunday morning, when the kids were at his parents' and he and Aisha had a graceful morning of slow, easy, delightful sex, and he'd wrapped his arms around her and whispered, I love you, you are my greatest joy, you are my greatest commitment, she'd turned around with a sardonic smile and replied, No I'm not, cigarettes are your true love, cigarettes are your true commitment.

The fight was cruel and exhausting—they'd screamed at each other for hours. She had wounded him, shattered his pride, especially when he'd been mortified to realise that it was only his feverish sucking on cigarettes that had allowed him any measure of control in the argument. He'd accused her of being self-righteous and a middle-class puritan and she had snapped back with a litany of his weaknesses: he was lazy and vain, passive and selfish, and he lacked any will-power. Her accusations hurt because he knew them to be true.

And so he resolved to quit. To really quit this time. He didn't bother telling her; he couldn't bear her scepticism. But he was going to quit.

The morning was warm and he stripped down to his singlet as he sat down at the verandah table with his coffee. As soon as he had lit the cigarette, Melissa flew out of the back door and ran screaming into his arms.

'Adam won't let me play.' She was howling, and he dropped her onto his lap and stroked her face. He let her cry till she was spent. He didn't need this, didn't want this, not this morning of all mornings. He wanted the cigarette in peace. There was never enough peace. But he played with his daughter's hair, kissed her on her forehead, waited for her tears to end. He stubbed out his cigarette and Melissa watched the smoke extinguish.

'You shouldn't smoke, Daddy. It causes cancer.'

She was parroting admonishments she had learnt at school. His kids struggled with their eight times tables but they knew smoking gave you lung cancer and that unprotected sex caused venereal disease. He stopped himself from scolding her. Instead, he picked her up and carried her into the lounge room. Adam was intent on his computer game and did not look up.

Hector drew a breath. He wanted to kick the lazy little bastard but instead he plunked his daughter next to his son and grabbed the game console from the boy.

'It's your sister's turn.'

'She's a baby. She's no good.'

Adam had wrapped his arms tight around himself and glared rebelliously at his father, his soft belly bulging over the waistband of his jeans. Aisha insisted that his puppyfat would disappear in adolescence but Hector wasn't convinced. The boy was obsessed with screens: with his computer, with television, with his PlayStation. His sluggishness unnerved Hector. He had always taken pride in his own good looks and fit body; as an adolescent he'd been a pretty good footballer and an even better swimmer. He could not help but see his son's corpulence as a slight. He was sometimes embarrassed to be seen with Adam in public. Aware of the scandalous nature of such thoughts, he'd never revealed them to anyone. But he could not help feeling disappointed, and he seemed always to be telling off his son. Do you have to sit in front of the TV all day? It's a great day, why don't you play outside? Adam's response was to be silent, to sulk, and this only fed Hector's exasperation. He had to bite his lip to not insult the child. Occasionally Adam would glance up at him with a look of such hurt bewilderment Hector would feel a crushing shame.

'Come on, mate, give your sister a go.'

'She'll wreck it.'

'Now.'

The boy threw the console onto the floor, rose unsteadily to his feet, and stormed off to his bedroom, slamming the door behind him.

Grabbing her father's hand, Melissa stared after him. 'I want to play.' She was crying again.

'Play by yourself.'

'I want to play with Adam.'

Hector fingered the cigarette pack in his pocket.

'It's fair that you have time to play video games as well. Adam was being unfair. He'll come and play with you in a few minutes, just wait and see.' He was keeping his voice deliberately even, almost making a sing-song childish rhythm of the platitudes. But Melissa would not be pacified.

'I want to play with Adam,' she wailed, and gripped tighter onto his hand. His first instinct was to push her away from him. Guilty, he tenderly stroked the little girl's hair and kissed the top of her head.

'Do you want to come to the market with me?'

The wailing had stopped but Melissa was not yet prepared to concede defeat. She stared miserably at the door that Adam had slammed behind him.

Hector shook his hand free from hers. 'It's your choice, sweetheart. You can stay here and play video games by yourself or you can come with me to the market. Which would you prefer?'

The girl did not answer.

'Right.' Hector shrugged his shoulders and put a cigarette to his lips. '*Your* choice.' He walked out to the kitchen with her renewed cries following him.

Aisha was wiping her hands dry. She indicated the clock.

'I know, I know. I just want one fucking smoke in peace.'

He thought Aisha would also join in the chorus of resentment directed towards him that morning but her face broke into a grin and she kissed his cheek.

'Right, which one of them's to blame?'

'Adam. Definitely Adam.'

He sat on the verandah and had his cigarette. He could hear Aisha talking calmly to his daughter. He knew that she would be on her knees beside Melissa, playing with the console. He also knew in a few minutes Adam would emerge from his room and sit on the couch to watch his sister and mother play. Within moments the children would be sharing the console and Aisha would have slipped back into the kitchen. He marvelled at his wife's patience, felt the lack of his own. Sometimes he wondered how his kids would respect him when they were older—whether they even loved him at all.

Connie loved him. She had told him. He knew that it had almost caused her physical pain to say the words, that she'd almost choked on them. Her agony underlined his own shame. Aisha, of course, often told him that she loved him, but always calmly, nonchalantly; as if from the very beginning of their relationship she had been sure that he loved her in return. Telling someone you loved them should never be dispassionate. Connie had spat out the words in terror, not knowing or trusting their consequences. She hadn't dared look at him as she said it, and immediately flicked a lock of her hair straight into her mouth. He had gently flicked it away and then kissed her on the lips. 'I love you too,' he had answered. And he did, he certainly did. He had been incapable of thinking of much else for months. But he hadn't dared speak the words to Connie. She said them first. She had to say them first.

'Have you got any valium left?'

'No.' He heard the reproach in Aisha's answer and he noticed her quick look at the kitchen clock.

'I've got plenty of time.'

'Why do you need valium?'

'I don't need it. I just want it. It's just to take the edge off the barbecue.'

Aisha suddenly smiled, her eyes glistening and mischievous. He screwed his cigarette into the ashtray, walked through the glass doors and scooped his wife into his arms. 'I've got plenty of time, I've got plenty of time,' he sang. He kissed the fingers of her left hand, sniffed at the sweet tang of cumin and lime. She kissed him back and then gently pushed him away.

'Do you mind that much?'

'No, of course not.' He certainly would have preferred not to have to give up Saturday evening to play host to a mixture of family, friends and work colleagues; he certainly would have rather spent the last day of his smoking life doing something just for him. But for Aisha, the evening's small party was a way of repaying countless dinner and party invitations. Aisha believed they owed it to their circle. Hector felt no such obligation. But he was a genial host and understood the importance of the evening for his wife. And he had always been proud of the fact that they shared a respect and tolerance for family.

'I don't mind but I'd like some valium. Just in case Mum decides to break my balls tonight.'

'It's not *your* balls she's going to break.' Aisha's eyes darted back to the clock. 'I don't know if I have time to go to work and pick some up.'

'That's okay, I'll drop by and get them after the market.'

In the shower, with the warm jets of water falling onto his head and shoulders, and the steam rising around him, he looked down at his lean body, at his thick limp cock, and cursed himself. You are such a prick, such a fucking lying prick. He was surprised to find himself speaking out loud. A jolt of humiliation flashed through him, and he sharply turned off the hot water tap. The shock of ice-cold water on his head and shoulders could not banish his remorse. Even as a child, Hector had never had time for make-believe or rationalisations. He knew he had no need for the valium and the only reason he was saying he did was so he could see Connie. He could simply choose to drive past Aisha's clinic and not stop for the pills. He could, but he knew he wouldn't. He did not once dare catch his own eyes in the mirror as he was drying himself with the damp towel that smelt of soap, of himself and his wife. Only in the bedroom, running a small squirt of wax through his hair, did he dare look at his reflection. He saw the grey at his temples and at his unshaven chin, the wrinkles at the edge of his mouth. He also saw that his jaw was still firm, his hair still full, and that he looked younger than his forty-three years.

He was whistling as he kissed his wife. He grabbed the shopping list and his car keys from the kitchen table.

When he started up the car, an appalling bleating pop song assailed his ears. He quickly changed to another radio station, not jazz but comfortable acoustic drone. Aisha had picked up the kids from school the day before and allowed them to choose the station. He never let them dictate what was to be played in the car, and Aisha often mocked his sternness.

'No,' he would insist. 'They can play the music they want when they develop some taste.'

'Oh, for God's sake, Hector, they're kids, they have no taste.'

'Well they're not going to get any listening to crap top-forty shit. I'm doing them a favour.'

This would always make Aisha laugh.

The market carpark was packed and he weaved slowly in and out of the crammed lanes before he managed to find a space. The Commodore—reliable, comfortable and dull—had been a concession. Their previous family cars had included a rusted late-sixties Peugeot that was missing a hand-brake and which they ditched as soon as Adam was born; a sturdy Datsun 200B from the seventies that had given up the ghost somewhere between Coffs Harbour and Byron Bay when Adam was six and Melissa just a baby; and a monstrous late-model Chrysler Valiant that was seemingly inde-structible and which had taken the family back and forth across the country a number of times to visit Aisha's family in Perth. The Valiant was stolen by two young men high on alcohol and petrol who smashed it into a phone box in Lalor and then poured petrol all over the interior and set it alight. Hector had almost cried when the police told him. Then Aisha had declared that she was no longer interested in any car older than ten years. She wanted something safe and less expensive to run. Reluctantly Hector had agreed. But he still dreamed of another Valiant—or a two-door ute, or an old EJ Holden.

He stretched out in the car seat, rolled down his window, lit a cigarette and pulled out the shopping list. As usual, Aisha was thorough and meticulous, listing the exact quantities of the ingredients she wanted. Twenty-five grams of green cardamom seeds (she never bought spices in bulk because she believed they became stale too quickly). Nine hundred grams of squid (Hector would ask for a kilo; he always rounded up, never down). Four eggplants (then in brackets and underlined, she had indicated European not Asian eggplants). Hector smiled as he read down the list. His wife's orderly habits sometimes made him frustrated, but he admired her efficiency and he respected her calm manner. If left to him, the preparations for the barbecue would have been chaotic and resulting in panic. But Aisha was a marvel at organisation, and for that he was thankful. He knew that without her his life would fall apart. Aisha's steadiness and intelligence had a benign effect on him, he could see it clearly. Her calmness assuaged the danger of his own impulsiveness. Even his mother—who had initially bitterly resented his relationship with an Indian girl—admitted as much.

'You're lucky to have her,' she would remind him in Greek. 'God knows what gypsy you could have ended up with if you hadn't found her. You have no control. You've never had control.'

His mother's words came back to him again after he'd loaded the box of vegetables and fruit into the boot of the car and was strolling back to the delicatessen. The young woman walking in front of him had denim jeans tightly cupping her round, tantalisingly small buttocks. She had long, swinging straight black hair and Hector guessed she was Vietnamese. He walked slowly behind her. The noise and clamour of the market had fallen away; all that existed was the perfect sashaying arse before him. The woman darted into a bakery and Hector awoke from his fantasy. He needed to piss.

Washing his hands and staring at the grimy mirror, he shook his head at his reflection.

'You have no control.'

He sat in the car outside the clinic, smoking while he listened to Art Blakey and the Messengers. He always found the sharp discordant horns of 'A Night in Tunisia' both sensually charged and calming. When he found himself reaching for a third cigarette, he abruptly switched off the music, jumped out of the car and walked across the street.

The waiting room was full. A thin elderly woman was clutching tightly to a cardboard cat box that emitted regular distressed, pitiful cries. Two young women were sitting on the couch, flicking through magazines as a black Pomeranian sat desolately at their feet. Connie was on the phone. When she saw him walk in, she offered a small, tight smile and then looked away. She placed another caller on hold then resumed her conversation.

'I'm going through,' he whispered to her, pointing down the corridor.

She nodded. As he walked past the closed door of the consulting room and into the surgery, he felt breathless. The girl made him anxious. Seeing Connie was always difficult, confusing, as though seeing her peeled away the years of his maturity back to the shy, tongue-tied boy he was at school. But he was also aware of a deep and satisfying pleasure, a warmth that flooded his whole body: when he was with her it was as if he had stepped out of the shade and into the warm invigorating sunshine. The world felt colder to him now when Connie wasn't around. She made him happy.

'What are you doing here?' There was nothing menacing in her question. Her arms were crossed and her blonde hair was tied back in a thick ponytail.

'It looks busy.'

'Saturdays always are.'

She moved over to the X-ray table, and started picking pieces of lint off the pale blue sheet that covered the machine. He could hear a dog growling in the consult room.

She was refusing to look at him. She had no idea how to treat him when they were together in public and it always made him acutely aware of her youth: the ridge of pimples below her bottom left lip, the freckles on her nose, the awkward droop of her shoulders. Stand up straight, he wanted to say to her, don't be ashamed of being tall.

'Aish asked me to pick up some valium.'

At the mention of his wife's name, Connie looked at him and sprang into action.

'They're in the consult room.'

'It can wait till Brendan's finished with the client.'

'It's alright, I'll get them.' She rushed down the corridor and returned with five tablets in a small plastic bag. 'Is this enough?'

'Sure.' He took the bag and as he did so he rubbed his finger softly across her wrist. The girl looked away, but did not pull back her arm.

'Can I have a cigarette?' She was now looking straight at him, her sharp blue eyes daring him with the request. Brendan was notorious for his objections to smoking and he would disapprove of Hector giving a cigarette to a teenager. No, not a teenager, Connie was a young woman. Connie's dare seemed deliberate, provocative; her insistent stare aroused him. He gave her a cigarette. Connie opened the door to the back verandah and he was about to follow her.

'Keep an eye out for Brendan, will you? Or if someone comes through the front.' When she gave instructions she still sounded like a Londoner. He nodded and she slammed the screen door behind her.

Through the surgery window he watched her smoke, drinking in every aspect of her. The thick, fair hair, the plump bottom and long, strong legs in too-tight black jeans. The gracious curve of her neck. The phone rang and she pitched the cigarette onto the ground, stubbed it into the earth, picked up the butt and threw it in the industrial bin. She brushed by him to answer the phone.

'Good morning, you've called the Hogarth Road Vet Clinic, Connie speaking. Do you mind holding?' She turned back to him. 'Is there anything else?'

He shook his head. 'I'll see you this afternoon.'

A look of confusion shadowed her face and again he was struck by her youth, her adolescence, the naivety she so detested about herself. He wanted to praise her for throwing her cigarette butt into the bin but stopped himself because he knew she would interpret any comment as patronising. Which in part it would be.

'The barbecue, at our place,' he reminded her.

Without a word, she turned her back to him.

'Thank you for holding, what can I do for you?'

Back home he helped Aisha unpack the groceries then went to the toilet and, over the bowl, he masturbated furiously. He was not thinking of Connie. He was picturing the luscious buttocks of the Vietnamese woman he had spied at the market. He came in a minute and he wiped the semen off the seat, chucked the toilet paper in the bowl, pissed, and flushed it all away. He had no need to fantasise about Connie. Connie was inside him. He looked into the bathroom mirror as he was washing his hands, and again he noticed the grey amid the black bristles on his chin. He wanted to smash his fist into the face staring back at him.

Just before the guests were due to arrive, Adam and Melissa started a fight. Aisha had laid out a feast on the kitchen table: a lentil dahl, samosas and curried eggplant, a potato salad and a salad of dill and black beans. He was standing in front of the stove, waiting to throw calamari into a sizzling pan, when he first heard his daughter's angry scream. He was about to yell out when he heard Aisha running from the bathroom. She started to mediate between the children but Melissa's cries were rising in intensity and he could hear that Adam too had begun to wail. His wife's voice was drowned out in the commotion. Hector threw half of the calamari rings into the pan, lowered the heat, then went to investigate.

Melissa had her arms around her mother's neck and Adam was sitting on his bed, sulking defiantly.

'What happened?'

It was the wrong thing to ask. Both children started shouting at once. Hector raised his hand. 'Shut it!'

Melissa immediately went silent, except for a series of low, sad moans. Tears were still running down her face.

He turned to his son. 'What happened?'

'She called me a fat pig.'

You *are* fat.

'What did you do to her?'

Aisha stepped in. 'Listen, I want both of you to behave this afternoon. I don't care who started it. I want both of you to go and sit in the lounge and watch TV until the guests come. Deal?'

Melissa nodded her head but Adam was still scowling. 'Something's burning,' he muttered.

'Fuck!' Hector raced into the kitchen and quickly began turning the rings. Oil splattered across the front of his shirt. He swore. Aisha was standing in the kitchen doorway and started laughing.

'What's so bloody funny? I just changed into this shirt.'

'Maybe you should have changed after cooking the calamari.'

For a lightning moment, he imagined throwing the frying pan straight at her. She came up and slipped her hand under his shirt, her fingers cool and soothing.

'I'll do it,' she whispered. 'You go change again.'

It tickled where she had touched him.

His parents were the first to arrive. He watched them from the bedroom window as they unloaded bags and boxes from the boot of their car. He went out to greet them.

'Why did you bring all this?' His father was holding a tray of chops and steaks. 'I bought all the meat we need at the market this morning.'

'It's alright, Ecttora,' his mother answered in Greek, kissing him on both cheeks, two large bowls of salad in her hands. 'We're not barbarians or English to bring nothing to a barbecue. What we don't eat today, you and the children can have tomorrow.'

Have tomorrow? They would be eating the leftovers till the following weekend.

His parents put their trays and bowls onto the kitchen bench. His mother gave Aisha a small pet on the cheek then rushed into the lounge to greet the children. His father hugged Aisha warmly.

'I go bring the rest of food from car.'

'There's more?' Aisha's voice was warm and cordial but Hector noticed the tightness around her mouth.

'Just dips and things?' Hector queried.

'Yes,' answered his father. 'Some dips and drinks and some cheese and fruit.'

'There's going to be too much food,' Aisha whispered.

Just leave it, he wanted to say, they have always been this way. They will always be this way. Why are you still surprised by it?

'It's alright,' he whispered back to her. 'What we don't eat today we can have for lunch through the week.'

Within an hour the house was full. His sister, Elizabeth, arrived with her two children, Sava and Angeliki. Aisha popped *Toy Story* into the DVD; the film was a durable favourite. Hector had lots of time for his nephew Sava, who was only a year younger than Adam, but already seemed more assured and knowledgeable, more daring, than his own son. Sava was lithe, agile, secure in his body. He was sitting close to the screen, mouthing the dialogue off by heart, pretending to be Buzz Lightyear. Adam was sitting cross-legged next to him. The girls, Melissa and Angeliki, were sitting side by side on the couch, watching the movie and whispering to each other.

'It's a beautiful day, you should be outside playing.'

The four children ignored their grandmother.

'It's alright, Koula, let them watch a movie.'

His mother ignored Aisha and instead turned to Hector, speaking in Greek. 'They're always in front of that damn television.'

'So were we, Mum.'

'That's just not true.' And with that, his mother brushed him aside and went into the kitchen. She took the knife from Aisha's hands. 'I'll do that, love.'

He noticed that his wife's back had stiffened.

The weather was perfect, a lush late-summer afternoon, with a clear blue sky. His cousin Harry arrived with his wife Sandi and their son, eight-year-old Rocco, and soon after Bilal and Shamira arrived with their two kids. Little Ibby ran straight into the lounge and plonked himself next to Adam and Sava, barely acknowledging them, his eyes riveted to the screen. The toddler, Sonja, at first refused to join the other children, nervously clutching her mother's knees, but the laughter from the lounge room slowly enticed her away from the women in the kitchen and she eventually, quietly, went to sit on the floor next to the girls. Aisha placed a tray of party pies and sausage rolls on the coffee table and the kids swooped on them.

Hector went out into the backyard with Bilal, and his father handed them both a beer.

Bilal refused the alcohol with a slight shake of his head.

'Come on, just one drink.'

'I don't drink alcohol anymore, Manoli. You know that.'

Hector's father laughed. 'You must be the only Aboriginal in Australia who not want drink.'

'No, I'm not. I hear there's also this other guy in Townsville.'

'I go get you a Coke.'

As his father shuffled slowly to the verandah, Hector pulled his friend aside and apologised.

Bilal raised his hand to stop him. 'Don't worry about it. He remembers me from when I was drunk all the time.'

'We were, weren't we?'

And as young men they had been. It was the tail end of school, back when Bilal was a bloke called Terry. Hector's memories of his late adolescence were of seemingly endless nights of parties, clubbing, seeing bands, taking drugs, drinking, chatting up girls. Sometimes there were fights—like the night outside the doors of Inflation in King Street, when a bouncer had taken one look at Terry's proud black pockmarked face and refused the youth entry. Hector swung at the massive bouncer and punched him square in the nose. The man bellowed and rushed at both of them, throwing Hector against a parked car—he still remembered it was a Jaguar— and with one arm keeping Terry at bay, he kept punching into him, a volley of jabs, into Hector's back, his face, into his belly, his groin, his jaw. He'd been crippled for a week, and on top of that Terry had been furious with him for starting the incident in the first place. 'Fucking useless wog, did I ask you to defend me?'

Hector's mother, of course, had blamed it all on his friend. 'That Terry is an animal,' she screamed at him. 'Why are you friends with that *mavraki*, that blackie, all he knows to do is drink.' But they had always been good friends, since sitting together in Year Eight in school, a friendship that continued even when Terry left to go to tech to start his sign writing apprenticeship, that flourished even as Hector went off to uni to do his commerce degree. They were still good friends—now in their forties, still living in the same neighbourhood in which they had grown up and gone to school. It was a continuity they both cherished even though they saw each other rarely. Terry had found Islam, changed his name, and stopped drinking, dedicating himself to his new faith and to protecting his family. Hector watched fondly as his friend took the Coke from Manolis, thanking him for it in the school-yard Greek that Hector had taught him when they were both fourteen. He knew that his friend was happier than at any other moment in his life. Bilal no longer lost himself in destructive rages, no longer hurt himself or dared death. But Hector also missed those nights of drinking and laughing and listening to music and being high. He wished he could split his mate into two: mostly he wanted him to be Bilal, but sometimes he wanted a night with Terry. It had been a long time since such a night.

Hector's work mates from the State Trustees Office arrived. Dedj walked in carrying a carton of stubbies. Leanna was with him, a bottle of wine in her hand. A dark-faced man followed silently behind them. The man was younger than the rest of them—Hector figured he must be thirty—unshaven and sullen. His face was familiar. Hector wondered if he was Dedj's date or Leanna's. Dedj put the stubbies on the lawn and grabbed Manolis, hugging him and kissing him on the cheeks three times in the Balkan way. Dedj gestured to the stranger.

'This is Ari.'

Hector's father started making small talk in Greek but Ari's own Greek was broken and clumsy. Manolis turned away and focused his attention back on the coals.

'Leave it, Dad. We've got plenty of time before dinner.'

'No, Manoli, you look after the barbecue. It will take a couple of hours to fire up.'

'See?' his father responded triumphantly. 'Your wife is smarter than you.' The old man placed an arm around his daughter-in-law and Aisha squeezed his hand.

'Aish, this is Ari.'

Hector noticed the young man's approving stare and felt proud of his beautiful wife.

'You look familiar, Ari. Have we met?'

The man nodded at Hector. 'Yep, we go to the same gym.' Ari pointed westwards. 'Just around the corner.'

'That's right.' Hector recognised him now. He was one of those men who always seemed to be at the bloody gym. Hector's attendance was sporadic at best. His morning routine was the one constant concession to exercise in his life. He'd have to go to the gym this week, to get rid of the night's calories. And then it could be weeks before he'd go again. He figured Ari must be one of those wog guys who seemed to spend all their time at the Northcote gym, making it the centre of their social life.

Aisha's friends arrived next, Rosie and Gary, and their three-year-old, Hugo. Hugo looked like a cherubic, gorgeous child. He had Rosie's straw-coloured blonde hair, and shared the almost ghostly translucent blue of her eyes. He was a delightful-looking kid but Hector was wary of him, having once witnessed the boy's vile temper. As a toddler Hugo had kicked Aisha when they were babysitting him. They had always had a firm bedtime rule with their own children but Hugo knew no such discipline. He had cried and screamed and then started kicking when Aisha picked him up to carry him to bed. He was like a wild animal, lashing out with his feet, and one of his kicks found her funny bone. She had yelled out in pain and nearly dropped the child. Hector had wanted to smash the kid against the wall. Instead he wrenched Hugo from his wife's arms and without a word carried him into their bedroom and chucked him on the bed. He couldn't remember what he said to him, but he had screamed out an order so loud and so close to the little boy's ear that the child had recoiled and started a long, disbelieving sob. Realising he had terrified the boy, Hector scooped him into his arms and rocked him to sleep.

'So what's to drink?' Gary was rubbing his hands and looking expectantly at Hector.

'I go bring,' his father answered. 'You want beer?'

'Yeah, thanks, Manny, whatever.'

'It's alright, Dad, I'll get it.'

Gary was going to get drunk. Gary always got drunk. It had become a running joke in his family, one Aisha disapproved of because of her loyalty to her friend. Gary and Rosie have been attending their family Christmases on and off for years, and every time, once they had walked out the door, Rosie usually trying to support her staggering husband, Hector's mother would turn to the other Greeks, raise her eyebrows and exclaim, *Australezi*, what do you expect? It's in their blood!

Hector took a beer from the mounting pile of bottles sitting in ice in the bathroom tub. From the lounge room he could hear the DVD. He could hear Adam introducing Hugo to his cousins, and smiled. He sounded like Aisha, polite, gentle, welcoming.

Anouk and Rhys had also arrived. Anouk looked like she was dressed for a cocktail party, not a suburban barbecue. Her black denim skirt came to just above her knees, leaving a gash of pearly white flesh visible over the top of her black patent leather boots. She was wearing a see-through dark chocolate silk vest over an intricately patterned lace black bra. Hector noticed that on seeing Anouk, his mother's lips had tightly drawn together: she started chopping lettuce with fury at the kitchen bench. But her face brightened when she was introduced to Anouk's boyfriend. Rhys was an actor in the soap opera that Anouk scripted and, although Hector never watched the show Rhys's face was blandly familiar. He shook the man's hand. Anouk kissed him on the cheek. Her breath was sweet and her perfume was intoxicating; he could smell honey and something tart and sharp in it. Expensive, no doubt.

Hector was about to put on a Sonny Rollins CD when he felt a tap on his shoulder. He looked up to see Anouk brandishing a disc.

'No jazz. Aisha's sick of jazz.' She spoke firmly and he obediently took the CD. It was burnt and the words Broken Social Scene were scrawled in thick blue slashes of Texta across the disc.

'Put it on. It's one of Rhys's. Let's listen to what the kids are up to these days.'

He pushed in the disc, pressed play and stood up, grinning at her. 'The kids, eh. Then it'll be shite r'n'b, won't it?'

The smoke was now streaming from the barbecue and he resisted the urge to yell at his father. Instead he circulated, pouring more drinks for the guests while Aish brought out the samosas. The women had gradually come out of the house and everyone was standing on the lawn or the verandah, drinking and biting into the delicate pastries. Hector noticed that Ari had walked away from the main group and was examining the garden. Harry announced that he had enrolled Rocco into a beachside private school and Gary immediately challenged him. Hector stayed silent. Sandi argued that the local school was inadequate for their son, that the facilities were degraded and the class sizes too large. She had wanted to send their child to a government school but there were no decent ones in the local area. Hector knew that this could not possibly be true. Sandi and Harry had left their westie childhood and adolescence far behind them: they now lived in prime blue-ribbon real estate.

'Look,' Harry interrupted his wife, and Hector could tell that his cousin was annoyed by Gary's challenge. 'You don't have to tell me about government schools, mate, I went to the local tech. It was fine back then, but I'm not sending Rocco to the fucking local high school. It's a different time—no government, Liberal or Labor, cares a flying fuck about education. There's drugs, there's not enough teachers.'

'There's drugs everywhere.'

Harry turned away from Gary and whispered in Greek to Manolis. 'The Australians don't give a fuck about their children.'

His father laughed but Hector's mother suddenly spoke up.

'But what if all people send children to private schools. Bad for government schools. Only very very poor people can then go and the government gives no more money. I think this is terrible. I'm happy I send my children to government schools.'

'That was a different time, *Thea*. The world's gone to the dogs now. It's every man for himself. I still support public schools, don't get me wrong, but I'm not risking Rocco's education for my beliefs. Sandi and me both support public education—that won't change.'

'Will that be possible?' Bilal, who had been listening silently, suddenly spoke up. 'You won't know what's going on in the high schools. How are you going to know the issues and stuff my kids are facing?'

'I can still bloody read the papers.'

Bilal smiled and said nothing further. Aisha remained quiet. Hector knew that she disliked the conversation. It was an argument that arose between them with increasingly uncomfortable regularity. She was concerned about Adam's poor academic abilities, and wanted to enrol him in a private school. Hector doubted any school would help; the boy just wasn't that smart. With Melissa it was different. The girl was lazy but she probably would be okay at school. But that was precisely why it wasn't an issue with their daughter. She would be fine at Northcote High, more than fine. He was a reverse snob. He thought private education was no good for a child's character. Private school boys always seemed effete; private school girls were up themselves and cold.

'You don't mind what that school will do to your son?'

It was as if Gary had read his thoughts.

Harry ignored Gary and asked Hector, in Greek, for another beer.

Gary was insistent. 'You don't mind that he'll be with all those rich snobby kids?'

'Look, mate, Rocco's grandparents on both sides were factory workers. His old man's a mechanic. I'm sure he won't forget where he comes from.'

'You own your own shop, don't ya?'

Hector knew that Gary's questions were not sinister, that the man had a real curiosity for people and their lives, that he was trying to work out where exactly Harry and his family fitted into the social order. But Hector, who knew his cousin detested obtrusive questions into his personal life, thought it best to intervene now.

'I reckon it's time for the sausages. What do you think, Dad?'

'Five minutes.'

Gary went quiet. Harry had turned his back to him and was talking sport with Dedjan. To broker the peace Sandi initiated a discussion with Rosie about children.

At first reluctantly, Gary joined in, but soon became animated, describing the delight he received from watching Hugo grow, from trying to answer the child's increasingly complex questions. 'You know what he asked me the other day, when I took him to the swings at the local park? He asked me how his feet knew how to make steps. It bowled me over. It took me a long time to answer that one.'

Yeah, yeah. Whose kid hadn't asked that bloody question? Hector walked over to where Ari was standing smoking a cigarette, looking over the vegetable garden, at the late-season eggplants, full and black, hanging precariously from their thick pale stalks.

'Want a drink?'

'I'm still on this beer.'

'These are the last of the *melentzanes*, we'll have to use them over the next couple of weeks.'

'You'll have to make a moussaka.'

'Maybe. Aish uses them a lot. The Indians love them.'

The men stood silent. Hector struggled to make conversation. Ari's face remained stony, his eyes ungiving.

'What do you do?'

'Courier.' Just the one word, that was all the younger man was going to give. No indication if he worked for himself or for a business or was in a partnership. Come on, man, Hector wanted to plead, help me out a little.

'You're a public servant too?' Ari was gesturing towards Dedj who was still chatting with Harry.

'I guess so.' Ridiculous. Why did he always feel embarrassed when he mentioned his job, as if it was somehow not quite legitimate, not real work? Or was it just that he hated that it sounded so dull?

Ari's demeanour changed. 'You're lucky,' he said, and then grinned wickedly. 'Good job,' he added, giving the phrase a deliberately exaggerated wog accent.

Hector had to laugh. 'Good job,' he echoed in accent—it was exactly what his parents said about him. Which he did. Fuck being embarrassed. What did he want to be instead? A rock and roll star, a jazz muso? They had been teenage daydreams.

He looked across to where Dedj and Leanna were making his cousin laugh. When he had finished his degree, Hector was twenty-three and idealistic. He had searched for and found work as an accountant for a respected overseas aid agency. He did not last out the year, hating the chaos of the office, the earnestness and antagonism of his colleagues: The books have to balance if you want to feed the world, motherfuckers. And the pay had been lousy. From there he'd gone into an internship for a multinational insurance company. He enjoyed working with numbers, appreciated their order and purity, but he found the people he was working with tediously conservative. Confident, physically capable, he had never found any need to enter into pissing contests or exaggerated jock humour. In the time between Adam and Melissa's birth he'd drifted in and out of four jobs. Then for a three-month period he worked on a tender with the state government. Dedj had been the public servant liaison on his team and the two men had hit it off from the beginning. Dedjan was a hard drinker, a party animal and a fellow music freak. He was also disciplined and good-humoured at work. Hector was offered a contract with the service for a year, and though Aisha had queried the opportunities for advancement, she'd reluctantly supported his taking the position. He had discovered that he enjoyed the collegiate environment of the public service office. Twenty years of economic rationalism had sliced out most of the flab. It certainly wasn't rock and roll, it wasn't *sexy*, but he was respected, did meticulous work and was given increasing managerial responsibility. He now sat comfortably on top of the bureaucratic fence negotiating compromise between the old-school bleeding hearts and the capitalist young turks. He had become 'permanent', the Holy Grail, and long-service leave was just around the corner. The most important part for Hector was that Dedj and Leanna, three or four others, they were like family.

'What's that?' The low rumble of the man's voice snapped Hector out of his contemplation. Ari was pointing towards the back fence, at the rain-worn handmade crucifix they had planted over Molly's grave.

'It's where we buried our dog. She was mine, a damn stupid Red Setter I had for years. The kids loved her as well. Aish hated her, blamed me for never training her. But, *entaxi*, you know the Greeks. As if my parents were going to pay money to train a bloody dog.'

'They'd be expensive, Red Setters?'

'A friend of a friend of a friend. I named her after Molly Ringwald. Remember her?'

'*Pretty in Pink*.'

'Yeah, the fucking eighties, man. All shit.'

Ari turned to him now and Hector was startled by the fiery intensity of his jet-black eyes.

'I've got some speed on me. Dedj said you might want some.'

Hector hesitated. It was a long time since he had taken speed. The last time was probably with Dedjan, at a work Christmas party. He was about to refuse when he remembered that he was giving up the cigarettes the next day. He wouldn't be able to go near drugs for a long time after that.

'Yeah, sure, I'll have some.'

'It's a hundred for a cap.'

'For a fucking cap? It used to be sixty for a gram.'

'And that was back in the fucking eighties, wasn't it, *malaka*?'

They both laughed.

'It's good. It's real good.'

'Yeah, yeah.'

'No,' Ari's tone was insistent and serious. 'I promise. It's good.'

Hector tapped out half the speed onto the toilet lid. The amount suddenly seemed enormous as he cut two thick long lines. He rolled up a twenty-dollar note and snorted the lines quickly. It hit him almost immediately—he couldn't tell whether it was the amphetamines or just the old unforgotten rush that came from indulging in something illicit—but he was suddenly flushed and he could feel his heart thumping. Rhys's CD was still playing and he found the music was whiny and jarring. On his way back outside he switched off the CD mid-song and replaced it with Sly and the Family Stone. He turned up the volume. Anouk, in the backyard, turned around and shook her head, mocking him. Beside her, Rhys was nodding to the music.

'The kids love it,' he yelled out to her.

The late afternoon sun was soft and low in the sky, sending sheets of incandescent red cloud across the horizon. Hector stood on the verandah and lit a cigarette.

From behind him, inside the house, came the sounds of squabbling, then a child was howling. Rosie rushed past him.

Hugo was in the kitchen, inconsolable. Rosie picked him up and hugged him tightly. The child couldn't speak, couldn't get his breaths out.

Hector walked into the lounge where the four boys were sitting mute and fearful on the couch. Melissa had been crying but she was now wiping away her tears. Angeliki spoke first.

'He didn't want to watch the DVD.'

Suddenly there was a rush of accusing voices.

'We wanted to watch *Spiderman*—'

'He hit me—'

'We didn't do anything—'

'He pinched me—'

'We didn't do anything—'

Aisha came into the lounge room. The children immediately fell back to silence.

'*Spiderman* is rated PG. I don't want you to watch it today.'

'Mum!' Adam was furious.

'What did I say?'

The boy crossed his arms but he knew better than to protest any further.

'You let Hugo watch what he wants, that's an order.'

'He wants to watch *Pinocchio*.' Sava's disgust was clear.

'Then you'll all watch *Pinocchio*.'

Hector followed Aisha into the kitchen. Hugo was now quiet and suckling contentedly at Rosie's breast.

'Why are you smoking in the house?' asked Aisha.

Hector looked down at his cigarette. 'I came in to see what the fuck happened.'

His mother marched up to him, took the cigarette from his mouth and proceeded to drown it under a torrent of water from the kitchen faucet. 'It's finish,' she announced disdainfully, placing the soggy butt into the bin. 'Children fight for nothing all the time. Nothing to worry about.' His mother could not take her eyes off the suckling child. He knew she was disgusted that Rosie was still breastfeeding Hugo at his age. He agreed with her.

Brendan arrived next. Connie wasn't with him. Hector shook the man's hand and welcomed him to the gathering. He wanted to ask, Where is she? Why hasn't she come with you?

Brendan kissed Aisha. 'Connie's coming later. She went home to change.'

Connie was going to be there. A rush of pure pleasure ran through Hector. He wanted to shout and sing and grab the whole damn backyard, the whole house—yes, even Rosie and that brat Hugo—grab everyone and hold them tight.

'It is good stuff,' he whispered to Ari.

'I've always got some if you need it.'

Hector grinned widely and said nothing. He was thinking, not me, I don't need it after tonight. Not me, mate, I've never *needed* it.

Aisha's brother arrived. Ravi was over from Perth for a few days on a working holiday, staying in a swish hotel in the city. He had lost weight and was wearing a tight-fitting, pale blue short-sleeve shirt that showed off his newly muscled chest and arms. His dark hair was shorn close to his scalp.

'You look good, man.'

Ravi hugged his brother-in-law and then went straight to Koula and Manolis, hugging them as well and kissing Koula on both cheeks.

'Nice to see you, Ravi.'

'Nice to see you as always, Mrs S. When are you going to visit me in Perth? Mum and Dad are always asking after you.'

'How is your mama and father?'

'Good, good.'

Whatever issues his mother might have with her daughter-in-law, she adored Aisha's younger brother. Hector knew that at some point during the evening his mother would sit down next to him and whisper in Greek, That brother-in-law of yours is so handsome. And his skin is so light, not dark at all. She wouldn't elaborate, but her meaning would be clear. Not like your wife.

Adam and Melissa ran out and fell onto their uncle. He raised his niece to the sky and kept a firm grip on his nephew's shoulder. 'Come out to the car with me.'

Ravi spoiled the kids. Hector heard them shouting and laughing as they followed their uncle to his car. They came back each hugging a large box. The other children came out onto the verandah while Adam and Melissa ripped into their presents.

'What is it?' Sava knelt down next to Adam. The packaging was thrown away to reveal a new computer game. Melissa, always more patient, was carefully stripping away the pieces of tape and folding the wrapping paper neatly beside her. Ravi had given her a pink and white doll's house. She hugged her uncle, then grabbed Sonja by one hand and the box by the other. She turned to her cousin.

'Come on, let's go to my room and play.' Angeliki promptly followed her.

The boys whipped round and looked at Hector. He wanted to laugh; their shining faces, their bright expectant eyes. Adam was holding tight to his gift.

'Can we play with this?'

Hector nodded. With ferocious whoops, the boys rushed into the house.

'You spoil them.'

'Shut up, Sis, they're just kids.'

Aisha wasn't offended. Hector knew she was overjoyed that her brother was in Melbourne, that he could be at the party. Ravi threw his arm around Hector and they strolled over to the barbecue.

Gary had started another argument, this time with Rhys and Anouk. Manolis nudged Hector, speaking in Greek. 'Go get the chops.'

'Is it time yet?'

'It's time. That Australian hasn't stopped drinking since he got here. He needs food.'

Gary's face was indeed flushed and he was slurring as he fired a volley of questions at Anouk, his finger accusingly jabbing at her chest. 'It's just crap. That's not how real families are.'

'It's television, Gary, commercial television.' Anouk managed to sound cutting and bored all at once. 'No, it is not how real families are.'

'But you're perpetrating bullshit that has an influence on millions of people around the world! Everyone thinks that Australian families are exactly like those on the show. Don't you want to do something better with your writing?'

'I do. That's why I work as a scriptwriter on the show. To make money to pay for the writing I do want to do.'

'And how much of that are you doing?'

'Forty thousand words so far.'

Anouk turned to her boyfriend. 'Shut up, Rhys.'

'Why? It's true.' He turned to Hector. 'She told me this morning. She's got forty thousand words down on her novel.'

Gary shook his head and looked mournfully down at his beer. 'I just don't know how you can write that shit.'

'It's easy, Gazza. You could write that shit.'

'I don't want to. I don't want to be part of that cock-sucking toxic industry.'

Harry winked at Anouk. 'I like the show.'

'What do you like about it?'

Harry ignored Gary.

'What do you like about it?' Gary raised his voice.

What a whinger. That's where Hugo got it from. Hector caught his cousin's wink. 'It's good to veg out on. Sometimes that's all you want, something to entertain you for half an hour.'

Sandi linked her arm through her husband's. She was smiling at Rhys who smiled back at her. 'And I think you're very good in it,' she added shyly.

Hector stifled an urge to laugh. He looked across to where the others were sitting on the garden chairs, all keenly listening in to the argument. Dedjan caught his eye and Hector mock-winced. I think you're very good in it, Dedj mouthed sarcastically. Hector, who genuinely liked his cousin's wife, made no reply. He turned back to the circle and smiled warmly at Sandi. She was almost as tall as her husband, slim and long-limbed. The combination of a model's body and a wog woman's style—the teased, dyed hair, the long painted nails, the too-bright make-up—made people think that she was a bimbo. She wasn't. Sandi might not be a uni graduate but she was smart, warm-hearted and loyal. Harry was damn lucky. She still worked a few days a week behind the counter of one of the garages that Harry owned. She didn't have to do that; Harry was rolling in money, riding the seemingly endless wave of the economic boom. His cousin was one lucky motherfucker.

A flush of excitement ran through Hector, like a jolt of electric current surging from his feet to the tips of his hair. His eyes darted over to the gate that separated the backyard from the driveway. Where was she? She should be here by now.

'Why do you think he's good in it?' Gary was a dog with a bone—he would not let the argument go. He was looking directly at Sandi, who was flustered by the fierceness of the man's stare, unsure if his question was a taunt. Hector thought it was possible that he was genuine. Gary's world was not their universe and it was one reason Hector preferred detachment in his interactions with him, had always avoided conflict with him. There was no small-talk, no frivolity to be had in conversation with Gary; even when they were innocent or harmless, his questions and statements seemed under-scored by threat. Gary didn't trust their world, that was very clear.

In her confusion, Sandi was reduced to silence. Hector placed a hand on her shoulder and she suddenly lifted her head. She ignored Gary, she was looking at Rhys.

'I thought you were very good in those scenes last year when they wrongly arrested you for Sioban's murder.' There was a hint of flirtation in her smile now. 'I wasn't sure myself you hadn't done it.'

Jesus F Christ. She *really* watched that shit?

Gary was nodding, seeming to take her words in. He then turned and faced the actor, looked him up and down, taking in the casual but expensive fine cotton cowboy shirt, the black jeans, the confederate flag buckle of his belt.

'You shot a man in Vermont, eh? Just to watch him die.'

Hector couldn't stop himself, he laughed out loud. He was pretty sure that Anouk would be trying to suppress an outraged but treacherous grin. Gary was a prick, but he was an astute prick. Hector had only caught snatches of the soap opera, it was only ever background, but he had seen enough to know Rhys was never going to be the real thing. He was a second-rate Joaquin Phoenix playing Johnny Cash. He was destined for a lifestyle show flogging holidays or home renovations. Vermont was perfect, Vermont was frigging spot-on. The young actor screamed private schools, nutritious breakfasts as a child, the immense bland spread of the eastern suburbs.

At least Rhys had the decency to blush.

'I don't get it.'

'It's a line from a Johnny Cash song,' Hector explained to Sandi.

'I still don't get it.'

Gary tilted his beer bottle towards Rhys. 'I'm just acknowledging the tortured artist in our midst.'

Was it the amphetamines? Hector sensed Anouk's body ready to spring, to pounce. Fast, dangerous, like a shark.

'Gary's a tortured artist as well. One of our most tortured.'

'I'm just a labourer, Anouk.' Gary's voice was a snarl. 'You know that.'

'That's his day job.' Anouk's expression was both innocent and lethal. 'Gary's not content with being salt of the earth. He's really a painter, a visual *artiste*.' She was like Cleopatra and the asp rolled into one, poised and calm, but her words stung. When Rosie first introduced Gary to them all those years ago, he had called himself a painter. Hector doubted Gary had worked on a canvas in years— which was a good thing; he was shit.

Anouk's words had indeed found their target. Gary was looking like he wanted to explode. Hector surveyed the scene as if from a distance. He waited for the tension to fracture, then to break, for Gary to lose it. It wouldn't be a party without some kind of verbal stoush between Gary and Anouk. His father was turning the chops and sausages, ignoring everyone. I am my father's son, Hector thought to himself, I don't want to get involved. I just don't want to get involved.

He crashed to earth. Another burst of hysterical wails came from within the house. Anouk's smile was arctic as she turned away from Gary. 'I think that's your child again.'

Hugo had snatched the game remote and smashed it against the coffee table. The black plastic casing was cracked and there was a milky gash across the red gum surface of the table. Surprisingly, Adam was not crying or in a temper. He just looked genuinely astonished, finding it impossible to believe the evidence of his own eyes. Rosie was hugging Hugo who was pressed into her chest, as if clamouring to escape inside her. He was hiding his face from the world. Rocco was staring at Rosie and Hugo, also incredulous, but his vicious temper—exactly like Harry; they were all their fathers' sons— was about to erupt. The other little boys, terrified of the tension, were looking down at their feet; the girls had come out of Melissa's bedroom and were standing silently in the doorway, Sonja, afraid, uncomprehending, was weeping softly. Hector had come in and was standing behind Aisha and Elizabeth.

His mother, holding a knife in one hand and a souvlaki skewer in the other came up behind him. 'See? Stupid computers games, they cause too much trouble.'

Anger flooded Adam's face. 'That's not true, *Giagia*, we were just playing.' He pointed a challenging finger towards Hugo, who was still hiding in Rosie's arms. 'He just lost it because he can't play very well.'

'Well, he's young,' blurted out Rosie. 'He's impatient to learn, to play with you boys. How about you teach him how to play?'

'Is he going to be punished?'

Hector shook his head in warning to Rocco. The boy ignored him.

'He bloody broke it. He should be punished.'

'He didn't mean to.'

Rocco's face was flushed with rage. 'That's so fucking unfair.'

Hector noticed that Sandi had slipped quietly into the room. She went to discipline Rocco and he fled to his cousin's bedroom. Adam took one quick look at the adults—father and son locked eyes; Hector's nod was imperceptible—and scurried after his cousin. Sonja started sobbing and her mother rushed to console her. Aisha and his mother were both trying to get the girls to go back into Melissa's bedroom, as Sandi continued yelling at her son. Hector turned and walked away. He felt like shaking Rosie, he couldn't look at her. He was fucking sick of children. Let the women sort it out.

Gary hadn't moved from his spot next to the barbecue. He'd started on another beer, his face set in a scowl.

'What happened?'

Hector shrugged his shoulders and didn't answer Anouk's question. She turned to Gary. 'Shouldn't you go in?'

Hector realised that Gary was exhausted, working at a shit job, not his own boss, raising a family. Anouk had no idea.

'Let Rosie deal with it. She's the one who spoils him, so let her fucking deal with it.' His voice softened; the sadness was unmistakable. 'You were right, 'Nouks, I shouldn't have had a child. I'm no good as a father.'

'You are speaking rubbish. You are a very good father. Your son loves you.' Manolis took a charred piece of sausage from the barbecue and offered it to Gary. Hector stood next to his father, their bodies touching. He was much taller than his old man. There was a time he had thought of his father as a giant. 'Do you want some help, Dad?' he offered in Greek.

'It's nearly ready. Tell your mother.'

In the kitchen the women were busy preparing plates and glasses, tossing the salads. Rosie's face was tear-stained, as was her son's who was sucking hard on her nipple.

'Dad says the meat is ready. We can eat.'

In the lounge room the boys were sprawled across the couch and on the floor watching another DVD. It was *Spiderman*. Hector didn't know how their anger had been defused but he assumed Aisha had something to do with it.

'Turn it off,' he ordered. 'Time to eat,' and the boys complied. He was suddenly aware of a snatch of rhythm, a sensual roll of bass. A melody from the past, a song he had not heard for years—before children, before the streaks of grey in his hair and on his chest. Neneh Cherry was singing. Someone had changed the CD, probably Anouk. It was the right choice.

It was a feast. Charred lamb chops and juicy fillet steak. There was a stew of eggplant and tomato, drizzled with lumps of creamy melted feta. There was black bean dahl and oven-baked spinach pilaf. There was coleslaw and a bowl of Greek salad with plump cherry tomatoes and thick slices of feta; a potato and coriander salad and a bowl of juicy king prawns. Hector had been completely unaware of the industry in the kitchen. His mother had brought pasticcio, Aisha had made a lamb in a thick cardamom-infused curry, and together they had prepared two roast chickens and lemon-scented roast potatoes. There was tzatziki and onion chutney; there was pink fragrant tara-mousalata and a platter of grilled red capsicum, the skins delicately removed, swimming in olive oil and balsamic vinegar. The guests lined up for plates and cutlery and the children ate seated around the coffee table. There was hardly any conversation: everyone was too busy eating and drinking, occasionally stopping to praise his wife and his mother for the food.

Hector nibbled at everything but could taste nothing. The amphetamines still rushed through his body and each mouthful he took seemed bland and dry. But he felt proud of what his wife had made possible. He heard the slam of a car door and he eagerly looked up, counted the steps coming up the drive and sprang up to open the verandah gate. Tasha kissed him on the cheek. There was little resemblance between Connie and her aunt; Tasha was short, with a squat body and dark straight hair. Connie was dressed in a blue sweater that was too big for her; it hid her entire body. When Hector went to kiss her she jumped back, bumping into the timorous teenage boy who had walked in behind them. At first Hector didn't recognise the youth, then realised he was the son of Tracey, the vet nurse at Aisha's practice. He was all acne and shyness, his eyes almost hidden beneath the navy and red baseball cap that he had drawn tight over his skull and forehead. Hector mechanically shook the youth's hand. His eyes were on Connie and she was staring right back at him. The challenge in her eyes shot a jolt of heat through him.

He led the trio into the kitchen. 'There's heaps of food,' he gushed. 'Here, let me get you something to eat.'

'They can do it themselves, you organise the drinks.' Aisha kissed them all by turn. The boy blushed a deep scarlet, his rash of pimples flaring.

'Where's your mum, Richie?'

Tasha answered for him. 'Trace can't make it. Her sister's across from Adelaide.'

'But I told Tracey to bring her along. There's certainly enough food and drink. Hector's parents have made sure of that.'

Richie mumbled inaudibly and there was an awkward silence. Clearing his throat the boy began again. His sentences were short, confused, a rapid jumble.

'Only one night. Then friends, going to Lakes Entrance. Only has one night. She and Mum have to catch up.'

Aisha was amused by the almost incoherent statements, but didn't show it, smiling sweetly at the youth who suddenly beamed back at her.

'Well, I'm glad you came.' Aisha turned to Hector. 'How about some drinks?'

Richie asked for fruit juice and Connie diffidently asked for a beer. Hector glanced over at the girl's aunt but Tasha seemed oblivious. He looked back at Connie and he couldn't help but register a hint of disappointment behind the stiff smile on her lips. He had made a mistake in seeking her aunt's permission.

His eyes followed Connie. He watched her fill her plate, observed the fine ripples on her pale long throat as she swigged at the beer. She ate delicately, slowly, but with obvious relish, enjoying the rich food. She wiped at her mouth, casually, unconcerned. The boy ate with gusto; in minutes, his lips and chin were shining. Jealousy suddenly erupted in Hector. Connie and Richie had moved to the back of the garden, sitting on the bluestone bricks which bordered the vegetable patch. They ate and drank in silence under the giant fig tree. As quickly as it had occured, his jealousy was gone. There was no reason to be threatened by the nurse's son. The boy was still trapped in the awful confusion of adolescence; it was clear in everything he did. The boy had his mother's fair colouring and freckled skin. One day he would be a striking man. He had strong, fine features, high cheekbones and attractive, kindly eyes. But the poor kid had no inkling of such a possibility. Hector put a cigarette to his mouth. Ari was smoking as well. He, too, had only grazed at the meal. Leanna had little appetite as well. Hector smiled at her and she made a grimace of apology.

'It's amazing food,' she whispered. 'But I'm just not hungry.'

He sat down beside her on the blanket. Her eyes, with the delicate hint of her Burmese ancestry, were glistening, mischievous.

He tapped her nose. 'I know why you're not hungry.'

She chuckled and looked across at Dedjan who had gone and filled his plate with a second serve. 'Nothing stops Dedj.'

Dedjan was wolfing down his food. It was a running joke at work how much the man ate and how he managed to stay slim. Though time was telling on him as well, thought Hector, looking across at his friend. There was more flesh on his jowls, and perhaps the first evidence of a belly?

As Hector lit his cigarette he promised himself, now that he was finally giving up smoking, that he would start swimming again. He knew Connie's eyes must be on him, that she would be wanting a cigarette. He deliberately did not look her way.

As his mother began clearing away the plates, Hector saw Ravi get up and walk into the house. He emerged minutes later with the children forming a conga-line behind him. Adam was laughing, first behind his uncle. If Hector had not been speeding, it was possible that his next thought would have hurt: he loves his uncle unconditionally, in a way he will never love me. In a way I will never love him.

'We don't have any wickets, Uncle Raf.'

'Use your imagination, amigo. Where's a bucket?'

Sava and Adam immediately ran to the garage, Adam emerging triumphant with a green bucket. Sava followed with an old scarred children's cricket bat, its skin now dotted with green patches of mould, the result of too many winters left out in the rain. It had been Hector's cricket bat when he was a boy. Melissa had been scrounging in the undergrowth and emerged with a tennis ball. Ravi expertly and quickly assigned the children into teams. The adults drifted into the house. Hector, his hands full of plates, looked back and saw that Connie and Richie had scrambled up the fig tree and were watching the children take their allotted positions. In the kitchen, Aisha had begun to brew coffee.

'*No! No no no no no!*' It was as if the child had become lost in the very word, as if all the world was contained in the screaming of this one negative syllable. '*No no no no no!*' It was Hugo. All of them by now, Hector figured, must know that it could only be Hugo. It was the men who rushed outside, as if the child's screams were somehow connected to the rules of the game and therefore it was the men who should arbitrate in the dispute. Hugo was awkwardly slamming the bat on the ground; he needed to hold on to it with both hands but his grip was strong, he would not let it go. Ravi was trying to plead with the little boy. Rocco was frowning behind the wicket.

'It's alright, Hugo, you're not out.'

'He is.' Rocco was standing his ground. 'He got lbw'd.'

Ravi smiled at the older boy. 'Listen, he doesn't even know what that means.'

Gary jumped off the verandah and began to walk towards his son. 'Come on, Hugo, I'll explain why you're out.'

'No!' The same piercing scream. The boy looked as if he was going to hit his father with the bat.

'Put the bat down now.'

The boy did not move.

'Now!'

There was silence. Hector realised he was holding his breath.

'You're out, Hugo, you bloody spoil-sport.' Rocco, at the end of his tether, went to grab the bat from the younger boy. With another scream Hugo evaded the older boy's hands, and then, leaning back, he lifted the bat. Hector froze. He's going to hit him. He's going to belt Rocco with that bat.

In the second that it took Hector to release his breath, he saw Ravi jump towards the boys, he heard Gary's furious curse and he saw Harry push past all of them and grab at Hugo. He lifted the boy up in the air, and in shock the boy dropped the bat.

'Let me go,' Hugo roared.

Harry set him on the ground. The boy's face had gone dark with fury. He raised his foot and kicked wildly into Harry's shin. The speed was coursing through Hector's blood, the hairs on his neck were upright. He saw his cousin's raised arm, it spliced the air, and then he saw the open palm descend and strike the boy. The slap seemed to echo. It cracked the twilight. The little boy looked up at the man in shock. There was a long silence. It was as if he could not comprehend what had just occurred, how the man's action and the pain he was beginning to feel coincided. The silence broke, the boy's face crumpled, and this time there was no wail: when the tears began to fall, they fell silently.

'You fucking animal!' Gary pushed into Harry and nearly knocked him over. There was a scream and Rosie pushed past the men and scooped her child into her arms. She and Gary were shouting and cursing at Harry who had backed against the garage wall and appeared to be in shock himself. The children were watching with clear fascination. Rocco's face was filled with pride. Hector felt Aisha move beside him, and he knew, as host, there was something he should do. But he didn't know what—he wanted his wife to intervene, because she would be calm and fair and just. He couldn't be just. He could not forget the exhilaration he had felt when the sound of the slap slammed through his body. It had been electric, fiery, exciting; it had nearly made him hard. It was the slap he wished he had delivered. He was glad that the boy had been punished, glad he was crying, shocked and terrified. He saw that Connie had dropped from the tree and was moving quickly to the crying mother and child. He could not let her be the one to assume responsibility. He ran in between his cousin and the enraged parents.

'Come on. We're all going inside.'

Gary turned to him now. His face was contorted, he was hissing and a spray of spit fell across Hector's cheek. 'No, we're fucking not.'

'I'm calling the police.' Rosie had her fists clenched.

Harry's shock turned into outrage. 'Go fucking call the police. I fucking dare you.'

'This is abuse, mate. Fucking child abuse.'

'Your child deserved it. But I don't blame him, I blame his bogan parents.'

Connie had come up and touched Rosie's shoulder. The woman swung around angrily.

'We should clean him up.'

Rosie nodded. Everyone was now on the verandah and they cleared a path for the three to walk through. Hugo was still sobbing.

Hector turned to his cousin. 'I think you should go.'

Harry was enraged but Hector spoke quickly in Greek. 'He's drunk too much. You can't reason with him.'

'What are you saying to him?'

Gary's face was right in front of him, nose to nose. He could smell the man's acrid perspiration and the stale odour of the alcohol.

'I'm just saying Harry should go home.'

'He's not fucking going anywhere. I'm calling the cops.' Gary took his mobile phone out of his pocket and held it up.

'See? I'm calling the cops. You're all witnesses.'

'You can do that later.' Sandi's voice was shaking as she walked up to Gary. 'I'll give you our details. If you want to make a charge later, then you can. But I think we all need to go home tonight and look after our kids.' She began to cry.

Gary looked mutinous, and sneered, as though he was about to turn his abuse on her, when Rocco silently came up and stood beside his mother. His eyes were defiant as he looked up to the man.

Gary's next words were quiet. 'Why are you with that bastard? Does he hit you too?'

Hector gripped tight on his cousin's shoulder.

'My husband is a good man.'

'He hit a child.'

Sandi said nothing.

'What's your address?'

She shook her head. 'I'll give you our phone number.'

'I want your address.'

Aisha was beside him.

'Gary, I've got all the details. Sandi's right, you should all go home.' She had her hand on the man's shoulder and the small gesture calmed him.

Hector was filled with love for his wife. Aisha knew exactly what to do, she always did. He wanted to kiss her neck, to just hold on to her. Melissa had come up to her mother, she too was crying. Aisha curled her hand around her daughter's. Adam came and stood beside him. Hector took the boy's hand.

What the fuck am I doing? All that I have, all that I'm blessed with, and I'm putting it at *risk*? The boy's moist hand felt glued onto his own skin.

Abruptly Hector dropped his son's hand and walked into the house.

As he passed his mother in the kitchen, she whispered to him, in Greek. 'Your cousin was not in the wrong.'

'Shh, Koula,' his father warned. 'Don't make trouble.' His old man looked frightened. Or maybe he was just tired of this new world.

Hector walked into his bedroom and froze. Hugo was suckling on Rosie's breast and Connie was sitting next to her, stroking the child's head.

'I can't believe that monster did that. I've never hit Hugo—neither of us have. Never.'

Hector felt the boy's eyes on him.

Hugo pulled away from Rosie's teat. 'No one is allowed to touch my body without my permission.' His voice was shrill and confident. Hector wondered where he learnt those words. From Rosie? At child care? Were they community announcements on the frigging television?

'That's right, baby, that's right.' Rosie kissed her son's forehead.

How about when he kicks someone or hits out at another kid? Who gives him permission to do that?

'Yes.' Connie was nodding vehemently in agreement. 'That's right, Hugo. No one has a right to do that.'

She was so young. It suddenly repelled him.

'Gary's ready to go home.'

Rosie picked her handbag off the bed, picked up Hugo, and walked past Hector. They did not exchange a word.

Hector closed the door, leaving him alone with Connie. He wanted to be kind but he didn't know how.

'We can't see each other again. Not the way we have been. Do you understand?'

The girl looked away, sniffing. 'I can't believe he hit him. What kind of arsehole hits a child?'

He couldn't believe what he had risked. It was so clear to him. He wanted her out of this room, out of his house. He wanted her out of his life.

'Do you understand?' He softened his tone.

'Sure.' She still couldn't look at him.

'I think you're so special, Connie. But I love Aisha, I really do.'

Her response was almost violent. She started shaking. 'Don't you know I do as well? I hate what we're doing to her.' She took a shuddering breath. 'It's . . .' she was struggling for the word, 'It's disgusting.'

She was so young, everything was an exaggeration. He wanted to push her out of the room, out of his life. She wasn't mature. She was a bloody child.

'I'm sorry.'

You'll never tell? It was the terror he had been living with for months, always there, beneath the thrill. He'd imagined the shame for months—cops and divorce and jail and suicide.

She read his thoughts. 'No one knows.'

'I'm sorry,' he repeated.

She wouldn't look at him. Instead her foot was swinging, she worried at a lock of hair in her mouth. A child, she was a child.

She said something so softly he couldn't hear it.

'What?'

This time she looked at him, poisonous. 'I said your arms are ugly, they're so hairy. You're like a gorilla.'

He was shocked. And he wanted to laugh. He sat down next to her on the bed, not daring to let their bodies touch. 'Connie, nothing really happened between us.'

She flinched. He could smell her cheap perfume; over-ripe,

sugary, it tickled his nose. It was a young girl's perfume. He wished he could touch her, stroke her hair, kiss her one more time. But he couldn't bring himself to show any affection. Any touch between them now would be loathsome. He looked up, into the mirror, at a man and a child sitting on the bed, and in that moment she did the same. Her eyes were pleading, tormented, and almost against his will, not wanting to hurt her anymore, he shook his head.

Connie jumped off the bed, jerked open the door, and bolted. For a moment he sat still, enjoying only the relief. He had done it, he had finished it. He closed the door after her and sat back on the bed. His chest hurt, a cord wrapped tight around his lungs. He tried to breathe but couldn't. He knew he must not panic, this wasn't a heart attack, it couldn't be, it mustn't be, he just had to breathe. His fucking throat, he couldn't open his throat. He was dripping sweat, couldn't see his reflection in the mirror. He wasn't there, where was he? Where the fuck was he?

With a gasp that sent him sprawling to the floor he convulsed and drew sweet life into his throat and lungs. He rocked back and forth, remembering again how to breathe. He wiped his face, his neck, with a handkerchief and found himself in the mirror. His face was pale, his eyes red. He looked bloated, grey and old. He realised he was crying. Snot trickled from his nose, tears marking his cheeks. He didn't cry—he hadn't cried since he was a kid. He massaged his chest. I will change, he promised. I will change.

When Hector came back out of the house, Richie was the only person in the backyard, still sitting on a limb of the fig tree. Gary, Rosie and Hugo had gone. Wordlessly, everyone else was collecting their gear, muttering muted feeble goodbyes. Out on the street Hector asked where Leanna, Dedjan and Ari were going. There was talk of more drinking, a bar in High Street, maybe some dancing. He felt separated from them totally and finitely: cleaved from their childless lives.

Back in the house, he could see that Harry was close to tears himself; to see his cousin so wretched was the worst thing. Fury rose within him. He was glad that Gary and Rosie had left. He couldn't bear to see them, to enact the forced pretences of friendship and compassion. Rocco was standing by his father, close, their bodies touching. Sandi kissed Hector and Aisha goodbye, but it was his parents who walked the family to the car. Hector had gripped tight to his cousin's hand but he was unsure what Aisha expected of him, where her sympathies lay. He knew that as his mother and father walked Harry to the car they would be soothing him in Greek, that their anger would be directed against the bloody Australians. Hector agreed with them, but he had no idea what Aisha was thinking. He dreaded the argument ahead.

In the backyard, Connie was calling up to Richie.

The boy made no move. Hector lit a cigarette and offered one to Tasha.

She put an arm around him. 'I'm really sorry.'

'For what?'

'That it ended so badly.'

Hector shrugged.

Richie was looking behind, down into the alley, across the rooftops. He yelled down to Connie. 'I think I can see your house from here.'

'Come down, Richie.' Tasha ordered patiently.

The boy jumped. Hector closed his eyes; he half-expected to hear the crack of a bone but Richie landed on his feet, stumbled, and righted himself. He had a big grin on his face. He ran up to the verandah and stopped abruptly before Hector. He grasped the man's hand and shook it vigorously.

'That was great. The food was awesome.' Then, just as abruptly, he blushed and stepped back.

Hector couldn't think of a word to say in reply but fortunately Aisha emerged from the doorway. 'Thank you, Richie. But I think the party's over.'

'We'll help you clean up.'

'No, Tasha, it's fine. We'll do it.'

Connie shook his hand limply, without looking at him. But she threw her arms around Aisha and held onto her tight. Hector stared out into the darkness. It was only when he heard Tasha's car start up that he let out his breath. He pulled Aisha towards him. She said nothing but leaned into him, his arm tight around her waist. Her hair smelt of barbecue smoke and lemon juice. He was glad they could stand together in silence, a peace broken when he went to butt out his cigarette.

She pulled away from him. 'I'll put the kids to bed.'

'It's still early.'

'I want them in bed.'

'It's Saturday night.'

'Please, Hector, help me on this one.'

He hesitated, wanting to put off the inevitable conversation, wanting to remain in the blissful, uncomplicated silence. 'So, what are you thinking?'

'I'm furious.'

'With who?

Her eyes flashed angrily at him. 'With your cousin, of course.'

'I'm not.'

'If that had been your child you would have never stood for it.'

But it hadn't been their child and it would never have been their child. Not because of him, he knew that, not at all because of him, but because of her. She was a terrific mother. Aisha was watching him warily, he knew she was preparing her arguments. He was suddenly glad for the drugs. He didn't want to fight—he couldn't summon either annoyance or self-righteousness. She was already there, he could tell, she was spoiling for a fight. She wanted to insult Harry, to excoriate him because, in part, Harry was his family. He had not even noticed Ravi leaving and it dawned on him, there and then— how could he have been so stupid?—that in part the day's gathering had been meant to celebrate her brother's visit.

Aisha's eyes were alive and shining, she was clenching her right fist. All he could think about was how to seduce her.

'It's true,' he said quietly. 'Harry had no right to hit the child.'

She was taken by surprise; he even thought a shadow of disappointment might have crossed her face. She unclenched her fist. 'No, he didn't.' But her response was muted, unconvincing.

'You put the kids to bed. I'll start cleaning up.'

He was stacking the dishwasher and he felt like dancing. He flicked Benny Goodman into the kitchen stereo, feeling like something jaunty but solid. He was whistling as he closed the machine and started clearing the benches.

'How the hell can you be so cheerful?' She was standing with her hands on her hips, her expression unamused.

He danced up to her and kissed her lips. ''Cause I got you, babe.'

And it was true. It was so fucking true. He put his arms around her, lowering his hands to cup her buttocks. He kissed her eyes, her cheeks, her earlobes. He tightened his grip.

'They're not asleep yet.'

'I don't fucking care,' he whispered. His cock was hard and he took one of her hands and placed it on his crotch. She giggled, and it reminded him of Connie. He closed his eyes, realising that he'd been hoping the girl had faded from his imagination forever. But of course she hadn't. He gave himself over to the fantasy. He was undoing the buckle of his wife's belt, lowering her skirt, stroking her belly, reaching for her breast. With his eyes closed, he was recalling the soft, sparse bristles of Connie's cunt.

'I don't need a rubber, do I?'

Aisha shook her head. 'It shouldn't be a problem,' she whispered close to his ear. He shivered, the sound, her breath, entering and invading his body, waves of euphoria rollicking through him, again and again.

'Let's go into the bedroom.'

He did not reply. Instead he lifted Aisha's arms in the air, and began kissing her neck. He pulled her top up and first cupped, then he began kissing her breasts. She tried to pull away from him but he would not let her. His lips closed over a stiffening, obliging nipple, then he was sucking it, biting it, till Aisha let out a small whimper of pain and reluctantly he stopped. He straightened, faced her, her eyes were sparkling, and then, suddenly, they were both giggling. He wondered, briefly, if the children could hear, then the thought was gone. His zip had lowered, his cock had been released from the cavity of his Y-fronts and he could smell Aisha's desire. He pushed a finger inside her, she moaned, and he pushed his jeans down and his cock was inside her. Like that, standing up, her skirt bunched around her ankles, his jeans pulled down to his knees, moaning into each other, the drug keeping him hard and allowing him to forestall climaxing, they fucked for ages. When he came he could not help crowing out his rapture and Aisha, laughing, placed her hand across his mouth. He left his softening cock inside her, thrusting gently, whispering he loved her, whispering her name. He heard her gasp, then she was kissing him hard, almost biting his lip. His eyes were still closed, he wanted to stay inside her. He had banished all thoughts of Connie—now that he had come. Not before, he couldn't before. He had merged them in the fantasy of his exertions, fucking his wife, fucking the girl, all at the same time, their bodies, their cunts, their skins both one and distinct for him. Aisha shifted and his cock slipped out of her. Still grinning, they pulled up their clothing.

Aisha went to check on the children and came back. 'I think they're asleep.' It was years since he had seen her look so sheepish.

'We were quiet.'

'No, we were not.' She went to the kitchen sink and started clearing the remains of the salads into the compost bin.

He went up behind her and clasped her tight. 'Let me do it. I'll clean up.'

'We'll do it together.'

'I'll do it.' He was firm. The drug, though less relentless now, was still in his blood and he wanted to move, to be active. The sex had re-energised him.

'What am I going to do? It's too early for sleep.'

'Watch TV, read. I'm going to clean up.' He'd pop the valium, enjoy the comedown as he put the house in order.

She twisted around, his grip still tight on her, and she stared into his face. She was calm, a tremor of sweat still lay sheening her top lip. He licked at it.

'What are you going to say to your cousin?'

Nothing.

'I don't know.'

'Hector.' She just said his name. There was an urgency and a potency in it. He wondered if he could manage to fuck her again, like this, her arse against the kitchen bench.

She repeated his name. 'I want you to be kinder to Adam.'

Where the hell had that come from? He let go of her and fumbled for his cigarettes. Opening the sliding door, he stood under the doorway between the kitchen and the verandah. She followed him and pinched the cigarette from his hand. He couldn't remember the last time he had seen her smoke, it was certainly before she was pregnant with Lissie. It was as if that night he was seeing her and their life together in a different way. He wished he could confess, tell her about the last few months, how he had betrayed her, how he had almost come to be indifferent to her. He wanted to confess because he was, at that very minute, assured of his love for her, for all of her, for everything they had together. This house, their children, their garden, the still comfortable queen-size bed that had begun to sag in the middle from years of their bodies linking in sleep, his arms always around hers, shifting only when she, still asleep, nudged him, still asleep, to move and to stop his snoring. He could not bear life without her. His chest tightened, his fists clenching in determination. He would not allow her to see his fear.

'I promise I'll change. I won't be so hard on the boy.'

ANOUK

Anouk looked in the mirror and smiled wryly to herself. There were more wrinkles around the edges of her mouth, she was sure of it. You're getting vain, girl, she lightly scolded. She flushed the toilet, switched off the bathroom light and slipped back into bed. Rhys protested in his sleep, then turned and wrapped an arm around her. He felt warm and sweaty. Anouk peered at the alarm clock: 5.55. No way she would get back to sleep now. She kissed Rhys's arm, brushing her lips against the coarse hair and soft, boyish skin, tasting his salt as she slid out from under him.

'You okay?' he mumbled.

'Yep.'

A moment later, she was throwing up into the toilet bowl. She raised her head and found Rhys staring anxiously down at her. His right hand was dangling protectively over his genitals and this made her want to laugh. She pointed at the towel and he bent down to wipe around her mouth. That's very nice of him, she thought gratefully, and then almost immediately, and almost comically, He must be very much in love.

She got to her feet and kissed him lightly on the brow. 'I'm alright.'

His green eyes were still anxious.

'Rhys, it's nothing. Just a bit of flu.'

'Take the day off work,' he yawned.

'As if.'

'Go on. I'll do the same.' He was pissing into the bowl. She had not yet flushed her vomit away and his unconcern disgusted her. She suddenly wanted to wound him, to say that the last thing she wanted to do on a day off was spend it with anyone. She rubbed her belly and looked at her lover's firm behind, the graceful curve of his back. There were probably hundreds of girls more than half her age around the country whose dreams of Rhys were about to be rudely interrupted by their alarms. Maybe thousands. Some of them would gladly tear her eyes out for the way she was treating their idol.

Rhys flushed and turned to her, smiling.

'You're really disgusting.'

He scratched his balls and ignored her. She pushed him out of the bathroom. She wanted warm water falling on her head and shoulders, she wanted solitude. She had a long, extravagant shower. She felt better after it. She felt she was herself again.

Though they both had to be at the studio this morning, Rhys drove while Anouk took the tram. She preferred public transport because it gave her time to read or to prepare notes or just gave her time to herself. Rhys argued his was now too public a face to risk taking the train or tram. She thought this was mostly affectation. It was certainly true that a few giggling schoolgirls could be annoying but Rhys's upmarket rockabilly wardrobe was far enough removed from his alter-ego's surfer style—especially when coupled with over-sized sunglasses and a musty smelling Bombers footy beanie—to allow him relative anonymity. And, as she often teased him, most people heading off to work in the morning aren't going to give a toss about some soapie star. That made him grin but he insisted that she didn't understand the ignominy of being fawned over—or worse, being humiliated—in public. She had to admit it wasn't all affectation. When they had first got together a drunk had come up to them at a bar and inexpertly punched Rhys in the face. 'Fucking poofter soapie wanker,' he screamed as his reason for doing so, as the bouncers converged.

Fucking poofter soapie producers. She was not looking forward to the morning meeting. During the last month her writing had become florid, deliberately theatrical, and at the same time, self-aware and mocking. Her recent script had a young girl quoting Verlaine, both the poet and the rock singer. But this wasn't why it was going to be a tense meeting. The producers and the network had been congratulating each other for introducing an incest scenario into the early evening soap opera's storyline. They were being 'brave', 'socially responsible'. Anouk had no illusions about what they were doing. It was basically a recycled child abuse theme which included an unspecified and vague sexual torment. The victim and her father were also secondary characters, newly arrived neighbours living next door to the central family. In this way, had the advertisers protested, it would have been relatively simple to immediately drop the storyline. Not that anyone had protested. As the executive producer kept reminding them, they had 'managed to remain tasteful'. When she first heard this, Anouk had burst into laughter. Another of the writers, Johnny, told her a story about a friend who was working in Hollywood, involved in the production unit putting together a mini-series set in World War II. She'd sent Johnny a confidential email that had circulated among the writers. One sentence had been highlighted: *All scenes set in the gas chambers must be tastefully executed and not upsetting to the viewers' sensitivities.* Anouk had stuck the copied email above her desk at home. If she ever fell into the delusion that her career was glamorous, or worse, important, she would remind herself of the email. She took her most recent script out of her bag, squashed next to a friendly old man on the tram seat, and began to read. She smiled to herself. They probably did want to kill her this morning.

She had made the supposed victim a liar, exposed her as a sadistic vixen. She had set a scene in a high school corridor where the fifteen-year-old asked her sympathetic teacher to kiss her. When the shocked teacher refused, the girl warned him that she could get him into trouble. That had been it. A jarring scene which she had written to confront the viewers and to make the plot more interesting. She was also bored with the sugary niceness of the girl. The soap was filled with wholesome, buxom blondes and that made Anouk feel decadent and amoral, made her want to fuck them up. She smiled again. He was going to kill her.

He screamed at her for ten minutes. She didn't interrupt him, smirked superciliously throughout, tactics which she knew would infuriate him further. None of the other writers looked her in the eye or offered their support but this neither surprised nor annoyed her. This was commercial television: they would all be loyal to her at the pub afterwards. The script was trashed and he told her she would not be paid for it.

That was the only point at which Anouk answered back. 'You have to pay me.'

'You're not fucking getting one cent for that rubbish, you useless bitch.'

She didn't miss a beat: working in Australian television stank of the locker rooms.

'And if you don't pay me, you fat ugly faggot, I'll shut this production down so fucking quickly that you'll have advertiser dollars gushing out of your overstretched arsehole.'

It was a bluff. She doubted she could muster enough union support from the writers to shut down the canteen for an hour. But her bravado made him hesitate for a moment and in that moment she won.

'Well, you're not getting a fucking dollar more for the rewrite. And I want the rewrite tomorrow morning. Got it, sweetie?'

'I've got plans tomorrow morning, *sweetie*. I'll talk to Rhys.' She usually avoided referring to her relationship at work. It had become public only a few months ago and, by now, everyone knew, but she did not want to discuss it with anyone at the studio. However, she had a hunch the producer fancied Rhys. It was too good to resist.

'I'll get him to bring it in.'

She was meeting Aisha at a bar across from Federation Square and had arrived early. Her hand shook as she smoked. She had felt elated walking out of the meeting. She had not lost her temper; she knew she'd made the bastard feel insecure because he wasn't able to intimidate her. Afterwards her colleagues had privately sought her out and congratulated her on standing up to him. But the feeling of triumph soon dissipated. There was bravado on her part, but precious little bravery. Bravery would have meant walking out, telling him what she really thought of him, of his laziness and rudeness and incompetence, of the contempt she felt for the imbecilic program they made. Her hand shook because she was confronting, yet again, her own weakness. She fingered the bracelet on her wrist, a helix of copper and silver that she had bought near Split when she was working with the Croatians on developing their version of the soap opera. She looked down at her fine leather sandals: she had bought them in Milan on a weekend off from work in Zagreb. She knew what she wrote was infantile and moronic. She knew that she assisted in exporting stupidity to the world. But she loved her shoes and her jewellery and her apartment that looked over the bay across to the skyline of Melbourne. She loved the money. And tonight, when she could be working on her book, she would be rewriting the script instead. And the good guys would be wearing white hats and the bad would be wearing black. She rang her GP to make an appointment for the morning, she phoned the library to extend her loans, and she was on her second martini when Aisha walked in.

'How did it go?'

'I hate my job.'

'You like the paypacket.'

As Aish went up to the bar to order a white wine, Anouk laughed to herself. She loved her friendship with this woman because they knew each other so well. Aisha had known Anouk well before she'd become a successful, confident woman. Aisha had been there from the beginning, when Anouk was the gauche Jewish girl with vomit on her too-tight red dress at the end-of-high-school ball.

Aisha returned with the wine and sat down. 'I still hate my job.'

'Rosie and Gary have got the police involved.'

For a moment, Anouk had no idea what her friend was referring to. Then, with a groan, she remembered the incident at the barbecue.

'You are fucking joking, surely?'

'Harry hit their child.'

'He should be given a medal.'

'Hugo's just a kid, Anouk.'

'He's a monster. I hate that bloody child.'

Aisha looked incredulously at Anouk, who took a deep breath. She didn't want an argument but it was inevitable if the subject was going to be Rosie. They'd all been friends since they were teenagers in Perth, but it was an uneven friendship. Aisha loved them both but the truth was that Anouk and Rosie no longer had much time for one another. Not that Rosie would ever admit that—she could never acknowledge darkness or confusion in life. Rosie was always about the light and the good and the positive. That way she never had to admit to cruelty or malice within herself; she could always be the victim. Anouk thought of the plain-speaking burly Harry who had slapped Hugo at the party. She knew next to nothing about him but that he seemed decent enough, good-natured, probably insufferably dull and bourgeois except for the faint linger of a once-dangerous prole virility. He was definitely more of a man than Rosie's Gary. Anouk also liked Harry's charming, unpretentious wife and his good-looking son. The man probably liked his life. And now her unthinking friend, no doubt encouraged by her resentful alcoholic prick of a husband, was going to try and damage that life. She breathed out slowly and waited for Aisha to speak.

'Hector's furious with me. He thinks I am betraying his cousin.'

'Why, what have you done?'

'He's so fucking Greek at times.'

'Don't evade the question.'

'Rosie wants me to make a statement.'

Anouk exploded. It was as if all the tensions of the day had collided and found a release through her scorn for Rosie. No, it was more than that: she was furious that her good, smart friend could be led into making this mistake because of the self-righteous whims of a doormat like Rosie.

'Don't get involved.' She would not let Aisha interrupt. 'If you get involved not only do you fuck things up between yourself and Hector but you pander to Rosie and Gary and their paranoia. Hugo is a basketcase. He has no boundaries, he is uncontrollable. If she wants to act like some hippie earth mother, that's fine, but Hugo's no longer a baby and he's going to have to learn about consequences. What happened on Saturday was a good thing.'

Aisha was composed. 'He hit a child. Are there no consequences for that?'

'He was defending his own child.'

'Rocco is twice Hugo's size.'

'Aisha, don't get involved.'

'I *am* involved. It happened at our house.'

Anouk rolled her eyes. 'And what does Hector think?'

Aisha was silent. She ran her finger along the rim of her wine glass.

Anouk smiled. 'He agrees with me, doesn't he?'

Her friend slapped the air in a gesture of annoyance. Anouk's anger dissipated. Aisha's dad does that, she suddenly realised. Mr Pateer's plump face was kind, genial, but it had always been inescapably Indian, unavoidably *foreign*, whereas Aish was her familiar best friend, undoubtedly Australian. She always thought of her as more the daughter of her English mother than of her Indian father. But looking across at Aisha now, she could see some of the old man's features in her friend's tense, proud face. We are ageing, mate, we're ageing. And with that, the anger and frustration she was feeling was replaced by tenderness. Aish would forever be picking up after Rosie; there was something in her character that led her to look after the weak and the helpless. It was what drew her to animals. Yet there was little that was sentimental about her friend. Aisha's kindness was tempered by a steely, objective intelligence. That's what made her such a good vet.

I love you, thought Anouk, and she was suddenly shamed by tears welling in her eyes. It was just a moment, just the blink of an eye, and the tears were gone.

Aisha's hand rested back on her wine glass. 'Hector is impossible at the moment. He's quit smoking again.'

Anouk reached for a cigarette and lit it.

Aisha laughed. 'You're never going to quit, are you?'

'No. I don't want to.'

'Neither does Hector. He's doing it for me. But it makes him hate me.'

It was Anouk's turn to laugh. 'Oh please. Hector does not hate you.'

'I think he hates me at the moment,' she hesitated.

Anouk could see that Aisha was agitated, that it was getting to her. 'They say a month. Give him a month of being an arsehole and then the cravings will go. Just ignore him for a month.'

'It's not the quitting smoking. It's this business with Hugo. Fuck him!' Aisha gulped down her drink and rose to order another. 'It's his mother. She has to interfere. She's furious with me for supporting Rosie, and Hector won't stand up to her. Of course.' Her tone was sarcastic, bitter, and as Anouk waited for her to come back from the bar, she found her own anger returning. It's not his fucking mother, it's you, it's you taking Rosie's side without question, and then resenting the fact that we are not all bending over backwards to lend you support. Of course Hector is furious, of course his parents are not going to support you causing trouble in the family. You are the one who should be standing up to Rosie.

'You are being unfair.'

Aisha's eyes flashed as she sat back down.

'Unfair to whom?'

'Hector.'

They sat in silence. Anouk could see that her friend was thinking, weighing up arguments and positions in her mind. It was the way Aisha worked. She made lists, she was organised.

Anouk enjoyed her cigarette and waited.

Aisha sighed. 'I'll tell Rosie that I'll support her emotionally but I can't be a witness in any legal or official capacity. It places me in a compromised position with Hector and his family. She'll just have to understand that.'

She won't. She'll pretend to.

'She will.'

It was a good decision. They could relax back into gossip and laughter now, shop, maybe catch a movie. Anouk was slightly drunk now, and she felt happy for the first time that day.

The house was dark when she got home. She ordered Thai, poured a gin and she began to rewrite the script. She was quick, efficient, reducing the narrative to exposition and small, dramatic arcs that resolved snugly within commercial breaks, peppering the mundane dialogue with easy, disposable slang. She felt like a fake and she did not care. Her treacherous, vengeful teenage girl retreated back to being a damaged imbecile and the teacher a supportive drone, mouthing all the acceptable platitudes of victim rights and girl power. The only character she felt any affection for was the rapist father.

She had printed the redraft and was proofing it when Rhys came home.

'That was a late shoot.'

'I went to the gym.'

He had taken a bite of leftover green curry chicken and she wiped away a grease mark where he had kissed her neck. He sat beside her on the couch and lifted her leg onto his lap. He began massaging her foot, kissing her ankle. She pretended to continue reading. His hand was creeping up her thigh, to her groin. The phone rang and her sister's voice, pleading, breathless, was coming through the answering machine. He dropped her leg.

'Leave it,' she whispered, as though her sister could somehow hear her. 'I'll call her tomorrow.'

Her mobile rang next. They both laughed.

'I'm dying to meet her. The born-again Jew as you call her.' His fingers were stroking her now, the script discarded, her eyes closing in pleasure. He was a great lover, his fingers both determined and gentle, a combination she had rarely encountered in a man. She opened her eyes for a second to see him smiling at her. She was awed by his youth, it was almost overwhelming, the softness of his skin. She was both aroused and sad. He would never meet her sister. His beauty and his youth would only make her sister suspicious. Anouk could not bear having to justify herself. She arched her back and pushed her body forward, as Rhys's fingers teased her clitoris, slipped inside her. His lips were on her neck, her cheek, her chin, her mouth. She unzipped his jeans and felt for his cock, pulling his free hand to her breast, moaning as he squeezed her nipples. Everywhere, all over her skin, every part of her was aroused. It was as if her body had been asleep for years and had suddenly awoken, refreshed but hungry. Fuck me, she whispered into Rhys's ear. She shook, shuddered, as he pushed his cock inside her. She wanted to bite him, scratch him, devour him. Fuck me, she ordered him sharply now, and she wondered, Is this how a man understands sex? This ravenous animal desire? She came before he did and then came again. And as he began to spasm, as he withdrew, as his semen pumped warm against her thigh, she reached for his cock, feeling the blood still throbbing underneath the silken skin, and shuddered once again.

* * *

She walked straight out of the doctor's office, not registering the noise and traffic on Clarendon Street, and claimed the first yellow cab she saw. The driver was smoking a cigarette and he quickly ground the remains into the asphalt before ducking into his seat.

'You can smoke in the cab,' she muttered absent-mindedly. 'It's alright by me. In fact, I may have one myself.'

'Sorry, lady, I can get a fine.'

She didn't even hear him. She looked out of the window. An old lady, the kind you rarely saw in public anymore, her hair dyed chemical blue, wheeling an out-sized shopping trolley, was standing blinking at the lights.

'Where to?' The man had been patiently waiting for her to speak.

She apologised and gave him her destination. Her fingers were tapping against the vinyl covering of the seat. She did want a smoke. Fucking stupid regulations, fucking nanny-state ideology, fucking puritanical death-fearing Protestantism. Fuck! Why was this country so over-regulated? At times like these she desperately missed the anarchy and disorganisation of the Balkans. She badly wanted a cigarette. It would be real defiance to have one now. She was aware that nothing seemed to be penetrating her consciousness. The buildings, the other cars and vehicles on the road, the driver, the sky, the city. It was as if she was under the effect of some drug but there was no reciprocal pleasure permitted to counter the loss of what she could only describe as her intelligence. She felt as if she was floating, incapable of decision.

'Which way do you want to go?'

She glanced at the reflection of his eyes in the rear-view mirror. She was numb, she couldn't think. Would there be too much traffic on Swan Street? Should they take the tunnel? Her mind cleared, irritability smacking away the fog, and she replied bitchily, 'You're the driver, shouldn't you know the best route to take? Isn't that why I'm paying you?'

His face tightened and he focused on the route ahead. He was a young man, probably younger than Rhys, his skin the rich honey shade of roasted chestnuts, and his eyes wide and striking, set deep in his sharp-edged face. She hated the wiry, immature beard that seemed stuck onto his chin. Why do you do that to yourself, she wanted to ask him, why do you make yourself deliberately ugly? Why does your God demand that of you? This was not like her at all. She was usually courteous to taxi drivers. They were invariably immigrant men, and she told herself that in treating them with respect and dignity she was separating herself from the immense sea of indifferently racist Australians out there, a world that existed—as far as she could tell because she never visited 'out there'—somewhere beyond the yellow lines that marked the inner-city zone-one train and tram tracks on the Melbourne transport maps. But she felt neither courtesy nor respect at this moment. Fuck him, she thought sourly, ignorant fundamentalist Muslim pig. She received an illicit thrill from the jolt of hatred.

'I'm sorry for snapping at you,' she began sweetly, 'but I'm a little shell-shocked. I've just found out I'm pregnant.'

The young man looked at her again in his mirror, smiling now. 'Congratulations. You are very fortunate.'

'You think so?'

She saw confusion spread across his face and he turned his eyes away from her again.

'I don't think I want it. I'm not married, you see, and the father is almost half my age. There's so much I want to do. I don't feel fortunate at all.' Her eyes were focused on the rear-view mirror. She could see a corner of his face, but his eyes were averted.

Talk to me, you bastard.

They sat in silence as the cab weaved fitfully down the clogged South-Eastern freeway. Nearing the studio she realised that she was red-faced. She felt ashamed and then furious. Who the fuck was he to judge her?

She leaned forward as he stopped the car. 'I know what you think of me.'

'I not think anything at all.'

'You're a liar,' she hissed. 'I know exactly what you think of me.'
The vitriol shocked them both.

'Your change,' he said, as she went to leave the car.

'Keep it,' she mumbled.

He looked at her, still unsmiling. 'Please do not presume to know
what I think of you. We do not know each other.'

She did not say a word at the script meeting. She hardly listened.
When it was finished she called Rhys and left a message on his phone
that she was fine, the doctor said it was just a bit of gastro, and that
she preferred to be alone the next couple of nights. She was relieved
to not have to speak to him. The taxi driver who took her home was
an elderly Greek man and she was sweet and courteous with him.
She rang Aisha as soon as she walked into her apartment.

'Are you free tomorrow?'

'Thursday is a bad day. I'm working till eight.'

'Friday?'

'What's this about?'

'I need some advice.'

'Rhys?'

'Friday?'

Aisha laughed. The sound of her chuckle made Anouk feel sane
again for the first time that day.

'Let's meet in the city. How about somewhere on the river. South-
bank or Docklands?'

'Friday night? Forget it. Too crowded.'

'How about Doctor Martins? It's got a courtyard.'

'Great. But you sure the city's alright? I can come up to your side.'

'Hector can get off early on Fridays. He can pick up the kids.'

Anouk felt her belly. Was this going to be life for her from now on?
Was she, for the first time in her adult life, to be beholden to another
being's whims, demands, needs?

'And I'll call Rosie.'

She could have said it then. She *should* have said it then. She didn't want Rosie there. She understood why Aish did. Aish wanted them to be girlfriends again. Aish wanted the tension between them to go away. Aish wanted them to get drunk together, be friends together, talk shit together. Anouk could have said, No, I need to talk to you, just you. That's what she should have said, but she didn't.

'Fine. Can you get off early?'

'I'll be out by three-thirty. Brendan won't mind.'

'Let's make it for four-thirty. We can score a table before happy hour.'

'Perfect.'

Anouk hung up the phone and looked at herself in the mirror. She raised her shirt and looked at her stomach. It was flat, she still had a young woman's stomach. With Rosie there on Friday, she knew how the conversation would go. She'd tell her friends and they would be excited for her. Rosie would gush and Aish would probe her for her feelings. She'd explain her reservations and Rosie would tell her that there was nothing like the experience of having a child, that all women should go through childbirth. She'd listen and then put forward more objections. Aish would consider them all in turn and tell her that she shouldn't make up her mind straight away. That they should talk about it together again later. Anouk would chain-smoke and Rosie would make a joke about her not being able to do that for much longer. Anouk would then say that word—she would not say termination, she would say abortion—and Rosie would look fearful and Aish would look inscrutable. Rosie would have tears in her eyes and Aish would order them all another drink. Rosie would plead with her and Aish would try to intervene. Rosie would go off to the toilet and Aish would ask, Are you sure? Rosie's eyes would be red when she returned and she would not look at Anouk. Anouk would then take her hand and tell her that she did want to know what it would be like, that she did dream of having a child, she did, but she was scared and confused. Rosie would be placated and they'd start gossiping about other things and they would laugh and get drunk. Anouk would leave, promising her friends that she had not yet made up her mind.

Anouk then realised that she wouldn't say a word about being pregnant to her friends. She looked critically at herself in the mirror. She was not a beauty, but she held herself well, she had style and she was striking. She was chic, and with age, that mattered more than looks. Chic didn't desert you. She did look her age but she looked fantastic. She was secure, comfortable and she had a good life. She knew this but it was not enough. She wanted to do great things. Television was not a great thing. Rhys was not a great thing. She wanted to write a book that would shake or move or be known throughout the world. She wanted the grand success. Or the grand failure. It did not matter. She did not want the pleasurable and comfortable mediocrity in which she now wallowed to be the sum of her life.

It was possible that a child could change all this, but a child would not make her a success. All the child would succeed in doing would be to transform her finally, irreversibly, into her own mother. She had no doubt she could nourish and educate a child—she would be encouraging, loving. She could also be suffocating, smothering, demanding that the child fulfil her dreams to repay the debt she would always feel it owed her. She would not be a mother; she would be a gorgon. It was in her blood—her mother had been that and her sister was becoming that with her own children. Not that Anouk bore ill-will towards her mother, not at all. Her mother had been fierce, courageous, had challenged family, society and love. She had raised her daughters to be equally relentless, equally brave. But her mother had been resentful, unable to submit to having no talent for anything but being a mother. She had raged against the unfairness of destiny to the end of her life. No, all of them, all the women in her family, they should have been born men. She shut her eyes tight and tried to will the desire for a child, to really feel a sense of achievement about the life developing in her womb. I'm sorry, she whispered, it's not enough. She flinched as she recalled her churlish behaviour with the young taxi driver that afternoon. It was not his difference that annoyed her: his accent, his beard, his unforgiving God. It was not that at all. What had shamed her was that he was not at all different. She had assumed he spoke for all of the world.

On Friday morning she awoke with a dream still freshly sketched in her imagination. She was walking with Jean-Michel, he was holding her hand and his grey hair was cut short in a military style. She preferred his hair like that and wanted to tell him that she was glad he had finally taken her advice and cut it. But she found she could not speak. They were walking through a cold, sun-starved cityscape that she did not recognise. It was a little like what she had imagined Zagreb to be like before she got there. Jean-Michel's grip on her hand was firm and she felt safe. There was no one else in the city. She was pregnant, she was huge. She was happy.

She showered and dressed quickly. She hadn't thought of Jean-Michel for a long time. She remembered that even back then his chest was beginning to sag and grey hairs had begun to spread across his thickening stomach. He was always going to age badly, and he would be an old man now. She blushed as it struck her that he had been the age she was now when they were lovers, and she herself had been even younger than Rhys. She found herself mouthing him an apology in the morning light of the apartment. Maybe it wasn't mere cowardice or professional fear that had made Jean-Michel reluctant to leave his wife and pursue the passionate affair with his Master's student. Maybe he was only too aware of the ruthlessness of time, saw ahead to the moment when she would no longer find him attractive. She had not possessed such wisdom then and overcame her sorrow by first detesting and then pitying what she had thought was Jean-Michel's weakness.

Before leaving her apartment she looked at herself, up and down, critically, in the mirror. She was tall, yes, she was glamorous, her figure was still strong and supple. But she was an ageing woman. In twenty years' time she would be sixty-three. And Rhys would be a handsome and still-attractive man of forty-four. The thought of her young lover brought a smile, tender and amorous, to her lips. She felt a spasm of desire. Was this pregnancy, this constant awareness of eroticism, this helpless surrender to the body?

Aisha and Rosie were already sitting in the beer garden. Anouk kissed them both, and she gave Rosie a big hug as well. They had been friends for what amounted now to more than a generation. They'd always been different. She did not want to wallow in spite or resentment of her old friend. The glue that bound them together was certainly not history. Their glue was Aish. They both knew this. An open bottle of white wine was at the table and Anouk poured herself a glass.

'I nearly got run over by three little bitches, just outside the pub.'

'At the lights?'

'No.' Anouk shook her head and smiled. Rosie was frowning, concerned and anxious. 'They weren't in a car. This was on the street. They bumped into me and then walked off as if I didn't exist.'

'How old were they?' asked Aisha.

'God knows. They looked like hookers but they could have been sixteen. They were probably twelve.'

'Well, you probably don't exist for them. None of us do.' There was resignation in Aisha's tone.

'Well, I do fucking exist and I want my existence acknowledged when I'm physically dealt with. God, I hate young women. I much prefer boys. They are so much more polite.'

Rosie shook her head in mock derision. 'We're turning into our mothers. I'm sure we were bitches to older women when we were young.'

Anouk lit a cigarette and looked down at the table. They needed an ashtray and she quickly surveyed the tables around her. Two men, in suits and with their ties loosened, were engaged in spirited conversation at the next table. She indicated their empty ashtray and one of the men smiled and handed it to her. He was roughly handsome, paunchy but virile. She registered his assistance with a small smile but she was thinking of what Rosie had just said.

'You're probably right. We were arrogant. But we weren't deliberately rude. That is what I'm complaining about and, much as I hate to say it, I think we feminists have helped create it. These little bitches think they have the right to do anything they want but they don't care about consequences.'

'Now you sound like some right-wing shock jock.'

Anouk snorted out loud at this. 'Rosie, that's bullshit. I think the age of consent should be twelve, I think heroin should be sold legally and I think the American president and our prime minister should be prosecuted for war crimes. I'm not a fucking conservative and I resent the implication. It's not only the right who can speak on morality.'

Rosie and Aisha glanced at one another and then started laughing.

Anouk blushed. 'Rant over. I'm sorry. I just wish I could have slapped those stupid little cows.'

As soon as she said it, her thoughts flew back to the barbecue at Aish's place. She knew all three of them were flashing back to that instant when Harry had hit the child. The man who had handed her the ashtray kept looking up at her. He would be in his late forties, with salt and pepper thinning hair. Strong forearms, fat fingers. No wedding ring.

'It's how slutty they look that I can't stand.'

For a moment, Anouk and Rosie were confused at Aisha's statement, then they both burst out laughing.

'It's true, we *are* turning into our mothers.'

But Aisha wasn't laughing as she poured herself another drink.

She reached out and without asking took a cigarette from the packet on the table. 'I worry about Melissa. I know she's still a kid but she's already asking for bikini tops to wear when she goes out to a friend's birthday. I don't want her to grow up thinking that she has to look like a streetcorner whore to be attractive.'

Rosie shook her head at this. 'You're forgetting what we were like. You're forgetting how much your mother bitched about the clothes we wore.'

'Because she thought we were making ourselves look deliberately ugly. That's true. But our reality was different, we wanted to be punks, to stand out from the crowd. But we were all aware of what it meant to look slutty and we felt sorry for those girls. They were the girls that dropped out of school, the ones that became single mums. They were the girls that boys fucked and fucked over. I wanted to look like Siouxsie Sioux and Patti Smith. I did not want to look like the Happy Hooker. You know who Melissa thinks is wonderful? Paris Hilton. Paris fucking Hilton. Now, there's a role-model.'

'At least she has some attitude. I don't mind her.'

Anouk gulped down her wine and poured another one quickly. Her good will towards Rosie was dissipating. Rosie was a few years younger than both her and Aish, not yet forty, but as an adolescent Rosie had been reckless and harsh: it came from having a puritan mother and an alcoholic loser dad. It had made her suspicious of pieties. But since meeting Gary and especially since having Hugo she had slowly taken on a New Age moral code that retained elements of her mother's religious ethics but which resisted the hardline dictates of her Calvinism. Rosie had been a beautiful young woman. She could have been a model, an Aryan model, Anouk thought a little spitefully. Rosie had also been a mean-tongued bitch when she wanted to be, with an intolerance of hypocrisy. She could do with some of that cruelty now. She could do with not being bloody earth-mother to both her husband and kid.

The man from the next table had risen to go to the bar. He smiled again as he walked past them. He was tall. It was the one thing that she regretted about Rhys as a lover, that he was not a tall man. A sensuous glow, intensified by the alcohol, spread through her body, waves of pleasure emanating from her loins. She wanted to fuck all the time. She wanted to fuck the man at the next table. She wanted to fuck him tonight. She drifted back into the conversation. Aisha and Rosie were still engaged in a heated debate.

Anouk raised her hand in protest. 'Enough!'

'Okay,' Rosie conceded, then added quickly, 'But I still think you two are being tough on younger women. You're forgetting that we had it easy. Free education, social services, feminism. You name it.'

Anouk's resentment dissipated. Rosie had a point.

'I think I hate that they are so generic, so Hollywood.' She was remembering her fury at the young girls' refusal to acknowledge her physical encounter on the street. Their swagger, their look, their style was qualitively different from the arrogance they themselves had as young women. The teenagers on the street were emulating a look and a pose of sneering indifference that was manufactured by the media. It was individualistic, it was selfish. There was no world outside the image. And she herself worked in the industry that created these young monsters. She felt sick to her core. The luscious sexual euphoria she had been quietly experiencing completely disappeared. She felt tired, old, her lungs hurt. She looked up to find that Rosie and Aish were nodding in agreement.

'I hate that too.' Aisha finally lit the cigarette. 'I hate how everything is becoming the same.'

'I'm part of it.'

'What do you mean?'

'I mean I spent a year in Zagreb teaching Croatian writers and directors how to faithfully recreate a soap opera based on a suburban Melbourne family that was itself based on a concept that originally came from a failed German soapie. I don't think I have any right to accuse anyone of being a whore.'

'We're all whores. I get free trips for my family from drug companies who get me to give vaccinations to animals that I know they don't really need. It's the modern world, Anouk. We are all whores.'

Rosie was silent.

Anouk grinned evily at her. 'Except you, of course. You're a saint.'

Rosie blushed. Anouk saw a glimpse of something like fury, something vicious flash across the woman's piercing eyes but it vanished, disappeared back deep inside her where so much had gone since marrying Gary, since going straight.

Rosie answered with an insincere smile. 'I'm no saint, Anouk. I just think you don't have to engage with all that is terrible about this world. You can separate yourself from it. That's why Gary and I will only let Hugo watch DVDs and videos, absolutely no television but the children's shows. We want Hugo to get a chance to develop his imagination independent from that vile world.'

Rosie turned to Aisha. 'I've caught up with Shamira a few times. I like her. That's what her religion is, a way of protecting herself and her family from the shit in this world.'

'Who the fuck's Shamira?'

'You know her,' Aisha reminded Anouk. 'Bilal's wife.'

Anouk nodded. The Aboriginal Muslim and his white Muslim wife. The odd couple. She had found that she had nothing to say to either of them at the barbecue. She could see why Rosie would like them. The three of them had all obviously shed their pasts and grown new, vastly different skins. She glanced over at Aish and she was suddenly convinced that her friend was thinking exactly the same thoughts. It was a shared moment in which they were both pitying and ridiculing the experiences of the three true authentic Australians. Aish and herself, they had real pasts, real histories. Jewish, Indian, migrant; it all meant something, they had no need to make things up, to assume disguises.

'I had no idea you knew each other.'

'We exchanged numbers at your party. She's lovely. And she's obviously been a good influence on Terry.' Rosie quickly rectified her mistake. 'Bilal, I mean.'

'Yes, they seem happy.' Aisha's reply was curt, offering nothing.

Rosie leaned across and almost whispered. 'We can't meet anywhere where they serve alcohol. That feels so odd.'

That means you can meet without having to take your husband, doesn't it? You don't have to risk Gary getting drunk and embarrassing you. Their wine bottle was almost empty. 'I'm going to the bar.'

The pub was getting crowded, full of smoke and it was a wait before she could get served. Just as the bartender asked for her order, she felt a tap on her shoulder and she turned around. The man from the table next to them was grinning at her. His face was flushed, pink. His mouth was wide and his lips full.

'Can I buy you this round?'

'That's very kind of you, but I'm getting a bottle for the table.'

'That's alright. I'm happy to shout all you ladies.'

Anouk smiled ruefully and shook her head. 'Afraid not.' She had let go of the fantasy the second he began speaking. His voice was thin, reedy. Men should not have little boys' voices. 'I'm with someone.'

'Lucky bastard.'

'Thank you.'

The bartender returned with her order and the man slipped a fifty-dollar note across the counter. She began to protest but he interrupted.

'My shout. I'm Jim.'

'I'm Anouk.'

His eyebrows rose. 'Like the actress?'

It pleased her that he knew this. This was not common for Australian men.

'Yes, like the actress.'

Jim assisted her back to the table. The noise from the crowd was amplified in the narrow bar and they found they had to shout.

'Your parents French?'

'No. My parents were francophiles.'

She found herself a little tongue-tied when she reached their table. Jim placed the bottle before the women and introduced himself. He pointed to his friend, who rose, and walked over.

'This is Tony.'

Tony was also tall, younger than Jim, slimmer with a thick moustache. He was balding. They all shook hands and then there was an uncomfortable moment of silence.

'Do you want to join us?' Aisha finally asked.

Jim raised his eyes at Anouk. He slowly shook his head. 'You ladies look like you're having a girl's night out. We'll do the gentlemanly thing and leave you alone.' He looked straight at Anouk. 'Enjoy the night. I just wanted to buy you all drinks. In celebration of gorgeous women.'

Anouk left it to Rosie and Aisha to thank him. She was making sure she could memorise everything about him. The colour of his hair, his ruddy cheeks, the strong, heavy jaw, the fading sunburn visible under his unbuttoned collar, the thick neck, the smattering of fine blonde hair on his arms and wrists. His eyes, his mouth, his hands.

Aisha waited till the men had seated themselves again at their table before speaking. She leaned forward conspiratorially. 'I don't want to giggle but I feel like giggling.'

'Don't you fucking dare giggle.' Anouk's eyes were imploring her friends to behave. 'What did I miss?'

The grin departed from Aisha's face. It struck Anouk that Aisha looked too thin. Her cheekbones seemed too sharply defined beneath her dusky skin; there were dark shadows beneath her eyes.

Anouk took her friend's hand beneath the table and held it tight. 'You alright?'

Aish nodded and Anouk loosened her grip. Their hands slid apart.

'Rosie was saying that Shamira is the first veiled woman she has ever spoken to.'

Rosie looked embarrassed. 'Not quite, Aish. Obviously, I have shared greetings with strangers or across shop counters. But I've never had a conversation with a Muslim woman before.' Rosie dropped her voice. 'I feel a bit ashamed, but I can't take my eyes off her headscarf. I want to forget it but I can't.'

'That's because it appears strange to you.'

'And it isn't strange for you?' Rosie shot back.

Aisha didn't respond. God, thought Anouk, let's not have this conversation.

'Aish simply meant she's Indian, it's not strange for her. Or for me.'

'Because you're Jewish?' Rosie sounded incredulous.

Anouk remembered as a child her parents taking her to Sydney for a wedding, and in Bondi, at some stranger's house, she had first seen women covered. They had not mixed with any Orthodox in Perth. They had scared her, these women; even the young ones had seemed ancient.

'Yes, some Orthodox women cover their heads. I think they're doormats as well,' she added emphatically.

'Shamira says it gives her strength. It's given her confidence.'

I'm not going to have this conversation, thought Anouk, let us not have this fucking conversation again. She was sickened by the return of questions of religion and God. Increasingly she felt restricted by the morality and the confusion of this new century. She had abandoned God a long time ago when still a child. Her atheism had seemed normal, expected. Of the world. This new century seemed to stretch out before her with an unrelenting, atavistic resolve. She wished that she had been born twenty years earlier. Born a man, twenty years earlier.

'I hate it when I see women covered. I detest it. It makes me furious that they let men do that to them.'

Rosie's face registered shock and disapproval. Anouk too was surprised by Aisha's vehemence.

'But, Aish,' Rosie answered, 'not all Muslim women are forced into the veil. You know that. Surely you support their right to wear whatever they want.'

Anouk couldn't keep silent. 'I'm not having this fucking conversation. Let us not have this conversation.'

'Why?' Rosie would not back down. She was directing her questions to Aisha. 'Do you think Shamira is lying to herself when she says the veil gives her strength?'

'Shamira's strength comes from being with Terry. Shamira's mother is a drunk, her sister's a junkie and her father is God knows where. It's Terry who gives her strength, not a piece of cloth over her head.' Aisha's fingers moved towards the cigarette packet but she didn't take one.

'And Bilal's faith is what gives him strength.' Rosie would not back down.

Anouk knew she was right. She remembered Terry before his conversion, his wit and boyish charm, but also the violence that seemed to lie just beneath his jovial, egalitarian demeanour, the aggro that would surface whenever he got drunk. His open, friendly face was inexorably falling to dissipation and fat, there was always the toxic smell of grog emanating from his body. She had been amazed by the different man who had shaken her hand years later at a dinner at Hector's and Aish's house. He had not yet taken on his new Muslim name but he had converted and was studying Arabic and his new faith. His eyes and skin were clear, he had gained weight, filled out. He was calm, as though he had finally found repose. She had never thought him a happy man, but he looked content then. Truth be told, the lacerating awareness of her country's racial history and her own prejudices had made her assume that he would never be happy, that he would always be aggro. That he would die aggro—aggro and young. She grinned at a blasphemous thought, one that she knew she could never share with Rosie: he had been young and aggro and now he was pious and boring.

Instead she nodded. 'It's true. But can we not talk about religion? I thought God had died just before my ninth birthday but it seems that was not the case. I hate being proved wrong. Let's talk about something else.'

Jim was still glancing over at her. She was glad to be a woman, drinking, flirting, having fun.

Rosie laughed. 'Done. No God talk. It's just that she's been such a help to me. I think we're going to be friends.'

'Who?'

Anouk, distracted by the flirtatious game she and Jim were playing, had lost track of the conversation. Was this muddle-headedness also a curse of pregnancy?

'Shamira,' replied Rosie, stealing a glance at Aisha and then quickly looking away. They've talked about this already. Anouk felt a piercing jolt of adolescent jealousy.

'How is she being a help?'

'She's been such a rock. With this business of Hugo being bashed.'

I will not go there, I will play dumb.

'We've charged Hector's cousin with assault.' Rosie could not bring herself to look at Anouk.

'Rosie, don't do this.'

'Gary's determined.'

Anouk, in frustration, glared at Aisha. 'You say something to her.'

'It's Rosie's choice,' Aisha answered firmly.

'Then I'm going to be a witness for Harry and Sandi.'

Rosie swung around. 'You saw that bastard bash Hugo.'

'I saw Harry slap Hugo. And I saw that Hugo deserved it.'

'No one deserves to be hit, let alone a child.'

'That's just a platitude, a new age bullshit platitude. You need to teach a child discipline and sometimes that discipline has to be physical. That's how we learn what is acceptable and what is not.'

Rosie was furious. 'Just shut it, Anouk. You have no right to say what you are saying.'

Because I'm not a mother? She nearly said it, she had to choke back on the words: I'm pregnant. She must not raise her voice, she must state her argument calmly.

'My point is not about your son. My point is a general one. We're raising a generation of moral imbeciles, kids who have no sense of responsibility.'

'You do not teach children responsibility by bashing them.'

'Harry did not bash Hugo.'

'He hit him. He assaulted him. That's illegal.'

Anouk exploded. 'That's crap. Maybe he shouldn't have slapped Hugo but what he did was not a crime. We all wanted to slap him at that moment. You're going to fuck up Harry and Sandi's lives just because Gary has it in his head that he was done wrong and because Gary always has to be the victim.'

Anouk wasn't shouting but she was loud, dogged, her tone urgent. She was aware that Jim and Tony had fallen silent at the next table but she did not care. She wanted her words to be knives, to hurt Rosie. She felt as if she had never detested anything in her life with more passion than her friend's self-righteous conviction.

'Or is it that he's bored? Is that it, Rosie? Gary's bored and he wants some drama in his life?'

Rosie was quietly sobbing. 'You have no right. You have no right.'

'Hugo's problem is not that Harry slapped him. Hugo's problem is that neither you nor Gary had the control over your child to stop him acting like a brat.'

'Anouk, that's enough.' Aisha was livid.

It was enough. She had nothing more to say. She had wanted to say these things to Rosie for a long time, but there was no pleasure or satisfaction in saying them. She felt guilty and wretched at seeing the effect her words had on her friends.

Aisha was holding Rosie's hand. 'You don't have the right to say any of that, Anouk. Rosie is right.' Aisha's tone was icy, her eyes were black steel. 'You aren't very interested in our children, we know that and we can deal with that. You don't like babies and you don't like talk about babies and children. You've made that clear over the years and we've respected that. But don't then assume that you can start being an authority now.' Aisha was struggling to hold back her own tears, her voice was shaky. 'Harry didn't have any right to hit Hugo. Yes, maybe we all felt like slapping him at that moment but the point is no other adult did. We exercised self-control, which is what makes us different from children. We didn't slap him because we knew that was the wrong thing to do.'

No, some of us didn't because we were too scared. But Anouk was tired. She was not prepared to argue further. This is why I will not have this baby, she said to herself, why I am going to have the abortion. I don't want to become like either of you. I'm not on your side, not in this. This is not the only way to be a parent but it is the only way this world now allows. And to do it my way would be an exhausting struggle and maybe I could do it but I couldn't do anything else. Anouk realised that she was repeatedly clenching and unclenching her fists. There was silence at their table, made more insistent by the buzz of the now crowded beer-garden, all the drunken laughter and conversation. She knew that the women were waiting for her to fill the silence, to renew their camaraderie, to make them all feel safe again. It had always been this way. It came to Anouk with the force of a revelation. She was the risk taker, the cool one, the glamorous one. She had the actor boyfriend, the high-powered job. She was not a mother, she was not a spouse. She was different and they must have always seen her as different. Even Aish.

Anouk stood, leaned across the table and kissed Rosie's brow. 'Darling, I'm sorry,' she said simply. 'I agree. He had no right.' Rosie smiled tearily. 'Thank you.'

Aisha gripped Anouk's hand and looked straight at her. I'm sorry too, she mouthed. Carefully, Anouk wrested her hand free and lit a cigarette. Aisha furtively, guiltily, took one from the packet and this made Anouk and Rosie suddenly snigger.

Aisha ignored them.

'Has it struck you that smoking is the new adultery?' Anouk whispered with a wink to Rosie.

'That's what Gary says,' Rosie answered and Anouk let that pass without comment.

Aisha changed the subject. 'So what did you want to speak to us about? You said on the phone you wanted our advice.'

I wanted *your* advice, thought Anouk, but instead said, 'I'm thinking of quitting the job. I want to see if I've got it in me to write the novel I've always bloody talked about and have kept putting off.'

Rosie and Aish squealed as if they were girls again. They were overjoyed for her.

'Of course you should,' said Aisha. 'We've been wondering how long it would take for you to make this decision.'

'You've got to,' agreed Rosie. 'You've just got to. And you can, Anouk.'

'I know,' and she finished the sentence with the words that the others did not dare speak. 'I don't have children to worry about.'

Rosie poked her tongue out at her. She had been forgiven. 'Gary's in the same head space. He's talking about painting again.'

Anouk and Aisha shared a quick, covert glance. There was no similarity between her creative ambition and Gary's. He had no discipline, no talent. The idea that he was a painter was a joke to them.

'Let's get another bottle.'

They proceeded to get riotously drunk. Later that night, Anouk got home and rushed to the toilet where she threw up, again and again, something that she had not done for over twenty years. She drained her body of everything, of the food and the wine, and it seemed to her that she was expelling her child with every retch.

The next morning Rhys came over before she awoke and she rose to the smells of eggs and bacon being fried. She ran to the bathroom and vomited again.

'You must have got hammered last night.' He was kneeling beside her, wiping her brow.

'That I did,' she groaned ruefully as he helped her back into bed. 'Sorry, Rhysbo, I've got no appetite.'

'You girls can drink us guys under the table.'

No we can't, she wanted to answer, not because we're women but because we are no longer twenty-five. It takes days for us to recover. She thought about saying, Rhys I'm going to have a baby. Will you take time out of your career to help me raise it while I write my novel? She looked at him as he reclined alongside her. He'd probably say yes. He'd probably be happy to do it and wouldn't start resenting her till years later.

She tickled his nose. 'Aish asked me last night if you could sign some photos for Connie and Richie.'

'Are they her kids?'

She rolled her eyes. 'You smoke way too much pot.' God, she did sound like a mother. 'Aisha's children are called Adam and Melissa. Which I've told you a dozen times. Connie was the teenage blonde girl at the barbecue, a cute kid, a nice girl. Remember?'

'Vaguely.'

'Richie was her boyfriend.'

'Yeah?' The hint of doubt in Rhys's voice intrigued her.

'What?'

'I just thought he was gay.'

Gay? She thought it preposterous. Richie was just a normal, boring kid.

'My God, you are vain.'

Rhys looked wounded. 'I didn't mean it that way. It's just a feeling I got.' He looked up at her, teasingly. 'My generation has got a good gaydar, you know, not like you uptight old baby-boomers.'

This made her laugh. 'Watch it, I'm not that old. Anyway, I don't think it's true, but just in case, get them both a photo of you topless. Unless your gaydar is telling you the girl's a dyke?'

He rose, laughing as well, and headed to her kitchen. She heard him put on a coffee. She threw the sheets off her and looked down at her stomach. It was flat, it seemed impossible that life was commencing inside there. Rhys and I would make great parents for a gay kid, she mused, they'd be lucky to have us. She patted her stomach. But that's only one chance in ten, kiddo, and only one chance in twenty if the God-botherers are right. I just don't like the odds, she whispered to her belly.

She went to the clinic on her own. She returned on her own. The taxi driver was a Serb and he was a grandfather. He was delighted that she could remember a few Yugoslav words from her time in Zagreb and he made her promise that one day she would visit Belgrade. He was a gentleman and seeing that she was pale and unsteady, he walked her to the door. Inside her apartment she glanced at a photocopy the nurse had given her on things not to do after a termination. She scrunched up the sheet and flung it in the bin. She found that she could not stop thinking of the taxi driver she had insulted the week before. She stripped, slipped on her robe and switched on the television. She could not forget his face. She muted the volume, rang the taxi service and waited for a human voice. She gave the details of the fare and asked if she could have the address of the driver. The woman on the other end sounded stern.

'We can't give you those details. Do you have his plate number?'

'No.'

'Do you wish to make a complaint?'

'God no, I want to send him an apology. I'm afraid I was terribly rude to him and he did not deserve it.'

The woman's voice softened. 'I'm sure you weren't rude.'

'No, I'm sure I was.'

There was a pause and then the woman said that she would make enquiries, she would get an apology to the driver. Anouk gave as many details of the fare as she could—the time, the date, the pick-up, the destination—and when she was finished, she asked shyly, 'Will you make sure he gets my apology?'

'I'll try.'

'Do you want my name?'

'No,' the woman replied firmly. 'That's not important.'

She slept soundly and awoke with her head pounding and what felt like a laceration in her abdomen. She could not bear the thought of breakfast or of a shower. She slipped on a pair of track-pants and a shirt and she rang Rhys. She left a message on his phone for him to come over that night. She turned on the computer, put on a coffee and sat down at her desk. She wrote her letter of resignation quickly and efficiently: she said all she wanted to say in four lines. She then opened up another Word document. She looked at the terminal screen. The cursor blinked. She sipped her coffee and lit a cigarette. The cursor was still blinking.

'Well, fucking write then,' she said out loud.

So she began to write.

HARRY

Harry stood on the verandah, naked except for his Dolce & Gabbana sunglasses and his black lycra Speedos, looking over on the flat calm waters of Port Phillip Bay. The setting sun painted the horizon in swirls of red and orange and the spires and flat-topped skyscrapers of Melbourne were just visible through the late afternoon smog that sat over the city. Harry's body glistened from the suntan lotion and sweat; the day was still scorching hot and there had been no breeze since the early morning. He could smell the meat that Sandi was sizzling in the kitchen and he rubbed his hand over his stomach, anticipating dinner. Cars were crawling slowly, bumper to bumper, along Beach Road. Fuck you, losers. Harry smiled to himself. From his newly finished verandah he had a clear view below to the sand and water. Four young girls in thin strips of bikinis were showering in the park. They had pert adolescent tits, they were blonde and lithe. Grinning, he pushed his crotch hard against the dark tinted glass of the balcony wall. He breathed long and hard, his eyes still focused on the girls below, who were now giggling and squealing, splashing water at each other. His penis lengthened and hardened, stretching against the lycra. Slowly, he rocked back and forth against the glass. Come on, bitch, he mouthed to himself. One of the girls had bent over and he let out a small groan at glimpsing her full, toned buttocks. Wouldn't you want my cock up that hole, you little whore.

He stepped back from the glass. The girls were now drying off, collecting their towels and bags, but his interest had waned. He took one more look at the world below him, and then turned and dived into the pool. He smacked the water's surface and entered the blissfully cold world beneath; he emerged for air, grinning. He dived once more beneath the surface and then rolled like the seals Rocco loved watching at the zoo. He turned on his back and stretched his limbs out over the water. 'I am the king of the world!' he shouted to the sky.

'Is his majesty hungry?'

Sandi was standing at the edge of the pool, her skin tanned a rich honey. She too was wearing a bikini, but whereas the girls' swimsuits had seemed sluttish and vulgar, his wife seemed to him to be as exquisite as the elegant European models on the covers of the magazines she read. He had bought the bikini for her. The pearl-coloured fabric straps were held in place with small coils of gold. He looked up at her and regretted having wasted time fantasising over the cheap floozies on the beach. Sandi was a real woman. She was wearing one of his old denim work shirts over her bikini and she still managed to look spectacular. I am the king of the world, he repeated silently.

'I'm famished.'

'Then dinner is served, your majesty.'

The television was on in the kitchen and there was catastrophe on the screen. A bomb? An earthquake? A war? He didn't fucking care, let the towelheads and the yids wipe themselves out. He punched a button on the remote control, found images of nature and colour on one of the cable stations, and turned down the volume. He poured wine for himself and for Sandi, lit a cigarette and sat on a stool watching her prepare the dressing for the salad.

'Where's Rocco?'

'Watching tele in the lounge.'

Harry belowed out his son's name and waited for a response.

'What?' Rocco yelled back.

'Get in here.'

Rocco, as if in childish defiance of his parents' ease with their near-naked bodies, was wearing track-pants, a baseball cap and an over-sized black T-shirt with some garish gangsta insignia on its front. He had his socks and runners on.

'Aren't you hot?'

His son shrugged and carefully lifted himself onto the stool next to his father. 'What's for dinner?'

'Chops.'

'With chips?'

'You eat too many chips,' his mother warned.

'You can never eat too many chips.'

'Thanks for the support, your majesty.'

Rocco, quizzical, was chewing on his bottom lip. Harry resisted the urge to tell him off. Rocco made himself ugly when he did that.

'Why are you calling Dad "Your majesty", Mum?'

'Because I'm the king of this house.'

Rocco stopped chewing at his lip and Harry playfully tweaked the boy's earlobe. 'And one day you will be king.'

But Rocco had lost interest in the subject and instead swivelled around in his seat and stared at the television. He picked up the remote control and started switching channels.

Sandi leaned across the bench and took the remote off him. 'Leave it till after dinner. You watch too much television.'

'You can never watch too much television.'

Sandi's exasperated face made both father and son laugh out loud in guilty, masculine complicity.

'Have you called the lawyer?'

Rocco had gone to bed and they were watching a DVD on the new plasma television. It had cost the frigging earth but it was worth it, as large as a small cinema screen, situated in the centre of their feature wall. On either side of the screen sat granite stone slabs, lit by faint orange light, the water a constant softly burbling sheet down the surface of the stone. It all cost a bomb but it was ideal. He was paying the film little attention, some tedious rom-com; it was only Sandi's head lying on his lap that made him put up with it. He didn't want to disturb her by reaching over for the remote control. But it was she who suddenly sat up and muted the volume. He groaned out loud at the question.

'Have you?'

'I'll do it tomorrow.'

He watched her warily. Sandi rarely argued with him. She had learned early in their courtship that he reacted to a direct confrontation by a woman with implacable stubbornness. She nodded, unsmiling.

'I'll call him.'

Fuck. You.

'I'll call him tomorrow.'

Her expression was still petulant, unconvinced.

'I promise.'

Her face relaxed into a warm smile and she leaned over and kissed him on the lips. 'Thanks, baby.'

He ran his fingers against her neck, her shoulders. She was still wearing his shirt and he rolled it off her. But her question had made him tense, reminding him of the working week ahead, shattering the relaxed comfort of his Sunday evening. 'Sorry, honey. I'm too tired.'

Sandi moved away from his embrace and slipped the shirt back over her shoulders.

He kissed her brow and she turned up the volume on the television and rested back on his lap. But he was now too agitated to sit still. He rose gently, putting a cushion under her head, and went to the bar and took a Crown from the fridge. He wandered through the house and stopped outside Rocco's bedroom. The boy was curled up, quietly snoring in bed, the white sheet tangled around his body. The night was still hot and there was only the slightest flutter of a breeze coming off the sea. Harry looked up at the icon of the Mother and Child above his son's bed and he quickly made the sign of the cross. Thank you, *Panagia*, he whispered. It once seemed likely that he and Sandi would never have a child. She had difficulty conceiving and the first three pregnancies had ended in the pain of miscarriage. Thinking of his wife's ordeals, Harry winced and reaffirmed the promise he'd made to God. To protect her and love her always, and as he looked down at his sleeping son, he was grateful for the home and family they had made together.

And that cunt wants to fuck it all up. He couldn't decide who he hated more: the hysterical wife who had hissed at him with unconcealed contempt, the drunk, weak faggot of a husband, or the whining little prick he had slapped. He wished the three of them were dead. Fuck the lawyer. If he had real balls he'd take his shotgun and fire three quick bullets in each of their heads. He knew these people—freeloaders, whingers, complainers. Victims. They were the clients who weasled and begged for the cheapest deals and then when it came time to pay there was no money in their accounts. It had all gone on bongs or smokes or grog or whatever filthy shit they used to fill up their miserable, ugly lives. They were trash, should've been sterilised at birth. He shouldn't have slapped the child, he should have grabbed the bat off him and smashed it once, twice, a hundred times into the little fucker's head, made him pulp and blood. Almost tasting the blood, seeing the boy's face collapse into jutting bones and squashed muscle, Harry felt calm for the first time since Sandi had brought up the subject of the lawyer. He took a swig of beer and walked back into the lounge. Sandi was half-asleep. He switched off the television and lifted his wife into his arms.

'Bedtime,' he whispered.

He and Sandi awoke at six and he went straight down to the beach. He tried to get in a swim each morning, even in winter, but if the water proved impossibly cold he would make do with a long walk the length of the cove and back. But the morning sky was clear and the bay still, and though the first lunge into the water was a punch in his stomach and a kick to his balls, within a minute his furious strokes had propelled his body into the deep and he had forgotten the cold. Rocco was still asleep when he got back home and Sandi had put on some hippie-shit music and was performing a series of smooth yoga exercises. He showered, had a hurried breakfast of toast and coffee and went into Rocco's room. The boy had pushed the sheets to the edge of the bed, his body shiny from the night's sweat. He smelt good, thought Harry. He smelt innocent and clean.

'Wake him,' Sandi was behind him, her arms around his chest. Harry glanced at his watch. It was still only seven o'clock and the boy could have another half-hour of sleep. Harry shook his head. 'Not yet.'

He kissed his wife and headed down the stairs to the garage. He'd have a clear run at this hour all the way to the Westgate Bridge.

Alex had already opened up the shop and was working underneath the bonnet of an early 1990s Mitsubishi Verada. Harry slid his four-wheel drive next to the petrol pumps and beeped the horn. Alex turned around, spotted Harry, nodded, then went back to work. His grimy navy track-pants were sitting precariously on his thick hips. A prickly bush of black coils peeped out from the top of them and dived into the plunging crevice of the man's arse-crack. Harry screwed up a McDonald's bag that Rocco had dumped underneath the passenger seat, and as he withdrew from his vehicle, he expertly aimed for Alex's arse.

'What?'

Good shot.

'What?' mimicked Harry and started laughing. 'Pull up your dacks, you ox,' he said in Greek. 'Who wants to look at your fat, hairy arse?'

'They don't fit.' Alex was incapable of complex sentences. He was still determinately working on the engine.

'You're getting fat, mate.' Alex had gained at least twenty kilos since his divorce. Much of it was the fault of his mother. Alex had moved back to his parents' house and Mrs Kyriakou was cooking for him three times a day and that didn't include the greasy take-away lunches that Alex ate at work. Nor did it include the chips and chocolate bars he had on his break. It was not all his mother's fault. Alex had always lacked ambition and since Eva left him he'd surrendered to the assault of time on his body. He and Harry were the same age—less than a week separated their birthdays—but Alex looked at least ten years older. It was still possible to glimpse in him the attractive youth that Harry had gone to school with, who'd been his best friend for over twenty years and his best man at his wedding, but no girl would bother to look twice at Alex now.

When Harry had first thought of buying the autoshop in Altona he had asked Alex to be a partner. His friend had taken his hand, shook it proudly, with tears in his eyes. But I'm no businessman, mate, he had answered, I'd be bad for you. He was right. Harry would have killed him years before if they had been in partnership together. Alex loved working on cars and trucks, he was an excellent, thorough mechanic, but he hated paperwork and he loathed communicating with clients. He couldn't stand to be accountable for money, it made him tighten up, made him silent and non-communicative. He had been working for Harry for twenty years now and every year Harry gave him a bonus and steadily and loyally increased his wages. Alex was grateful but Harry was sure that if he had been less than fair to his mate, Alex would not have complained. It was this passive lethargy that had made Eva walk out on her husband. Alex's parents had put a deposit on a small worker's cottage in Richmond when Alex had finished his apprenticeship and, steadily over the years, Alex had paid off the house. But even with the arrival of a baby, Alex couldn't contemplate moving and searching for a bigger home. Harry thought it unlikely that Alex would have even bothered with marriage if his parents had not become obsessed by the possibility of being without grandchildren. He'd married out of duty, as he did everything else. Harry was not surprised by the divorce and did not blame Eva for leaving. Alex would never change. He was happy in his room, drinking with mates who went back three decades, seeing his kids every fortnight and at Orthodox Easter, and working full-time at Harry's shop. Alex probably thought his life was good. It probably was, thought Harry, there was no stress, but it was also a life that seemed finished. It was as if there was nothing more that the world could offer his friend.

'You've got to lose weight, mate. Those extra kilos you've stacked up aren't good for your health.'

'You're right.'

'You should go back to playing soccer on the weekends.'

'Sure, mate.'

'And no more fucking junk food. Salad sandwiches for lunch from now on.'

This made Alex raise his head from underneath the bonnet and look at his friend. 'Fuck that. What's the point of living to be an old man if I have to eat like a fucking rabbit to get there? I like my pies and burgers.'

'What's up with the engine?'

'The car's over-heating. Can't find a leak in the radiator so I'm just checking out the fan.'

'Whose is it?'

Alex shrugged. 'Dunno. Con booked it in.' It suddenly dawned on him that it was unusual for his boss to be at the shop so early on a Monday morning. Harry and Sandi had recently opened a third garage in Moorabbin and for the last few months most of Harry's time was taken up with the new business.

Harry grinned to himself as if he could see the thoughts slowly taking shape in his friend's head.

Alex wiped his hands, put down his work towel and offered a cigarette. 'So what are you doing here so early?'

Harry took the cigarette and Alex lit it for him. 'I've come to look at the paperwork.'

Alex raised an eyebrow. 'Is there a problem?'

Harry looked down the road. Traffic had started the long crawl into the city. The suburb stretched out flat and monotonous around him, all grey and muted, functional and drab. Even though the beach lay a few blocks south, that too seemed grim and unappealing when compared to the sparkling emerald stretch of sea that lay just outside his front yard. God, he thought, I can't stand the fucking western suburbs.

'Yes,' he answered finally. 'I think there's a problem.'

Alex picked up his towel, butted out his cigarette and turned back to the engine. Harry knew that this meant the conversation was finished. Whatever opinion Alex might have—if he did, in fact, have an opinion—the man would keep it to himself.

Harry finished his cigarette in silence, then walked over to the small makeshift office, a lean-to he'd built himself when he had first bought the shop. He searched the filing cabinet, found the account books, turned on the radio and sat down to work.

Sometimes, when the cumulation of life's responsibilities made him anxious and stressed, Harry wished he could go back to the simplicity of being a tradesman. Unlike Alex, he had never been obsessed with cars, but he'd always had a fierce curiosity to understand mechanical failure. His mother—God bless her departed soul—had been constantly afraid that her beloved only child would be electrocuted as he went about tinkering with faulty toasters, dead batteries and malfunctioning electric toys. Do something, she would scream at her husband, stop him, he's going to kill himself. Shut up, his father would roar back, leave the kid alone. You want to turn him into a fucking *pousti*. Leave him alone. Instead, his father—God bless the poor fucker's soul as well—would assist him in exploring the intricate world of circuits and electrical cords and eventually he allowed Harry to work on the family car. When they were bent over the engine together, father and son had an impenetrable bond which Harry's mother could not touch. It was only in the kitchen and in the intimate interiors of the house where Harry had felt unsafe. His mother and father could go for weeks without exchanging more than perfunctory communications. Harry learned early on to love these periods of silence. What he could not bear were the occasions when this silence was rent apart by the hatred that husband and wife had for one another. His mother would always start the fights. You're an animal, she would suddenly announce over a meal. You're a rapist, a degenerate. Her husband would continue to eat his food silently. You don't know what your father is like, she would insist to her son. You don't know his whores, his sins against God and nature. And Harry would wait for the moment that his father would rise and hit her. He'd pray then that one punch or one slap would be enough. Sometimes he'd see his father unbuckling his belt and he'd call out to his father to stop, try to intervene. But Tassios Apostolous was a strong man, and he'd push his son out of the way. One day you'll understand, he would often say to his child, women are the form the Devil takes here on earth. Harry would go into his room, lose himself in fixing his toys, the radio, the old black and white television his father had given him to work on. When he emerged back into the main part of the house, his father would be sitting in front of the television, his mother would be ironing or sewing in the kitchen. There might be a rip in his mother's blouse, blood in the corner of her mouth, but the shouting, the tearing into each other had stopped. Harry would be thankful that the silence was back.

Harry crossed himself. He prayed for the souls of both his parents. They had sheltered him, paid for his training, left him enough to get a start in the world. No one could ask for more than that.

Now he had little time for tinkering. He checked his mobile and already there were messages piling up. He rarely worked on cars these days, except for long-standing clients. Alex and Con worked at the shop in Altona and he had three guys working for him in Hawthorn and another three at the new garage. Moorabbin also had a twenty-four-hour convenience store attached to the motorshop and he employed a roster of young people to staff it. His time was spent managing wages, superannuation, deliveries and ordering. Sandi had always helped out but he had been insistent after Rocco's birth that she should feel free to give up work altogether. She had for a year but then asked to come back to work part-time. He had agreed and secretly been proud. He loved his new house, loved living by the beach—it had been a dream since childhood—but he had little time or respect for the rich skip bitches who were his neighbours, useless fake-tanned women with plastic smiles and silicone tits who spent their husbands' money on afternoon teas, endless shopping and personal trainers. He leaned across from his chair and touched wood. Thank you, *Panagia*, he silently prayed. Thank you for everything.

Sandi's hunch was right. There was something odd about the books. Alex claimed that business hadn't declined, that if anything it had increased over the past year. But this was not reflected in the profits. Sure, the shitfight in the Middle East had played havoc with the price of petrol, and they had laid out a fair amount of money refitting the garage over the last two years, but all of that had been factored into the accounts. He heard Con's car entering the yard. He lit a cigarette and looked up at the clock. The face was smeared with a thick cocoon of spider webbing and three dead blowflies were trapped behind it.

He heard Con greet Alex. The young man stopped, surprised, when he saw Harry sitting in the office.

'Yo, Boss.'

The silly fuck had his hair cut in the fashion of the yuppie English soccer players, cut short at the sides and up in a thick bouffant that rose to a point in the middle of his head. There were blond tips in front.

'The clock needs cleaning.' Harry glanced around the office. 'In fact, the whole office needs a clean.'

'Sure, I'll do it today. How's Sandi? How's the kid?'

'Sandi's fine, so's the kid.'

'What brings you here?'

Harry's mobile whirred and beeped.

'Take the call.'

'Forget it. I'm looking at the books.'

Con threw a cigarette to his lips and smiled. He was a cocky bastard. 'Any problems?'

'Yeah. I got problems. You're my problem.'

Con's smile faded and he fumbled with his cigarette. There was an edge to his voice. 'Man, I don't know what you're talking about.'

Harry said nothing. He watched his employee.

'Jesus, Harry. Are you going to fire me?' The young man's voice cracked and collapsed and he started sobbing. Harry saw Alex at the pump. A young woman had stepped out of a scarlet Toyota Corolla and was looking around. She was Asian, young and up herself, clutching a handbag with pink and yellow roses imprinted on the cloth, her chin raised in haughty expectation. Wait all you like, darling, Alex won't notice shit. Harry did not turn back to Con till the man had stopped his blubbering.

'Sit down.'

Con immediately sat on the chair opposite, wiped his eyes and looked anxiously at his boss.

'There's no fucking way I'm going to figure out exactly how much you've ripped me off, *pousti*. You care to name me a figure?'

'Man, I've done something stupid. I know it, man. I'll pay you back everything, Harry.'

'You care to name me a figure?'

Con looked wary, afraid. 'I've no idea, man.'

'Ballpark.'

'Twenty thousand?'

Harry let out a long low whistle. It was a good answer. Anything lower and he would have taken a club to the silly cunt. 'Double that, I reckon. You owe me forty grand.'

Con nodded slowly. He stretched out his hands. 'Mate, I don't have it.'

'Where's it gone?'

Harry knew exactly where it had gone. On the ridiculous mortgage that Con was paying for that piece of shit apartment in the city, on the new Peugeot, on coke and pills and dinner for that stupid skip prick-tease that Con was trying to impress. How long did he think she'd stick around now?

'I don't know, I don't know where it's gone.' Con had started crying again.

He was a weak piece of shit but Harry felt sorry for the boy. Not too sorry. He made up his mind there and then. He'd give him a chance. Sandi would disapprove, but Con hadn't attempted to lie or bullshit him. He'd give him that due.

'You're going to give me a third of your wages every week. I'm going to calculate interest on forty thousand starting today. Deal?'

Con was breathing heavily, he was unable to speak. He nodded.

'And Con, you dare walk out on me or pull this kind of shit on me again and I go straight to the cops. But before I do I'll put a wrench through your fucking teeth and I'll fuck you up the arse with a screwdriver like a faggot at a choir boy's picnic. You understand me?'

The man's tears had dried. He stood up. 'Thanks, Harry.' Con extended his hand but Harry refused to take it.

'Fuck off and start work. I don't shake your hand until you pay me back every cent you owe me. I'll shake hands with you when you're a man again.'

There was a moment of fierce hatred and resistance in the young man's eyes. Then it disappeared and Con lowered his head. 'Sure, Boss.'

His walk was slow, defeated as he went to work alongside Alex.

Harry checked his messages. An old Italian client wanted him to look at his car. He hesitated then rang back and confirmed he'd meet Mr Pacioli at eleven in Hawthorn. There was also a message to call

Warwick Kelly. What the hell, he thought, I might as well kill some time till the rush hour is finished.

He punched in the number and Kelly's youngest daughter Angela answered the phone.

'Is your mum there?'

'How are you, Uncle Harry?'

'I'm good. How are you sweetheart? Are you getting ready for school?'

'I'm sick.'

'Really sick?'

'Yeah, my stomach hurts.' The girl sounded offended by his doubt.

'Guess I won't get you a chocolate then. It won't do your tummy any good.' He grinned to himself at the long silence.

'I can have it when I feel better.'

Kelly came onto the line. 'Angela's sick.'

'So she says.' He could hear the girl's protests. 'I'm coming over.'

Kelly lived in a flat on the Geelong Road and he was there in ten minutes. She was on the phone when he rang the bell; she opened the door and kissed him, all the while speaking loudly in Arabic to whoever was on the other end. Harry guessed from the frustrated tone that she was talking to her mother. He walked past her and into the kid's room. Angela was lying in her bed, a pink teddy bear on her pillow, watching a children's show on a small TV. In an attempt to be a convincing invalid, she did not even raise a hand to greet him. He sat beside her and kissed the crown of her head.

'Did you get me a chocolate?'

'Yeah, but you can't have it now. You look too sick.'

'I am too sick. Put it in the fridge.'

'Sure, sweetheart.' He kissed her again. As he was about to leave, she rose and called after him. 'What kind of chocolate is it?'

'Cherry Ripe.'

'Yay,' she shrieked, and then, remembering, she lowered herself back to her pillow and let out a weary whimper. 'Thank you, Uncle Harry.'

Kelly was still on the phone and she mouthed at him to take a seat. He sat by the small round kitchen table and looked over the water, gas and telephone bills. He pulled out his wallet and laid out a hundred and fifty dollars on the table. He paid all the bills except for the telephone. He had given Kelly the mobile that she was to use when calling him and he only paid for that. Kelly was a good woman. She only ever used that phone, never exposed him to danger with his wife. He watched her as she walked around the flat. She was tiny, with a cushiony, fleshy arse and large, low-hanging breasts. She was also dark and plump, a real contrast to Sandi's tallness and Serbian fairness. The difference excited him. She grimaced at him and he cheekily unzipped his jeans and began stroking at his cock. She threw him an exasperated look, then closed the kids' bedroom door and came over to him.

'Sure, Ma,' she said suddenly in English. 'I'll bring them over Sunday.' With her free hand, she started tickling his balls, then slowly her fingers tapped along the shaft of his fattening cock. 'Of course I won't fucking forget.' Harry looked up at the Madonna staring down disapprovingly at him on the kitchen wall. He closed his hand around Kelly's fingers to tighten her grip around his cock, and he thrust up and down on his seat, jerking himself into her hand. He pulled at her nipple, twisting it till she slapped his hand away. He was conscious of the young girl watching television behind the wall. He could smell his lover's sweat, and he kissed her arm, her neck, her hair as she finished the conversation. He shuddered, stifled his groan and blew into her hand. Kelly put down the phone.

'Look at me,' she hissed, showing him her coated hand. 'You're a pig.' Then, expertly, as if performing a routine household task, she grabbed a clean Chux wipe, wet it at the sink, and cleaned her hands. She threw the Chux at him.

'You want a coffee?'

'Sure.'

He wiped his cock, rubbed at a spot of cum on his jeans, and threw the Chux back at her. Kelly flicked it into the bin.

'Van called this morning. His equipment has fucked up. He needs some money.'

Jesus Christ. This was not his morning. 'How much does he need?'

'A couple of grand.' Kelly glanced down at the money on the table. 'Thanks, honey.'

'Shut up. You know I adore my Lebo chick.' He grabbed her and sat her on his lap. He wondered if there was time to get hard again and fuck her. He looked at his watch. No way. Kelly turned off the kettle and poured the boiling water into the cups. She sat down across from him, smiling, scratching at her left breast underneath her sweatshirt.

'Van doesn't bullshit, Harry. You know that.'

She was right. Van was an old Vietnamese schoolmate of Kelly's who duplicated DVDs from home. He was sent the original masters from Shanghai or Saigon, mostly Hollywood new releases and some porn, and like old-style travelling salesmen, he and Kelly went around to people's houses, hosting DVD afternoons and selling the illegal copies. It was a good, steady business and Harry and Sandi had a cupboard full of DVDs they had scored from Van.

'He's got the money.'

'He's over-extended. Like the nation. He's cash poor this week.'

Harry grinned. 'I want twenty per cent of the next drop.'

Kelly's reply was immediate. 'Ten per cent and the full two grand in your hand next week.'

Harry laughed out loud. She had balls, Kelly. He thought of Con an hour ago, blubbering like a bitch. 'Done. I'll drop off the money to Van this arvo.'

'Thanks, honey. When am I going to see you next?'

'Soon.' She was not his wife. He didn't owe her commitment.

He drank his coffee quickly, kissed his mistress on the lips and dropped the Cherry Ripe on Angela's bed. School had definitely started, and secure in her deception, she was sitting cross-legged on her bed playing with her dolls. She hugged him tight. She smelt like Rocco—they must use the same soap. He was whistling as he walked to the car.

His mobile rang as he was slowly circumnavigating the edge of the city. It was his own home number that was flashing on the screen and he decided not to take the call. It would be Sandi checking if he had called the lawyer. He turned the music on the stereo up to near distortion levels and rocked along to the churning, violent hip-hop beats. A new model Pajero Cruiser on his left was trying to enter his lane; he didn't give the prick an inch. He sped ahead and laughed as he saw the furious face of the old fat *malaka* in his side mirror. A twinge of guilt, not uncommon after visiting Kelly, led him to decide to buy his wife roses when he returned to the house that evening. She was right. He had to call the lawyer.

At first, the secretary refused to put him through. 'Mr Petrious is busy with a client.'

'Tell him it's Harry Apostolou.'

There was a pause. 'Is this about an appointment?'

What's it to you, cunt?

'Andrew knows what it's about.'

The casual use of his friend's first name did the trick. The girl's bored, supercilious tone changed in an instant.

'One moment, sir. I'll consult with Mr Petrious.'

Harry watched from his office as the guys worked on two cars, a Ford ute, a couple of years old, and a late-nineties BMW coupe. Of the three businesses he owned, he liked the one in Hawthorn the best. The site itself was a solid old thirties brick deco building. They built things to last back then. The garage was down an alley off Glenferrie

Road and that meant that it was only a short walk for lunch. Glenferrie Road was always busy and Harry enjoyed strolling down the
strip, stopping at the Turk's coffee shop and sitting down for a long
read of the paper, a few cigarettes, coffee and a chat to Irzik. The
Altona garage was in the middle of ugly bogan suburbia, and though
he was proud of the scale of the Moorabbin yard, it too sat off the
wide asphalt hideousness of the Nepean Highway: eight lanes of
cars, waves and waves of them, they never seemed to stop. And as for
finding a decent coffee, forget it. No, he preferred Hawthorn, even
the smell of it. A row of eucalypts stretched above the back wall of
the garage, lining the railway track that ran parallel to the alley. The
air in Hawthorn smelt clean. Not as good as the sea air in Sandring-
ham—no way near as good as the bracing, fresh air on his balcony at
home—but a million times better than the stink of salt and sewage
in Altona, so much healthier than the dry carbon-monoxide fog of
Moorabbin. When Rocco was old enough, he'd close down the yard
and get the site rezoned as residential. He'd renovate the garage so it
would become a house for Rocco. It would be close to the city, close
to the action, a good, safe, rich suburb. No mortgage. His son's first
home.

Andrew's deep voice interrupted his reverie. 'How's it hanging,
Doggy Dawg?'

'They're hanging right over your lips, bitch.'

Andrew roared like he was at the footy, at that moment when
there's three minutes before the siren and your team is one goal
behind. Harry held the mobile away from his ear.

'You want to see me today?'

'Yep.'

'What are you doing for lunch?'

'Meeting you.'

'Too right you are, *malaka*.'

'Where?'

'Where are you?'

'Hawthorn.'

Andrew named a pub in Richmond. 'Meet you at one.'

'Thanks, Andrea.'

'Shut the fuck up, Apostolou. You're paying.' With a chuckle, Andrew hung up the phone.

Harry rang Sandi immediately.

'Sorry, sweetheart. I was in traffic.'

'Did you ring the lawyer?'

'Done.'

He could almost taste her happiness. She liked white roses, he'd buy her white roses.

He bought her a music box instead. He finished up in Hawthorn sooner than he thought he would and had strolled down Burke Road for fifteen minutes, window shopping. In one of the shop windows he had spied a copper-plated box studded with shards of silver and what looked like an Arabic inscription in gold-raised lettering. Sandi liked that Buddhist shit. He went inside and indicated the box to the shopgirl.

'It's beautiful,' she gushed. She raised the lid and the inside was lined with a velvet crush fabric the colour of rubies. As soon as the lid was opened a pleasing oriental melody hummed from within the box. Harry pointed to the script.

'You know what that says?'

'It's Sanskrit.'

'And what's that?' He had no concern about showing his ignorance. He knew his education was limited and he saw no reason to hide it from the young girl before him. He had money and that's all that mattered.

'It's the ancient Indian language.'

She had hesitated. She didn't know what she was talking about.

'You don't know what it says?'

The girl bit her bottom lip apologetically and shook her head.

Harry smiled at her and picked up the box. 'It probably says *Fuck You, Yank.*'

The girl's mouth formed a shocked perfect circle and then she laughed out loud. Harry winked at her.

'Wrap it up for me, honey, make it look nice. It's a gift for the ball and chain.'

Andrew was at the bar with a beer when Harry entered the pub. It had been recently renovated but the new owners had kept as much of the original detailing as possible and any new additions were in keeping with the late Victorian edifice and interiors. Harry surveyed the room quickly, approvingly. He made a mental note to take Sandi there for dinner. He whacked Andrew on the back. The lawyer was sweating, still wearing his suit jacket with his tie neatly knotted at his neck. He was astonishingly thin, a stick insect, and so tall that seated he was eye to eye with the standing Harry. The two men embraced and Andrew called over the barman for another beer. Harry gestured in the negative but Andrew ignored him.

'*Uno, per favore.*'

'Mate, I'm driving all arvo.'

'We'll eat, we'll have a coffee. You'll be fine.' Andrew looked at him suspiciously. 'Don't tell me the nanny state's taken your soul, as well?'

'What the fuck are you talking about?'

Harry plonked himself on the stool beside Andrew and stared up at the lunch menu scrawled on a blackboard.

'Food good?'

'The food's fucking excellent.'

It was. Harry had ordered a plate of grilled calamari, conscious that there would be no time to get to the gym that afternoon. Andrew obviously had no such concerns. He ordered a burger and chips and a bottle of wine for lunch, most of which he consumed on his own. Harry marvelled at the lawyer's ability to eat as much of whatever he wanted and yet never add an ounce to his frame. It was because he never could stand still. Andrew had always been that way, since they were neighbours in Collingwood. At school, one bitch of a teacher with a sadistic streak had spent day after day attempting to beat the agitation out of him. If she saw him jittery or fidgeting she would stand him in front of the class and whenever he moved she would bring a metre ruler smashing against the back of his legs. Andrew would flinch, grimace, and try for a minute to stand as still as possible. He never succeeded. By the end of class the back of his legs would be crimson and purple from the whallops he had received. The teacher's vicious punishments came to an end when Andrew's mother attacked her at a parent–teacher night by grabbing her hair and slapping her. Andrew was not expelled for the simple reason that he was the brightest and smartest pupil at a school that was dependent on his winning the state Mathematics and English competitions to justify its appalling lack of educational success with the other students in the school's care. Andrew bore no obvious grudge against the teacher who had hurt him. She was an animal, thought Harry, but schools these days could use some of her ferocity. There had to be a middle path. No one back then had thought of going to the police or the lawyers to deal with their problems. Andrew's mother had apologised and the teacher had—possibly not with good grace—accepted the apology.

'Remember Miss Ballingham?'

'Who?' Andrew asked with his mouth full.

'Miss Ballingham in grade four.'

'Jesus, that psycho. She's probably in a maximum security prison somewhere. Guarding it, I mean.'

'She wasn't that bad.'

Andrew gulped down his mouthful and looked across at his friend. He put down his fork and sipped from the wine.

'What's this about, *malaka*?'

Harry could hear the *tap-tap-tap* of his heel on the floor. He made his foot go still.

'People will think I'm just like her.'

Andrew looked genuinely appalled, then pissed off.

'You're no Miss Ballingham.'

'Of course I'm no fucking Miss Ballingham.' Harry cursed in Greek.

Andrew wiped his lips and chin with his napkin, scrunched it into a ball and threw it on the table. He grabbed a cigarette, leaned back in his chair and let out a loud burp.

'I'm done. Let's get to business.' He rocked back and forth in the chair. '*Malaka*, I'm taking care of it. You have no record of assault, you have one misdemeanour stretching back to when you were a kid, you're a good father, a good husband, a good businessman. They're not going to hang you for belting some little prick kid that deserved it.'

'Should I say that in court?'

Andrew laughed. Ash had fallen on his shirt and he absent-mindedly brushed it off.

'No, you are going to look contrite, you are going to look like a loving husband and father. Which you are. I'm going to do all the talking. That's why your pocket is bleeding, *malaka*, you're paying for the opportunity to see me shine.' Andrew burped, again deliberately loud, to shock the tables around them. 'And if we're in luck that waste-of-space loser will turn up drunk. Don't worry about it.'

'Sandi wants to know when it will be.'

'Bah.' Andrew flung his hands in the air and looked unconcerned. 'It's months away.'

'I want a date.'

'We'll probably get a notice over the next month. What's the hurry?'

'I just want it done. I just wish the whole fucking thing was over.'

Andrew made a contemptuous wave over the food and drinks. 'Nah, it's nothing, mate. What's the worst that can happen to you?'

'You said I can get a conviction. My second one.'

'Shut the fuck up, Apostolou.' Andrew's tone became urgent and he leaned across the table. 'You got into a fight at sixteen. That's it. No judge is going to condemn you for that. You slapped this brat because he was threatening your child. Okay, they can try and make something of it but they're not going to get far. The charge of assault isn't going to stick. Worst-case scenario you get a slap on the wrist because the judge is some femo nazi or raving loony survivor type who sees abuse in everything. But even if they are loonies, what you did is nothing, do you understand me, it's fucking nothing. Nada. Zero.' Andrew's voice hardened. 'You know what the judge will have seen before you, Harry? I'll tell you because I've seen it in court. The judge will have seen two-year-olds with their jaw shattered and their skull caved in because some drug-fucked boyfriend of some drug-fucked sixteen-year-old took her son and banged him against the wall because he couldn't score his fix that morning. The judge will have seen some sick pervert pig who fucked his five-year-old daughter so often up the arse that poor girl can't shit and for the rest of her life is going to have a colostomy bag attached to her. This is the real world. Welcome to Australia in the early twenty-first century. No wonder the Arabs are so envious of us. Wouldn't you be? Isn't it fucking great?' Andrew stopped, embarrassed at his outburst, sniffed, and finished off the wine in his glass. When he spoke again, his usual mocking drawl had returned.

'You're gonna be alright, Harry. You, Sandi, Rocco, you're all normal. You got nothing to worry about. So, tell me what the fuck is really worrying you?'

'What are you talking about?'

Andrew silently scrutinised Harry while rocking back and forth in the chair. Harry looked across to a table at the edge of the courtyard where three young women were finishing their lunch. The blonde one was a looker. She had long legs, nicely tanned under the thin, tight denim of her miniskirt. Rock and roll, thought Harry, rock and roll. He turned back to his friend. Andrew's eyes had not moved off him.

'Sandi's scared that the television stations will find out.' For one ludicrous moment he thought he was going to cry. Don't you dare fucking cry, he threatened himself. He reached for his cigarettes and lit one quickly, inhaling deeply. He felt relieved. It was good to confess his anxieties to his friend. Sandi's fear had become his, a seed that had sprouted, and slowly, obstinately, it had taken root and flowered in his imagination. All that they had created could be smeared and trashed by that animal manipulating and twisting what had happened to his kid to make out that Harry was some kind of monster.

He had felt it when the cops had come around the day after the barbecue to interview him and Sandi. The female cop in particular. She was blonde, a looker. She despised him, he could tell. You could always tell with the pigs. He had tried to be polite, used all his charm but nothing worked. She had gone off separately with Sandi and left him alone with the male cop. He too had been unfriendly, young, barely out of cop diapers.

'So you hit a kid?' he had asked with an ugly sneer, as if Harry was some kind of pervert. 'You do that often?'

Harry had wanted to murder him. Instead, he laughed it off as a joke. The cunt cop didn't return the laugh. Harry's humiliation had deepened. Later, Sandi told him that the female copper had tried to get her to say that Harry beat her, beat Rocco, that he had a violent temper. Sandi politely denied that there was any violence or aggression in her husband's character, that he'd only hit that child because he was scared that Hugo was going to hurt Rocco. He's a saint, is he? the copper had taunted. Sandi's lip curled in distaste as she told Harry about the encounter. Then a sly grin spread across her mouth. I took a chance, she said to Harry, I asked the bitch if she had children. Of course, she didn't. It shut her up. No, it didn't thought Harry, what had shut them up was asking to see Rocco. Their child had shut them up because it was obvious to anyone, even to some dim fuckwit copper, that Rocco was a wonderful, sane, normal, blessedly normal, good kid. Thank you, God, that he is normal, thank you, *Panagia,* that he is a good kid. That's what shut them up.

'This case is not going to get in the news.'

'Yeah?'

'Why would it?'

'That loser, Hugo's father, he told Sandi over the phone that he was going to *A Current Affair* with it.'

Andrew started to chortle.

'It's not fucking funny.'

'Being concerned about something as stupid and ridiculous as *A Current Affair* is funny. Who cares what *A Current Affair* or any of those crap shows say or do? That's not news, that's just moving pictures on a screen for morons.'

'You may not care, but my neighbours care, Rocco's friends' parents care, my workers care, my *thea* cares. We're the morons that watch that show.'

Andrew's tone softened, turned apologetic. 'You're not going to be on *A Current Affair*. You're not a story. You're not fucked-up enough. If you want to be on a show like that, next time send the kid to hospital.'

'You know what happened after the cops came that day. None of the neighbours will look at us. Sandi and I and Rocco don't exist for them. Just because they saw a cop car outside our place.'

'Your neighbours are the kind of people who expect the police to be on call twenty-four/seven but otherwise don't want to know they exist.' The steel in Andrew's tone returned. 'I'm sure your neighbours weren't shocked. I'm sure that's what they expected to happen as soon as wogs moved into the neighbourhood.'

You sarcastic lawyer cunt. I could do you, I could fucking do you now.

'I'm trying to make you understand why Sandi is so scared, why we're so nervous. I spent years building this house. And this arsehole, this nothing piece of Aussie yobbo shit is trying to destroy it all. Why do I have to go to court? Can't you stop it? This isn't fair.'

'No, it isn't.' Andrew picked up his cigarettes and pocketed them. 'I've got to go. I'll ring you as soon as the court notice comes through. Tell Sandi not to worry about *A Current Affair*. That freak probably got on the phone while raving drunk and I doubt he got further than the receptionist. As for your neighbours, better learn to live with them. If you wanted friendly neighbours you shouldn't have bought a big motherfucking block of land right across the road from Brighton Beach.'

He was regretting the beer and the wine by the time he got home that evening. All afternoon he'd felt light-headed and by three he had developed a dull but steady headache. He'd lost his temper with the young Indian guy working the store in Moorabbin. The lazy bastard was always trying to change his roster and as soon as Harry walked in Sanjiv had come out from behind the counter and demanded Saturday off.

'How about a fucking hello?'

'Please, Mr Apostolou, I cannot work Saturday night.'

There was a group of school boys in the back, probably shoplifting. A young tradie pushed through the doors. Harry nodded towards him. But Sanjiv ignored the customer and instead patiently waited for an answer from his boss.

I wish I could fire you on the spot you butt-ugly Hindu cum-rag.

'No,' he said curtly. 'I need more notice. I can't get anyone to fill in for you Saturday. You're just going to have to do the shift.'

The boy's expression did not change. He slowly nodded and turned and walked back to the counter. Harry touched his forehead, his eyes felt heavy and there was a distinct throbbing in his head. He passed the schoolboys and for a moment was tempted to grab one of their bags and tip the contents on the floor. He was sure they were lifting from him. There were four of them, two skips, two Asians, giggling, the tall white one speaking loudly about smut and sex, trying to impress the others. Harry had bitten his lip. He wished he could say to the little bastards, Hey, if you're not going to buy anything, fuck off from my shop. But he couldn't risk it. He couldn't risk one of the little fucks saying something smart-arse in return. The way he felt at the moment, Harry couldn't risk his temper worsening. He felt horribly, inescapably trapped.

The electric hum of the store, the air, the schoolboys' voices were a fog around him. His hand was shaking as he fumbled with the key to open the storeroom. He crashed through the door, slammed it behind him, and rested his head on the cool metal of the shelf. He looked up at the clock on the storeroom wall and he shamelessly indulged in a little boy's fantasy that he could turn back the time, to before the barbecue at his cousin's, to before hitting that little cunt. He had been so happy. He lifted his head, shook away the world. You don't deserve this shit, he told himself. You did nothing wrong.

He did the wages, some bookkeeping and then locked up. In passing, he told Sanjiv he'd find someone to do the shift on Saturday night.

'How about a massage?'

It was the first thing she said to him when he walked into the house and her solicitude, her sensitivity to his mood, her care and her affection immediately routed his headache. He hugged her and Sandi relaxed into him. His grip tightened around her and she submitted easily, without anxiety or fear.

After a few moments she gently pushed him back. She held on to his arms. 'What's up, lover?'

'Nothing. I'm just tired and glad to be home.'

'What did Andrew say?'

'It's all fine. There's nothing to worry about.' He felt the buzzing in his head return.

Sandi was about to speak, but she stopped herself. He saw that she was tense and he wished there was something he could say to eradicate all her worries, to take away every single one of her fears. It was at that moment he made up his mind to lie.

'I tell you, he said there's nothing to worry about. Some journo from a TV station did contact him but Andrew put him straight. The journo told him he thought that that was the case because the prick was pissed when he phoned up. He abused the receptionist and everyone he spoke to. No one is going to take the arsehole seriously.' As his story unfolded he found himself enjoying the lie, almost believing it himself.

His wife made no reply. She moved to the sink and began to dry dishes.

He came up beside her and took the hand towel off her. 'Let me do it.'

'He's just going to go somewhere else.'

Jesus Christ, I'm so fucking tired.

'He'll get the same response everywhere he goes. Don't you get it, Sandi, the arsehole's a loser.'

'You can't be sure. Someone's going to listen to him, someone can smell the story.'

He threw the towel onto the bench. 'What fucking story, Sandi, what fucking story? I slapped a kid. That's all. No one's interested.'

She was standing very still. It was like an advertisement: his wife in the middle of the expensive, perfect, modern kitchen he had built for her.

He touched her hair, kissed her softly on the lips. 'I'm not going to let the bastard hurt you.'

She grabbed the towel. When she spoke her voice was small. 'I don't care about me. It's you I care about. It's what he's doing to you that hurts.' She began to sob. He felt paralysed and was suddenly aware that Rocco must be somewhere in the house, in his room. Her sobs were loud, and he didn't want his son to hear them. He pulled her into his body and held her.

'Shh,' he whispered. 'We are going to be alright.'

Her body gradually relaxed, her sobbing stopped. She kept holding on to him.

'I could kill him,' she mumbled into his chest. 'I could kill him and that arrogant bitch.'

And that stupid cunt of a kid. I could fucking kill *him*.

'I'll put the dishes away. Go say hello to Rocco.'

His son was in his room, on PlayStation. Harry sat cross-legged next to him on the floor.

'Want to play?'

'Sure.' He leaned over and hugged Rocco. 'How was school?'

'Same.'

'What did you do?'

'We watched a video.'

'What kind of video?'

'On Eskimos but they called them another name.'

'Was it good?'

'It was okay. A bit boring.' Rocco was setting up another game and his eyes were fixed on the television screen. 'It looked really really cold. There was this family and they had to live in an ice house under the ground for months and months and ages and all they had to eat was seal blubber. It looked gross.'

'Did they have PlayStation?'

Rocco glanced at his father and then grinned. 'Nah, but they have the internet. How amazing is that?'

As he played the computer game with his son, both their backs resting against Rocco's single bed, as he chuckled over the boy's competitive streak, Harry felt his headache fade. He didn't feel like a drink, a pill, even a smoke. By dinner time he was ravenous. Sandi had cooked steaks and served them with mashed potato and the simplicity and heartiness of the meal was gratifying. As she washed up, he slipped the music box into the bathroom cabinet, next to her toothbrush. He showered, jumped into bed naked and waited. He heard her squeal of delight from the ensuite bathroom. She jumped into bed and straddled him.

'I love you.' She was holding the music box, opening and shutting the lid, the tinny oriental music kept starting and stopping. He unhooked her bra and drew circles around her left nipple. Sandi was still playing with her gift, but with her right hand she reached back and softly cupped his balls. She placed the music box on the windowsill and she moved down his body, kissing his chest, licking his belly, teasing him. Her lips brushed his cock and she had him in her mouth. He closed his eyes, and tried to think of nothing but what his wife was doing to him. But suddenly he returned to the moment earlier in the day when Kelly had aroused him in her kitchen. He opened his eyes and raised his head to look at his wife. He tried to pull her up.

'No,' Sandi whispered. 'I want you to come in my mouth. I want you to fuck my mouth.'

'Are you sure?'

The pornographic words excited him.

'Fuck my mouth,' she urged and took his cock once more inside her. He closed his eyes again and this time he thrust his body into her mouth. 'That's it, honey, that's beautiful.' Silently, not wishing to offend her, he mouthed words to Kelly. Suck me, bitch. Come on, bitch, suck me off. He lifted himself on the bedhead, got onto his knees. He continued fucking his wife in the mouth. He could see her gagging but when he stopped his thrusting she clutched his arse and pushed him deep into her. He blew his cheeks out, stifled his shout and came with savage force. Sandi refused to release him. He spasmed and fell against the bedhead. He didn't look at Sandi as she went to the bathroom. He heard the tap run and he knew she would be cleaning her teeth again. He smiled sheepishly at her when she returned to bed. She picked up her gift again and lay in bed looking at it. He rolled over and spooned her into his body.

'That couldn't have been much fun for you.'

She was examining the music box.

'I enjoy making love to you. You don't have to thank me. You're my husband.'

'My cock thanks you.'

She was still opening and shutting the music box. He tightened his arms around her.

'Tell me about your day.'

He stroked her hair as he told her about his warning to Con, told her about Sanjiv breaking his balls, the loan to Van. He told her about the car he started work on in Hawthorn, a late-sixties Valiant that the owner wanted to restore back to its original condition. Sandi listened till he finished.

'I want to get the girls around on Saturday, look through some DVDs. Do you want to ask Van?'

He murmured an assent. He was falling asleep.

'And ask Hector. We haven't seen Aish and Hector for ages.'

He froze, waiting. They hadn't seen his cousin since the barbecue. But Sandi seemed relaxed, unconcerned. He hugged her close to him.

'I'll call them.'

The lie seemed to work. Sandi came into Moorabbin with him on the Wednesday and she was cheerful, laughing and joking with the customers and the staff. Harry watched the appreciative glances the Indian boys threw at her and he was pleased. Seeing her happy, calm, he relished the lie and became seduced with it himself. There was nothing that anyone could do to them. They would be fine— they were protected. Delighted with the return of normality he phoned Kelly and cancelled a dinner he had promised her. She was, as always, unperturbed.

'Cool. So when will I see you?'

'Not sure.'

'Call me when you're lonely.'

'I call you when I'm horny.' He was excited by her giggling on the phone.

'I hear you've got Van coming around on Saturday.'

He was pissed off that she knew. But he was not surprised. Van was the only other person who knew about their affair. He knew the Vietnamese cocksucker would never say a thing to Sandi but he hated that there was a witness to his infidelity. He wished that Kelly was a pure whore, that the transactions were only financial, uncomplicated. He was learning a lesson. Once it was over he'd not repeat the same mistake. He'd find a beautiful hooker, see her once a fortnight and pay his way. Christ, it would probably work out cheaper.

Kelly judged his silence correctly. 'You can trust Van.'

You can only trust family. Period. And even that can be a risk.

'Sure, I know.'

He rang his cousin straight after.

'*Yia sou*, Ecttora, it's your cousin.'

'How are you going, matey? How's Sandi, how's the kid?'

Fine, fucking fine, do we always have to go through this bullshit?

'All good. Everyone's good. How's Aish, and Adam and Lissie?'

'No complaints.'

Harry realised he felt self-conscious speaking to Hector. He knew his cousin supported him but he could not forget the clenched, disapproving face of that Indian bitch that night of the barbecue. She should be ashamed of herself. She wasn't a fucking witless Aussie, she was Indian, a wog. She should know about family.

'We're having our mate over on Saturday arvo, he's got a heap of new DVDs. Why don't you, Aish and the kids come over?'

Harry registered the moment of hesitation.

'Sure, Adam would love to see Rocco. But Aish is working at the Clinic this Saturday. I'll bring the kids.'

'No worries, we'll catch up with her soon.'

Harry waited for his cousin to switch off the mobile then he banged his phone hard on the desk. He lit a cigarette and walked out to the yard. The guys were busy working and paid him no attention. Harry walked to the end of the garage, looked up and down at the unrelenting drone and rush of the highway. He knew exactly what he was dreading, telling Sandi, telling Sandi that Aisha wasn't coming over.

But his lie had done its job. When he told Sandi that evening she just nodded.

'That girl works too hard.'

He kissed his wife on her bare shoulder.

Saturday morning came around and the sky was clear and the weather mild. Sandi had risen early to go to the market and spent the morning preparing salads. Harry had a bong after his swim and then sprawled on the couch watching music videos. Rocco joined him and they silently watched the monkeys going through their motions on the television. All the black girls acted like sluts and he wondered momentarily whether it was a good thing for his son to watch these baby whores rubbing their arses and tits. But before he could say anything Rocco got up.

'This is boring.'

Harry held out the remote for him. 'You can change it if you like.'

'Nup,' responded his son. 'I'm going for a swim in the pool.'

'Good. I should do the same.' But the dope had made him lethargic and he dropped the remote and kept watching the screen.

'What do you think of her?' he called out to his son. A teenage black girl dressed in a yellow tank top and a denim miniskirt was circling around a fat rapper who was sprouting some bullshit about guns and bitches and crack. Harry liked hip-hop but he thought this particular song ridiculous and ugly. There was no tune, there wasn't even a proper rhythm. God, it was awful. Rocco stood in front of the television and watched the girl who was now miming an orgasm and rubbing her hands up and down her thighs.

He turned to his dad. 'It's okay.'

'You like this?'

'Nah. But it's okay.'

'What do you think of her?'

Rocco was confused. 'What d'you mean?'

'Do you think she's sexy?'

'Shut up, Dad.' Rocco's disgust was obvious.

Harry cackled and muted the volume. 'One day you'll understand, Rocco baby. There's no escape from the evil clutches of women.' He pointed to the screen. 'She's gorgeous but she's cheap. Cheap women are never any good.' Except for one thing and we'll talk about that in the future.

Rocco watched the model who was now gyrating away in silence. Bored, he turned away. 'They're all hos,' he said to his father as he headed to his room to change. 'Black chicks are all hos. Everyone knows that.'

Van arrived at noon on the dot. He parked in the driveway and yelled up to Harry to open the garage. Harry, who had just fired up the barbecue, leaned over the balcony and grinned.

'Why don't you ring the doorbell, you crazy Chink bastard? That's what civilised people do.'

Van grinned back. 'Go screw yourself, you hairy butt-ugly wog dog. But before you do, open the fucking garage.'

He had brought along five large albums of DVDs and Harry helped him carry them up to the living room. Sandi wiped her hands and kissed Van. He smiled at her.

'You're a beauty, Miss Sandi. Why don't you leave this mad wog bastard and come live with me?'

'And what's Jia going to say about that?'

'Sandi, darling, you come live with me, I'll get rid of Jia today. I promise.'

Rocco emerged from his bedroom and he shook Van's hand. Van grinned and opened one of the albums, took out three DVDs from a sleeve, and handed them to the boy.

'You like Adam Sandler, don't you? I've got his new one.'

'Cool. Can I put one on?' The boy looked expectantly at his mother.

'Sure. But you turn it off when the others arrive. Promise?'

'Promise.' With a whoop the boy dived for the DVD player. He turned around.

'Thanks, Uncle Van.'

Within the hour the guests had all arrived. Alex had immediately walked over to the food and then spent the rest of the afternoon playing computer games with Rocco. He had made no effort with his clothes: he was dressed in black track-pants and an Olympiakos T-shirt with a hole under his left armpit. The women paid him no attention at all. Most of them were married, anyway, but Tina was still single and Annalise divorced. But Alex seemed oblivious to the women there. Hector, however, certainly made an impression. Harry felt a smug pride at the attention his cousin received that afternoon. They were a good-looking family, no fucking doubt about it. Here they were sliding towards middle-age and they still turned the chickadees' heads. As if a deliberate contrast to Alex, Hector was wearing a pressed short-sleeve shirt that fitted snugly across his chest and torso. His cotton shorts were conservative and expensive. After kissing and greeting his cousin at the door, Harry had whispered in his ear, You look so good I could fuck you. Now, outside on the verandah, turning the sausages on the barbecue, he looked through the glass doors of the living room and watched his cousin talking to Annalise on the couch. The woman was staring at Hector with open admiration. Harry grinned. He liked Annalise. She talked too much, but she was generous, friendly, and had certainly not deserved that loser of a husband. Maybe she and Hector could get together and he could divorce that uptight bitch of a wife. He heard the squeals of delight, the splashing and laughter from Rocco, Adam and Melissa who were diving and playing in the pool and he felt ashamed. She's the kids' mother, and that's that.

He called out to them. 'Food is on!'

'Ten more minutes, Dad.'

'Out. Now.' His tone softened. 'If you get out now maybe we'll take you guys out to the beach this arvo, what do you reckon?'

'Fooking A!'

He pointed the skewer warningly at his son. 'Watch your mouth.' He turned the sausages one last time. 'Come and get it!'

Van sold a shitload of DVDs that afternoon. He had boxed sets of all the hit TV shows and all the latest movies, including the new Tom Cruise that hadn't even opened in Australia yet. Harry sat back on the couch and watched the women search through the album sleeves. Sandi bought a few romantic comedies, the new season of *Lost* and the complete set of *Sex and the City*. She also paid for a few action movies for him. Alex was only interested in the Hong Kong martial arts selection and he and Van got into an animated discussion about the genre.

'This is the boss, man.' Van was excited and pulled out a DVD with a lurid image of a Chinese girl in a bikini kneeling before a leather-geared man in sunglasses holding a rifle to her head. 'This shit is wild.'

'I'll take it.'

Sandi had looked across at him, questioningly. 'Do you want it, honey?'

Harry shook his head. Some of that chink stuff was alright, but it was all the same. He'd seen enough of it. His cousin was politely sifting through the albums but had not yet made a choice.

'Come on, Ecttora, seen anything you like yet?'

Hector smiled and shook his head. 'Sorry. Aish and I prefer seeing films at the cinema.'

'Fuck that shit, man.' Van looked outraged. 'The cinema is dead, brother. What's your home entertainment system like?'

Hector laughed. 'It's called a TV.'

Nadia, one of Sandi's oldest friends, stopped flicking the sleeves and looked up. 'Ben and I haven't been to the pictures in years.'

Van ignored her. 'What kind of television are we talking about?'

Hector hesitated. 'Sony. Yeah, I think it's a Sony.'

'How old?'

'Maybe eight years? We got it when Melissa was born.'

'You're fucking having me on, man? Get your wife a new television, a flat-screen mother with surround sound.'

Annalise smiled across at Hector. 'I'm with you, Hector, I prefer going out to the movies as well.'

Van snorted and lit a cigarette. 'Right, so I pay fucking thirty bucks for me and Jia to see a film, another fucking thirty bucks for popcorn and drinks, and then have some doped-out kid usher me to a seat that some sweaty-arsed motherfucker has been sitting in for hours just so I can watch a movie that I could have downloaded for myself for free.' Van shook his head in disbelief. 'I hate the fucking movies.' He stared at Hector combatitively. 'Come on, man, there must be something you want.'

'You got *The West Wing*?'

Harry rose and walked to the bar to refill his glass, ill-humoured. He loved his cousin but, Jesus, Hector and Aish were wankers. The fucking *West Wing*? All they did on that bloody show was talk. Talk talk talk talk. And the women were all butt-ugly. He poured himself a long shot of whisky and stayed standing at the bar. Maybe he should take Sandi to the cinema soon. She liked it, and it had been a while. But he agreed with Van. What for? He looked over proudly to the giant plasma screen on the wall.

'Which series you want?'

Harry grinned. He could tell Van hated the show as much as he did.

'Aish and I have seen series one and two. We never got to see the rest. You know how it is with television channels these days. They play them Tuesday one week, Thursday midnight the next. You can't keep a flow going.'

Then why don't you invest in cable, you cheap fuck? The whisky felt nice going down. Harry walked back, sat cross-legged on the floor next to his wife and began to pack the bong.

'Bro, I don't have any of *The West Wing* with me.' Van looked around at everyone, winked at Nadia and smirked. 'I didn't think anyone would be interested. But I'll get them all for you next time.'

'Deal,' said Hector. 'Have you got *Six Feet Under*?'

You had to hand it to his cousin, the cocksucker wasn't intimidated by Van's obvious contempt for his loser trendoid taste.

'Wog man, wog man,' Van sang out to Harry, in a deliberately Ching-chong voice. 'I think your cousin's a *pousti-malaka*.'

Harry spluttered into his bong. Hector just smiled. He closed the album in his hands, handed it back to Van and got up from the couch.

'Sandi, I'm going to take the kids to the beach.'

Van took the bong from Harry. 'Hey, man, I meant no offence.'

'No offence taken. You'll get me *The West Wing*?'

Van inhaled, the bong water spluttered and gurgled, and he exhaled. 'Sure, man. A deal.'

'For me too? I've always wanted to see it.'

Harry nodded to himself. Annalise definitely wanted to fuck his cousin.

'You want it too? Sure, darling.' Van packed the bong and handed it to Annalise. His tone was innocent, charming. 'You can call Hector, you could get together and discuss which season's the best.'

Harry burst out laughing and covered it up by pretending it was a cough.

'Coming with me, Harry?'

He looked up at his cousin. He felt good, stoned and a little pissed, sitting next to his wife, all he felt like was going to sleep soon. He had no energy for the beach. But Hector's gaze was sharp, pressing.

'Sure, man.' Unsteadily, he got to his feet. 'Let's go.'

* * *

'That guy's an arsehole.'

Alex had decided to come with them.

'Van's alright.'

'That slope dickhead is a fucking prick. You let him talk to your cousin like that?'

Harry was surprised. It always looked as if Alex and Van got on fine. He waited for Alex to explain further but true to form, his friend went silent. They crossed the road at the lights and walked down the bush path to the beach. The kids ran ahead of them, in their bathers, with towels wrapped around their shoulders. On the sand, the kids impatiently waited for Hector and Harry to rub them down with suntan lotion and then ran screaming into the water. Harry was proud of his son. Rocco dashed down to the water's edge and ran into the sea; without hesitation he dived under the soft, small waves. Adam, his fat bulk shivering, took ages to muster the courage to dare the water. Even little Melissa was under the water before him. He lit a cigarette and stretched out on the towel. Alex had taken off his shoes and was standing knee-high in the water, watching the kids, or most probably the two blonde women who were swimming bare-breasted in the water near the kids.

'Sandi wants me to organise it so you and she can meet Rosie and Gary and have a talk.'

He groaned. The lie hadn't worked after all. Harry sat up and stared out to the sea. Rocco was fearless, he was further out than any other swimmer. Pride and anxiety battled within him. He nearly rose to call out, then he watched as his son dived under the water, and emerged, swimming towards his cousins.

'When did she ask you?'

'Just before lunch.'

How dare she?

'She's really worried, Harry. But that guy Gary is an arsehole. There's no way to make him see sense. I don't think you four getting together is going to do any good.'

It would if it meant I could fucking murder the cunt.

'What else did she say?'

Hector was looking longingly at the cigarettes lying at the foot of the towel. Harry took a perverse pleasure in lighting another one even though he had just butted one out. The intake of smoke and nicotine calmed him down.

'Come on,' he insisted in Greek. 'What else did she say?'

'She's worried about you. She thinks you're not handling it. She says you're angry all the time.'

Hector was looking straight ahead, out to the kids, they could hear their laughter.

'I'm handling it, mate. She's the one not handling it.' He butted out the cigarette in the sand; he had only had a few drags. 'She can't stop thinking about it.'

'I understand. Charging you with assault, that's all bullshit. He can't live without drama in his life. It's the way he is.'

'And she's innocent?'

Hector hesitated. 'No one's innocent in this.'

You fuck.

'You mean me.'

'You shouldn't have slapped him.'

'Fuck off, Hector. That little bastard deserved it. I was looking after my child. I was protecting him. That's what fathers do.'

Harry's fists were clenched. He felt the heat of the sun, the stretch of the sky, they were heavy weights descending onto him. There was a hammer at his chest. He felt his cousin's hand on his shoulder. He shrugged it off.

'Harry, listen to me. You're a good man. You don't deserve this.'

'But?'

'But you shouldn't have hit him.'

He wanted to cry. Take back that moment, fix that moment, change that moment, so that he had never hit that child. That fucking cunt of a child, that fucking animal of a child. *Panagia*, he whispered to his God, I want that child dead. He was back on the sand, the warm sun on the back of his neck. He could hear Rocco's laugh. Rocco brought him back, as he always did.

'Okay. Sure. I'll go and apologise to them. Can you organise it?'

Hector was shaking his head. 'I know him, mate. It's not going to do any good.'

'I'll give it a go. For Sandi's sake. But she's not coming with us— I don't want her to have anything to do with that *vroma*, that filth. Will you do it?'

Hector slowly nodded.

'Are you going to tell Aish?'

Hector's face was grim, determined. 'Of course I'll tell her. She'll find out from Rosie. Don't worry about Aish.'

Harry looked out to the water where the three children were playing. 'I'm glad they get on so well.' He cleared his throat. 'It's good for Rocco, he doesn't have any brothers or sisters. It's good he has Adam and Lissie.'

'They're family,' Hector answered simply.

Harry laughed and indicated the sea. 'Don't they remind you of us when we were kids?' He reached for his cigarettes. 'You sure you don't want one?'

'Don't tempt me, you evil bastard.' Hector turned and faced Harry. 'You ever going to give up?'

'When I stop enjoying it. I still love it.' Harry lit his cigarette. 'Man,' he said, putting on a fake gangsta accent. 'All my money goes on alcohol, nicotine and gasoline.'

'Yeah,' replied Hector with a laugh. 'Who'd have guessed it's probably the gasoline that will finish us all off.'

Harry groaned. 'Jesus fucking Christ, cuz, you think too much.' He placed an arm around his cousin's shoulder. 'Don't think about all that shit, global warming and terrorism and the war and the fucking Arabs and the fucking septics. Fuck them all. Fuck them up the arse.' Harry nodded out to the dazzling sea, the brazen, endless sky. 'We got it good. Just think about how fucking good we've got it.'

They sat, in silence, watching their children play.

It cost him—for he was full of such fury he could gladly have struck at God—but he remained polite, courteous, a classy host, on his return from the beach. He was confident that as far as his cousin, his son, Alex, Van, and his wife's friends were concerned that he appeared to be content; possibly only a little detached from the effects of the mull. He was proud of how he contained his fury, maintained an easy humour throughout the interminable afternoon. He nursed that pride, consciously submerging himself in the role of generous host, so as not to lose it and snap, to lose it and grab his wife and shake the stupid bitch over and over till he could hear her teeth rattle in her head, till he could see her eyes bulge, till he had her crying for forgiveness on her fucking knees. On. Her. Fucking. Knees. He was affectionate saying goodbye to his cousin and the kids, cracking jokes and smiling all through the quick supper that Sandi prepared for Van, Alex and Annalise—would the arseholes never leave? He read Rocco a bedtime story. Van offered Alex a lift, and Harry was glad he had drunk and smoked just a little too much to feel any obligation to drive Annalise home to Frankston. He was smiling as he walked her down the drive to the cab. She kissed him clumsily on the lips and he thought, You are such a slut.

'Sandi's so lucky,' she called out as the cab reversed, screeched out onto Beach Road. Annalise leaned her head out of the window.

'But you're the real lucky one,' she yelled. 'Don't you forget it.' He could hear the rush of waves from the beach and her voice sounded ugly, a squawk, like one of the seagulls. He smiled again, waved a goodbye, nodded in pretend agreement. He watched the cab drive away. He was no longer smiling. He walked slowly back up the drive.

Sandi was loading the dishwasher. She was a little bit tipsy herself and swung around eagerly on hearing him behind her. A coffee mug fell onto the floor, jumped, and rolled again and again on its side before coming to a stop, unbroken.

'That was lucky.' She shrugged good-naturedly and stooped to pick up the mug. He could kick her in the face right now. She stood up, a delirious smirk on her face. 'That was a fantastic day.'

As she spoke she must have become aware of the danger in his eyes because she took a step back, bumping the back of her knee on the open dishwasher door.

'Honey, what's wrong?'

'How dare you go to Hector behind my back?' He saw fear spread across her features and a surge of excitement flooded through him. He grabbed her hair and tilted her head towards him. 'How fucking dare you?'

She went limp. She did not struggle. 'Harry, I was going to tell you.'

'You stupid bitch, you don't talk to anyone about our business. Not to Hector, not to your mother, not to your sisters, not to your girlfriends. Our business is our business and nobody else's.' He kept his voice low. He would not awaken his son. He pulled again at his wife's hair, a thick strand was now curled tight around his fist. 'Do you want that stuck-up Indian bitch of Hector's knowing your business? Do you? You don't think she'll run straight to that slut friend of hers and tell her everything? What the fuck were you thinking?' Now he wanted to scream, he wished he could yell, that he could slam his fist into her face. He pulled at the coil of her hair around his fist and brought her face right up next to his.

He could see the terror in her eyes. She was petrified, shivering like a desperate animal, and he realised, looking into her eyes, that he had failed her. She would never be able to forget his violence, never forget the slap. He could hit her now, he could, like his father would have, to see how far he could go, how far she'd let him and how far he'd let himself.

He freed her hair from his hand, pulled her into his arms and hugged her hard, tight through her confusion, her crying, that blessed moment of relief when her tense body collapsed into his and he realised that her fear had gone.

'I'm sorry,' she kept repeating. 'I'm so sorry, Harry.'

'It's alright.' He kissed the top of her head. 'I'll go and see that bastard, I'll go with Hector. I'll go and see him and that bitch of a wife. Fuck! It will cost me, but I'll apologise to the cunts. I'll do that, sweetheart, I promise. But you're not coming with me. You and Rocco are going to have nothing to do with them ever again.'

She nodded, eagerly, glad of his love. Again, he was reminded of a faithful dumb animal.

Hector swung the car into a small side street and Harry was suddenly reminded of his childhood. His old man had once taken him for a walk down these very streets. He must have been younger than Rocco—six? seven?—and it must have been a Sunday because his father, he recalled, had been wearing a freshly ironed white shirt, not his usual overalls. The neighbourhood had been bare of trees back then, the sun had scorched the asphalt streets and Harry remembered being mesmerised by the shimmering heat that seemed to rise in opaque waves from the concrete. The houses had not seemed so pretty back then, they had seemed small, ugly and squat. Now that the wogs had moved out and the yuppies had moved in, the houses had been renovated, beautified, the streets stank of money. The council had planted bushes and plane trees along strips of concrete that had once reeked of dog shit, petrol and sewage. Not that he would ever move into any of them. They cost a bomb but they were still tiny shitboxes. His father had taken him into a small worker's cottage. The men had played cards into the evening and he had gone off with a young boy who lived in the house and spent the day playing in the small unkempt park across the road.

Hector turned into another street and Harry was sure that they were passing that very same park. Back then there had been no swings for children, no benches, nothing. It had been more of a vacant lot than a park. When they had returned to the house at dusk, he remembered that heaps of wogs had been sitting outside on the porches of their houses, drinking coffee, smoking, yelling across to the neighbours. Evening was falling now but the houses they passed were all silent.

Hector braked and parked the car. Harry looked out of the window and his cousin pointed to a small weatherboard house sitting desolately between two newly renovated red-brick ones. The weatherboards were originally painted white, God knows how many decades ago, but years of rain and wind had stained them a murky jaundice. The small front garden was overgrown with weeds, and the one lonely rose bush was dying.

'That's their place?'

Hector nodded.

It figured, thought Harry, the fucking pricks didn't even have enough pride to look after their home. He would be ashamed to have his neighbours think that he was so lazy or indifferent or hopeless that he could not even manage to maintain this small shitty excuse of a garden.

'Do they own it?'

'They rent.'

Of course. Perfect. They were the types that would be renting all their lives. Still, it was their home for the moment; were they so degenerate that they did not care at all for having a beautiful place to come home to? And how about the kid? What example did they want to set for him? Or didn't they care about such things either?

'Come on, let's do it.'

Harry hadn't even unbuckled his seatbelt. He sat still for a moment, then nodded.

'Sure.'

The doorbell didn't work and Harry belted the thick red wooden door with the ball of his palm. They heard a child call out, then rapid footsteps along the corridor. It was the man who opened the door. He was wearing overalls, his paint-splattered shirt unbuttoned. The moment was awkward, tense. Harry extended his hand. Gary looked at it, he seemed unsure, confused. The resulting handshake was limp.

The house smelt of incense. Harry was the last in the file down the corridor and he peeked into the rooms. They were all darkened, dishevelled. He noticed that the bed was unmade and he couldn't see a room for the child. They walked into a brightly lit kitchen. A wide table dominated the space. She was sitting at one end of the table, her child in her lap suckling on her bosom. She did not even acknowledge his smile.

'Hello,' he growled. 'Thanks for seeing me.'

Her voice was cold, distant. Was she stoned? 'I didn't want to see you.'

She was ice-bitch beautiful, a stunner blonde with crystal blue eyes. But he did not find her attractive at all. There was something sly, something he did not trust in her eyes. They were serpent's eyes.

The child looked up at him and Hector, quizzical but friendly eyes. There was something both obscene—and possibly because of that—something erotic about seeing such a grown child still drinking from his mother. A quick thought came to Harry. What would she do once the brat started school? Would she be sticking her jugs through the school fence?

'How are you, Hector?'

Her tone was cool towards his cousin as well. Gary had returned from a small room, adjacent to the kitchen, holding three stubbies of beer. There was no room in the kitchen for a fridge. How did people live like this? She had not offered them a seat and Gary indicated that they take a chair.

Harry sat, took a sip of the beer, but he found he had no thirst.

'Do you remember this man, Hugo?'

The boy had inherited his mother's fairness, the uncanny opaqueness of her eyes. There seemed to be no bile or fear in them as he looked at Harry. The boy slowly nodded.

'This is the bad man who hit me. He's going to go to jail.'

The men all laughed, as if the boy's innocent words had allowed them to confront and therefore relax into the situation. The boy, surprised at the reaction to his statement, looked from man to man with glee. Rosie's face remained stony. She shifted Hugo on her lap, capped her breast into her bra, and then flopped out her other tit. Hugo immediately turned and fell upon it. You stupid bitch. Harry couldn't bring himself to look at them. He glanced over at Gary. The man didn't approve of this. The man obviously didn't approve of this at all but didn't have the fucking balls to do a thing about it.

'Why are you here?' Her tone was contemptuous.

'I've come to apologise.'

'Not fucking accepted.'

'Rosie, at least hear him out.'

Christ, the man was a whiner. Harry noticed that he had nearly finished his stubbie.

'I have. He's come to apologise.' She turned back to Harry. 'Well?'

He was unsure of her taunt, confused. He realised what she was demanding. 'I'm sorry I hit Hugo. I shouldn't have done it. You've got to understand it was because I was scared for Rocco . . .'

She interrupted him. 'Your son is twice his size,' she sneered.

And thank you *Panagia* that he is my son rather than that little faggot you are breeding on your tittie there. Why had he come? He just wanted to belt the silly cow.

'Harry's really sorry, Rosie. Trust me. It happened so fast, he was scared for Rocco.'

'This is none of your business, Hector.'

None of his fucking business? This had all happened at his cousin's barbecue. Of course it was his business.

'I know this is not my business, but I've come here today to see if I can help resolve it. I am affected, I can't help but be. Harry is my cousin, you are my wife's best friend. I'm fucking involved.'

'No,' Gary called out from that back room where he had gone to get more grog. 'You aren't involved. The only people involved are me, Rosie and this arsehole here. It's simple.' He returned holding three more stubbies. Harry and Hector had hardly drunk any from the bottles in front of them.

Gary slammed them down on the table and sat, grinning. 'Simple,' he repeated, looking across at Harry. 'It's between us.'

'And Sandi.'

'Sure.' Gary's grin disappeared. 'She's involved too.'

'We don't blame her at all.' Rosie's voice was steel. She hated him as much as he hated her. 'It's not her fault she's married to a pig.'

That was it. Fuck them, let them do their worst. He looked around the room. The lazy bitch hadn't even started dinner yet. In a few years Hugo would probably be joining his old man in an after-school stubbie. He'd make one last attempt, just one.

'Whatever you guys think of me, Sandi is so messed up by all of this. Please don't take it any further. It's a waste of money, a waste of all our time. It's unfair. It's unfair on her.'

The sneer had not left Rosie's face. She sat in silence when Harry had finished, not taking her eyes off him. He forced himself not to blink, he kept his gaze on her cold blue eyes. Gary, the kid, his cousin, they had all disappeared. There was only the battle with Rosie. The child dropped the nipple and hiccuped. A flash of concern crossed the woman's face and she dropped her gaze. Harry breathed out. Rosie was stroking Hugo's hair. She sat him on her lap and the child started playing with his father's keys.

'I am sorry for your wife. But she's made the choice to be with you. You hit my child. Do you hit her?'

Harry sat still, breathing in, slowly breathing out.

'I bet you hit her. Do you hit your kid? How often do you hit your kid?'

Breathing in, breathing out.

'I hope all this makes her leave you. I hope she has the sense to walk out on you, you disgusting sexist pig.'

It was the sniggering that did it. Gary's drunk, nervous giggle, as saliva dribbled from the edge of his mouth.

Harry jumped up and the force of his chair hitting the wall was so loud that the child began to howl. Rosie shrank back in her seat.

'Mum!' The child was terrified and his wailing would not stop.

Rosie hugged him to her and stood up. 'Gary,' there was a triumphant smile on her face. 'Call the police.'

The bitch. She had trapped him.

'Gary. I said call the cops.'

'Calm down, for God's sake, it's alright. Hugo's just frightened.'

Rosie ignored Hector. 'He's threatening us. He's made Hugo scared. Call the bloody cops.'

Gary was on his feet, staggering, looking in confusion from his wife to Harry. Harry did not take his eyes off the cunt. If he could only smash his fists into her pretty face, if he could only bruise her, hurt her. The boy was still howling, enfolded in his mother's arms, but he stole furtive glances at the angry stranger and then immediately curled back into the protection of his mother.

'Should I call the cops?'

What a fucking pussy-whipped creep. What a fucking lame excuse for a man. Harry saw the opportunity, saw what he could do. He could reduce the man to pulp, he could beat him senseless, here in this room, in front of the man's son. Hector would not be enough to stop him. He could smash the man right in front of his son and that bloody useless child would never ever forget it. That would be one of his earliest memories, forever. He would never be able to forget it, to forget what a coward his father really was.

He breathed in.

Then they would have him. Then they would crucify him. What a world, what a lousy, ugly, unjust world that allowed the weak and fucked-up and hopeless scum to survive, to have the upper hand. A bullet into each of their heads, three sharp pops.

He picked up his jacket and walked calmly down the hall. He heard the witch shouting that she would call the cops, he heard his cousin clammering to follow him. He heard the child's howls, now almost hysterical, as if he was choking, gasping for air. He kicked the front door open and emerged into the clear cool night.

He breathed out.

He waited by the car for Hector. He lit a cigarette and the first intake of smoke felt pure, righteous.

'Aish doesn't want anyone to smoke in the car.'

Pussy-whipped. They were all fucking pussy-whipped. He butted out the smoke.

'I'm sorry.'

'Forget it. It was a stupid idea to talk to those scum anyway.'

They drove to Hector's place.

'You want to come in?'

Can I belt the bitch you're married to?

'Nah, I'll head off. I'm too wound up.'

'They're . . .' Hector could not find words to describe the night.

'What the fuck are you doing hanging out with degenerate trash like that, cuz? Why the fuck do you do it?'

He left Hector staring at him open-mouthed, embarrassed. Harry started up his own car, pushed in the cigarette lighter, drove off without a wave and lit his cigarette. He'd allow the car to fill up with smoke if he wanted, let it burn if he wanted, smash it up and drive it in the river if he wanted. He drove carefully, steadily. The smoke felt good. It felt real fucking good.

He had not even been conscious that he was driving to Kelly's flat. He banged loudly with his fists on the door and Kelly answered, in a yellow singlet and a baggy grey tracksuit. Her hair was up in a ponytail and there was no make-up on her face. It made her look younger. He leaned over and kissed her hard, biting her bottom lip. She drew back and looked at him with alarm.

'Baby, what's wrong?'

Without answering he barged into the flat, and started dragging her into her room. Kelly pulled away from him and looked into the girls' bedroom. Harry stood in the living room, he could hear their voices but he could not make out the words. Kelly emerged and shut the bedroom door firmly behind her.

'You scared them. Are you drunk?'

He looked at her without answering. She seemed so dark, so dark and small and fat after the poised brittle aloofness of that Australian bitch.

'I'm not drunk.' He started pushing her towards her bedroom. 'I'm horny, I want to fuck you.'

Kelly resisted him again. But a smile started spreading across her face.

'You are horny, aren't you? I'll just wash up.'

He lunged at her.

'Forget that. Get into the fucking bedroom.'

She leapt aside, poking out her tongue, and evading his grasp.

'I'll be there in a sec.'

Her room smelt of incense, and of the sharp citrus of her perfume. He opened the bottom drawer of her dresser and started searching underneath the T-shirts and singlets.

'What are you looking for, honey?'

She was standing in the doorway, her singlet off, her bra un-strapped. One enormous tit had loosened, and hung plump and soft. She threw off her bra and came towards him. She took his hand and slid it through her clothes in the drawer, right to the back, where he felt the cold metallic surface of a tin box. She took out the box, which had an image of Tupac Shakur on its top, and lifted out a small plastic bag of white powder. She cut up three small lines on the lacquered wood surface of the dresser.

'Here you go.'

He kissed her tits, first the left, then the right. He thought back to the child on his mother's breast and he felt himself harden. He rolled up a twenty-dollar bill and hoovered two of the lines. Kelly bent over and finished the third. She was so good, Kelly, she asked no questions, demanded nothing of him. Why couldn't all women be like Kelly? The cocaine was good; slowly he felt his head clear and a warm rush sweep through his body. His gums went numb and he sighed. This was what he needed.

He kicked off his shoes and fell back onto the bed. 'Come here.'

He closed his eyes. He felt her hands all over him, underneath his shirt, rubbing at his belly, his chest, softly sucking on his neck. She unzipped him, slipped her fingers underneath the elastic of his jocks. He imagined Rosie's face, the jutting cheekbones, the cryptic pale eyes. Kelly was kissing him now on the lips, urgently, her tongue darting into his mouth. He opened his eyes. She lifted her head and looked down at him. She suddenly seemed so ugly, so dark, such a wog. She was not Rosie.

He pushed her off him, got up, buckled his belt and zipped up.

Kelly did not rise from the bed.

'What's up?'

'Must be the drugs. I'm not into it.'

Kelly reached for his crotch. He slapped her hand away.

'I'm not into it.'

'Okay.'

He looked down at the dresser. 'Can I have another line?'

'Sure, honey.'

As he was leaving he looked through his wallet. He took out two hundred dollars and he handed it to her. She stared at the money. 'Harry, I'm not a whore.' She took a fifty from him. 'That's for the coke.'

She was good. She was very good. Why couldn't all women be like Kelly?

Stepping outside, the night felt fantastic as it wrapped itself around him.

He drove across the bridge but instead of heading south down Kings Way he turned north and drove through the city. He kept driving and turned into Brunswick Street. The traffic was heavier and there were people everywhere. He kept driving north and he found himself weaving across the small streets of Fitzroy. He found the street. He parked the car and sat in the darkness, looking at the house. Even in the dark the house looked ramshackle, uncared for. The grass hadn't been mown for months, their kid could get lost in it. He took a deep breath. The creek and the river were close by—weren't they scared of rats, mice, tiger snakes for God's sake? He would never take such chances with Rocco and, as he thought that, he realised that he and Sandi had nothing to worry about. The people who lived in this house were vermin, no more than animals. He was a drunk and she a fool. It was no wonder the child was a brat. For the first time since the barbecue Harry felt something that was not quite, but close to, compassion. It wasn't the kid's fault—what could he be but what he was with parents like that? Some people should be sterilised. He turned the key in the ignition. He shouldn't have come; one of them could have come out, spotted him across the street. On the cocaine high he had fantasised about a bullet in each of their brains. There was no need. It would be a waste of bullets. They were scum. He and Rocco and Sandi weren't even part of the same species. They were as far above them as the moon was from the earth. There was nothing for him to do. The future would exact his revenge.

He drove. He drove south, heading towards the water, heading towards home. He thought of his house that he loved, with the pool and the new kitchen, the double garage, the sound system, the plasma television, he thought of his barbecue and fishing lines, and then he thought of his beautiful wife and his beautiful son. He drove urgently, in silence, the windows up. Music and the noise of the world outside would only spoil his thoughts, his pure thoughts of happiness and contentment. He was a lucky man, he was such a lucky man.

The car seemed to fly down Hotham Street and then he turned and could see glimmering lights on the dark water of the bay. He was nearly home. The moon's rays sparkled on the water and he pressed a button, the window slid down, and he could smell the sea. He filled his lungs with the sea and the moon and the night and the cleansing air. As he slid into his driveway he looked up and saw that his bedroom light was still on. Sandi was waiting for him. She probably had a meal waiting. He would eat, he would slip into his son's room and kiss him goodnight. He would then get into bed next to Sandi and fall asleep with her nestled in his arms. Thank you, God. He parked the car in the garage, he pressed the remote and the garage door began to roll down. Thank you, *Panagia*. He was home.

CONNIE

It was during a surprise test on genetics in her biology class, that Connie realised that her father would have turned fifty today, if he were still alive. She had just answered a question on inheritance when she happened to look down at the date on the bottom right corner of the sheet. The thought hit her on seeing the numbers, and she did her best to put it out of her mind, to try to concentrate on answering the questions in front of her. But the thought was alive now, and would not be banished. She started to etch a face on the margins of the page; it was her face she was drawing, in fine blue biro lines. Her aunt Tasha always said of her that she had her father's features, and it was true that when she looked at a photograph of him she recognised as her own the strong, square jaw and the slightly over-sized ears that she hated about herself. But she had also inherited her mother's thick blonde hair and large mouth. (She also hated this about herself. Her mouth was too big, her lips were too full, her teeth protruded—that was why she rarely smiled in photographs.) She turned the page and tried to concentrate on the series of diagrams, charts and data detailing the frequency of respiratory illness in four generations of human twins. She had to evaluate both the genetic and environmental factors on the inheritance of disease. Again, her eyes kept straying to her father's birthdate on the bottom right-hand corner of the page, but she forced herself to focus and soon enough was finished and leaned back in her chair.

Behind her, Jenna had finished as well. 'How'd you do?'

'Alright,' whispered Connie, furtively looking over to where Mr De Santis was standing. He had his hands behind his back and was staring out of the window. What could he be looking at? The empty basketball court? Her eyes drifted across to the clock next to the whiteboard. Ten minutes to go. He was probably as bored as she was. Ten minutes—six hundred seconds—left before the bell rang. Beside her, Nick Cercic was still frantically writing out his answers in his rough scrawl. His tongue was sticking out of one corner of his mouth; he looked feverish, anxious. He was one of the best students in her year but unlike herself, it did not come easy to Nick C. He wasn't naturally smart; everything was an effort for him. He was now scratching at his mop of unruly red hair, sending flickers of dandruff onto the paper and across his desk. He must have played football over lunch—she meant soccer, but she had never been able to bring herself to call the sport by its Australian name—and he smelt of boy, a pungent male stink. She fought back the urge to lean over and whisper an answer. De Santis had turned and was facing the class, his hands still behind his back. Probably still bored. Four hundred and thirty-one, four hundred and thirty.

She would not think of Hector. She would not think of Hector. She wished she hadn't finished so quickly. One hundred and twenty-six, one hundred and twenty-five. She did not give up on her backwards count and when the bell finally did ring it gave her a jolt. De Santis walked up and down the aisles of desks, picking up the tests. Chairs scraped back, everyone rushed to the door. Jenna had ear phones on and was scrolling through her iPod. Most of the students were checking their mobile phones or already shouting into them as they pushed into the hallway. Connie was back at her desk, slowly packing her bag. Nick hadn't moved and he looked over to her with a sad, puzzled smile.

'That was hard,' she lied.

He was rocking back and forth on his chair, his hands behind his head. There were dark sweat stains on the armpits of his white school shirt. The sight offended her.

'See ya.' She swung her bag over her shoulder and marched out.

The tram was packed with schoolkids—from her school, the girls' school up the road, the Catholic boys' school—and she and Richie pushed their way through the crowd and sat on the dirty steps of the emergency exit. Richie was leaning his elbows on the sportsbag on his lap. He was humming a song.

'Hey, faggot. Shut it.'

Richie fell silent immediately and slumped over his bag. Connie turned around and gave Ali the finger. His dark, sharp-featured face broke out into a grin. He simulated the motions of oral sex.

'Gross.' She turned away in disgust. 'He's such a pig,' she called out loudly. She could hear Ali and his mate Costa laughing behind her but she pretended to ignore them.

Richie still looked hurt, but suddenly he straightened up and winked at her, leaning across to whisper in her ear. 'Yeah, but he's such a sexy pig.'

It still shocked her, to hear him say things like that. She tried not to show her discomfort. 'You reckon?'

'Don't you?'

'No way.' She shivered in mock horror. 'He's a totally sexist creep.' She screwed up her face and pretended to vomit. Richie started to rock back and forth with laughter. His loud chortle rang through the tram.

'Faggot, you sound like a fucking horse.'

An old woman sitting behind them coughed and then said something sharp in Arabic. That shut Ali up.

Connie turned around and peeked at him. He *was* good-looking, pretty hot, really; the bastard had smooth skin that seemed untouched by the blemishes and insults of adolescence. His hair was cut short, thick coils, jet black. Costa caught her staring and whispered something to Ali. She blushed and turned back to Richie.

'What was that you were singing?'

'Just a song.'

'Duh, but what song?'

'Jack Johnson.'

'Yuck.' She lowered her voice to a whisper. 'Your taste in music is as dumb-arse as your taste in men.'

She was forcing herself to be cool, pretending to be unaffected by her friend's recent coming out to her. But she wished he hadn't said a thing, not yet, not when they were still at school. It had made them closer, of course, more intimate, but the fact of his homosexuality seemed to dominate their conversation, their time together. Even when they weren't talking about it, the subject seemed to be all around them, raw, present, uncomfortable. She missed just hanging out with Richie. She missed thinking of him as her friend, not her fucking *gay* friend. She wondered if tolerance could be an inherited trait from a parent. If so, that was her destiny—she had it from both sides. If it was true it was a good thing, of course. But she wished she could let herself be intolerant from time to time, spew forth casual derogatory remarks like everyone else around her did. But she couldn't, she had never been able to.

'Jack Johnson is so fucking gay,' she said cruelly, as they stepped onto the road. And then, instantly regretting her words, she linked hands with Richie as they ran across the lights on St Georges Road. Everyone thinks you're my boyfriend, she was thinking to herself, everyone thinks we're a couple. I will not think of Hector. I will not pretend it is Hector's hand I am holding.

Don't ever get married. It makes you boring. She and her mum had been baking a chocolate cake in the dingy little kitchen in Birmingham. It was her seventh birthday and it was the only cake she ever remembered her mother baking. At the time she had thought that her mother was talking about her own marriage. Connie was still such a baby back then, the comment really had not made much sense to her. But she had never forgotten it. It was only after her mother's death that she realised her mum was probably referring to the other man she was in love with. Dad told her about it soon after the funeral, that they'd moved to Birmingham because her mum had fallen in love with a married man, a Pakistani who would not leave his wife. And looking back, it was unlikely that her mum would have referred to her own marriage as boring. There were a thousand other words she could use to describe it—weird, infuriating, deranged—but not boring. Her father had never told her the man's name, but she was pretty sure she knew who he was. She remembered a well-built man with a trim beard, who carried himself regally, wore a suit, and drove a BMW into which her mother would disappear from time to time. He never came to the door; she was never introduced to him. The affair must have ended because within the year they had moved back to London. Birmingham is a fucking hole, her dad had complained, and he was probably right. Though he too had a thing for South Asian men, so he probably didn't have such a terrible time there. For herself, all she remembered was that it was bitterly cold in winter and that she was one of the few white girls at the local comprehensive. She had even picked up a few words and phrases in Urdu; that was her Birmingham legacy.

'Will you marry me?'

'What the fuck?'

Richie stopped dead and dropped her arm. She giggled at the look on his face and she punched his shoulder.

'Why not?'

His tongue was doing that weird thing he did whenever he was thinking to himself, jutting out and licking his top lip. It sometimes made him look a little slow. His face brightened. 'Sure.'

'Cool.'

'When?'

'We've got to have lots of affairs first and travel the world.'

'Done.'

She filled the cat bowl with biscuits when she got home, and Lisa purred around her ankles. It was still daylight and Bart wouldn't stop prowling the neighbours' yards until dark. She switched on the computer and connected to Messenger. She did the maths and worked out that it was just after eight in the morning in England. Maybe Zara was online. But only Jenna's and Tina Coccoccelli's avatars were visible. She quickly typed a message to Zara and sent it off into digital space. She chatted with the girls for a few minutes but signed off when she heard her aunt enter the front door. She went into the kitchen where Tasha was standing, her backpack still on, rubbing her hands together.

'It's getting cold. Winter is definitely on its way.'

'Guess so.'

'How was school?'

'Okay.'

'Have you got much homework tonight?'

'A little. Why?'

'I thought we could go out and see a movie and have something to eat. I can't be bothered cooking.'

'Sure.' She looked at her aunt. Tasha was due a haircut, and there were dark rings under her eyes. Connie kissed her on the cheek. 'I can cook dinner.'

'No, I want to take you out.' Tasha chucked her backpack on the kitchen table and started sorting through the mail.

'A movie would be great, Tash. Thanks.' She hesitated, then blurted out: 'It would have been Dad's birthday today.'

Her aunt did not look up from the bill she was examining. 'I know. He would have turned fifty.' She put the bills to one side and started filling the kettle. 'You want a tea?'

'I'm fine.'

'You know how terrible I am with dates. But I never forget your father's birthday. Everyone else's I forget, just as I forget faces and phone numbers. But since I could talk I always remembered Luke's birthday.'

'How about Uncle Pete?'

'The fifteenth of August,' Tasha laughed.

'I reckon it's a sibling thing. I think siblings must always remember each other's birthdays.'

Tasha sat down then looked up at her niece. 'You're perceptive, aren't you, Connie?'

That was a nice word. Perceptive, it sounded like a good thing to be. At school last week Mr Dennis had a go at her for not putting enough effort into a history assignment. He was right. She had left it to the last minute and had completed it while watching an episode of *The OC*. You're so much smarter than the others, he said to her, just apply yourself a little bit harder. Smart, she'd wanted to yell back. Smarter? What the fuck does that mean? You think the rest of them are morons and bogans, so what's so great about being smarter than them? She had been surly and made a half-arsed apology. But her aunt never made a compliment that did not have some insight behind it. Inheritance.

'Maybe it runs in the family.'

Her aunt looked confused, was about to say something, then her face softened, and she sank back in the chair. 'I thoroughly hate work.' She straightened up and smiled. 'Do your homework fast and then we'll catch the movie. I'll tell you what I want to see: *The Squid and the Whale*, that French film *Hidden* and the new Jennifer Aniston movie. You can pick from those three. Look up session times after you've done your work.'

Connie had nothing urgent to do except some Maths reading. The English report she could do the next night. She clicked on Messenger again but there was nothing from Zara so they probably wouldn't talk until the weekend. There were more kids from school online but she clicked off without bothering to join in. She did her Maths, and then searched for information about the movies. *The Squid and the Whale* sounded interesting, a little arty-farty, all about smart, educated people and divorce, and it was playing in Carlton, which she knew Tasha would enjoy. The food would be good. *Hidden* was French and had amazing reviews. But it sounded complex and like it needed a lot of thought. And it required reading, it would be subtitled. She knew that her aunt had picked it because she thought it was good for Connie to be exposed to challenging films. She was probably right, but after a day at school the last thing she felt like was more education. The new Jennifer Aniston was called *The Break-up* and half the girls at school had already seen it. People seemed to like it. It also starred Vince Vaughn. She looked at the actor's face. He looked like Hector, just not as handsome, but he had the same big, slightly boofy face. She really wanted to see the movie and it was playing in the city, so they could eat in Chinatown.

She switched off the computer, zipped up her jacket and pulled on her boots. She knelt before the mirror and carefully started applying lipstick. It was her father, not her mother, who had taught her how to apply make-up. Marina never wore it. Her dad had done his own face. The secret, he'd said to her, powdering his cheeks, his chin, his nose, is foundation. You can hide any blotches, he added, pointing to a sarcoma underneath his chin, and you don't get any shiny patches anywhere. She puckered her lips. Her dad would have wanted her to choose *Hidden*, he always went for the obscure, the difficult, the arty, what the Australians called wanky. Wasn't that why he had left Australia? What would have her mother chosen? A thick-set, tall Pakistani man in a suit. He looked a little like Vince Vaughn as well. She carefully drew on the eyeliner.

Tasha had combed her hair and changed into pants and an op-shop fifties lavender faux-fur jacket with wool lining around the collar. Connie loved that jacket. It made her aunt look so cute.

'What's the choice?'

'*The Squid and the Whale*. It sounds cool.'

Tasha rubbed her hands together eagerly. 'Perfect. We can have pasta after the movie.'

She'd go and see *The Break-up* with Richie. Or Jenna if she hadn't seen it yet. Or maybe she would go on her own. And pretend. Shut up, don't think about him. She clutched tightly onto her aunt's arm as they strolled to the station.

When they got home there was a message from Rosie on the machine, asking if Connie could do some babysitting on Thursday evening. She glanced at the clock. It was not yet eleven, so she picked up the phone.

'Are you going to say yes?' Tasha had poured a red wine and turned on the television.

'Yeah, I think so.'

'Do you have time?'

She wished her aunt would lay off a little. She could make her own decisions. 'I can do school work at their place. It's no big deal.'

She could see that her aunt wanted to say more. She held her breath. But Tasha had turned away. Connie quickly dialled. Their answering machine clicked in and she began to leave a message. There was a loud squeal, an electronic cacophony, and then she heard Gary's voice on the other end.

'Connie, that you?'

'Yeah. I can look after Hugo on Thursday. What time do you want me to come around?'

'You're good, aren't you? You're a good person, Connie.' Gary was slurring his words. She figured he was pissed. 'Come around seven.'

'Sure.'

'Bloody Rosie has booked us into some Mickey-mouse parenting workshop. I fucking hate those things. I always feel like the bad boy at the back of the class.'

She bit her lip. She didn't have anything to say in response. She couldn't imagine Gary as a student. She wasn't thinking of the learning part, he would enjoy that part of school; he read all the time. She thought he probably regretted having dropped out so young, Form Four he'd told her, which was now their Year Ten, but she didn't have the guts to ask him why he had. She figured a person like Gary couldn't stand the discipline, obeying rules and following a timetable. He could never sit still. She was always slightly anxious whenever she was alone with him.

'Okay,' she finally blurted out, realising there had been a long pause in the conversation. 'See you Thursday.' Maybe he was stoned.

'Yeah, yeah, thanks Connie, you're an angel.'

Her aunt was channel-surfing, going from Iraq to *Big Brother* to some American crime show. She took the remote off Tasha and flicked back to the news. A black, charcoal shell of a car was smouldering in a stretch of desert highway. Scarfed women were howling.

'Please turn it off, Con, I can't stand watching this.'

She pressed a button. Two women were in a sauna, discussing anal sex.

'Oh, for Christ's sake.' Her aunt tore the remote from her hand. The screen flicked over to the crime story.

Connie yawned, leaned over and kissed her aunt on the cheek.

'It's all rubbish, isn't it? Maybe we should get cable?'

Jenna had cable but all they ever did at her place was channel-surf as well. Connie shook her head. 'There's only rubbish on that too. Goodnight.'

'Goodnight, angel.'

She lay in bed and listened to the muted sound of the television. She kept the light on and looked at all the pictures on her wall. Last summer she had stripped the room bare of all her posters, all the images of movies stars, celebrities and pop stars; she chucked out

Robbie Williams and Gwen Stefani, Missy Elliot and Johnny Depp. The only picture she couldn't bring herself to part with, was one she had ripped out of a *TV Week*, a small black and white photo of Benjamin McKenzie from *The OC*. It reminded her of Richie and she kept it Blu-Tacked at one edge of her bedroom mirror. Across from her bed the wall was dominated by a large print of nineteenth-century London that her aunt had bought and framed for Connie's sixteenth birthday. Her desk sat underneath it. There were only two posters on the walls now. One was of a clear blue desert sky shot through with razor wire, protesting the inhumane detention of refugees in Australia. She had snaffled it at an anti-racism rally the year before. The other poster was a stark image of an Arab child with a petrol pump murderously aimed at his head. In Arabic and in English the stark red lettering read NO TO BUSH'S WAR FOR OIL. Zara had sent it to her for her sixteenth birthday. The walls were now full of photographs of real people, people she knew: Tasha in a blue raincoat holding an over-sized black umbrella; Richie grinning mani-acally at the camera, wearing his daggy Thank Drunk I'm a God T-shirt; she and Jenna and Tina dressed up for a party; Zara in a long-sleeved white hoodie with an image of Kurt Cobain stenciled across the front; her own Year Ten school photo, the one in which her legs didn't look fat. Then there was the photograph of her mum and dad, looking like she had never known them. Her father was pencil thin, his hair cut short except for a greased quiff at the front and dyed a peroxide salt-white, her mother in garish eyeliner and lipstick, her hair in a mohawk. They looked like gangsters, not like in rap videos and ads for Coca-Cola, but like romantic outlaws from deep in the last century. Her mother wore white lace stockings and had a brooch of the Japanese imperial flag pinned to a cup of her exposed bra. Her dad was smoking a cigarette, had a white shirt on, the top button done up and a thin black tie; he was leering comically into the camera as her mother gave him a look of open adoration. Just above the photograph of her parents she had stuck a photo of last year's work Christmas party, everyone a little drunk, smiling stiffly into the camera. They all formed a semi-circle around the table, Aisha in the centre, with her and Hector at either end. He wore a suit, elegant as always, and he looked so good. He looked so good it hurt. Her eyes drifted from her father to Hector, and then back to her mother and then to herself. In the photograph she was looking at Hector with the exact same expression as on her mother's face. How was it that she had never noticed it before? She blushed, and quickly turned off the light.

Lisa, who was asleep on her pillow, miaowed in indignation at being disturbed. Sorry, girl, she whispered, and tickled the cat underneath her chin. There was a scratching at the door. She waited. Bart pushed opened the door and she heard him scampering across the carpet. He jumped on her bed and she lifted the covers, making a space for him to nestle into. Lisa jumped off the pillow and onto the dresser. She could hear the cat lapping at the water in the glass. Bart curled into a ball and began purring.

She tried to think of schoolwork, she tried to think about the movie she had seen—the actor reminded her of her father and she wondered if that was how her dad would have looked now if he hadn't died, if he had lived to fifty, gotten fat, maybe grown a beard— but she couldn't stop thinking of Hector. Bart edged further under the sheet and blanket; she could feel his purring, the rise and fall from his breathing, the warmth of him next to her stomach. The sound of the television was just audible from the lounge room. She closed her eyes and fantasised.

She was in the *Big Brother* house. It was the first episode of a new series and the house was filled with the contestants she had liked from previous series. She was sitting on one side of the couch, Hector on the other. She looked older and thinner. Hector was only about twenty-five. Big Brother was speaking, explaining the house rules. The other contestants were excited and abuzz, interrupting, squealing. She and Hector were silent, they could not avoid contin-uously glancing over at each other. The cameras were picking up the stares and everyone knew exactly what was going on. Hector winked at her and she blushed. The cat was purring. She fell asleep.

'Jordan's having a party. He wants you guys to come.'

'When?'

'Saturday night. You want to go?'

Last period on a Wednesday was meant to be study time in the library but, as usual, she, Tina and Jenna had skipped class and gone to the Juice Bar on High Street instead. Connie slurped from her watermelon and ginger drink and looked out the window. The weather was cruel, one of those Melbourne days that reminded her of the savagery of London's weather. She had put on a skirt that morning and the wind had nipped at her legs all day. She shivered.

'I said are you coming?' Jenna, her voice indignant, was frowning at her.

Connie apologised and turned back to the conversation. 'Maybe.'

'Good. And you?'

Tina nodded lazily.

Shit. Connie remembered that she had just promised Richie to go out to the movies with him on Saturday.

'Has he invited Rich?'

'How the fuck should I know? I'm not his social secretary.'

Connie and Tina shared a quick, surprised raising of their eyebrows. Tina stretched back on her chair. 'Hey bitch, just cool it. She was only asking a question.'

To their horror, Jenna burst into tears. Tina, mortified, glanced around the café, then put her arm around her friend. Connie played with her straw. Jenna's heaving slowly came to a finish, and she sniffed, took a napkin off the table and blew her nose.

'I'm sorry,' she whispered. 'I'm a fucking retard.' She breathed in heavily and Connie thought she was going to start crying again. Connie grabbed her friend's hand and squeezed it.

'What's wrong?'

'I had sex with Jordan last night.'

Tina rolled her eyes and withdrew her arm from around her friend's shoulders. 'So why are you crying? You've been wanting to sleep with him for ages.'

'It was just a sympathy fuck.' Jenna had emptied the contents of a sugar sachet on the table and was sifting the grains between her fingers. Tina looked across at Connie in confusion. Connie shrugged.

'What's a sympathy fuck?'

A sympathy fuck is when a straight guy lets you blow him or fucks you up the arse because he knows you are in love with him and he feels sorry for you—had she heard her father say this once or had she dreamt he had said it? Or was it something she thought he might likely have said?

Jenna didn't answer Tina, she was busy playing with the sugar.

'Jenna, what the hell do you mean?'

'Have you got a cigarette?'

Tina shook her head.

'I need a fucking cigarette. How much money have we got?'

The girls checked their pockets. After what they owed for the juices they had five dollars thirty cents between them.

Jenna stood up, and swung her schoolbag over her shoulder. 'I'm going to rip some off now.'

They paid the bill and followed their friend through the mall. Jenna marched into the tobacconist but the woman behind the counter took one look at their uniforms and mouthed, Out, out.

'Bitch.'

Connie debated taking off. Jenna had a foul temper and when she was in one of her moods she didn't care what trouble she got herself or her friends into. She was almost running to the supermarket. When Connie and Tina caught up with her, Jenna was leaning over the unstaffed smokes counter. The girl at the nearest cashier was oblivious, serving a customer, an old *giagia*, who suddenly looked up disapprovingly, catching sight of what Jenna was doing. The old bitch pointed to the smokes counter and the cashier turned around. Connie pulled her friend back.

Jenna screamed at the girl. 'Well, if you losers employed enough people I wouldn't have to get them myself, would I?' She then poked her tongue out to the old woman and added a few curses in school-yard Greek. The *giagia* pursed her lips in distaste. She had no teeth and so her mouth looked exactly like a shrivelled prune. Through the glass doors of the mall entrance Connie could see Lenin walking towards them, still in his school uniform, his untidy black curls bouncing around his head in time with his loping, gawky walk. The glass doors opened, he walked through and she called him over.

'What's up?'

Jenna swung around and glared up at him. 'Have you got any fags?'

'Nah. I don't smoke. It gives you cancer and makes you impotent.'

'Fuck off.'

Lenin looked at Jenna and then across to Connie.

'What's up with her?'

'Can you get some?'

Lenin looked nervously across to the girl at the cashier. He nodded slowly. 'I don't start my shift for another fifteen minutes,' he whispered. 'Come back then.'

Jenna's mood lifted immediately. She raised herself on her toes to kiss the boy, but even then Lenin had to stoop for her to reach his cheeks. Connie marvelled at his clear white skin. He had the palest skin she had ever seen. It was like milk. They watched him as he sauntered down the aisles to the storeroom out the back. His tall, thin body jerked sluggishly to a rhythm playing only in his head.

The girls wandered the mall, checked out the music shop and the pet shop. When they returned to the supermarket, Lenin was behind one of the registers in his soiled orange work vest, scanning a man's groceries. His nametag sat lopsided on his chest.

Jenna called out to him and, without turning his head, he dropped something off the register shelf and kicked it towards them. A packet of cigarettes slid across the floor. Jenna stooped, pretending to tie her laces—which looked completely suss, thought Connie, since her runners had velcro straps—and picked up the smokes.

They blew a kiss to Lenin, who ignored them, and ran laughing across the carpark, up the rise of All Nations Park where they fell, giggling and panting, onto the bench at the top of the mound. They sat looking down at the city below. Jenna passed the smokes around. Connie looked at the gold packet, opened and shut the box, then took out a smoke and let Tina light it for her. The first gulp of nicotine and smoke tasted foul.

'So, what is a sympathy fuck?'

'A sympathy fuck is when someone sleeps with you because they feel sorry for you.'

Her father *had* said it. He'd said it to her mother. Her mother had been weeping, distraught, crying about some man, and her father was comforting her. Connie was painting with watercolours in the middle of the room. They must have been in the house in Islington that they shared with Greg and his boyfriend Clem, and Shelley and Joanne. She had loved that house even though it was cold and the hot water never seemed to work properly. It was full of places to hide—it even had an attic. She had three mothers and three fathers in that house.

Jenna seemed to smoke the cigarette in a few quick drags then threw the butt into the shrubbery. Connie resisted the urge to tell her off. Jenna knew what would happen to that butt. It would end up in the sea. She got up from the bench, picked up the butt and put it in the side pocket of her backpack. She'd dispose of it later.

'I'm sorry.'

Connie dismissed the apology with a shrug. 'Why do you think it was a sympathy fuck?'

'Because all night all he could do was talk about Veronica. He's still crazy for her. We were meant to be working on the prac but all he wanted to do was talk about Ronnie. Then his mum made us dinner and we went over to the park across the road from his house. He had half a pill from the weekend so we shared it and he talked some more about bloody Veronica. He was so sad. He was so sweet. I just had to kiss him.'

Tina and Connie were silent.

'He said that I was his best friend. That we shouldn't do anything. I told him I wanted him to fuck me.' Jenna shook her hair defiantly and threw another cigarette to her mouth. 'So we fucked.'

'In the park?' Tina sounded so shocked that both Jenna and Connie broke out in laughter.

'No, we went back to his house.'

'Where was his mum?'

'I dunno.' Jenna looked like she wanted to hit Tina. 'Don't be such a wog, bitch. She was probably asleep.'

'He does know that Veronica's with another guy, doesn't he?'

Connie drifted. She nodded occasionally, but she had stopped following the conversation. Jenna had been in love with Jordan for years. On, off. On, off. She wasn't quite sure if her friend really wanted a relationship with Jordan or preferred the drama and emotional pain of unrequited love. Did Jenna really know what love was, how much it hurt, how intoxicating it was, how sick it made you feel? Did she know that love was being drunk and stoned and sick all at the same time? Absent-mindedly Connie took another cigarette from the stolen packet and bent over for Tina to light it.

'Was it good?'

Tina had never dated a boy, and was fascinated by sex. She wanted descriptions, intimate details. Jordan Athanasiou was probably the best-looking guy in their year. He had a great body without being at all sporty. Which they preferred. He always wore band T-shirts, The Cure or Placebo or the Pixies, and his skin was gorgeous. He was hot. All the girls thought so—even her aunt Tasha had drawn in a breath when she'd met him: My God, Connie, that boy looks like a young Elvis. Your father would have loved him.

Jenna started to cry again. Connie put her arm around her and Jenna curled into a ball and sobbed.

Connie stroked her friend's hair while Tina whispered, 'It'll be alright. It'll be alright.'

It was bitterly cold and Connie's teeth had started to chatter. Jenna got up, dried her eyes, and blew her nose on her shirt sleeve.

'Sorry,' she whispered to the girls, without looking at them. She sniffed. 'So that's why you have to come to the party. You have to.'

There was no getting out of it. They promised.

'Nick Cercic was asking heaps of questions about you. Heaps.'

She and Richie were studying in her room. She was cross-legged on the floor and Richie was lying across her bed. He had thrown his shoes off and had his feet up against the wall, just under her photographs. He was looking at the picture of her mother and father, his book closed beside him. The last two buttons of his untucked school shirt were undone and she could see fine blonde hairs on his belly. Richie found concentrating hard. She always had to be the one getting him focused back on work. She ignored him. He twisted his head around and looked askance at her. 'Did you hear me?'

'I heard you.'

'Do you like him?'

'He's alright.' He was nice. A nice boy who smelt a little off, who was a bit of a nerd. He was alright.

'I reckon he thinks you're more than just alright.'

Richie was waiting for a response. He turned back to the wall.

'Were your parents punks?'

'I think so.'

'That's so cool.'

'Your mum's cool.'

'My mum's great but she's not cool. She's a bogan. She knows that.'

'So's Nick Cercic.'

'Why?'

'He just is.'

'Am I a bogan?'

He was. He wore sports tops from Target, cheap jeans from Louis's Economy Store and no-name runners from Northland. She didn't want him to change, she didn't want him to start wearing cologne, tight T-shirts, get all faggy on her. She liked him being a bogan.

'You're a bogan in a good way.'

'Is Nick Cercic a bogan in a good way?'

She was concentrating on an algebraic equation but the numerals and the symbols were starting to swim. She had lost the thread of her concentration. She sighed and shut the book. She crawled over to her desk and launched Messenger. Richie rolled off the bed and knelt down beside her. He leaned across and flicked the switch on her stereo. A screeching guitar and a staccato backbeat filled the room.

'Turn it down.'

Richie twisted the knob slightly.

Connie pushed him aside and turned the volume down sharply. She entered her password on the computer. Richie crouched on the floor and started searching through her CDs. She sent a smiley face to Jenna who was online. Her friend quickly responded: *Thank you for yesterday*. Connie typed back, *No worries*. She forgot her homework completely and she spent the next half-hour messaging back and forth. Richie sat cross-legged on the floor beside her, playing CD after CD, hardly ever a complete track. There was a pile that belonged to Tasha, some of which she knew had been her father's. The first Madonna album, someone called Jackson Browne. He played three songs from *Nino Rojo*.

Without asking whether he could, without Connie or Tasha bothering to invite him, Richie sat down to dinner with them. After the meal Tasha pulled out the fold-up camp bed in the sunroom and dropped a doona over it.

'Ring Tracey.'

Richie, who had been lying across the lounge-room floor watching television next to Connie, lazily pulled out his mobile phone and dialed his mother.

'Mum, I'm staying at Connie's tonight. That okay?'

He dug his phone back into his pocket and smiled at Connie. His grin was wide, huge, he seemed so excited, so happy, like a little boy. His eyes were gargantuan, so vivid, shiny and bright. Connie, lying next to him, could smell the musty pong of his socks. She smiled back and he touched her finger. They watched the end of *Law and Order* together.

'Do you want to go to a party instead of the movies on Saturday?'

'Whose party?'

'Jordan Athanasiou.'

'I'm not invited.'

Richie was slurping on his yoghurt and fruit, he ate messily and quickly, milky stains around his mouth.

'I'm inviting you.'

'He won't want me to come.'

There was no whingeing, no hurt in her friend's response. She was astonished at Richie's calm understanding and acceptance of the world. It was true, Jordan probably didn't want him at the party. She wasn't sure she wanted Richie at the party. She didn't want to sit with him all night, look after him. She was such a terrible friend.

'I really want you to come.'

Richie vigorously wiped his chin. 'Okay.'

He hadn't showered, he didn't have his toothbrush with him so he hadn't brushed his teeth. She had offered him hers and she was glad when he declined. Sometime during the day, she knew one of the boys would tease him about his smell. They were in the last year of high school, nearly adults, but still, more than any other insult, the childish, You smell, You stink, hurt more than anything.

In English she and Mr Thompson argued furiously over her interpretation of *The Quiet American*. She hated the passivity of the woman in the book and wanted her to take responsibility for her fate. She didn't answer Mr Thompson when he interrupted her and asked if she was wanting to absolve the Europeans and North Americans of their colonial exploitation of Vietnam. She was furious at his accusation. This is not at all what she had meant. She wanted the female to do more, say more, be more. She hated that the character had given herself over to drugs.

That lunchtime she, Jenna and Tina watched the boys play football—*soccer*, she reminded herself—in the back oval nearest the creek. One of the boys kicked the ball hard in their direction and they all had to jump. Nick Cercic came rushing over and apologised. You didn't do it, thought Connie, why are you apologising? He was sweating, out of breath. She squinted up at him, he was a shadow against the sun. She knew then that he wanted to kiss her. The thought made her slightly nauseous. He was just a big, clunky boy, he wouldn't know how to kiss. Men knew how to kiss. Hector knew how to kiss. She launched a savage kick at the ball and it flew high over Nick's head and landed in the middle of the oval, to the whooping astonishment of the boys.

'Nick said you bent it like Beckham this arvo.' Richie was on his knees on the floor, slowly building a railway circuit for Hugo who was staring at him with rapt attention, interrupting from time to time with an anguished cry, No, not there, Don't put that there, put it there.

Connie didn't answer. She had given up on the game, bored with it, but Richie seemed to have endless patience when it came to Hugo. The room stank of cigarettes and bongs. Rosie used incense to mask the stench but the sweet scent of sandlewood was too fragile to combat the dank odour of the other smells. While the boys played, Connie composed random text messages to various friends. *Wot is it with boys + trains?* Within a minute there was an answering beep: *Its all about cock*—Tina.

Richie suddenly jumped to his feet, an abrupt movement that startled both her and Hugo.

'I've got to go to the loo,' he announced, his look almost pleading, as if he was asking for her permission.

Hugo also scrambled onto his feet. 'I want to come.'

Connie and Richie looked at each other in confusion. Hugo swung his head towards her as well, as if he too sensed all decisions lay with her. Shit, she didn't know what to say. Was it a boy thing? Did little boys have an obsession with penises and pissing? She thought it strange, but maybe that was because she was a girl and had no experience of brothers. Shit. She didn't know what to do. She glared at Richie, raising her eyebrows at him. Idiot, she mouthed, Do something.

'Buddy, I'm just going for a wee. I won't be long.'

'I want to see.' The child was adamant. His last word had tailed off into a wail. The last thing she wanted was for him to start crying. It would be at least another hour before Rosie and Gary came home. At least. If Hugo lost his temper the tears and tantrums and howls could go on for hours.

'You can't. Some things are meant to be private.'

Hugo was frowning, his stare defying her. Richie made for the door and the boy threw himself onto the older boy's legs. 'I want to come, I want to come.' He would be screaming any moment now.

Richie was still, his hand on door. She laughed. He looked so frightened it was comical. The little shit had them wrapped around his finger.

'Oh, alright. If you want, go for it.'

For a moment, she thought Richie was going to cry as well but then he just shrugged his shoulders and ushered Hugo out of the door.

She shook her head and walked over to the bookcase. Unlike the one at home, it was crammed with so many books that a pile had fallen onto the carpet. She touched the stained dark wood and looked at the film of dust on her finger. The bookshelf was high, almost reaching the ceiling, with deep recesses; you'd need to get a chair from the kitchen to reach the books at the top. The selection of books intrigued her. There were art books, biographies of writers and artists, stained dog-eared copies of books on philosophy and eastern religions. There was one whole shelf of DVDs, another of old videos, mostly European and Asian movies. Gary, provocatively, had four porno videos lying on their side, under a thick biography of the German playwright, Bertolt Brecht. She wanted to read Bertolt Brecht. Her father had loved him, and had once taken her to see a strange play called *Mother Courage*. She remembered the experience of watching actors live on stage more than she recalled anything about the play itself. She pulled out the book. She had imagined the playwright to be old and bearded, but he was young and clean-shaven on the cover, not exactly good-looking, his eyes piercing and sharp. She wondered if she would ever know any playwrights, any artists. Gary was a painter. She knew him. But would she ever know anyone *famous*? On the lowest shelf there were two photo albums lying underneath a copy of Irvine Welsh's *Trainspotting*. She put the biography back on the shelf and removed one of the albums. She sat back on the couch—it too stank of stale tobacco—and opened the album.

They were Gary's photographs and they were exquisite. Secretly she thought he was a much better photographer than he was a painter. The first few sleeves were full of close-ups of flowers. The colours were brilliant, vivid, the subjects clear and distinct. She could see the veins in the petals and in the leaves. She turned the pages. Rosie, her cheeks fuller, heavy shadows under her eyes, was breastfeeding an infant Hugo. She turned the pages again and there were photographs of an even younger Rosie, her hair peroxided, in a sunflower yellow bikini, her skin tanned to a rich copper. She recognised a photograph of a young Aisha. Wow, she looked like a kid. She must have always been slim. There were dozens of photographs taken at a beach. The sky and water were an intense seductive blue, the light was the glare of a hot Australian summer. She turned another sleeve and gasped. She drew in her breath. She felt as if her heart was going to splinter.

She recognised him instantly. His features were the same except he was so much younger. His dimpled chin, the cruel haughtiness of his eyes, the soft fleshiness of his lips. She was shocked by the smoothness of his face, his hairless, suntanned chest and plump, crimson nipples. Hector wasn't looking at the camera; his brow was creased as if there was something urgent he was searching for out to the sea. She was sure he was looking out to the water, she was sure of it. He was like a monument, a heroic man of stone, but more breathtaking than any sculpture she had ever seen. The next photograph in the sleeve must have been taken the same day. He was wearing long, daggy board-shorts, his short-cropped black hair was glistening, wet, so you could see scalp beneath it, and he had his arms around Aisha. She was wearing a white bikini, and it was such a contrast against her dark skin that it made it seem black. Aisha was grinning widely at the camera and Connie had a sudden ugly thought. Her teeth were too big. Her grin was toothy, she looked stupid. She was furious at herself, but more than fury she felt a piercing, wounding jealousy. I wish you had died. She had mouthed the words before she was conscious of them. Shame punched through her body. She hated herself. She was the worst bitch in the world. She fucking hated herself.

'What you looking at?'

She snapped the album shut. 'That was a long piss.'

It sounded like an accusation. She had not meant it to be.

'He had to do number twos.' Hugo was laughing gleefully.

'And you watched?' She was appalled.

'Yeah,' the boy chuckled again and held his nose. 'It stank!'

Richie playfully lurched towards him. 'That's why what people do in toilets should remain private.'

Hugo squealed, delighted, and evaded Richie's clutches. The boy knelt on the floor and began to play with his train set. Richie fell onto the couch next to Connie and grabbed the photo album. He began to flick through the sleeves. She stared up at the painting of a clown on the wall above the heater. It was one of Gary's, a wild caricature done with thick, vivid splashes of oil. She guessed her art teacher in Year Nine would have called it Expressionist. The leering mouth was mocking her. She found the painting repellent but she kept staring at it. She was fully aware of her friend next to her, turning the pages. Richie stopped flicking. He was looking at the photograph of Hector, she was sure of it. Lucky, lucky Aish, to have known him, to have had him back then. The clown's nose was bulbous, the thick dabs of scarlet oil were like blood. It was a dumb painting to have on the wall. It was dumb and ugly. Dumb dumb dumb. Richie had turned the page. Her hands were trembling.

As soon as Gary and Rosie walked through the door she knew they'd been arguing. She and Richie had tried to put Hugo to bed but he had refused and was lying on the lounge-room floor in his pyjamas watching *Pinocchio*. He rushed to his mother. Rosie loosened the clasp on her bra and began feeding the child. Gary groaned. He walked out and yelled from the kitchen.

'Do you guys want a beer?'

Richie looked across at her, Up to you, she mouthed.

'Sure.'

Gary returned with three beers. She still found the taste of beer unpleasant but she was determined to master the drink.

'How was the class?'

Gary didn't respond to Richie's question. His eyes were fixed on his wife and child. Rosie's smile was stretched across her face. She was faking it. Connie wished she wouldn't do that.

'The class was fucked.'

'Gary, it was alright. We learned a lot.'

'We learned fuck all.'

'Connie and Richie don't need to know about our arguments.'

'They don't need to know. But I want to tell them.'

Connie sucked savagely at her beer. Richie was sipping his slowly; she wished she could rush him. If they were going to fight she didn't want to be here.

When Gary next spoke his tone was calm, reasonable. This almost frightened her. 'We argued because I think Rosie should stop breast-feeding Hugo. He's nearly four. I think she's been doing it long enough.'

'And the woman said it was fine, didn't she?' Rosie's voice was rising. 'There's no right age to stop breastfeeding.'

'Of course she would say that. That whole class was about vali-dating middle-class women's whims.' Gary turned around to the teenagers. 'What do you guys reckon?'

She and Richie both shrugged.

'You don't have an opinion?'

Rosie sighed. 'Leave them alone. They don't want to get involved. I'm not going through this again. It is natural to breastfeed a child. It's just our fucked-up Western culture that puts all these prohibi-tions and regulations in place. Hugo will stop breastfeeding when he's ready. It's perfectly natural.'

'*It's perfectly natural*,' Gary was cruel, mocking.

'Fuck off.'

'I wish I fucking could.'

Connie placed her beer, not quite finished, on the coffee table and stood up. 'Sorry, I've got to go. I've still got some schoolwork I need to finish.'

'Of course, sweetheart.' Rosie rose slowly, struggling with the still-feeding boy in her arms. The strained smile was back on her face. Connie was worried that the woman would stumble and fall. Richie looked at the half-empty beer bottle in his hands.

'Take it, mate,' Gary urged him. 'Drink it on the way home.' He started searching his pockets for his keys.

'Don't worry about driving us home, Gary. We'll walk.'

'It's freezing out there.'

'I don't mind, I like walking in the cold.' Richie was nodding as well. His grin was as effusive as Rosie's had been. But he wasn't faking it. He seemed oblivious to the tension, not bothered by the argument. How did he do that? She knew he listened. But he didn't seem to take on other people's shit. How the hell did he do that? She wished she could. She now felt guilty and a little sordid—it was silly, the argument had nothing to do with her.

'Suit yourselves.' Gary brushed his lips across her cheek and staggered off to the kitchen for another drink. He was probably too blind to drive them anyway. 'Thanks,' he called out.

Rosie walked them to the front door. She gripped Connie's hand and pulled it shut over two oily notes. It was thirty dollars.

'You don't have to.'

'Shut up. 'Course I do. How was he?'

'He was fine. He was great.' Richie nodded in agreement.

'Can I ask you one more favour?'

'Sure.'

'Can you look after him for an hour on Saturday? Gary's got to work.'

'I'm working at the clinic till four. The morning's free or the afternoon. Does that fit in with what you need to do?'

'That's fine. I'll drop Hugo off at the clinic at four if that's alright. I don't have to be at my appointment till four-thirty. In fact, it's perfect, thank you. It's just for a couple of hours.'

Hugo had dropped Rosie's nipple from his mouth and jutted his chin out for a kiss. Rosie, impulsively, gathered up Connie in a hug. 'I really mean it, thank you. I feel so guilty.'

Connie kissed the child. She adored his smell, the rich succulent nectar of his mother's milk.

'Why are you guilty?'

'It's just yoga. It's my one indulgence.'

'Rosie, it's not a problem.' She tickled the boy's hair. 'See you Saturday, Hugo.'

'Can Richie come?'

Connie looked across at her friend. He nodded.

Richie tweaked Hugo's ear.

'See you then, buddy.'

As they walked across the park, they shared the remaining beer.

'That was full-on, wasn't it?'

'What was?'

She looked at her friend in amazement. And then she laughed.

By the time she finished her schoolwork it was nearly midnight. Her aunt was in bed and the house was quiet. She shivered. She closed the bathroom door and began to run a bath. She stripped and looked at herself in the mirror. Her legs were too fat. She wished she could have a body like Aisha. She patted her stomach and groaned. Her pubes were too thick, too bushy. She would shave. She would get a Brazilian the first chance she had. She was hideous. She turned off the taps and slowly put her feet into the water. It was scalding. She shivered, enjoying the excruciating contrast, her legs burning and her torso freezing. Slowly, she eased herself into the tub.

She could hear the steady metallic whirl of the fan. She stretched her body out fully and watched as her breasts bobbed in the water. She closed her eyes. She was at the beach. Hector, the young Hector, was in the sea. He was running to her. He lay down next to her and she dried him with a towel. He kissed her. She loved how he kissed her. Hard, with his bristles rubbing at her skin, but he never hurt her. His kisses were long and confident, they weren't like the kisses of boys. She imagined him putting his arms around her, feeling her breasts, kissing her neck, touching her cunt. This is how he had made her come, in the car, fingering her, telling her how beautiful she was. She opened her eyes. She lifted herself half out of the water and reached across for the shampoo bottle. It was cylindrical, thick. She placed her hand around the bottle. When he had been hard, he'd been this thick. She lay back in the water and lifted her feet up against the end of the bath. She closed her eyes. She was back at the beach. Hector had her in the sand. It was hot, much hotter than the water. Slowly she pushed the shampoo bottle into her vagina. It wouldn't go in and the pain was piercing. She gritted her teeth and tried again, but it felt like it was ripping her flesh apart. Her eyes filled with tears. Would it have hurt like that if he had put his cock inside her? She tried to force the bottle in further but the pain was unbearable. It stung, it really stung. She opened her eyes and blinked back the tears. She turned on the hot water tap and washed the bottle. He had not let himself fuck her. She had tried to blow him once, in the car, but he had not let her. She hated him for that, she fucking hated him for all of that.

The clinic waiting room was full when she got into work on Saturday. Tracey was on the phone and had given her a wry smile as she walked in. She heard the phone ringing and ran into the office and picked up the line. She scanned the computer. Every consultation was taken, they were booked up till closing.

The woman on the other end of the line was insisting on an appointment. 'My dog hasn't eaten for a week.'

Then why the hell didn't you bring him in earlier? She scanned the appointments. There were two vaccinations in the next half-hour; they looked straightforward.

'Excuse me, I'll just put you on hold and consult the vet.' She stripped off her cardigan, took a clinic vest from the cupboard and quickly slipped it on. She knocked on the consult door and went in. Aisha was finishing up with a client, an old woman, who smiled sweetly at her. Connie walked over to the consult table, tickled the black and white cat, and waited for a pause in the conversation.

'What is it?'

Connie was now used to Aisha's curtness when they were at work. For the first few months she had thought that she was always doing something wrong.

'There's a lady on the phone. Her dog hasn't eaten for a week.'

'And she's decided Saturday afternoon is the best time for me to see it?'

They shared a complicit, frustrated smile.

'Is she a regular client?'

Connie shrugged. 'We've seen the animal twice in the last five years.'

Aish sighed. 'Tell her to bring it in.'

The phone was ringing again and she let Trace take the call from the front. She picked up her line.

'Can you come in immediately?'

'I have a lunch appointment.'

Not even five minutes in at work and she felt like screaming.

'I'm very sorry. We are always booked heavily on Saturdays. You'd need to come in now with Monkey.'

There was a long pause. Tracey poked her head through the office door, her bag swung over her shoulder. Connie waved her goodbye. Trace blew her a kiss and rushed out the back.

'Fine, I'll come in now.'

The bitch was pissed off. Fuck her.

Connie made the appointment. Just as she finished entering it into the computer, the phone rang again.

There was no time for a break. But even though it was rushed, even though there hadn't been a moment when the waiting room wasn't full or the phones weren't ringing, she enjoyed the shift. Aisha was quick, thorough and kept to a martial pace.

Monkey, the dog who hadn't eaten for a week, was a fat, sad-eyed labrador. Suprisingly, as the breed was usually docile, Aisha had called for Connie to bring in a muzzle and to assist holding the dog while she examined it. It was a big dog and they had to examine it on the floor. Connie had to put all her weight on the animal to stop it trying to get to its feet. The owner was hopeless at controlling it.

Aisha felt along its belly and abdomen. 'What do you feed it?'

'Oh, just the usual.'

Connie suppressed an urge to giggle. There was nothing that would piss Aish off more than such a silly, unthinking response.

'And what is the usual?'

'Pal. Dry food. Some leftovers.'

'Bones?'

'Monkey loves his bones.' Monkey? What a dumb-arse name for a labrador.

Aish sighed and got to her feet. Connie unmuzzled the dog. He growled and then plonked himself next to his owner's feet. He was huge, way too fat for a labrador. He would be doing enormous damage to his legs.

'Can I go? I've got the phones on hold.'

Aisha did not answer. She was looking at the dog, weighing up the options. She turned to Connie and nodded.

Aisha followed her into the office.

'How busy are we?'

'Booked up. Why?'

'There's something stuck there, I can feel it. We can do an X-ray but I'm convinced it's a bone. I'd like to do an enema.'

Connie did not answer. An enema would mean that they'd have to be there for hours. There was no way they could do it before consultations finished.

'Do you want me to set up for it?'

The older woman looked at Connie. She was smiling.

'Fuck her. There's no time and the dog should be monitored overnight. I'm going to refer her to the emergency clinic.'

Aisha went back into the consult and Connie started preparing the paperwork for the referral.

Trace had left a few slices of chocolate cake she'd baked the night before in the office fridge. There was a note beside it, in Tracey's hurried, oversized handwriting. *Richie ate over half of it last night. He is NOT having any more. Enjoy.* In between consults, Aisha and Connie hurriedly crammed scoops of the cake into their mouths. It was sweet and oily and satisfied Connie's hunger. The phones had finally quietened and the last consult of the day, an elderly Italian woman with her yappy Maltese Terrier, was waiting her turn. Connie had started counting the money in the till, preparing for closing. The bell on the front door began to violently clang and a young woman rushed into the clinic holding a dog in a bloodied towel. The animal, a kelpie, was breathing with difficulty. Connie banged the till shut and rushed over to the woman.

'What happened?'

'He tried to jump the fence. I don't know what the fuck he's done to himself.' The woman smelled of cigarettes and the faint sting of perspiration. Tears were welling in her eyes. Connie lifted the towel. The gash along the side of the dog's left hind leg was deep. She could see through to the bone. She didn't dare touch it, not trusting how the dog would react. She asked the woman to take a seat and walked into the consult room.

'We've got an emergency.'

'What is it?' Aisha had just finished administering a vaccine to a large unhappy tortoiseshell.

'A dog has cut itself pretty bad on its leg.'

'How much blood has it lost?'

Connie felt stupid. The towel was soaking. It looks like a lot. And then, resentfully, she couldn't help thinking, How the fuck do I know? *You're* the vet.

'A fair bit.'

The owner, a bearded gentleman in his forties, took his recalcitrant cat from Aisha and pushed it back in its cage. 'We're fine here,' he insisted. 'You deal with the emergency.'

Connie ushered the woman and her kelpie into the consult room and then fixed up the gentleman's bill. She started to apologise to the Italian woman who promptly raised a hand to stop her.

'Don't you worry, love. You look after that dog. That's what's important.' She lifted her fluffy terrier to her face and kissed the dog's snout. 'My little Jackie O, my little Jackie O, how I'd hate anything terrible to happen to you.' The dog happily licked at the wrinkled old face.

'It needs surgery.'

Connie nodded.

'Can you stay back?'

'I was going to babysit Hugo.'

'Connie, if you need to go, that's fine. I'll get them to go to the emergency clinic.'

The girl shook her head. 'Do you want me to premed as usual?'

'Thank you.' For a moment she thought Aisha was going to kiss her. Instead, the older woman just smiled and went to vaccinate the terrier, beckoning to the old lady to follow. Connie switched the after-hours answering machine on. She weighed the kelpie, took down the details and placed it into a cage.

'He'll be alright.' The dog's owner was following her, loath to leave the animal alone. She knelt before the cage and the dog licked at her fingers. Connie repeated her assurance. 'He'll be fine.'

The woman stood. 'Thanks. I'll give you all my numbers.'

Connie rapidly wrote them down on a piece of scrap paper.

The woman said a last goodbye to her dog and Connie showed her to the door. As soon as the woman walked out, Connie locked up then ran to get her mobile phone from the office and was about to enter Rosie's number when she stopped. She rang Richie instead.

'What's up?'

'I've got to help Aisha with surgery.'

'Cool. What happened?'

'Rich, I haven't got time. Can you look after Hugo on your own?'

There was a pause. Please, Rich, please.

'Sure. No problem. Done.'

'Thank you. I'll get Rosie to drop him off to your place.'

'Nah. I'll walk over there now.'

'Rich, you're the best.'

He made a sound somewhere between a splutter and a groan. She had embarrassed him. 'Gimme a break.'

She hung up and rang Rosie.

Her experience assisting in surgery was minimal. When she had first started work at the clinic, she had just turned fifteen and for the first six months her duties were confined to cleaning the cages, washing up, reception. Slowly, however, Tracey had encouraged her to take more responsibility with the animals and to train during surgery. Connie found that she was not squeamish at all. She had no fear of administering pills or even giving subcutaneous injections to the animals. But she did find surgery overwhelming. Both Aisha and Brendan had stressed to her the importance of anaesthetic monitoring and she was drilled on emergency procedures in case of a negative anaesthetic reaction on the table. The cold reality was so different: the complicated respiratory tubing and dials of the monitoring machinery, her near paralysing phobia that the animal would go blue, fall into a coma. But she knew that being anxious or panicking about it would not help Aisha at all. The vet was finishing up with the last client and Connie retrieved a list she had typed up months ago from her work basket. With Trace's help, she'd listed everything she needed to remember for surgery. She pulled out the necessary surgical kit, the gloves and scalpel for Aisha, and then she prepared the injections for the animal.

She had always liked animals but they had never had any pets when she was a child—her parents had moved around too much. But her aunt loved cats and Connie too had come to respect the aristocratic nature of the species, and admire the independence and unrepentant indolence of the feline. There was no way she'd give up either Bart or Lisa. One day, though, she would really love to have a dog. A big, friendly, slobbering dog that she could take for long walks and that would sleep next to her at nights.

The kelpie had curled into a corner of the cage and was whimpering. Its eyes were sad, moist. The dog smelt scared, like it was about to shit and piss itself. Connie glanced at the post-it on which she had written the owner's name and details. The dog was called Clancy. She knelt, opened the cage door and softly rubbed the dog behind its ears. It's alright, Clancy, she whispered, and the dog obligingly licked at her hand. She pulled it close, cocked the syringe's cap between her teeth and fed the needle into the thick skin behind the dog's neck. It did not flinch. She capped the needle, placed the syringe behind her ear and took another from her uniform pocket. The penicillin was thick and creamy. She inserted the needle into the skin again but this time Clancy whined and withdrew into the cage, leaving the thick liquid to pour over his coat.

'Fuck!'

'You have to be careful when administering the penicillin. It stings.' Aisha had come in and walked over to the bench to get another syringe. 'Did he get any?'

'I don't think so.'

Aisha handed the syringe to Connie. 'Try it again. I'll hold him.'

Connie felt foolish and was furious at herself. Why was she feeling so intimidated? She knew Aisha trusted her. She pulled on the dog's skin and pushed the needle into the tent she had formed with her thumb and forefinger. The dog whimpered but Aisha's hold was firm. Connie gave the dog the injection. It whimpered once more than curled back into the cage. Aisha shut the door and walked over to the computer.

'What's the owner's surname?'

Connie cringed. She hadn't recognised either the woman or Clancy. She hadn't checked if they were already clients. That was the first thing she should have done. Stupid, that was stupid. She'd become flustered and panicked.

'His name's Clancy Rivera. I haven't check the computer. Sorry.'

Aisha walked to the monitor and punched in the details. 'It's alright, I've got him up.'

Connie let out a long, slow breath.

The surgery proceeded quickly and succesfully. Connie watched Aisha perform her work with admiration. Within twenty minutes she had turned the anaesthetic off and they were waiting for the dog to wake.

'Rosie says that Hugo adores you.'

Connie blushed and a big grin broke on her face. 'I adore him as well.'

'Well, I know Rosie appreciates the help you give her. It's a tough time for her.'

Connie looked up at her employer. It was always difficult to know what Aisha was thinking. Except for when she was displeased, when her mouth tightened to a thin line. That was the look they all feared in the clinic, the look that Brendan and Trace poked fun at, mostly in affection and good humour, when Aisha was away. Connie felt her age, but she was also proud that the older woman was taking her into her confidence. She stammered out a sentence.

'Yeah, she and Gary fight a lot, don't they?'

Aisha's lips immediately tightened. The off-milk look, as Brendan called it. For an instant Connie was worried that Aisha disapproved of what she had said, but then realised that Aisha did not like Gary at all.

'They always have. Or rather, *he* always has. Gary is one of those loud-mouthed insecure men who will forever be arguing with the world because the world refuses to lift him in its arms and wipe his arse for him.'

Connie was gently patting the dog. It was waking, starting to bite on the respiratory tube.

Aish quickly pulled it out. 'This upcoming hearing is consuming her. She can't think of anything else. I just wish they'd confirm a date for her.'

'That was a terrible thing that happened. He should never have slapped Hugo.'

'Do you think?' Aisha asked the question simply, unemotionally. Again, Connie had no idea what she was thinking. She went to the sink and started scrubbing the instruments while Aisha placed the kelpie in the cage. What did she think?

'I don't think an adult has any right to physically abuse a child, that's what I think.' She was surprised at the fierce, trembling passion in her voice. That was what she thought, exactly what she thought. Adults shouldn't hurt kids, they shouldn't touch them.

Aisha had come over to the sink and was wiping the instruments for her, placing them on a drape. Connie glanced over at the older woman. 'Isn't that what you think?' Her rush of indignation was gone. She was ashamed of the pathetic indecision that she could hear in her own voice.

'I think that hitting a child is a reprehensible action. I also think that Hugo needed to be disciplined that day, that he was totally out of control. I think Harry has a dangerous temper which he should learn to control. But he apologised and I think Gary and Rosie should have accepted the apology and left it at that. No one has behaved very well in any of this.' Aisha was neatly laying the surgery equipment across the drape in order of size. 'But in the end, Hugo is the child and Harry is the adult. Harry should have controlled himself. He's responsible.'

Connie wanted to ask so many questions. She wanted to ask what Hector thought. Had they argued about it all night after the barbecue? What if it had been Adam or Melissa? Connie felt a warm, comfortable blush spread across her shoulders and her neck. She adored this woman, she was so kind and generous to her, so sexy and smart—God, if only she could be like Aisha. And she had done such hurtful, shameful things to her. She tried to stop herself but suddenly her eyes watered and she gasped for breath. She wiped angrily at her eyes.

'Connie, what's wrong?' Aisha placed her arm around the girl. Connie hugged her back and then awkwardly tried to disentangle herself from the older woman's grip. She felt young and stupid. She guessed that both she and Aisha were glad to draw apart.

'Sorry, I'm an idiot.'

Aisha folded the drape. The bundle looked clumsy, misshapen.

'Trace always makes up the surgical kits so beautifully. And I have no bloody idea how she does it.'

Connie laughed. 'Yeah, she always says you vets are bloody hopeless. Don't worry, I know how to make them up.'

Aisha winked. 'Sweetheart, you've been wonderful today. I really appreciate it.' She gently flicked a blonde lock away from Connie's eye. 'It's not embarrassing to feel things strongly. It's nothing to be ashamed of that you get so indignant and mad about what adults can do. That's one of the great things about being young.

It just becomes a problem if you let that indignation become self-righteousness.'

Was that her problem? Was she self-righteous? What exactly did it mean? She was unsure of its definition but it sounded like it fitted her. She didn't like it. It sounded a heavy word, too big a weight to carry.

'But I don't think you need to worry about that at all.'

Aisha dropped her off at Rosie's. It was just after five in the afternoon. The front door to the house was open and Connie walked through the hall, past the kitchen, through the lean-to sunroom that always seemed to smell damp—even in the height of a dry summer—and into the backyard. Richie was stretched out on the grass, and he grinned, then winked, when he saw her. Hugo was crouching in the untidy vegetable patch, half-hidden amongst the tall shoots of the broad beans. He ignored her.

'What are you guys doing?' She sat next to Richie on the grass. His black Eminem sweatshirt was pulled tight across his torso and she could see a glimpse of his chalk-white flat stomach. There was a thatch of sparse copper-coloured curls disappearing underneath his trousers. She was tired and felt like snapping at him, I don't want to look at your pubes, mate. Confused, a little sickened, she turned her attention to the boy.

'Come on, Huges, what you doing?'

'He's looking for money.'

'Is there buried treasure?' Hugo did not even bother answering her stupid question. He made his disdain obvious by a click of the tongue.

'I threw some coins in the vegie patch. Hugo's looking for them.' Richie rolled over onto his stomach and looked up at her, shielding his eyes from the subdued winter sun. 'Was it awful?'

'Nah. It was okay.' Connie closed her eyes, leaned back and felt the last warmth of the dying sun on her face and arms. She could still smell the clinic on her: the sharp chemical bite of the cleaning fluids, the musty carnal smell of cats and dogs. In a few hours she would have to be ready for the party. She wanted a long, long extravagant hot shower.

'You coming to the party?'

Richie nodded, bored. He turned over again onto his back. There was an excited squeal and Hugo emerged from the vegie patch with a gold dollar coin in his hand.

'Found it,' he exclaimed.

'Thanks, buddy. I'll have it.'

Hugo ignored Richie. He pocketed the coin and ran to his yellow and green soccer ball. 'Kick to kick,' he announced.

The teenagers glanced quickly at one another.

'Kick to kick,' Hugo insisted, a little louder.

Richie yawned and shook his head. 'I'm tired, Huges, you can play with Connie.'

She nearly hit him. She was the one who had been working. But she began to rise.

Hugo pouted. 'No. She's a girl. I want to play with you.'

Connie, grinning, fell back on the grass and stuck her tongue out at Richie. 'You heard him, you're the boy. You have to play with him.'

She lay in the setting sun, her eyes shut, listening to the thud-thud of the ball being kicked between the boy and the teenager. She had fallen in love with Melbourne when she experienced her first late autumn in the city, when the bitter cold was kept at bay by the determined effort of the hardy antipodean sun. The English sun was weak. She didn't have to open her eyes, she knew Richie and Hugo were there, that they were safe in the garden. This was like they were married, she thought, like Hugo was their child, this backyard was theirs and they were a family. Maybe this would be what the future would be like. Of course, Richie couldn't be her husband. She couldn't imagine a husband. Not if Hector couldn't be it. She heard Hugo laugh and then there was a sharp pain in her side as the ball slammed into her. It stung.

'You bastards.'

The boys cracked up, laughing hysterically at her outrage. She ran to Hugo, grabbed him, all writhing arms and legs, and carried him over to the pond. A large goldfish was lazily gulping at the surface of the water. At their shadow, it flicked into the murky deep and vanished from sight.

'I'm going to drop you in.'

'No,' screamed the boy, his legs thrashing furiously.

'Say sorry.'

'No!'

'Say it.'

'No!'

'In you go.'

She then held him tight and kissed him, and he placed his arms around her neck. He put his lips to her ear and whispered, I'm sorry. His skin was warm and sweaty, the sweetness of breast-milk coupled with a faint trace of earth. She rubbed her face in his hair.

'It looks like someone's had a great afternoon.'

Hugo released his grip, she lowered him to the ground and he rushed over to his mother, who scooped him into her arms. Rosie sat on one of the abandoned kitchen chairs that were scattered across the backyard, their once bright red vinyl now faded to a light pink. Hugo dived for her chest, and Rosie gave him her breast.

Richie was still playing with the soccer ball, kicking it from his foot to his head, from his head to his knee and back onto his foot. Hugo dropped his mother's nipple and watched the older boy.

'Teach me,' he called out to Richie, who beckoned him over. The boy dropped out of his mother's arms and ran to the older boy.

'I think I've been usurped.' Rosie fixed her bra. 'Probably a good thing. You want some tea, sweetheart?'

'It's alright, I'll go make it.' She called out to Richie. 'Do you want a drink?' The older boy shook his head. He was trying to get Hugo to kick straight. The younger boy, frustrated, couldn't coordinate his movements. Richie was patiently allowing him to fail and try again. Fail, and try again. Connie's friend was good with kids. They both were.

The blind was drawn in the kitchen and the room was dark and cool. That morning's dishes were still piled up on the sink. Connie switched on the kitchen light and then turned on the kettle. She could hear the boys playing, heard Rosie laugh, encouraging her son. Connie slipped into the lounge room and walked over to the bookshelf. Guiltily she glanced behind her, trying to ignore the ugly clown on the wall, and she pulled out the photo album. She flicked through the photographs, the young adults at the beach. She just wanted one more look. A blank rectangle stared out at her. The photograph of Hector was gone.

She felt light-headed and suddenly cold. It was exactly like a dream. She found herself pouring the boiling water into the teapot. When had the kettle whistled? When had she walked back into the kitchen? She heard Richie's laughter and felt rage run through her. She was silent as she handed the teacup to Rosie.

'Are you alright, Con?'

'Just tired. It was a long day at work.'

'Aish loves you, you do know that? She trusts you. She's told me she thinks you'd make a brilliant vet.'

Connie could not make sense of her emotions. The fury at her friend, the guilt. It felt toxic, like she had to try hard to get clean air into her lungs. The day that only minutes before had seemed so perfect, was spoilt, soiled. She hated herself and she hated Richie.

She gulped her tea too quickly, scalding her tongue. 'I've got to go.'

Richie handballed the soccer ball to Hugo. 'Home time for me, buddy.'

Hugo started to wail. She wanted to be out of the house, away from boys and their stupid babyish ball games. Richie had dropped to his knees and was trying to calm the crying boy.

'We'll play again, little man. In a few days.' Richie smiled over to her. 'Won't we Connie?'

She wanted to say, Nah, I've got to study. I've got no time. If you want to play with Hugo then you fucking arrange it on your own. She remained silent.

Hugo wiped his eyes. 'You promise.'

'I promise.' Hugo clasped his arms tight around the older boy, then he ran over to Connie.

'Promise.'

She hesitated. His blue eyes were looking straight at her. She grabbed him, kissed him. 'Promise.'

He was sweating. He smelt of boy, he smelt like Richie.

They walked across the park. She was deliberately silent, her face hard, but Richie did not seem to notice. He was humming beside her. It was really shitting her.

'Stop that.'

'What?'

'You're so off-tune.'

'What's up with you?'

'Fuck you.'

'Fuck you too.'

She stopped in the middle of the path. A young man with prickly short, grey hair, a half-dozen or so rings looped around his right ear, rock star looks and poise, was wheeling a pram, a little girl skipping at his side holding his hand. She was chatting away to him, something about school, and Connie stepped aside as they passed. Richie had turned around, was watching the man casually stroll away.

That would be right. He was such a fag.

Richie turned to her. His smile was gone. 'What's wrong, Con?'

She couldn't speak. He came up to her and placed an arm around her shoulder. She punched it away.

'What's wrong with you?'

'You took the photo, didn't you?'

His face went pale, then a deep rose shade, a blush that seeped down to his neck. He let out a silly weak whistle, like a frightened bird. She wanted to slap him.

'I don't know what you're talking about.'

He was a fucking liar.

'You took the photo.' She had no doubt about it. He was guilty and he was gutless. He'd lied to her. She resumed walking up the path, her strides long and furious. He tried to keep pace with her.

'Connie, what have I done?'

She refused to answer. Her eyes moistened and she pinched her palms, determined not to cry. But she couldn't stop it, the dumb tears fell. Richie grabbed her arm and she struggled against him. He tightened his grip.

'If you don't let go of me I'm going to scream.'

They were at the edge of the park, the station across the road from them was lit by the strong glare of the streetlights on Hoddle Street. A train was coming through. Richie, his grip still tight on her arm, glanced right and then rushed them across the road, onto the traffic island. She thought of kicking him, then rushing off. But she was crying now and her body seemed listless, lacking all energy. Richie waited for a break in the traffic and they hurried across to the other side. He dragged her under the railway bridge, pushed her through the gap in the fence and across the railway lines. She could hear the train coming and thought for a moment, I'm going to trip and I'm going to get killed by the train. He'll have to watch all of it. It will be his fault and he'll have to live with it all his life. She had a flash of the funeral, his distraught, panicked face. It would serve him right if he killed her. He pulled her up on the embankment and sat her on an old bluestone and sat down next to her. Her arm hurt from where he had tugged at her. The train thundered past, and they watched it slow down as it approached the station.

She turned to him, ready to yell at him, that she hated him, and noticed that he too was crying. She was suddenly terrified. She wanted to make it better, to stop the confusion of shame and fear and sadness that overwhelmed her. She wanted to take back the last half-hour. She wanted to be back in the garden with him again, outstretched to the sun, listening to the laughter and the bounce of the ball. She gulped and then started to really cry, her body heaved and rocked on the bluestone. Scared, Richie placed an arm around her. She wanted to make it better, she wanted it all to make sense.

'Hector raped me.'

The words were muffled by her sobs and she had to repeat them. Shocked, Richie dropped his arm from around her, then brought his hand awkwardly back up again, to comfort her. Her sobbing calmed. It was like being in a movie. Like she was floating above both of them, looking down, directing the action.

'When?' Richie looked stricken; he had turned pale. 'How, I mean . . .' He hesitated, swallowed and tried again. 'Tell me what happened, Con.'

She was suddenly confused. She didn't want to say any more. She didn't want questions, hadn't anticipated them.

She drew a shuddering breath. 'About a year ago. He gave me a lift home from work. It was in his car.' As she started to speak, she could suddenly fantasise the whole memory. She just let the words rush out. It was last winter, it was pouring outside. He'd come to pick up Aish and then offered me a lift home as well. He dropped her off first and then said he'd take me home. Except he drove to the boathouse, parked there and started to kiss me. I wanted to scream but he had his hand over my mouth. His hands were on her legs, then up her cunt. He was suddenly inside her. It had hurt but she couldn't scream. She should have bitten his hand. She wished she had bitten his hand. She didn't know why she hadn't. He had fucked her and it had hurt. He was kissing her neck and breasts. He had come and he had lit a cigarette afterwards. His zip was still undone. Her panties were still around her knees. She was bleeding. But she had asked for a cigarette. He had told her that he loved her. He had said that if she told anyone that would be the end of him and Aish. He kept telling her he loved her. She had told him that if it ever happened again she would go straight to the police. She told him he was a bastard. She told him that she hated him.

'He kept saying, I love you. Over and over. It was sick.' Richie's hand—hot, sweaty—was covering hers. The girl above them, the girl watching it all, the girl directing the movie, it had happened to that girl. It was real.

Connie wanted to pull her hand from under Richie's, but didn't know how to. The boy was the first to take his hand away and she sighed in relief.

'Have you told anyone?'

'No. I can't. I don't want Aish to know.'

'She should know.'

He couldn't say anything. He mustn't say anything.

'I can't say a word to anyone. Just you.' She was almost wailing, terrified now. 'You can't say a word to anyone, Rich, not a word, not fucking ever.'

The boy was silent.

She was panicking.

'Rich, you have to promise. You have to. You have to.' She was shouting. Hugo was like this when he wanted something he couldn't get. Almost desperate. 'You have to promise!'

'I promise.' It sounded like he was sulking.

'Promise?'

His face was fearful, sad and confused. 'I promise.'

They walked home hand in hand.

'You look great.'

Connie grimaced at her aunt's words. Their bathroom was tiny, an old alcove shoddily added to the main house, and the ruthless light from the overhead bulb above her seemed to accentuate every blemish on her skin. She pursed her lips and softly touched the freshly applied lipstick with the tip of her tongue. Tasha was standing in the doorway. Connie, her hair still wet from the shower, was in her underpants. She had slugged on an old gym sweater to keep warm.

'No, I don't. I look awful.'

Tasha laughed and came into the room, standing behind Connie. 'I said you look beautiful and you do. What are you going to wear?'

'My jeans. A T-shirt, I guess.'

'I think you should dress up.'

'Tash,' Connie moaned. 'It's just a party.'

'Exactly, it's a party, probably the last party before exams and before you finish school. You've been working so hard, you deserve a big night. Save your jeans and T-shirt for when you get trashed at the end of the year. I think you should dress up tonight.'

Connie examined her aunt's reflection in the mirror. Tasha was wearing a floppy moth-eaten lime-green jumper and faded grey track-pants. She had no make-up on and her hair was loose, uncombed.

'What are you doing tonight?'

'I'm staying in. Getting take-away and watching *The Bill*.'

Connie bit her bottom lip. The lipstick smeared and she gently rubbed at it. 'That doesn't sound like much fun.'

Tasha laughed. 'Darling, believe me. It's what I've been looking forward to all week.'

Connie didn't believe her. She was sure Tasha would much prefer to be going out to a bar with friends, or maybe on a date. It had been a long time since her aunt had been on a date. Years. Connie turned and wrapped her arms around Tasha. The older woman, surprised, squeezed her niece tightly.

'Thank you, Tasha.' Connie's words were muffled. Her face was covered in the light fleece of her aunt's woollen jumper. It felt soft and warm, the bristles tickling her cheeks. It smelt of Tasha, her faintly apple-ciderish perfume, her tobacco. It smelled good.

'Thank you for what?'

Connie couldn't answer. Her father had said, from his hospital bed, just days before he slipped into his coma, in the weeks where he was slipping in and out of lucidity, You'll love Tash. You'll hate all the other cunts in my family, but you'll love Tash.

It had not been exactly true. Neither of her grandparents, and no, not even her uncle could be described as 'cunts'. There are other 'C' words, Dad. Conservative, contrary, maybe even a little cowardly; even now, they couldn't speak words like AIDS or bisexual. Even now they couldn't bring themselves to say who he had really been, how he had really died. But they certainly weren't 'cunts'.

'I didn't hear you, angel.'

'Thank you for looking after me. Thank you for putting your life on hold.' Even as she said the words she knew her aunt would be furious. She knew she was being self-pitying, that she was seeking assurance that she was loved. She knew all this but still said the words. She wanted to be held, to be assured.

'My life is not on bloody hold, Con. What the fuck are you talking about?'

'I just meant . . .'

'I know exactly what you meant. It may seem strange and bizarre to you, but there will come a time in your life when you too will look forward to being at home on a Saturday night and watching the telly. Putting your feet up is what they call it. I'm raising you. I enjoy that. You know that.' Her aunt turned and stormed down the hall. 'That was a fucking horrible thing to say,' she called over her shoulder.

Connie couldn't help smiling as she looked at herself in the bathroom mirror. She walked into the lounge where her aunt had plonked herself on the couch and switched on the television. Connie sat on the arm of the couch.

'What do you think I should wear?'

Tasha ignored her for a moment, her eyes fixed on the images flickering on the screen. Connie turned to look. Something about bombs, somewhere overseas. She took the remote and switched off the sounds and the images. She looked back down at Tasha, who was trying not to smile. Connie leaned down and softly tickled her aunt's sides.

Tasha curled over laughing. 'Don't!'

'What should I wear?'

'Something elegant. Something sophisticated. Not some horrible brand sports gear.'

'No logo. Boss. I like that.'

'Please don't speak like a teenager, Con.'

'I am a teenager.'

'Yes, an unusually intelligent teenager. I just can't stand the way you young people speak. For God's sake, what is so wrong with complete sentences?'

And then Tasha started to laugh again. Even more loudly than before.

Connie looked at her, perplexed. 'What's so funny?'

Tasha touched Connie's cheek. 'What we were and what we become, angel.' She rose from the couch. 'Wait here.'

Tasha came back with clothes draped over both arms. Connie could see a swirl of fabrics. A black and scarlet vest, delicately embroidered with glittering ruby- and sapphire-coloured beads, a camel-hair long skirt with large silver buttons down one side. There was even a hat, made from some thick ivory-coloured material, with a squat conical top that abruptly tapered at the end at an oblique, steep angle.

'Where did they come from?' Her voice was high-pitched from excitement.

'They were mine.'

'You used to wear them?'

'I made them. No logo.' Tasha smiled. 'Is that boss enough for you?' She lay the clothes across the couch. 'Actually, it's not true that there was no label. We did have a label. Nietzsche. How pretentious was that?'

Connie was holding up a dress, part of a charcoal suit, the skirt and jacket made of the same coarse wool. She ignored her aunt.

'It was the early eighties. It made sense back then, nuclear winter and all that. We were all listening to Public Image and Joy Division.' Tasha smiled at her niece's delight in the clothes. 'You probably have no idea what I'm talking about.'

'I do. Dad loved Joy Division.' Connie picked up the long skirt, placing it against her hips. 'I like some of their stuff. They're a bit dark.'

'Dark is good. Better than all that fluffy pop you mob listen to.' Tasha snatched the skirt away from her. 'You can't wear that, sweetheart. It's too heavy.'

Connie picked up another dress. It was a simple design; a knee-length, strapless dress with two satin panels forming a double-diamond pattern across the front. The fabric was a fine cotton, ethereal and white, with a trace of light blue shimmer.

Connie hugged it to her body. 'I can't get away with this one, can I?'

'Of course you can. You'll look terrific in that.'

'I can't.' Connie ran into her bedroom and stood in front of the mirror. She looked at the dress against her skin. Her aunt came and stood in the doorway. When Connie turned around she looked so distressed that Tasha rushed to her.

'I can't.' This time it was a wail.

Tasha ignored her. She said nothing. Instead she gently sat her niece down onto the bed and looked around the room.

'I need a brush and some hair gel.'

Connie pointed to her sports bag on the floor. Tasha scrummaged through it and found what she wanted. She sat back on the bed and squeezed gel into her hands. She rubbed them together and then began to run the gel through Connie's hair. They were both silent. Tasha started to brush Connie's hair back over her head, pulling at it till Connie winced.

'I'm going to slick it back. That's the look for that dress. Unless you want to try the hat?'

Connie looked alarmed at that option. 'I don't know anything about hats.'

'It's the sad decline of civilisation. What can I say? It's okay. I don't wear them either now that I'm a hippie.'

'You're not a hippie.'

'It's not an insult. Put on the dress.'

Connie carefully stripped off the sweater and gingerly stepped into the dress. The fabric felt cool against her skin and the fit was perfect. She looked into the mirror. There was a mole on her left shoulder. That was visible. There were too many summer freckles on the bridge of her nose. Her breasts looked huge. Her legs were too fat. She could see all this, but it didn't matter. She had never looked this good. She felt wonderful, she felt like a movie star, like a model, she felt older and more sophisticated than she had ever felt before. She couldn't wait for Jenna and Tina to see her. She imagined Richie's reaction, his awe, and it made her want to laugh. She would sit up straight all night. She would be grown-up in this dress. No slouching, no being a teenager tonight. She'd have to be careful with any food or drink. She'd have to be careful where she sat. There would be a hundred things she'd never have had to think about at a party before, but it didn't matter. It didn't matter because she had never looked this good. She swung away from the mirror and looked at her aunt on the bed.

·'Tash, what do you think?' Her voice was a little girl's, eager, hesitant and excited.

Her aunt got up and put her arms around her. 'I think you look stunning. Beautiful.' Tasha looked her niece up and down. 'But you need a brighter lipstick.' She pointed down to Connie's feet. 'And you certainly cannot wear runners with that dress.'

Connie's face dropped. 'I've got no shoes.'

'Well, you are very lucky that we are the same shoe size, aren't you? And you are even more lucky that despite being an old hippie I still can't bear to throw away any of my old shoes.'

Connie hugged her aunt. 'I never knew you were so talented.'

'I wasn't.'

Connie shook her head in disbelief. She pointed down to the dress. 'This is talented.'

'I only kept the stuff I thought was decent. Four dresses, a couple of vests, a few shirts. It's not much. I wasn't the talented one.'

Connie was about to continue protesting when Tasha put a finger to Connie's lips. 'It was so much fun, angel. Vicky and I would make clothes during the week and we'd sell them at Victoria Markets on Sunday. She was the talented one. It was fun, but I didn't have the gift.' Tasha carefully adjusted the dress. 'But I'm proud of this one tonight. What time do you have to be at Jenna's?'

'Seven-thirty.'

'I'm going to get some Thai take-away from Station Street. Interested?'

Connie shook her head. 'I'm not hungry yet. There'll be some food at the party. Mrs Athanasiou always has heaps of food.'

'Well, make sure you eat. I don't want you to vomit all over the dress.'

'Yuck, of course I won't.'

Tasha slipped forty dollars into her niece's hand. Connie protested and tried to give the money back. 'I don't need it. We got paid last week.'

'You're not drinking bourbon with that dress. Promise?'

Connie nodded. 'Promise.'

'I'll go and find you the exact right shoes.'

Connie stood in front of the mirror. She wished Hector could see her. Maybe they could stop past their place on the way to Jenna's house. It was in the same direction. She could make an excuse, that she hadn't looked at the roster and was wondering when she was working next. She could see Hector opening the door, how he would stare at her. He would want her back. She opened her eyes. No, Aisha would be the beautiful one in this dress. Aisha's dark skin would be lovely against the alabaster fabric. She stepped back from the mirror. She looked like a girl playing dress-ups. A rush of scouring, over-whelming misery overcame her. She could not pull this off.

Fuck you, Connie, you're such a wimp. She stepped back to the mirror.

You're Scarlett Johansson tonight, she whispered to her reflection, You're Scarlett Johansson in *Lost in Translation*. She felt better. Hadn't Hector told her that she looked like Scarlett Johansson? She had not believed him but she had never forgotten it.

She would be Scarlett Johansson tonight.

Jenna had screamed when she opened the door. Tina, behind her, let out a series of gasps. They pushed Connie down the long, dark corridor into the living room, where Jenna's mother, Fiona, was curled up with her girlfriend, Hannah, watching television.

Hannah gave a low whistle and took the girl's hand. 'Connie. You look fabulous.'

The girls were touching the dress, feeling the fabric. 'Aunt Tash made it.' She did feel fabulous.

Tina and Jenna had also dressed up, but next to Connie, Tina's tight-fitting boob tube and Jenna's skin-tight jeans and scarlet halter-top seemed adolescent, and inelegant.

Jenna had scored two Es from her brother and they had decided to take them at once.

Tina had looked at the tablets nervously and initially refused to take one. 'Not this year,' she said hesitantly. 'There's so much schoolwork. I can't. I promise, I'll become a drug fiend once school's finished.'

'Just for tonight,' Connie entreated, echoing her aunt's sentiments. 'After tonight, there'll be no more parties until exams are over.'

Tina continued shaking her head. 'I'm scared of losing control.'

Jenna had rolled her eyes. 'Then don't take it. I'm not a pusher. That's fine, that leaves a whole one for me and one for Con.'

Connie, however, had bitten off a small corner from a pill and offered it to Tina who anxiously rolled it between her fingers.

'Dad told me that you should always try half the recommended dose of a drug the first time you take it. That way you can't like, totally lose control and, if you like it, you can have more in a few hours. I've just given you a quarter, maybe less. You'll be fine.'

Tina had stared incredulously at her friend. 'When did your dad tell you that?'

Connie found herself blushing. Her father, her mother, of course, they weren't like other people's. 'When I was eleven, I think. He was heading off to a party.'

'In that dress, when you blush, girlfriend, you look like a lobster.' Jenna's tone was bitchy. The two girls looked at each other: Jenna's speckled green eyes were cool and hard but Connie smiled. Her friend was jealous. No, not jealous, envious that she looked so good, so fabulous.

'Ta, I'll try not to embarrass myself then.'

Jenna wrapped her arms around Connie and kissed her full on the mouth. 'I'm so fucking jealous I could kill you. Let's go party.'

Walking to Jordan's house, her elation faded. The night air was sharp, and there were goosebumps all over her arms. At the last moment her aunt had given her a black lace shawl as protection against the cold but it was flimsy and she was shivering as they walked down Bastings Street. She also found the shoes difficult to manage, she had to walk slowly, deliberately, so as not to stumble. They were not very high heels, but the shoes felt tight and uncomfortable. She envied her friend's denim jackets and runners. Tina had three badges on her jacket: a peace insignia, a Robbie Williams pin, and one that read Vote for Pedro; Connie was tempted to ask to wear one, to counteract the formality of her own outfit. She was conscious of stares from the people they passed on the street. At High Street a group of wog guys and girls were standing smoking outside a reception centre. She heard one of the boys call out, Check her out, and a few of the younger men had wolf-whistled. She shouldn't blush. She was going to spend the whole evening trying not to blush. She glanced back at the group of wog boys, all smoking, in their best suits, looking like they owned the world. She was not going to think about him tonight. He would not spoil her night.

The Athanasious had a huge double-storey house on the crest of the hill on Charles Street. They walked up the drive, which was steep and long, and the shoes pinched at Connie's heels. Fairy lights decorated the verandah and music could be heard booming from the back of the house. The girls stopped at the front door and looked back at the city spread below. Melbourne was all lit up below them, and the night sky was a deep, satiny purple.

Jenna let out a low, slow breath. 'Wow, I just love this view.'

Tina's eyes were wide. 'Is it just the E, or does everything look fantastic tonight?'

Connie and Jenna laughed. No way the drug had kicked in yet.

Connie slipped her arm through Tina's and opened the door. 'Just you wait,' she whispered. 'Just you wait.'

Mrs Athanasiou was in the kitchen, sipping a glass of whisky. Mr Athanasiou was at the table scooping out dips into small bowls. Through the glass doors the girls could see Jordan turning sausages and chops on the barbecue. There were already fifteen or so kids outside. Jay-Z was on the stereo.

Mrs Athanasiou walked up to the girls and offered them each a peck on the cheek. 'Good, we need more women.'

She looked at Connie appreciatively. 'And you have made quite an effort.' She turned to her husband. 'Don't the girls look marvellous?'

But it was the Athanasious who were marvellous. Selena Athanasiou was from somewhere in Indonesia called Sulawesi. Or at least Connie thought it was in Indonesia. Maybe it was in Malaysia? She had silky raven hair that unfolded into one thick wave down her back. Jenna had once told her that Mrs Athanasiou belonged to a tribe whose ancestors were head-hunters. Jordan had boasted that his grandfather was a King. That would make Mrs Athanasiou a princess, and she could easily pass for one. Tonight she was wearing black jeans and a scarlet sweater, the look simple, eye-catching. An elegant line of mascara and a soft kiss of lipstick were her only make-up. Mr Athanasiou was, as always, unshaven, wearing baggy canvas trousers and a colourful batik shirt, but even in the daggiest clothes he could pass muster as a companion fit for a princess. His hair was a mess of shaggy black curls, speckled with grey. His eyes were twinkling, still youthful. His unblemished olive skin was tanned a rich chocolate brown almost as dark as his wife's.

Twenty years ago Mr Athanasiou had been a hippie trekking the globe, especially the parts the rest of the world had no interest in visiting. Evidence of his exploits stared down at Connie from the exposed red-brick wall of the kitchen: a black and white photograph blown up to the size of a poster of an even more youthful Mr Athanasiou, bearded, his unwashed hair down to his shoulders, standing next to a veiled old woman on a street in Kandahar watching the Soviet army leaving. But the photograph that always struck Connie was a postcard-sized, framed image of the youthful couple, Mr Athanasiou for once neatly shaven, his wife with her hands clutched over her pregnant belly, standing outside an ancient

Orthodox Church in Georgia. The icons painted on the wooden doors had eroded to rust-coloured ghosts. Not long after that picture was taken Mr Athanasiou set up an internet website supplying information for adventurous—or foolish—travellers wanting to risk more than sunburn and a pickpocketed wallet on their holidays. This must have been somewhere in the prehistory of computers. He had made a fortune. A filthy, amazing fortune.

Connie smiled as Mr Athanasiou kissed her cheek and looked through the glass sliding doors of the kitchen to where Jordan was standing over the barbecue, laughing over something his mate Bryan Macintosh was saying. Something stupid, no doubt. Bryan Macintosh only made dumb jokes. Jordan was as tanned as his father. And already almost as tall. His eyes and his smile were his mother's. Last holidays his parents had taken him to Uzbekistan, then to Trebizon in Turkey and ended the holidays at his grandparents' house in the Aegean. The holidays before that it had been Bolivia and New York City. Don't ever start envying the rich, Connie's mother had told her once, in Harrods. Marina would often take her there after school. Her mother would stuff shirts and skirts and little toys in her daughter's *The Little Mermaid* schoolbag. Don't ever start envying them, because once you do, you can never stop. You'll just end up wasting your life.

Did she envy Jordan his wealth, his good looks, his parents? No. She had taken her mother's advice. Nevertheless she'd smiled naughtily when Jenna informed her that Mr and Mrs Athanasiou had met and fallen in love in Paris. So perfectly romantic but also so pleasingly clichéd.

'Is there anything we can do to help, Mrs A?'

Mrs Athanasiou waved her glass of whisky in the air and glanced over to the oven. 'No thanks, Connie, you go outside and have fun. We're just waiting for these pies to be ready and then Antoni and I are off to the movies. The house belongs to you kids.' She pointed to the bar at the end of the dining area. 'There's beer, champagne and you have limited access to the spirits. Don't touch any of the top-shelf stuff. It will only be wasted on you teenagers.'

Mr Athanasiou walked over to the door and slid it open. He bowed and waved the girls through. 'Join the party.'

Jay-Z had been followed by a short rant of spoken word by Jello Biafra and now Jet's 'Are You Gonna Be My Girl?' was pumping through the outdoor speakers. Jordan had obviously been lazy when it came to programming the iPod, just searching and clicking through his selections alphabetically.

The teenagers had formed into three groups. There was a bunch of boys around the barbecue, tending to the sizzling meat. A cluster of girls was sitting around the patio table. Lenin, the only boy among them, was rolling a joint. Steps led down from the patio to the pool area where more people were seated.

As soon as the three girls stepped outside everyone turned to look at them. Connie was suddenly acutely embarrassed. She felt ridiculously overdressed. They waved at Jordan and went to stand by the table next to the girls who all started commenting on her outfit. She tried to be graceful in accepting their compliments but she crossed her arms and wished she could disappear. Was Lenin staring at her tits? She crossed her arms even tighter. None of the other boys said anything to her. She stared back out to the lawn. She could make out the shape of two figures underneath the huge eucalypts at the bottom of the Athanasious's garden. There was a bonfire flaring in an upturned metal drum and in the dance of a flame she saw that one of the figures was Richie.

She excused herself and walked past the boys congregated around the barbecue. She tried to be oblivious to their stares, but she felt like a fucking freak. She stepped off the patio and nearly tripped.

'You okay?'

It was Ali. He was by the pool. He was wearing an oversized white Chicago Bulls basketball singlet and had his jeans rolled to the knees, his feet in the water. What an idiot, she thought, he's going to freeze. He too was rolling a joint. His skin seemed to glisten, as if oiled. The muscles on his arms were prominent. He knew it, that was why the bastard was wearing the singlet, daring pneumonia just so he could look good.

'I'm fine.'

He turned back to rolling the joint. 'You're more than fine.'

Costa and Blake, who were sitting either side of him, started to snigger. Had she been insulted?

'Shut up, you idiots.' The boys instantly stopped laughing. Without turning to her he held up the finished joint. 'Want some?'

'Maybe later.'

'Suit yourself.'

She could feel them watching her as she walked carefully along the footpath to the end of the yard. Maybe they were laughing at her.

Was she going to feel like this all night?

'You made an effort.'

Richie was sitting on an upturned milk crate. He still wore the same T-shirt from the afternoon.

'So have you.'

He laughed. Nick Cercic was sitting on another crate. His hair was slicked back with gel and he was wearing the straightest of shirts, a Target special, and suit pants that were way too big for him. He reeked of aftershave. He had mumbled something to her when she approached, what she could only assume was a greeting, and then with an abrupt, jerky movement he stood up and offered her the crate to sit on. The three of them looked at it. Nick's pants had left an impression on the accumulated dust. Nick mumbled something again and then grabbed his jumper from the ground and spread it over the crate.

Connie was touched. He was being chivalrous. She had come across the word in books but had never before had an occasion to use it. She sat down. 'Thank you, Nick. That's very chivalrous of you.'

Richie snorted. She poked her tongue out at him. The bonfire was warm. She dropped the shawl from her shoulders and clutched it in a bunch in her hands. She leaned over and grabbed a cigarette from the packet Richie had at his feet.

Nick, again abruptly, turned and walked off.

'What's up with him?'

Richie shrugged. 'I dunno. Maybe he needs a piss.'

'He's a nice guy but . . .'

'But what?'

'I don't know.' Connie tried to find the words. Her brain was starting to feel mushy; even sitting next to the bonfire she was suddenly cold again. She spread the shawl back over her shoulders. The drug was coming on. 'I don't know . . . he's so nervous all the time. He makes *me* nervous.'

'We've had magic mushrooms tonight. He's a little out of it.' Richie patted his pants pocket. 'You want some?'

'Nah, I've taken a pill.'

'Any good?'

Her teeth were chattering now, her spine felt like it couldn't support her frame and she felt a little queasy. She wished she wasn't wearing the stupid dress so she could lie on the grass and watch the night sky. It would be so nice to lie down. Everything would look so pretty, the flickering of the flames, the stars through the canopy of eucalyptus. She tried to answer Rich but found that all she could do was laugh. Which made him laugh. Which made her laugh even harder.

'It's good,' she finally managed to wheeze. And it was, it was very good. She was not feeling sick anymore. She felt really really really good.

'Same.'

That started them laughing again. Richie was the first to stop. He looked serious.

'What is it?'

'Con, you're my best friend.'

'And you're mine.'

'You're tripping.'

'So are you.'

And they started laughing again.

Nick Cercic returned and sat cross-legged on the grass. Connie and Richie slowly exhausted their laughter. Again, Connie wished she could lie down. She envied Nick his cheap pants. He looked a complete dag but he was comfortable.

'I wish I'd worn my bloody jeans. I feel like a freakazoid.'

Nick was scratching at the earth with a twig. 'Everyone is talking about how great you look. Everyone.' He hadn't mumbled. He hadn't looked up from his scratching but he hadn't mumbled. He was such a gentle boy, there wasn't anything arrogant or macho or mean about him. Which was why all the other boys teased him and why all the girls laughed about it. None of it was meant to be cruel but probably most of it seemed cruel. Without thinking she touched the tips of his ginger hair. He flinched.

'Sorry.' It was like an electric shock.

'It's okay.'

'I love red hair.' Did she? She loved *his* red hair.

'Well they don't come more ginge than Nick.'

Nick looked up, his face glowering. 'You shut up,' he snarled at Richie. 'You're a ginge as well.'

'Bullshit, mate. I'm what's called a strawberry blonde.'

They fell into silence. Connie wondered whether she should speak but she didn't really care to. She was enjoying looking at the party. Jordan must have changed the iPod to shuffle because straight after the Kaiser Chiefs and Kraftwerk, the party was suddenly rocked by the thundering drums and guitar of the White Stripes' 'Seven Nation Army'. Beside her Nick and Richie started to argue about which was a better album, *Elephant* or *De Stijl*. Hector liked the White Stripes. Creep. He was too old to like the White Stripes. She noticed that Ali was lighting another joint by the pool. She stood up.

'I'm going inside.' She smiled down at Nick. 'Thank you for the seat. I think you're a gentleman.' That sounded so fancy. It must be the dress.

As she passed by the pool, she took the joint from Ali's hand. He too smelt of aftershave but the odour was discreet, smoky, a little like what she imagined a pipe to smell like. She had two quick puffs and handed the joint back. Their fingers touched. His chest underneath the singlet was smooth and muscled, like his arms. She wondered if he shaved. Weren't Lebos meant to be hairy?

'Thanks.'

He said something soft in Arabic.

'What does that mean?'

He didn't answer. She shrugged and walked up to Jenna and Tina. They were sitting around the table listening to an argument about politics between Lenin and Tara. Connie sat on Jenna's lap. Lenin was outraged that Tara was intending to give her virgin vote to the Liberals. He was shaking his head and calling her a moral idiot. She was yelling back at him, Give me a fucking alternative, give me a fucking real alternative. The girls began yelling at both of them to shut up. Costa and Blake had started up a chant: Boring, Boring, Boring! Connie whispered in her friend's ear: Let's go. The girls nodded at Tina and the three of them left the table.

They slid the kitchen door shut behind them. Jenna took each of them by the hand and marched them through the house. They walked through the master bedroom, through a walk-in wardrobe and into an ensuite bathroom. Connie stared around her at the white tiles, the old-fashioned Aegean-blue enamelled bath sitting on cast-iron feet in the middle of the room, the floor-to-ceiling mirror that covered one wall.

Jenna shut the door behind them and then let out a piercing squeal. 'Oh my God, how good is this E.'

Tina sat on the edge of the bath and nodded her head vigorously. 'This is amazing,' she agreed. 'I wish we had more.'

'Bad luck, girlfriend, you had your chance.'

Jenna grabbed Connie from behind and the two girls stared at each other in the mirror. Jenna nuzzled her face in Connie's hair. She kissed her friend's shoulder. 'You look like a movie star.'

Tina stood up and put her arms around the two girls. 'You're my best friends.'

Connie kissed Tina on her cheek.

'You're my best friends, forever.'

Jenna kissed Connie's naked shoulder again. 'And you're mine.'

Jenna suddenly squeezed her friend's left breast.

'And oh my God, how good are your tits?'

Connie shivered. The squeeze had felt good. Jenna's fingers were still applying light pressure on her nipple. Connie stared at her friends and at herself in the mirror. Their faces were so close. Were they going to kiss? Jenna pulled away. She pulled a pack of cigarettes from her jeans and lit one.

'That was close to a lesbo moment, wasn't it? Mum would have wanted a photo. I think I could do anything on this E.'

'Can we smoke in here?' Tina was looking nervously around the bathroom.

Jenna pulled out two more cigarettes and handed them to her friends. 'Mr Athanasiou smokes in here. In the bath. Jordan told me.' Jenna switched on the fan. 'It'll be alright.' She made a face. 'They're *bohemian.*'

Connie lit her cigarette and stared at the bath. 'I wish I could take a bath in this. It's huge.'

'Why don't we?'

Connie stared at Jenna. 'Are you serious?'

'Why not?'

Connie shook her head. 'No way.' She stared down at her frock. 'I'd have to get back into this. It would take ages.'

Jenna nodded her head slowly. 'You look fucking amazing but you look so uncomfortable.' She opened the door. 'Come on, let's go back. Let's hope that Lenin and Tara have stopped fighting.' Jenna switched off the light.

'Yeah,' agreed Tina, as they walked out into the bedroom. 'Or that he's punched out that silly bitch.'

By ten-thirty everyone was drunk or stoned. Or both. Jordan had brought out his decks and Ali and he were taking turns DJ-ing. Connie, who would usually have drunk bourbon, drank vodka with lime instead. She looked terrific, she looked just like Scarlett Johansson in *Lost in Translation*, and she had her aunt to thank for that. She nibbled at some food, but had no appetite. She was also scared of spilling something on the dress. All she really wanted to do was dance. Jordan called on Costa and Lenin to shove all the lounge-room furniture against one wall. He had set Christmas lights up in the room and placed an enormous Chinese lantern over the globe that dropped from the middle of the high ceiling. The lantern was so overwhelming that Lenin, by far the tallest person at the party, had to avoid dancing underneath it or his head would knock it. When he occasionally did, the lantern would swing, sending a shaft of light zigzagging across the bodies of the dancing adolescents. Jordan played old seventies metal and hip-hop and jagged punky rock and Ali played rap and urban, electro and top forty. And Connie danced. She danced to Justin and Christina, to Eminem and 50 Cent, she threw off her shoes and jumped around the floor to the Arctic Monkeys and to Wolfmother. She was dancing to an old-school Usher, 'You Make Me Wanna', when Ali came up to her. She had her eyes closed and could sense him dancing next to her. She opened her eyes and smiled at him. He was dancing around her, slowly, confidently. He knew how to swing his body, how to move his feet and arms. He was a great dancer. She moved in closer to him. He was mouthing the words of the song; a line of sweat, a teardrop, was running down his chest. She wondered what it would taste like. The song was fading to an end and Ali rushed to the decks. She closed her eyes and kept dancing. She would not think of him, she would not think about Hector. The syncopated rhythms of Destiny's Child flooded from the speakers. Connie opened her eyes to find Ali, behind the turntables, smiling shyly across at her. She lifted her arms and let out a whoop of delight. Then he was beside her, and they were dancing again.

By midnight Jenna was in tears on the front verandah. The city lights glittered below them as she sobbed in Connie's arms. Tina was sitting beside them, stroking Jenna's hair. Lenin was perched against the verandah wall, a mop and bucket beside him. The light from the moon and from the city behind him cast a faint tangerine aura around the mad frizz of his jet-black hair. He looked angelic, thought Connie. It was Lenin who'd mopped up Jenna's vomit. Jenna was distraught because Jordan had gone off to his bedroom with Veronica Fink. Everyone knew they were fucking.

Jenna lifted her head. 'Why?' she wailed.

She had been wailing the same word for the last ten minutes.

Lenin shrugged. 'Jenna, mate. I've said it to you. They're just fuck buddies, it's not like between you and him, it's not a relationship.'

Jenna raised herself, struggling to keep a balance. She savagely brushed saliva away from her lips and chin. 'What the fuck is there between him and me? What do you mean? He's fucking Veronica bloody Fink. He's not fucking me. I think that means he's in a relationship with Veronica. He's not in a relationship with me, I'm the fuck buddy.' The final sentence wasn't clear as Jenna once again began to wail. Connie hugged her tighter. Her dress was getting stained. It didn't matter. Her best friend was upset. Everyone was pissed, out of it, no one would notice. She looked up at Lenin. He looked embarrassed, caught out, as he stared at the front entrance. She turned to look.

Jordan was standing in the doorway. He mouthed something to Lenin.

'Come on.' Lenin gestured silently to Connie and to Tina. The girls rose.

Jenna, confused, looked around her. When she saw Jordan she crossed her arms. 'You can fuck off.'

The boy walked past Connie and Tina and held out his hand to the crying girl. 'Come on, let's go for a walk.'

'I said, fuck off.'

Jordan still had his hand outstretched. Connie stood still in the doorway, looking back, not sure if she shouldn't stay and look after her friend. Lenin gave her a gentle push and they moved down the hall.

'Let them sort it out,' he whispered to her.

They went back into the party.

Connie didn't feel like dancing now and walked straight through the house and into the yard. Nick and Richie were still sitting on the crates by the bonfire. She sat on Richie's knees and nuzzled her face in his hair.

He stroked her shoulders. 'You right, Con?'

'Mmm.' She lifted her head. 'Jenna and Jordan are having a fight.' She smiled at Nick. 'How are you travelling?'

The boy nodded his head vigorously, his face beaming. She laughed.

'You've had more, haven't you?'

Richie nodded.

'You want some?'

She thought about it. She was still warm and secure in the euphoria of the drug but the heightening of the senses had worn off. She was beginning to feel drunk. Reluctantly, she shook her head. 'Nah. I'll be completely hammered.'

'That's the best way to be.' Both she and Richie were surprised by Nick's vehemence. 'I want to be like this for the rest of my life,' he continued. 'I don't ever want to be normal again.'

'Mate, you are not normal.'

Nick glared at Richie. 'What do you mean?'

Connie intervened. 'What's so great about being normal? It's better to be different, not like everybody else. Who wants to be normal in John Howard's Australia?'

Richie made a rude farting noise. 'All the dicks at this party. I'm glad you're not normal, Nicky my boy.'

Connie gave Richie the finger. 'Nick seems pretty normal to me. You, well that's another matter.'

'Thanks very much.'

She slid her arms around her friend's neck. 'I don't want you to be normal. I don't ever want you to be normal.'

Nick stood up. Without saying a word he walked away from them, weaving his way precariously up the path.

'Another loo break?'

Richie nodded, and laughed.

'He's been going all night. I told him to just piss in the garden. No one cares.' He pointed past the eucalypts to a row of bushes and fading jasmine plants along the back fence. 'That's where I've been going.'

Connie looked up to the sky. Clouds obscured the stars and the moon. 'I wish I could piss standing up.'

'Maybe you can.'

'Not in this dress. I'd embarrass myself.'

Richie pushed her off him.

'Am I too heavy?'

'Yeah, you're a lard-arse.' He reached inside his pocket and pulled out what looked like a wad of torn paper. He held it out to her.

'What's that?'

'The photograph of Hector.'

She was silent. She wanted to say, forget everything I said this afternoon. She wanted to apologise. She wanted him to apologise. She knew he wouldn't and she knew she couldn't. Richie stood up and sprinkled the scraps of torn photo over the fire. They caught flame, danced above the heat for a moment, then curled into black cinder. There was a bitter, chemical smell. She tried to remember what

Hector looked like in the photograph. Young, like her, like Richie, like Nick, like Jenna, like Ali. Young like her. Except he wasn't. She looked at the curling scraps of the photograph. She wished she could burn him away from her, make him disappear. *He doesn't want me.* It still hurt, like a burn, a scald right to the centre of her being. She remembered the relief in his face when he told her it was over. A gorilla, that's what she had called him. What a stupid, childish thing to say. She was glad that the flames danced before her, that they camouflaged the mortification she was experiencing.

'Con, you okay?'

She stepped back from the barrel, and sat back on Richie's lap. She lay her head on his shoulder. He stroked her face.

Nick returned and stood nervously by the crate. 'You want to sit here? I can sit on the grass.' His eyes were wide, like an animal's. He looked vulnerable and a little afraid. She wondered if the mushies were as good as he said they were.

She stood up. 'It's cold. I'm going inside. You should come in and dance.'

Richie made another farting noise. 'Not with those arseholes.'

'They're alright.'

Richie turned to Nick. 'See, I told you she was a replicant. She's one of the normal ones.'

He could be such a dick sometimes. Everyone at the party was alright, everyone was fine. She liked everyone tonight.

She held out her hand to Nick. 'Come and dance.'

The boy, alarmed, shook his head. 'I don't dance very well.'

'That's okay. It's not a competition.'

'Nah, I'd feel like a freak.'

'You're not a freak.'

'Yes, he is. He's a freak like me.'

She ignored Richie, was still holding out her hand. 'Coming?'

Nick sat down on the crate. He looked down at the dirt and lawn.

She shrugged. 'See ya then.'

Behind her she could hear Richie singing, off-key, the Sugababes' 'Freak Like Me'.

Nick said, Shut the fuck up, but Richie kept on singing.

'You want a smoke?'

It was Ali. She nodded. He took her hand—his hand was huge, it completely covered hers—and pulled her with him towards a door at the end of the hall. Ali shut the door behind them. They were in darkness. The noise of the party had suddenly stopped. Ali turned on the light—they were in a bedroom.

'Whose is this?'

'This is the guest bedroom.'

'Wow, it's huge.'

There was a queen-sized bed, a large Manet print on the wall, and a little golden reclining Buddha perched on the bureau by the bed. Ali plonked himself on the middle of the bed, cross-legged. He pulled out a pouch of tobacco, his rolling papers and a tiny nugget of hash. He started rolling the joint. Connie, confused, wondered where she should sit. She kicked off her shoes and sat on the edge of the bed, watching him. There was no way she could sit cross-legged in this dress.

'You look so fine,' he whispered.

She touched the tip of his hair. The gel was sticky in her fingers. Her make-up was probably all runny from the dancing and the sweat. She looked around for a mirror. Ali read her mind. He indicated a door, its red paint chipped and faded, off the bedroom.

'Bathroom's through there.'

She went in and washed her face, combed her hair back. She didn't look too bad. She took a step back from the mirror and looked at herself. The dress seemed to shimmer in the faint bathroom light. She was beginning to grind her teeth, she probably needed another drink. Her mouth would stink tomorrow morning. She'd try not to have another cigarette, they made her lips dry. She opened her mouth wide. Were her teeth yellow? Her smile was too big for her face. She wished she had smaller lips, tinier teeth. But the dress was beautiful.

She returned and perched on the bed. Ali handed her the joint and lit it. After a few puffs the soothing wave of the hashish rolled through her. She lay down across the bed and handed the joint back to Ali. He jumped over her and walked into the bathroom. He returned with a small crescent translucent bowl that held sea stones and shells. He emptied them over the bureau and used the bowl to ash the joint in.

'Are Jordan's folks back yet?' It must be way past midnight. The movie would be finished by now. The house stank of marijuana and tobacco.

'They're not coming back. Mr A has booked a hotel in the city for tonight. They're not back till morning.'

'They put a lot of trust in Jordan.'

'They can trust Jorde. He's not a dick. He won't let things get out of hand.'

Connie was looking up at the ceiling. It was one of the old-fashioned ones with an intricate relief from a circle around the lamp-shade, swirls of flowers and leaves. They had been hand-painted, red and yellow, white and green. It looked like a watercolour. Ali passed back the joint and she looked at him. His hair was wet from sweat and there wasn't a mark on his cinnamon skin. He too had a big mouth but it suited his face. He could be a model except there was nothing soft or feminine about him. He was commanding. She rolled the word around her head. *Commanding*. She was a little afraid of being alone with him.

'What are you looking at?'

'Nothing.' She had one short puff and handed him the joint. 'I was just wondering how you and Jordan became friends.'

'Because he's so smart and I'm just a dumb-fuck Mussie?'

Connie blushed. She had gone red, she knew it, on her cheeks and neck. She was embarrassed because it was, kind of, what she thought—not the Muslim bit, not that, and not that Ali was not smart. He just wasn't academic. Ali laughed at her embarrassment.

'We've known each other since we were kids. We were in the under-eleven footy squad together.'

'Serious?' Jordan was straight humanities. He was applying to the Victorian College of the Arts to do film or acting or something like that. Jordan Athanasiou didn't even like sports.

'He wasn't very good, but he wasn't an idiot.' Ali stubbed the joint out into the bowl. 'Most people are idiots.' He got up on his knees and looked down at Connie. 'You're not.' Ali seemed enormous, a giant above her. 'Connie,' he said firmly. 'I'm going to kiss you now.'

His mouth was firm, but he didn't hurt. She fell into his mouth, tongue, lips, teeth, saliva. She realised that Hector always hesitated when kissing her, that he was holding back. She had always felt that she had been too aggressive, too eager. Ali was in control and her mouth and hands and body followed him. She could kiss him all night, she hadn't realised how simple, how uncomplicated, kissing could be. She wasn't thinking of anything—her mind was not floating above her body—she and Ali were the kiss. The kiss was all there was.

'Can I fuck you?'

She just wanted the kiss but she nodded. This was how it was going to be. With this handsome, dark boy who a few days ago she thought an arrogant, sexist pig. She was frightened but she was nodding her head. This was how it was going to be. She was drunk. I'm not going to throw up, she ordered herself. She touched his skin. She had to remember how soft his skin felt. She touched his singlet. She would remember that it was coarse, a blend of cotton and polyester, the huge red number 3 across its front. She would remember the flowers on the ceiling, the reclining Buddha, the smell of the hash. She must write all this down when she got home tonight. She must remember to record everything, everything in her journal.

Ali had unbuckled his belt and pulled his jeans to his knees. His jocks were black and when he slid them off his cock was already hard. It looked big, thick. She must pretend it did not hurt. If it hurt, she had to pretend it didn't. She looked away, embarrassed, from his crotch and stared up at his face. He was smiling at her. One hand caressed her face, the other was sliding up her thigh.

'You're on the pill, aren't you?'

Should she lie? No fucking way should she lie.

'No.'

'Shit.' His fingers were touching her pubic hair. He seemed doubtful, wary. Was she too hairy? Maybe she was too hairy? He pushed his free hand into his pocket and pulled out a condom.

'Put it on,' he ordered.

She and Tina had once practised on a banana, they had been in Year Eight and had laughed all afternoon. She couldn't tear open the packet. He took it from her and ripped it open with his teeth. He lifted her up towards him, so they were face to face. Come on, baby, he whispered, I'm so fucking hot for you. When they were kissing, all of herself had been there. Now her mind was floating high above her body, looking down. He sounded like a porn movie, a bad rap soundtrack. She felt a little stupid. And he was talking like an idiot. Her hands were cold and clumsy, she tried to unsheaf the sticky coil of plastic but she couldn't seem to stretch the mouth of it over Ali's cock. It was starting to go soft. He was looking at her with a quizzical expression.

'You've put on a rubber before, haven't you?'

She was blushing again. 'Usually the guys put it on.'

He seemed to accept that and took the condom. He'd thankfully wiped the leer off his face. Now he just looked embarrassed. 'Connie,' he began softly. 'Do you want to blow me? Just to get me hard again.'

She wasn't resisting. His hand was gently pushing her down there, not with any force as she was not resisting. This is what girls do. This is what she had so much wanted to do for Hector. She looked at Ali's penis, sniffed at it. There was an unrecognisable smell. It smelt of flesh but not a bodily smell she had ever encountered before.

She shook her head. 'No.' She sat up. She couldn't bring herself to do that. She wasn't quite sure why. It seemed slutty or maybe just too intimate. It seemed a much more intimate thing to do than be fucked. She shook her head again. 'I'm sorry.'

Ali was still looking strangely at her.

She felt mortified—she was such a pathetic virgin.

'It's okay. Kiss me again.'

They lay next to each other, kissing. Her body returned to itself. She pulled him closer to her. She wished they could just kiss. He was fumbling with the condom, she tried not to think about it. To only think of how good he tasted, of beer and dope and peppermint gum. His hand was between her legs and then his finger was inside her. She let go of his mouth and groaned. He held her head gently in the cusp of his broad hand and said, once more, You're so beautiful, and then he thrust.

She cried out. It felt like a knife had cut straight through inside her. He tried to push himself inside her again and she winced, whimpered, then cried out, a strange moan that sounded exactly like the cry a dog made when it woke terrified from the anaesthetic. Ali pulled back and she cupped her hands between her legs. She felt ripped apart. She was ashamed, her face was streaked with tears. Ali was holding her. She was crying into his chest. He tightened his grip. Slowly, very slowly, the pain began to dull. She didn't want Ali to loosen his hold on her. She didn't want to look at his face.

'Connie, Connie,' he finally urged, gently. 'My foot's gone to sleep.'

Reluctantly, she pulled away from him. He rose and began to thump at his calf. His jeans and underwear were still around his knees. She pulled up her own panties and, as she did, panicking, she searched her thighs, her legs, the bedspread for blood. She couldn't see anything. Ali grimaced, then carefully rose from the bed.

'I'm going to the loo. Will you please stay here?' Connie wanted to laugh. His cock was still hard.

'Promise?'

'I promise.'

She did laugh as Ali, his jeans and underwear around his legs, jumped to the door. His cock bobbed up and down. It reminded her of Terrance and Phillip fighting on *South Park*.

When he was gone she wiped her face and eyes with the pillowslip. She must look awful. Maybe she should go. But she sat on the bed, staring at the door through which Ali had disappeared. She didn't want to face the party alone. They had gone off together. Everyone would be gossiping. She couldn't bear to face the party alone.

She heard the toilet flush. Ali emerged, fully dressed. She looked down at the floor, polished boards and a thick, pure wool rug, floral patterns the same colours as the ceiling above.

Ali sat beside her. And then he placed his arm around her. 'You're a virgin, eh?'

She didn't reply.

'I'm glad. You don't act like a slut.'

This made her furious. 'I see, so if you had fucked me I'd be a slut.'

'Don't pull that femo shit with me. You're not a slut.'

'And sluts are bad, are they?' She jerked away from him.

He pulled her back. 'No. But you're not a slut.' He stood up, taking her hand. 'Let's get a drink.'

He held her hand for the rest of the night: when they danced, when they went to get a drink. He even held her hand at the end of the party when it was just her and Ali, Jenna and Jordan, Tina, Veronica, Costa, Lenin and Casey sitting in the lounge room listening to Devendra Banhart's *Nino Roja*. Jenna and Jordan were sitting together on the couch, his hand in her lap. Veronica didn't seem to care.

Jenna had winked at Connie when she and Ali had walked back into the party. Tina had mouthed at her, with a smile, *You ho*. She wouldn't say anything to them tonight. She'd tell them all about it at school. She'd tell them the truth. At one point Richie had walked into the party. He was frowning, searching the room. He saw her and Ali sitting on the couch, holding hands and went over.

'How's it going, Rich?'

Her friend ignored Ali. 'I'm heading off.'

'Where's Nick?'

'He's waiting for me outside, on the street.'

'Say goodbye from me.'

Richie grunted.

'What's wrong?'

'Nothing's wrong. You're just so normal. Sometimes you are so fucking unbelievably normal.'

He was angry at her. She had no idea why he was angry at her. She couldn't be bothered with it now.

'I'll call you tomorrow.'

'Yeah, right.'

Without saying goodbye, Richie turned away.

Ali called after him. 'See ya, Richo.'

He didn't bother answering.

'He's jealous, isn't he?'

Connie gripped tight on Ali's hand. 'No, of course not.'

'He's in love with you. It's obvious. He has been for years.'

'It's not like that.'

'What? He's some kind of fag or something?'

She was about to answer, Yes, he is, but stopped herself. She couldn't do that to Richie. She couldn't betray him. And not to Ali. Richie didn't know how good Ali was. She'd make them friends. They had to become friends.

'It's just not like that, okay?'

Ali was about to say something. He stopped.

'What were you about to say?'

'Nothing.'

'What?'

'You know when I say the word fag, I don't mean it in a bad way. It's like when you call me or Costa a wog.'

'I don't call you a wog.'

'You know what I mean.'

'No, what do you mean?'

He squirmed next to her. He whispered in her ear, 'I heard your Dad was gay.'

'He was bisexual.'

Ali grinned. 'Well, obviously.' His face straightened, he looked concerned. 'I just say things sometimes, without thinking. I don't give a shit what anybody is. I want you to believe me.'

'I do.' She smiled wickedly. 'My old man would have loved you. You are exactly his type.'

Ali kissed her again.

He walked her home, hand in hand. They didn't talk much. He had on one of Jordan's jumpers, black with a turtle neck. She liked the look of him in black. He walked her to her house. They kissed again.

'How are you getting home?'

'I'll walk.'

'To Coburg? That's going to take ages.'

'Nah. Forty minutes, tops.' They couldn't let go of each other's hand. He was shifting uncomfortably from one foot to the other. He finally let go of her hand—it felt limp, empty once out of his warm grasp. She was terrified of what she was going to say to him at school on Monday. He was still shifting from foot to foot.

'Do you want to see a movie?'

'When?' Had she just squeaked? She had just squeaked.

'Friday night?'

'Yes. Sure.'

'Good.' He kissed her softly, tenderly, on the lips. 'See you on Monday.'

She watched him walk down the street, his hands in his pockets. Under a street lamp he turned and waved at her. She waved back. He looked like a little boy. She went into the house.

There was a light underneath her aunt's door. She knocked lightly. 'Come in.'

Tasha was sitting up in bed, reading. 'I couldn't sleep.'

'I'm sorry. It's late, isn't it?'

'Three-thirty. Okay for a Saturday night. Good party?'

Connie pulled back the doona cover and slipped under the sheet next to her aunt. 'I think I just got asked out on a date.'

'Who by?'

'His name is Ali.'

'You are your father's daughter.'

'He's really nice, Tash.'

'I'll make up my own mind. He fell for the dress, didn't he?'

Connie looked around her aunt's room—the stack of books by the bed, the old feminist and socialist posters on the wall, the icon of the Catholic Jesus in Mary's arms. It was warm and comforting.

'Do you get lonely, Tash?'

'No. I have you.'

'But if you hadn't had to look after me, maybe you would be with someone now?'

Tasha was silent.

Connie turned and looked up at her aunt. 'I'm right, aren't I?'

'It's possible. It's also possible that I would be all alone in this house. I was thirty-seven when I started looking after you, Con. I'm forty-two now. There wasn't a Prince Ali around the corner for me at thirty-five. Who knows, maybe there will be at forty-three. I don't really care. I've had you. I've had you with me. I think I'm lucky.'

Tasha leaned down and kissed her niece on her cheek. 'Now, go to bed. You were just fishing for compliments. I love you. You know that.'

Connie jumped out of bed, grinning.

'I'm just going to message Zara and then I'll go to bed.'

She couldn't asleep. She fired up her computer and then opened the bottom drawer of her desk. Under the bottles of liquid paper, Post-it pads, notebooks and pencil was an old tin box; the image of the smiling Prince Charles and Lady Di had faded so she had no nose and he had no chin. She opened the box and shuffled through the papers inside, the cards, the ticket stubs to Placebo and Snoop Dog. The letter was at the bottom, where she always put it. Her aunt did not know she kept it. Her father had given it to her, when he was dying in the hospital in London. It's a copy he had told her, a copy of a letter I sent to your aunt. She's replied, he added: She said yes.

Connie started to read.

Dear Sister,

I am writing to ask you to take care of my child, my daughter who is my life. I realise that it is years since you have heard from me but I am hoping that the love and affection you have shown me—and I know that I have not always been deserving of it—will also extend to your niece. She is a wonderful child, Tasha. She is a terrific kid.

I am dying; I guess I have been for years. That's one of the reasons I have kept my distance. I knew you would be kind but I was not very hopeful of understanding from Peter and Dad. It was 1989 that I was diagnosed as positive. If you remember you were just finishing your final year at high school and I had returned home for a visit. You were pissed off that my return had seemingly caused so much anguish and strife. I was abrupt even with you, and you told me later, in London, that you had thought me cruel and arrogant, that you thought England had done this to me. I should have told you back then that I was HIV positive but I was scared to, and Mum begged me not to. Yes, she knew. She was, apart from being ashamed, very good about it. And no, of course, she never told Dad.

Connie is fine. She must have been conceived before Marina or I contracted the virus. Or, thank God, she was very lucky.

Oh, Sis, even now my first impulse is to lie. Even nearing the end, hiding behind this letter, I am gutless. It was _me_ who infected Marina. I'm sure I know the exact moment the virus entered my body. It was, appropriately, in bloody Soho. In a club toilet, some-where deep in the bowels of fag London, and this man called Joseph fixed me with a shot of heroin. I was drunk, I was enam-oured of his beauty, and I deeply wanted to fuck with a man that night. Well, we didn't fuck—the drug took care of that—but as I watched him pump the syringe into my vein, I knew that he was poisoning me.

This was always the hard bit to read. Always.

For a year I fucked Marina hard and often, hoping, I guess, for some miracle to save us. She died, as you know, five years ago. I never confessed to her the above and she never blamed me. And maybe she wouldn't have even if I had told her. Who knows what secret places her vices took her!

This is really a confession to you isn't it? Marina went Buddhist in her final years but I, unfortunately, am still too scared of our stern Monophysite God. I have not been a bad man, far from it, but though I know I am not destined for the final circle of hell I cannot completely do away with the idea that there is a logic and a truth to the ancient patriarchs. I have obeyed so little in my life. I am very unenlightened.

Connie is nearly fourteen, and she attends a comprehensive school in South London. She is bright and does very well at study.

She is, inevitably, quite mature for her age. She has certainly astonished me with her capacity to cope with her mother's death and with my being sick. If there has been prejudice or ignorance among her friends she doesn't let on, and I rather suspect that those she is close to have been supportive. Her friend Allen's mum is a dyke and her closest female friend, Zara, is an unbelievably cool Turkish child. (Zara saved her pocket money for two years to afford a bloody T-shirt from Prada! It's not so much the wanting a Prada shirt that impressed me—the mania for labels is everywhere and I actually find it a little distasteful—but the fact that she was determined enough to save for so long.)

I don't know, Sis, if you have been spending any time with teenagers, but I am fascinated by them and encouraged by them. I don't feel the same way about our generation at all. Not that I wish to romanticise today's teenagers either. They are fucking cruel, this young mob, very very much the children of Thatcher, even though they might mouth all the right ecological and anti-racist platitudes. They have little time for anyone who is not capable, for whatever reason, of being successful. Even the council boys sniffing around Connie are full of derision for those who are not dreaming of fast cars and of entrepreneurial futures. But they are not hypocrites and, unlike us, they do not pretend to know more than they do or wish to speak on behalf of anyone but themselves. Are they the same back home?

It is raining outside and I am to be visited soon by a day nurse who eats up nearly half of my dole. I'm still on the dole—I guess that is another thing not to pass on to Dad. Has he retired yet or is he still building, building, building and drinking, drinking, drinking and complaining, complaining, complaining that his children do not know the meaning of hard work? What utter crap! I knew very early on the meaning of hard work and I promised myself that I would never work that way, never destroy my body and my back in that way, never become bitter like Dad. Well, I have become bitter, but not like Dad. Unlike our father, I don't regret the things I have not done but rather the things I have done. So, no matter how at peace I say I am about this fucking disease, the reality is I keep going back to the moment I got it and wishing I hadn't been in that club, wishing I'd never laid eyes on the man, wishing I did not share that needle, most of all, most of all, wishing I had not kept fucking with Marina, wishing I had not been such a coward.

Pray for me, Sis. I do fear God.

Nothing has been said to Connie. She knows about you all in Australia, and in particular she knows how much I adore you. But please believe me when I say that if you are unable to make a home for her then feel no guilt. It is not exactly your responsibility, is it? I know that. She won't hear of me dying and so we have not spoken of the future. If you are unable to take her, Marina's old aunt Jessica lives up in Lancaster and she is a generous woman who will do her best for Connie. I want her to know her uncle and her grand-father but I don't want them to have any choice in her life and her future. Of our clan, I only trust you.

Tasha, if you can't, for whatever reason, take her in, please at least make contact with her? Marina and I have not been very successful parents but there is some money for her, five thousand pounds, that Marina and I managed to save and hang on to. All my funeral arrangements have already been made and paid for and there will be no debts outstanding. I will be cremated and buried here in London. I have no yearnings for Australia. In fact, from what we hear over here, some things about home seem to have changed very little. We're still screwing the blackfella, eh? No, I'm more than happy to be buried here.

Oh, Sister, I know five thousand pounds won't go far, I know I am asking the earth. But I think you will love Connie. I remind her of when you last saw her, all those years ago when she was not yet five, and you told her how scared you were of taking the Tube at night. Remember what she said? 'But Auntie Tasha, it's better at night. There's more light. It's safer.' She really requires little

217

effort. The other night she surprised me by asking if I had any Simon and Garfunkel music. Her being a London kid, I thought all she knew was hip-hop and dance. But she is developing a taste for the hippie era. She has also been enquiring about Joni Mitchell and Fleetwood Mac. God knows where she hears it. Radio 2? Surely not?

Yeah, Dad, Radio 2. Mum and I would listen to Radio 2 when you weren't home. I fucking hated Joy Division, I fucking hated The Clash. I fucking loathed techno. I loved Fleetwood Mac.

I am dying. I would appreciate you replying to this letter as soon as possible. Please, please decide what is best for you, for what is best for you will be the best for Connie and me. Of course, you can phone but I am so scared that on hearing your voice, dear sister, that I will break into long and terrible tears. Connie calls me a dinosaur because I do not use the internet-email thing but one of the few pleasures allowed the dying is the liberty to discriminate. As you know, I have always detested the television and the telephone: email and the internet sound hideous, a combination of the two. I obviously was not made for this new century and I have chosen my time for exiting quite well.

Please write. I wish I could have been a closer and more attentive older brother. I did fail you miserably. I am crying now, writing this, and I am thinking of how we used to laugh at old Mrs Radiç next door when she would soliloquise on the pain of exile. And now I feel it so deeply myself. Poor Mrs Radiç, at least here they speak my language. She blamed her exile on poverty and war. Have I only myself to blame for mine?

Dear Sis, tell our brother and our father the truth. If my Connie at her age can bear it, so can those two. I don't want lies around Connie, and since I want her to know my family, I want my family to be worthy of her. Don't you dare lie to her.

The nurse is here. She is asking me to whom I am writing and I replied, to one of the three women I have truly loved. There is Marina, my Connie, and there has always been you.

I kiss you, Natasha.

Your loving brother,

Luke.

Connie folded the letter and put it back at the bottom of the tin. There was a ting sound from the computer. Zara was online. She wiped away her tears and began to tell Zara everything about the party. She didn't want to think about Hector tonight. She wasn't going to think about Hector tonight. She told her about the stunning dress she had worn, about Richie and Jenna and Jordan, about taking the E. And she told her everything that had happened between herself and Ali, all she could remember about Ali in the finest detail, how he looked, and sounded, how he smelt and how he tasted. She told her everything.

It was midday when she woke. Her head throbbed and she groaned when she looked over at the pile of schoolbooks on her desk. She shuffled into the kitchen. Tasha was cooking lunch and the room smelt of lemongrass and coriander. Fillets of John Dory were sitting on a plate.

'I can't eat.'

'Yes, you can. God knows what you ingested last night, but fish is the best thing for you.' Tasha tapped the side of her head. 'Brain food. Good for your serotonin levels.'

Connie sat at the table. She searched the front page of the newspaper, then pulled out the television supplement.

'I'm not leaving the house today,' she announced.

'Rosie rang for you. She wants you to look after Hugo on Wednesday.'

Connie nodded. 'Sure.'

'I told her you couldn't.'

'I can do a few hours,' she protested.

'No. This is your final year, Connie. You have heaps of study, then exams. You do too much as it is. I told her you can't do it. I don't want them to get dependent on you.'

'It's hard for Rosie. She's got no family here in Melbourne. They've got that hearing case coming up any day now. That's all she can think about.'

'Some people make it hard on themselves.'

'He hit Hugo.'

Her aunt did not answer.

'There's no excuse for an adult to hit a child. I hope they put him in jail,' Connie finished sourly.

Tasha started spicing the fillets. 'You know, what I don't like about adolescence is how brutal you can be.'

Connie ignored her. Her head hurt and she didn't want to get into an argument. She was thinking of Ali. She didn't have his number and he didn't have hers. Would he get it off Jordan? Would he ring her or would they just talk at school? She scanned through the television page for Sunday. There was just shit on.

'Tash, if I do a couple of hours' work this afternoon, will you drive me to the video shop later? I'll need a DVD.'

Tasha heated oil in the wok and threw in slices of ginger and garlic. Connie realised she hadn't really had much to eat last night. She got up and put her arms around her aunt.

'I'll just have a quick shower.'

'Three minutes. This will be done by then. And there's no point in wasting water.'

'Three minutes.' At the doorway, Connie swung around. 'Is there any chocolate left?'

Tasha bit her bottom lip.

Connie feigned outrage. 'You ate it all last night, didn't you?'

'Okay, okay. We'll pick up another block when we go and get you a DVD.'

'Thank you, Tashie. You are a sweetheart. I'll be ready for lunch in fifteen minutes.' Connie turned, humming, on her way to the bathroom.

'Brutal,' she head her aunt say. 'Just brutal.'

ROSIE

Rosie lowered herself into the bath, her hands gripping tight to the rim as her body slid into the scalding water. She slowly allowed her body to slacken in the enveloping heat, sighing deeply and closing her eyes to the world. One ear was cocked for any sound from Hugo. He and Gary were watching *Finding Nemo*. Hugo would be on his back, his legs whirring fast, pretending to cycle. Gary would be on his second beer, his overalls dropped to his waist. She had promised him that she would not stay in the bath for too long, would not allow the water to get cold. She could barely hear any sound from the living room, just the movie's imperceptible chatter and music. Hugo had already watched it right through earlier in the day. It had become his favourite over the last few weeks and now she too almost knew it by heart. Sometimes she would pretend to be Dory to his Nemo. She wished he could be in the bath with her (except it would be too hot for him, the little fella). They could pretend to be Dory and Nemo, under the water, in the pretty sapphire world underneath the sea. She'd pretend to be Dory, forgetting everything he told her, trying not to giggle as Hugo got more and more excited and frustrated.

Her eyes flung open. Damn. It was around lunchtime that she received the letter, just after she had come back from the park with Hugo. Rosie had gone pale as she read the dry words stating the date and time for the hearing to be held at the Magistrates Court in Heidelberg. She had quickly sat down, feeling faint. Luckily Hugo was watching the movie and didn't have to witness her anxiety and fear. Rosie immediately phoned Legal Aid and fortunately Margaret, their lawyer, was in the office. This is great news, the young woman assured her, this means it will all be over soon. Rosie put down the phone, in a daze. Four weeks. It would all be over in four weeks. She was about to call Gary on his mobile and then quickly decided against it. It was then that she composed herself. She decided she wouldn't say anything to him till Friday. It was only two days away and it would be better that they spoke about it at the end of the week, with him having the weekend to look forward to. If she told him today he would just get drunk and not be able to sleep and be in a temper for days.

She had felt calm as she made the decision, but that had not lasted long. She couldn't help thinking of what lay ahead. Margaret had explained that they would not have to speak unless the presiding judge asked for clarification from any of the parties. She wished she could get up on the witness stand and tell the world how that animal had hurt her child. That's not the way it works, Margaret kept explaining, over and over, this is a matter between the police and the accused.

As the water released its delicious heat, Rosie allowed herself a small smile as she remembered what Shamira had said to her. Let me get on that witness stand—I'll tell them all how cruel that man was, the pleasure he took in hitting Hugo. The bastard enjoyed it, I was looking straight at him. He enjoyed hitting Hugo—he got off on it, everyone should know that.

She rang Shamira straight after receiving the letter. Her initial impulse, as always, had been to ring Aisha, but it was early in the afternoon and Aish would probably be still finishing surgery, not able to talk. In any case, it was too complicated to ring Aisha. Maybe Hector already knew; his cousin, that bastard, might have already spoken to them.

So she'd called Shamira. Her friend had responded exactly the way she had wanted her to, with warm, uncompromising, unquestioning support. That was what Rosie needed at the moment.

Damn, she mouthed again, sinking further under the water so it lapped over her chin, her lips, her brow. She could open her mouth, let the water flood into her, take her over, fill her lungs and guts and cells till she exploded. She jerked her body upright, splashing water across the floor and the tiles. Fuck that animal. She couldn't relax—she didn't want to. This was her fight, her battle. Fuck him. She hoped he would be crucified, that the world would know the crime he had committed against her son, against her, against her family. The waves of fury and righteousness were intoxicating. She gently squeezed her right nipple and a thin ooze of milk slithered across the surface of the water.

There was a loud rapping at the door. 'The water's going to be fucking freezing.'

She dipped herself under one more time and then stood up in the bath. Gary had shoved open the door. She turned around and faced him, her smile innocent.

'Can you pass the towel?'

She caught the desire on his face. It was like a reflex, animal in its urgency. The water was dripping off her. She flattened her damp hair against her scalp, took the towel he offered her and stepped onto the bathroom mat. She enjoyed him watching as she dried herself.

'Get in,' she urged him. 'It's just going to get colder.'

He stripped quickly. She pretended to ignore him, bending over the sink, drying her arms, neck and shoulders. His work overalls had dropped to his feet and she could see he had the beginning of a hard-on. He pulled off his singlet and underwear, tossed them on the floor, and stepped into the bath.

Rosie turned around. 'Warm enough?'

He nodded, a sly, boyish grin on his face. That grin was Hugo's, exactly the same. And just like Hugo, it came across Gary's face when he wanted something from her. His cock was jutting out of the water. He touched her hand and pointed towards his groin. From the lounge room she could hear Hugo calling her. She hesitated; Gary's touch had become a grip, his fingers beginning to twist around her wrist.

She pulled away. 'Hugo wants me,' she whispered.

Gary's fingers uncoiled. She did not look at him again. She wrapped the towel around her, closing the door shut behind her.

She was feeding Hugo on the couch when Gary walked back into the room. His damp hair was combed over his head, the wet claggy ends forming a smooth wedge that touched the back of his shirt collar. He was wearing his favourite track-pants, years old now, full of holes. He came and stood over them. He watched his son suck contently from Rosie's tit.

'I want some of that.'

Rosie frowned. 'Don't, Gaz.'

'I do. I want some of your boobie.'

Hugo dropped her nipple and looked mutinously at his father. 'No. It's mine.'

'No it isn't.'

Hugo looked at her for encouragement. 'Whose boobies are they?'

'They belong to all of us,' she said, laughing.

'Mine,' he demanded.

Gary plonked himself next to her and lowered her blouse. He pinched at her nipple, hurting her, and sunk his lips over it. There was a jolt of pain and then a numbing, agreeable tingle as his teeth gently slid over her nipple.

Hugo was looking at his father in astounded horror. He began to pummel Gary with his fists. 'Stop! Stop!' he screamed. 'You're hurting Mummy.'

Gary raised his head. 'Nah,' he teased. 'She likes it.'

'Stop it,' the child demanded, his face now twisted with rage. She could tell he was about to cry. She shoved Gary aside and placed

Hugo on her lap. Gary shook his head and got to his feet. She could hear him getting a beer out of the fridge. Hugo dropped her nipple and looked up at her. The poor little guy, he was scared.

'Is Daddy angry with us?'

'No, no,' she cooed. 'Of course not. Daddy loves us.'

When Gary returned with his beer, he sat on the armchair across from them and picked up the remote. The television screen screamed to white noise, then a news broadcast blasted through the room. Turn down the volume, she mouthed to her husband. For a few seconds Gary did nothing, then the volume dipped. Hugo looked up, shocked, as Nemo and his friends had disappeared from view. He looked across at his father, his mouth opening and shutting—just like a fish, thought Rosie—then he settled back in her arms and took her breast into his mouth. She stroked his hair as they all watched the news together.

She had wanted to keep Hugo away from television for as long as possible, and for the first few years Gary had acquiesced. Of course he had: he was always complaining that everything on television was moronic, and if it wasn't moronic it was compromised and capitalist, or compromised and politically correct. When they first met she had thought herself too stupid to keep up with the flow of his intellect. Whether art or politics or love or earthbound ordinary gossip, Gary's opinions were iconoclastic and impossible. Was he a communist or a wildly libertarian free marketeer? Was art for the good of mankind or was art only good when it was elitist and solipistically self-obsessed? He loved his neighbours or he wanted them dead. There was no middle ground and there was no logic. It was, Rosie now realised, after years of trying to keep up with his ever-shifting opinions, simply that her husband could not separate an intellectual thought from an emotional expression. For the first few years of Hugo's life television was bad, a deleterious influence. Now that Gary had been working full-time for over six months, television was a benevolent force.

Rosie did what she always did when her husband expected unquestioning obedience to his whims, she steered a median course, but reigned him in—gradually, so he wouldn't necessarily notice. The television was never on during the day when she was alone with Hugo; then she only allowed him access to videos and DVDs. She would also open a book or a magazine whenever Gary turned on the TV, a subtle protest which she believed he did not notice but would have an influence on Hugo. The television must not become the centre of their domestic life. She looked over to her husband. Gary was sucking on his beer, staring vacantly at the screen. She leaned over and picked up an old Meccano set she had found at the op-shop and began to slot the pieces into one another, constructing a lean, tall tower. Hugo disengaged from her nipple and, more importantly, his eyes drifted away from the television to the game his mother was playing. The boy began to add pieces to the tower himself. Rosie stole another glace at her husband. He was worn out, all he wanted at that moment was oblivion.

She knew she was right to not say a word about the court notice till Friday night. On any school night Gary was tired and liable to fly into a fit, lose his temper, colour everything with pessimism. We should never have gone to the police, he would snarl at her, you made me do this. On Friday evening, with the work week over, she could talk to him and he would listen. She had made up her mind as soon as she had seen the antiseptic bureaucratic letter. Their case had a number, a code: D41/543. That simple fact could set Gary off. That meaningless number could come to represent the banal evil of authority; it could mean that they were now locked in the grip of an unforgiving, oppressive system. And it would all be her fault. Paranoia, anger, resentment—Gary couldn't cope with it knowing he had to work the next day. On Friday night, with the weekend ahead, he could be tender, he could be sweet, he could be kind.

Fuck, Rosie thought to herself, watching her son build the tower, defying gravity as the structure swayed—I wish we had more money.

She took a quick peek at the TV. The weather report was on and she noticed the date on the bottom of the screen. Christ, she realised, it was *her* bloody birthday today. She could have sworn that she didn't speak out loud but Hugo looked up from the table and the tower, and asked, 'What's wrong, Mummy?' It sounded foolish, it was silly superstition, but she believed that she could sometimes read her son's thoughts and he could read hers. Not all the time, of course not, but every so often it did seem to be the case.

'Nothing, sweetheart,' she answered. 'I just remembered it's your gran's birthday.'

His grandmother meant nothing to him. It wasn't the way it should be, but there was nothing Rosie could do about it. Hers was not a loving family, and nor was her husband's.

Again, Hugo surprised her with his presentiment. 'Grandma's scary. She doesn't love me.'

'Sweetie, that's so not true. She loves you but she doesn't know how to show it.'

Gary snorted. Please don't, she silently pleaded, don't make him hate my family.

But encouraged by his father, Hugo was nodding in stubborn assent. 'She yelled at me.'

How often had he met his grandmother? Three times, and the first of those he had not yet been a year old, so he could have no memory of that meeting. That's you, Mother, Rosie thought ruefully, cold and distant. The remorse she felt was not guilt. It was a long time since she had connected that emotion to the way she thought about her mother. It was just so sad: her mother was a peevish, lonely old woman.

Rosie looked at her son. She wanted to say to him, Your grandmother is incapable of love. But she doesn't hate you or dislike you. She's just not interested in you. He was way too young to understand, so she grabbed him and pulled him onto her lap.

'Huges,' she said, burying her face in his tummy. 'Your grandmother loves you very much.'

It would not yet be six o'clock in Perth; there were still a couple of hours to go before the sun set over the Indian Ocean. But she knew her mother was ruled by routine, loved the order and sanity and safeness of it, and refused to answer the phone after seven-thirty. Rosie winced at the thought of leaving a message on her mother's machine. She could well imagine what her mother's opinion of *that* would be. *You always leave things to the last minute.*

'I'm just going to make a call,' she announced. Neither of them were taking any notice of her.

She picked up the hands-free and sat cross-legged on the kitchen table, under the poster of *Wild at Heart*. The table was her favourite piece of furniture, made of solid, stained redwood, both long and wide so it allowed for Gary to spread the paper across it in the morning, for crayons and notebooks and pencils to be sprawled alongside. It allowed them to be a family around it. She also loved it because Gary had made it.

Make the call, she pushed herself, make the call. Her fingers flicked across the touchpad, then abruptly she hung up and dialled another number.

Bilal picked up the phone.

She wanted to call Aish, but it wasn't the time. She could not have stood it if Hector had picked up the phone.

'Hi, Rosie. Sammi's just finishing putting the kids to bed. I'll grab her.' Bil's deep baritone contrasted with the lazy clip of his Australian accent, an unmistakable black accent, a jaunty melody in the vowels, distinctly different from the closed-mouthed thud of the white man's tongue.

Shamira came on the line. 'Sheez, why did we ever have children?'

'Who was it this time?'

'Ibby. Sonja was an angel. Ibby just complains all the time now. He doesn't want to eat anything, he doesn't want to go to bed on time, he doesn't want to sleep in the same room as his sister Is it just boys, are they all bloody whingers?'

They continued to talk, about their children, their husbands. Rosie looked over to the kitchen clock and reluctantly said goodbye. She and Shamira had talked for close to an hour. Hugo and Gary were still in the lounge room, probably both asleep. She must ring her mother. Her fingers flew quickly across the phone.

Anouk's answering machine kicked in, her friend's voice sounding cool, bored. Rosie began to leave a message when Anouk picked up.

'Hey.'

'Hey to you too.'

It was weeks since they had spoken.

'What's up?'

'Nothing.' Rosie tucked the phone under her chin. She went to roll herself a cigarette with Gary's tobacco, but realised she didn't need a cigarette. She was no longer a smoker.

'Actually, we just received a letter from the courts. They've set a date for the hearing.'

'Yeah?' Anouk's tone gave nothing away.

A flare of fierce anger took hold of Rosie. She wanted her friend to speak, to say something. She did not answer.

'Are you nervous?'

'Of course I am.'

Rosie realised that this was the first time they had spoken in ages without the conciliatory presence of Aisha. She wished she hadn't called, she was feeling almost sick with nerves, and afraid of showing her anger. But fuck it, she wanted Anouk's support.

'Good luck.'

Now she wanted to cry. The relief was a release. She rubbed a tear away from the corner of her eye. 'Thanks. I really appreciate that.'

'Don't get too confident, alright?'

That was so like Anouk: always a sting, always the bloody pessimist. But even so, she was heartened by her friend's backing.

'That's what Gary tells me.'

'Well, he's right.' Anouk's tone again betrayed nothing. 'He'll be glad it will all soon be over, I guess.'

There's no way she'd confess to not yet telling Gary. It would be humiliating.

'What are you up tonight?'

'I'm feeding Rhysbo his lines for tomorrow. I can't believe I wasted so many years writing that shit.' Anouk laughed out loud. 'He's giving me the finger.'

'It's Mum's birthday today.'

'Have you called her yet?'

'Not yet.'

'Hon, just do it and get it over with.' This time Anouk's voice was warm, encouraging.

Rosie felt the safe, sweet pleasure of shared history. 'I know, I know. Can you believe that I still get nervous after all these years?'

'They fuck you up your mum and dad.' Anouk's tone firmed, became cool again, took on an almost brutal directness. 'Just call her. She's going to make you feel like shit. But that's just what mothers do.'

That was *not* what mothers did. She would not be that kind of mother. 'Rachel wasn't like that.'

'I know, I know. My mother was a saint.' Anouk was being deliberately sarcastic.

'Alright, I've got to go. I'm going to call her.'

'Good girl.' Anouk hesitated, then rushed through her next few words. 'Do you want to call back?'

'No, no, it'll be fine. We should all get together.'

All meant herself and Anouk and Aisha. Without the men. Reluctantly, Rosie had to acknowledge that for Anouk that would also mean getting together without Hugo. *Without the boys.*

'Next week.'

'You're on.'

Rosie was about to say goodbye but Anouk had already hung up.

She couldn't yet make the call. She put it off further by going to check on Hugo and Gary. They were both asleep, her son slumped across the lap of her snoring husband. A glistening film of saliva coated Hugo's lips. Rosie always enjoyed seeing father and son together, envied their relaxed intimacy, so different from the intensity she shared with Hugo. He was never so loose across her own body, he would always have his arms wrapped around her, possessing her as she possessed him. Soon, soon, she knew, she would have to wean him off her breast completely. It should happen in the next few months, it should happen before he starts kinder next year. She resisted touching the sleeping child and she decided against waking them both and urging them into bed. They looked happy. She switched off the television and quietly took one of the photo albums off the bookshelf. She turned off the light and went back to the kitchen.

The frayed purple spine of the photo album instantly took her back to a time before Hugo, before Gary. She could still remember buying the album at a small, dusty newsagency in Leederville. She had been working as a waitress in the city, sharing a house with a morose couple called Ted and Danielle. She was doing too much speed, floating, directionless. It was the summer that Aisha had moved to Melbourne. Rosie swiftly flicked through the pages and found the photograph she was looking for. Jesus, she looked so young, she looked like *such* a slutty surfie chick. Well, she had been.

She was in the bright tangerine bikini that had been her favourite; the hallucinogenic fluoro intensity of the colour seemed shocking now. She was smiling ecstatically at the camera, pointing her chin forward because she had read in some teen magazine that this was the thing to do. Rachel was standing next to her, her bikini top a dull blue, a man's white business shirt draped casually over her shoulders.

Rachel had no need to jut out her chin. She looked calm, assured, a half-smile that seemed now to Rosie to be mocking her younger self's exuberant grin. Rachel was holding a cigarette. They were in Anouk's house, the one Rachel had finally died in, that overlooked the beach at Fremantle. Anouk had been trying to be a good friend earlier on the phone. There was no similarity between Rachel and her own mother. Rachel could be cruel, yes, but only in her honesty, never as a weapon. Rachel was smart and adventurous and cosmopolitan. She took risks. And she expected her daughters to take risks. Yes, in that way she was hard. It had been Rachel who had told her to get out of Perth, to follow Aish to Melbourne. And she had expressed it in her abrupt, direct way. Get out of fucking Perth, girl. You're just treading water here. You're going to end up a boring, pampered lawyer's housewife on Peppermint Grove, or worse, some bimbo wife of an ordinary dumb-as-dog shit bloke in Scarborough. Get out now, girl. Straight talking. Anouk was definitely Rachel's daughter.

It was cruel. Unfair. The cancer had spread across both breasts and she had died within a year; Rachel who loved life, who was unafraid, so unlike her own mother.

She had to ring. Rosie gently shut the photo album and picked up the phone again.

There was just one ring, then the insistent beeping of the interstate connection, and her mother answered.

'Happy birthday.'

'Rosalind, it's late.'

She would not apologise. 'It took ages to get Hugo to bed.'

'It's much too late for him.'

I will not answer her, I will not answer her. 'Did you have a nice birthday?'

'Don't be ridiculous, Rosalind. I'm over seventy years of age. Birthdays ceased to matter to me a long time ago.'

It baffled Rosie how her mother could have lived all her life in the backblocks of Perth and still manage to sound so English, so *proper*. Though it was an accent that Rosie had come to understand while living in London, it would be unrecognisable to anyone actually from the British Isles. It was an accent learned from the ABC and the BBC World Service generations ago.

'Did Joan call around?' Joan was her mother's best friend. Joan was her mother's *only* friend, she thought spitefully.

'She did.'

Ask about your grandchild. Will you ask about your grandchild?

'Did Eddie call?'

'No, Edward did not call.'

'I'm sure he will.'

The sniff from the other end of the line was almost coarse. 'Your brother will be propped against a bar getting drunk. I doubt he realises what day of the week it is, let alone it is his mother's birthday.'

Such spite, such sourness in her tone. Rosie felt her prickliness evaporate, felt only pity for her mother. She was relieved; soon the conversation would be over and there would be nothing to regret.

'Joan is the only one who thinks of me.'

She should answer, I called. She should say, you make it so difficult. She could say, we don't call because we don't like you. What Rosie did instead was not answer at all. Soon, soon it would be over.

'Your brother is a drunk. The men in our family are all drunks and the women in our family all marry them.'

Rosie felt herself blush. And as she felt the flush of warmth travel across her brow, her cheeks and neck, any sympathy she felt for the lonely old woman disintegrated. You malignant old bitch. It was not true. Gary was not an alcoholic. To drink at all was a sin in her mother's fucked-up middle-class Christian worldview. Why couldn't she be honest? The real reason she couldn't stand him was because he was a tradesman.

'Okay, I just rang to say happy birthday.'

'Thank you.'

'I'll let you get to bed.'

'You really should be putting Hugo to bed earlier.'

She could not think fast enough, could not find a way to disentangle herself from her mother's trap. So she did the wisest thing. 'He's usually in bed much earlier,' she lied. 'Maybe he's a little sick.'

'Are you working? Mothers always find the need to create problems for themselves when they're not working.'

Yeah, Mother, I am fucking working. I'm raising my child. 'I'll find work next year, when Hugo starts kinder.'

'Please don't tell me you're still breastfeeding?'

That could only be answered by another lie. 'No.'

'Thank God for that. I don't understand this obsession young women have to return to the days of being cows. I couldn't bear breastfeeding.'

I bloody know.

'When did you stop?'

'Four months ago.' She made it up.

'Totally ridiculous. My God, he's four isn't he?'

'Just turned four.' She couldn't resist it. 'You didn't call on his birthday.'

Rosie quickly glanced up at the doorway. Gary was stumbling towards the loo.

'*I sent a card*. Is that why you called me? To hurt me?' Her mother's tone was furious.

Game, set and match. There was nothing else to do but that which her mother expected. 'I'm sorry.'

'Good night, Rosalind. Thank you for calling.' With that the phone went dead.

For a moment Rosie couldn't move. She sat with the phone against her ear, listening to the phantom hiss of electricity. She slammed the phone on the table, feeling sixteen again, wanting to fuck a boy, fuck a man, fuck anyone, drink, shoot drugs, get paralytic, steal from a shop, curse and scream, anything to upset her, anything to make her mother hate Rosie as much as she hated *her*. She reached out for her husband's tobacco pouch. Smoking would have to do.

'You don't need that.'

She felt caught, guilty; but her hand did not move away. 'I just got off the phone with Mum. Yes I do.'

They stared at one another. She couldn't read her husband's face. Don't yell at me, don't be a smart-arse, don't get pissy. Gary walked over, leaned down and kissed the top of her head, squeezing her shoulder as he did so. The tenderness made her teary. He wiped at her eyes, took the pouch from her hand and started rolling a cigarette for her.

'She makes me feel like shit. She makes me feel like I'm a bad daughter, a bad wife, a bad mother.'

Gary snorted. 'You know that's bullshit. You're the best mother. You know that.'

She was a good mother. She did know that, though it had taken so long to discover. Being a mother was what had given her a sense of completion, had made sense of the anxiety and rage and fear that had so long dominated her life. Being Hugo's mother had finally given her peace. She sucked on the cigarette, prised a strand of tobacco from between her front teeth. She wanted to take advantage of this moment of rare, unguarded affection to say to Gary, please give me another child. She bit back the words, knowing he would withdraw from her, become angry. She feared the year to come, when Hugo would go to school and she would be left alone again. She knew her husband thought of the coming year as an opportunity in which she could find work and he could cut back his days, take up his art again. His bloody useless painting. They both needed to be working next year, to save up for a house. They needed more money.

'I'm going to bed,' Gary murmured to her. 'Hugo's asleep. You coming?'

'In a moment.'

He kissed her on the lips. She breathed a sigh of relief as she heard him make his way to the bedroom.

The smile on her face dropped away and she stared down at the phone. You're wrong, she swore at her mother. I am a good mother. I am.

Nothing any of her friends had said to her had prepared her for the shocking assault of the birth. She had so long fantasised about having a child—had pushed, needled, baited, nagged, threatened Gary into assenting to her desire—that she had not once thought she would hate it. She had loved being pregnant, was fascinated by the changes in her body, the independence of it to herself. She had loved the fact that she smelled and looked different. Her body had altered, turned from being angular and boyish into supple and feminine. But the birth had collapsed her back into herself. The only word for it was hell. If pregnancy had been an escape from herself into her body, the labour had been a rebirth in which she had confronted her duplicity, her falseness, her ugliness, her self-hatred. She had been convinced of the sanctity of a home birth and natural delivery. Then it had begun and she had immediately realised her mistake—and by then it was too late to ask for drugs. The actual memory of it was, thankfully, fragmented: opaque flashes from a hallucinogenic nightmare. But what she did remember vividly—could never forget—as they tried to prise the child out of her, was that all she knew, all she wanted, was that it be taken away from her. She had made a terrible, unspeakable mistake.

For the first six months, every time she held Hugo she shook with terror. She was convinced that she would kill him. Every time he cried she felt herself shrinking further from him. He was an alien being; he was going to destroy her.

For six months after the birth, she had continued to go to yoga, had kept wanting to meet regularly with Anouk and Aisha, had wanted to sleep, drink, take drugs, have sex, had wanted to be young. She did not want to be a mother. She'd felt as if she were about to break in two, that she was no longer Rosie but this strange, evil beast that could not feel love for the child it had brought into the world. She hated reminding herself of it: God, how she had hated the child. She couldn't even call him by his name. She *distrusted* him, was scared of him. She must have been mad, must have gone mad. The uncontrollable sobbing, the fantasies of drowning him in his bath, of snapping his neck.

For six months she had been insane and during that time she had not said a word about it to anyone—not to her husband, to Aisha, to the mothers' group, to her family, not anyone. She had not dared. She'd smiled and pretended to love her baby. Then one morning she had been frantically trying to organise herself to go to yoga. The child was screaming, crying incessantly. Feeding, lullabies, screaming, nothing would stop the terrible sound of him. She felt a moment's strange calm. She would let him cry, leave him in the house, the shitty little one-room box they were renting in Richmond, leave him there, let the little prick cry himself out, she wanted nothing of it. She was at the front door, keys in her hand, her sportsbag over her shoulder. She was going to get into the car and drive. Let him howl, let the little bastard howl himself to death. Let him choke.

She had opened the door and looked out to the street. It was summer, there was sunlight and no breeze and there was no one around. She had stood in the doorway for a good ten minutes, her bag still over her shoulder, her fist clenched around the keys, looking out to the world. You are not free, she'd told herself. If you want to survive this, if you don't want to kill yourself or kill your child, you must realise you are not free. From now on, until he can walk away from you, your life means nothing—his life is all that matters. It was then that she had stepped back and shut the door. She shut out the street, the world. She had picked up the screaming baby and hugged it close. Hugo, Hugo, it's alright, she whispered. It's going to be fine. I'm here.

He was the focus, he was the centre, he possessed her body. She lost herself in him. That's how she had set herself free. Not that the pain had ceased then. It was as if in the savage animal agonies of giving birth to Hugo a sadness had entered her that was to never go away. He had broken her, shattered her girlhood self. But she managed, slowly, with effort and determination, to put the pieces back together. The only evidence of the melancholy now was when Hugo or Gary were not physically with her, when she was left alone. For Gary had been wonderful in those first few months, had nursed her, comforted her, praised her, held her, saved her. It was always best between them when it was just her and Gary, when they were separate from the world. Without Gary, without her child, she could no longer survive in this world.

That night she dreamed of Qui; he returned to her so clearly that days after the dream she could bring his features to sharp relief in her mind. The firm grip of his dry, strong hands, the wariness and occasional reproach in his coal-black eyes, the cool, smooth texture of his skin. The dream narrative was less solid, it had almost completely evaporated on awakening in the morning—just fragments remained. They had been sitting at dinner, though there was no food on the table, in a restaurant high above the harbour in Hong Kong. Then sometime later in the dream he was fucking her, the flicker of image brutal and pornographic, which was faithful to the reality of the sex between them. He *had* been brutal, he *had* been dirty: on waking up she'd felt unclean. The way he had often made her feel. Hugo was curled asleep beside her, Gary was snoring, and she crept quietly out of bed. She walked naked to the bathroom and stared at herself in the mirror. Her skin was still white, unblemished, that of a young woman. Only her breasts betrayed her age. They were certainly fuller than when she had been with Qui, and now carried the telltale cruel streaks of stretch-marks and sag. Christ, Rosie, she admonished herself, you were eighteen. A woman stared out at her from the mirror. She had been a girl.

'I dreamt about my first lover the other night.'

'*Lov-er.*' Shamira elongated the word, her tone playful, teasing. 'My, that's such a big word.'

Rosie couldn't help laughing. 'No other word fits. I couldn't really call him a boyfriend.'

And it didn't. Qui had been twenty years older than her; lover was the only word that fitted. She was conscious that Shamira was hanging expectantly on the phone. Of course, Qui would mean nothing to her.

'It was nothing. It was just odd. I haven't thought about him in years.'

'How did Gary take the news about the hearing?'

'He was fine. He was happy.'

And he had seemed pleased, had quickly read the notice and given it back to his wife. Good, he said. I've been wanting this fucking thing to be over with for months. He walked over to the fridge and pulled out a beer. She'd been wary, watching him, but he betrayed no signs of anger or resentment. It had been a perfect Friday night. Fish and chips, falling asleep on each other watching crap English detective programs on the ABC.

'Can I tell Bil?'

'Of course.'

Shamira wasn't interested in Qui. She was right not to be. Qui was over twenty years ago. Qui was before marriage and child, before Melbourne. He was another life. She heard Hugo running helter-skelter down the corridor towards her and she knew Gary would be up any minute.

'I've got to go.'

'I'll see you at ten.'

'Sure,' Rosie assented. She put down the phone, put on the coffee, prepared toast for Hugo, whose clear blue eyes looked up at her, pleading hunger. 'Boobies,' he pleaded. She loved it when he said that. It was her favourite word.

Gary hardly said a word to her throughout breakfast, and bolted out the door as soon as he finished his coffee. She knew exactly why he was pissed off: he never liked it when she accompanied Shamira on her house-hunting. He started bickering with her as soon as she'd got off the phone to her on Thursday night.

'Why are you going with them?'

'To have a look?'

'Why?' He had been immediately suspicious.

'Sammi wants a third person there, another opinion.'

'Where are they looking?'

'Thomastown.'

'What the fuck for?'

'She wants them to be on the same train line as her mum. I think it makes sense.'

'Thomastown is a hole.'

'It's an affordable hole.'

He had pounced. 'Don't get any fucking ideas.'

'I'm not.'

He looked at her with fierce distrust. 'I'm not having a fucking mortgage round my neck. It's bad enough with a kid. I won't do it.'

'I know,' she snapped.

'Good. And I promised Vic I'd go around to his place on Saturday morning. He's got some songs he wants to play me. You'll have to get one of the kids to look after Hugo.'

Thank God for Connie and Richie. That had been the only good thing about that awful barbecue, getting to really know those kids. Connie had rung up the day after Hugo was bashed, to find out how he was. They were good kids—those kids were saving her life. Fuck

Vic and his songwriting. It was on a par with Gary and his art. You are bloody tradies, just workers—fucking deal with it.

She stayed calm. 'Fine, I will. I'll call Richie—Connie works Saturdays.'

But Gary had already stormed off, into the backyard. She found herself breathing rapidly, panting, really scared.

Hugo came to the door, staring up at her quizzically. 'Did you and Dadda fight?'

'Of course not.' She picked him up in her arms. 'We weren't fighting.'

'You were.'

'No, I promise.'

His face scrunched up, his eyes wary, and suddenly he reminded her of her own father. She hugged him close.

'I promise, we weren't fighting.'

A fucking house, Gary. A house. I deserve a fucking house.

She had been sixteen when they lost their home. She still could remember everything about it: the wide Formica bench in the kitchen where she and Eddie would complete their homework; the slowly creeping crack on the wall above her bedhead which her father never got around to plastering; the out-of-control weeds and spindly, parched rose bushes that struggled to survive in her mother's neglected flowerbeds, the soil dislodged by the heavy sand that continuously blew in from across the highway. It was a drab, late-sixties, cement-cladded house, the ceilings low, the walls thin, an oven in summer. But it had been her house, where she had grown up, and it was only a ten-minute walk to the beach. For most of the year she lived on the beach. Golden girl, they called her, because her tan never faded, her hair was bleached almost albino white from the sun and sea, and because she jumped the waves and rode the surf as if she was born in the very ocean itself. In Perth the golden sun—*her* sun—set on the calm, warm Indian Ocean. It was where the sea and the wind and the land all came together and made sense. The impossible blue of the Pacific was pretty but it did not contain the elemental harshness of *her* ocean, of *her* sea; it could never feel like home.

She often avoided the house, especially in summer, with the school year over and time stretching ahead. She had hated the toxic wall of silence between her mother and father. Later, older and experienced with men, she found a grudging respect for the way her lovers could scream at her, abuse her, make their venom and anger clear. She could never be like that—it was impossible for her to even form the words. She would shut down. She knew it wasn't healthy. That was one thing she was teaching Hugo: to be clear, to express himself, to not be repressed. Every emotion is legitimate, that was a mantra she whispered to him even before he had mastered speech. Every emotion is legitimate.

That final year before her parents divorced their house was almost explosive with emotion, things unsaid. She couldn't bear to live in it. Thank God for the beach.

We're losing the house, Eddie had told her. It was so like Eddie; he had sounded offhand, indifferent. That was the reason Aish had given about why she and Eddie split up. Your brother has no passion for anything, I mean, not for one bloody thing. Not cars, not the beach, not a career, not school, not girls. He's got no blood in him.

We're losing the house, Eddie said to her, almost yawning, Dad's gambled everything away. He's lost his job—Mum didn't even know. We've got nothing.

Where are we going to go? she asked him, terrified. He shrugged, jumped off the beach wall, picked up his surfboard and headed off to the water. Where are we going to go? she screamed after him. She stayed there, sitting alone on the wall, watching her brother paddle his board out to the thin line where the water and sky touched.

Richie turned up promptly at nine-thirty. As always, she was surprised at his punctuality, so unlike herself as a teenager. As soon as Hugo spied him through the screen door, he whooped and ran down the hall. It was so clear to her: Hugo needed a brother. They *needed* another child.

'Yo, little man.'

Hugo was jumping, struggling to reach the latch on the screen door but it was just out of his reach.

'Hang on, hang on,' she laughed. Rosie slid the latch across and opened the door. She leaned in and kissed Richie on the cheek. The boy blushed. Hugo immediately took the older boy's hand and pulled him along the corridor, heading to the backyard. Richie turned around and mouthed, Sorry.

She waved them on. 'Go play,' she called out.

It was a relief to get behind the wheel of the car, glance back at the empty baby-seat, turn up the volume on an old Portishead CD, to have the window down, to be driving. To be by herself. And the best part was knowing it wouldn't last long. In a few hours she would be so wanting to be with Hugo.

Shamira's sister, Kirsty, was going to look after Sonja and Ibby. Kirsty and her sister shared the same heavy-lidded eyes and pale Irish, oval face, but beyond that the contrast between the two women was staggering. Kirsty's T-shirt was low-cut, the logo of a Balinese beer stretched tight across her ample breasts. She was wearing skin-tight black jeans, sandals, and her blonde-tipped dark hair fell messily across her cheeks and down her shoulders. Shamira claimed that Kirsty had long ago accepted her sister's conversion, but the younger woman's suburban trashy look seemed a deliberate and pointed protest. Surely the choice of a T-shirt advertising alcohol could not be accidental? What was clear was that Ibby and Sonja adored their aunt, both of them vying for her affection and attention, Sonja sitting on Kirsty's lap, doodling in an exercise book, Ibby standing at her side, leaning in, seeking to be enveloped by her. Rosie sat down across from the trio as Bilal came into the room, holding a pair of boots in his hands. He nodded to Rosie, sat down and pulled on the shoes. He turned to his son. 'You are going to listen to everything your aunt says, you got that?'

Ibby nodded purposefully, his boy's face suddenly serious, determined.

Bilal winked at him. 'Good fella.'

To Rosie, the boy's answering smile was full of joy and pride.

She insisted on being in the back seat. As she was pulling the belt across her she glanced at Bilal's face in the rear-view mirror, and then almost shamefacedly looked away when Bilal returned her gaze. She could hear Gary's caustic rebuke. You're so fucking uptight, Rosie, you don't know how to be around a blackfella, do ya? You're so scared of saying or doing or thinking the bloody wrong thing. You're so fucking middle-class, aren't you, Rosie? That, of course, was the worst insult her husband could throw at her, for it was both truthful and unfair. It seemed absurd to her that she should have no money, that she didn't have a home of her own, that she should be so poor, shopping for her son's clothes at op-shops and relying on one- and two-dollar coins to complete the end-of-week grocery shopping. But the worst of it was that she *was* so stolidly, boringly, stupidly middle-class. She did always experience unease around Aboriginal people, and had done so from when she was a young girl being taken into the city by her father, clutching tightly onto his hand when they passed any Aborigines in the street. She was scared that if she looked directly into their eyes something evil, something abominable would happen to her. She had no idea from where her fear had originated. Her own parents' racism had been casual, was certainly never expressed violently or aggressively. Her mother pitied the blacks and her father had no respect for them; but beyond that they prided themselves on tolerance. Rosie's fear had somehow seeped into her from beyond consciousness and memory, imbued from the very air of Perth. She certainly did not experience a similar anxiety around blacks from Africa or the Americas. She had not felt scared as a teenage girl when the US navy frigates docked in the harbour at Fremantle and the streets of Perth would be full of swaggering black American sailors. She loved their attention: the faint obscenity, the seductive illicitness of their stares; their wolf whistles; their pleas: Come on, baby, have a drink with me pretty lady. And Aish, her best friend, she was Indian. That was black, wasn't it? But she did not risk another glance at Bilal.

She let out a deep sigh. Shamira turned around, her eyebrows raised in question. Rosie shook her head apologetically, briefly patted her friend's shoulder, and mouthed, I'm alright. It was the news of the imminent hearing, that was what had done it. She shouldn't jinx herself, not doubt the inherent rightness of the decision she had made. She *was* a good person and her unease around Bilal was not just because he was Aboriginal. She remembered him as a young man—she'd met him when she first arrived in Melbourne. He always used to laugh then, a sing-song in his voice, an attractive, youthful wildness. But he seemed to be wound up all the time, ready to uncoil with ferocious violence. She had not liked him, had feared him, even. Now in his forties, Bilal seemed to have no connection with that youth. She trusted *this* man, she preferred him, but she rarely heard his laugh. She was convinced that he detested her, that he still saw her as the silly white girl who'd come over from Perth and couldn't look him in the eye. In all that time they had barely exchanged a few dozen sentences. But now she was becoming friends with his wife, and she wanted to prove to him that she was no longer that silly, thoughtless *white* girl, that she had left all that a lifetime ago.

The unrelenting flat suburban grid of the northern suburbs surrounded them. The further they drove, the more Rosie thought the world around them was getting uglier, the heavy grey sky weighing down on the landscape, crushing down on them. The lawns and nature strips they passed were yellowing, grim, parched. The natural world seemed leached of colour. She thought it was because this world was so far from the breath of the ocean, that it was starved for air. She understood her husband's resistance to even thinking about living here, to settling into this dreary suburban emptiness. But it was all they could afford. Unless they moved to the country. Gary refused to even think of it as a possibility, but it would be good for Hugo, good for Gary's painting. But she knew he wouldn't hear of it. She looked at Bilal's reflection in the window. Here was a good man, a great father, an adoring husband. For a dizzying moment, the kind that took her breath away, she wished that she was the woman sitting next to the man in the front seat. She wished she was part of the couple going to look at a house. She shivered.

She leaned forward and placed a hand over her friend's shoulder. 'Are you excited?'

Shamira shrugged. 'We don't let ourselves get excited. We've been disappointed too often.'

Bilal's hand reached across the gearstick to grasp his wife's. 'We'll find a place, hon, don't you worry.' His voice was gruff, embarrassed. Rosie sat back in her seat. He didn't want her with them, it was obvious. She shouldn't have come along—this was an activity for husband and wife. But what other opportunity would come her way? She didn't want to look for houses on her own, to look for a *home* on her own.

The street was a small cul-de-sac a few blocks back from High Street. There was a school around the corner; the kids would be able to walk to it. The house itself was a low-ceilinged, square brick-veneer built in the early seventies. An auction sign was hoisted above the wire fence: Family Convenience. Rosie chuckled to herself. How Gary would hate that phrase. *Family values. Working families. Family First.* 'Family anything' he hated. Some neighbours were hanging over their own fences, looking on dispassionately at the steady stream of people walking in and out of the house. One of them was an old Greek-looking man, and further up the street a group of kids were playing soccer, chaperoned by an African woman, her head scarfed, anxiously keeping watch on the traffic. It would be a quiet street. She wouldn't be afraid of Hugo playing outside in such a street.

The house itself was drab, there was no other word for it. The tenants had moved out and the place seemed like a shell to Rosie, devoid of personality or charm. The rooms were small, the carpet faded, and there was a distinct smell of damp in the bathroom and laundry. However, it was on a large block, with a decent-sized work shed perched precariously in the far corner. The yard had not been tended properly for years; the small garden beds were full of sickly looking weeds. But Rosie could tell that her friends loved the yard, the space, the possibilities. Quietly, she slipped back into the house, feeling like a fool, the only one on her own. The place was packed with young couples flushing the toilet, tapping the thin walls, measuring the dimensions of the rooms. She walked back out through the front door. When she had first walked in, the round-cheeked estate agent had offered her a leaflet and she had refused. He was still standing under the porch and he went to offer her one again, before recognising her, smiling, and dropping back. On an impulse she stretched out her hand. The photograph on it had a view of the residence taken from the most appealing angle, shot from below to give the house much-needed height and width. She turned the leaflet over and examined the plan. There were only two bedrooms; the kids would have to sleep together, but that was no different to the arrangement in the flat Shamira and Bilal rented in Preston.

'You interested in Thomastown?' There was a note of sly cynicism in the estate agent's tone, as if he had examined Rosie closely, that he'd noticed her clothes, though obviously op-shop, were put together stylishly, that he'd observed she wore expensive Birkenstock sandals.

She avoided the question. 'How much do you think it will go for?'

The agent's reply was cautious, speculative. 'Two hundred and thirty to two hundred and sixty. But.' He did not need to add anything on to that damn *but*. Two hundred and thirty to two hundred and sixty—a bargain, close to shops, schools, train. A bargain that she could not afford and one that would most likely go for much more than the price quoted. Three hundred friggin' thousand dollars. For this dump, for this distillation of banal, ugly suburbia? She handed back the leaflet.

'Are you looking for an investment property?' The man slipped a card out of his pocket and handed it to Rosie. 'Call me any time.'

Was he flirting? What was he? Twenty-five? Younger? She was sure he was being flirtatious and she found the thought both gratifying and absurd. She looked down at the card in her hand. Lorenzo Gambetto.

'Thank you, Lorenzo.'

'Any time.'

'I'm just here with friends.'

'Ah, yes. I noticed the couple.' His tone was even, offhand, but she caught the inflection of curiosity. The couple. She had been aware of it from the moment Shamira and Bilal had got out of the car. The stares, most discreet, but some rude, a few even threatening. The man was obviously an Aborigine, the woman a Muslim, but with the complexion and face of a stereotypical Aussie working-class girl. *Who are they?*

'What did you think?'

She tactfully turned the question back onto Shamira. 'What did *you* think?'

'There's only two bedrooms but we can only afford two bedrooms, unless we find a place much further out. But I want to be close to Mum and Kirsty, and Bilal wants to be close to work. I could easily live here.' Shamira's eyes were bright, enthusiastic.

Rosie knew exactly what to say. 'I thought it was a real nice place. The street seemed really welcoming, lots of kids, and you've got a primary school around the corner.'

'There's also the high school up the road, for later on.'

Rosie smiled at Bilal, wondering if he could read through it, see the disbelief it was shielding. How long would you live here if you got it? How long could you bear to live here?

'It's perfect.'

She half-listened in the car on the way back, aware of her friends' excitement, their apprehension and nervousness. She was wondering how to convince Gary to even begin looking for a house together, to just turn up to inspections.

Spring Street turned into St Georges Road and the skyline of Melbourne suddenly came into view. This was where she wanted to be, this had been her world for years, where she dreamed of buying a house. But if some shit-box in Thomastown was going for three hundred grand then there was no way they could afford to buy here. The inner north. The cafés. Her favourite shops. The pool. The tram rides into Smith Street and Brunswick Street. The luxury of the Yarra River and the Merri Creek for long walks. It was unfair—it was here that they belonged.

'So when's the auction?'

'In a month.'

The weekend after the hearing. It would be an enormous week. Bilal would be full-time at work, Shamira would be doing all the running around. Rosie had no idea what was involved, but she assumed there would be banks to visit, lawyers, estate agents, God knows what.

Shamira read her thoughts, turned around, grabbed her hand. 'I'll be there.'

Rosie could not believe how grateful she felt.

At first she thought the house was empty, that Richie had taken Hugo to the park. But from the kitchen she was aware of noise out the back. She softly kicked open the screen door and walked into the yard. Through the broken pane of the lean-to shed she caught a glimpse of Gary smoking.

They all looked up when she entered the shed. She felt as if she had intruded on some masculine game, as if she had walked into an exclusive club. Gary's face was expressionless. Richie, who was sitting cross-legged on the dirt floor, a pile of magazines across his lap, looked up at her, his mouth open, shocked, guilty. Hugo's face expressed only uncomplicated adoration and pleasure. He rushed at her and she lifted him up, but in doing so almost stumbled back, had to support herself on the frame of the door. He was getting bigger, he no longer fitted snugly into her arms. His body was separating from hers and she felt a twitch of need; wished he could be a baby again, a tiny thing that fitted perfectly into her. She kissed her son once, twice, three times, then set him gently back on his feet.

'Mummy,' he exclaimed. 'We've been looking at boobies.'

Richie had swiftly snapped shut an open magazine when she'd come in, but she immediately saw what the pile on his lap was: Gary's collection of *Playboys*, a box he had purchased at a flea market in Frankston when they had first begun dating. The box had travelled everywhere with them since. The editions were largely from the late seventies and eighties, long past the magazine's heyday; they looked completely innocent these days. Still, what the fuck did Gary think he was doing? Showing centrefolds to a child and a teenage boy? Didn't he realise how *perverse* that could seem?

Gary took a final deep drag from his cigarette and stubbed it out on the dirt floor. 'Can you believe Rich has never seen a *Playboy* before?' Gary's wink was defiant, challenging. 'But I guess there's no need now, is there? He's got the internet.'

At that, the shame-faced youth rose to his feet, spilling the magazines around his feet. Sheets of centrefold slid out, Miss January

1985's boobs flopping next to Miss April 1983's arse. Further mortified, Richie knelt and began stacking the magazines haphazardly
into a pile. She felt pity and affection for him; the poor love couldn't
look at her. She knew exactly what Gary was doing. He'd planned
this moment, deliberately chosen to show the boys the magazines
when he knew she could be home at any moment. He was paying her
back for going off to look at houses. The best thing to do was to not
react. She'd known that the moment she had walked into the
shed. The best thing to do was to not get angry. Because the prick
was spoiling for a fight.

Rosie crouched and helped Richie stack the magazines. 'My dad
used to read *Playboy*,' she said simply. 'For the articles.'

The youth did not get the old joke, had obviously not heard of it
before. He could not bring himself to meet her gaze, his cheeks were
still blazing.

'I'm going to make lunch. You're welcome to stay.'

Richie's mumbled reply was almost inaudible, but she made out
that his mother was expecting him home for lunch.

She stood up and looked down at Hugo. 'You want a feed,
darling?'

With this she turned and walked out of the shed, holding her son's
hand. She was sure that Gary's eyes were following her.

Gary got what he wanted. Of course they fought. He needed an
altercation, an argument, an opportunity to shout, to belittle her, to
rant. An excuse to go down to the pub, to stay there till closing,
maybe go off into the night, then roll up home, stumbling, incomprehensible, insensible, sometime after dawn. That's what he wanted,
what he always wanted.

At first she refused to bite. I suppose you're pissed off I showed
Richie those magazines. No, I don't mind. Then he complained
about the lack of salt in the pepperonati she had made, sneered when
Hugo wanted to breastfeed after lunch. He walked up and down the
hallway muttering, cursing because he could not find the copy of the

Good Weekend he wanted, for the picture of a young Grace Kelly on the cover. You threw it out, didn't you? No, Gary, I didn't. You always throw my shit out. I didn't throw it out. Then where is it? I don't know, Gary. What the fuck do you know, do you know anything, you fucking moron?

She tried to take a nap but he played music loud, Television's *Marquee Moon*, something with no lightness, no melody, so that she could not sleep at all. He started drinking straight after lunch, had finished a six-pack by four o'clock and then had raged at her when she'd hesitated handing over twenty dollars for more beer: I work for that money, that's my money—you do shit-all. Give me my fucking money. While he was at the pub she quickly rang Aisha, but she only got the answering machine. When she tried to ring Shamira, the phone just rang out. She decided to go over to Simone's, who lived just a few blocks away. Hugo could play with Joshua. They were ready to leave when Gary came back from the pub.

'Where are you going?'

'I thought I'd take Hugo to Simone's.'

'Hugo doesn't like Joshua.'

'Yes he does.'

'No, he doesn't. Joshua pinches him. Isn't that true, Huges?'

'Joshua doesn't pinch you, darling, does he?'

'He fucking pinches him.'

'You tell Joshua that he isn't allowed to touch your body without your permission.'

'Oh, for fuck's sake, Rosie, what kind of PC bullshit is that?'

'Let's go, baby. Put on your jacket.'

'Yeah, go Hugo, and if Joshua does anything to you tell him that your mummy will sue. Tell him that's what your mummy does.'

That broke her.

That pissed her off.

That made her fly at him.

Later, when it was all over, when he had stormed out of the house, heading back to the pub, what astonished her as she lay crumpled on their mattress, quivering, exhausted, was how they had both seemed to forget that Hugo existed. They fought as ferociously as when they had not been parents. What terrified her was that Hugo did not respond with tears or with terror or with understandable childish, selfish outrage to their battle, but simply took off, went into the lounge, switched on the television, sat down in front of it, close to it, and turned the volume to loud. It was only when they fought that he did not demand to be the centre of her world, of their world. When they fought he had no wish to compete. What would that do to him? Would he retreat from conflict? Would he take after her? Or would he grow up to be like Gary? Hungering for conflict, being contrary, argumentative, needing the fight? But she only thought about all this later, in bed, trembling, as Hugo lay next to her, his mouth tight around her nipple, it calming them both. She only thought about all this later. First there was the fight.

What she wanted was simple: his support. She could not bear that he withheld it from her. She understood his apprehension about the hearing, his fear of being disgraced. She shared the same anxieties. She wanted them to share the weeks ahead, to plan, to work, to hope, together. So she snapped, told him to fuck off. That was all, two abusive words that slipped out of her, but they were enough to set him off. *You got us into this.* It was the unfairness of the charge that rankled. What had got them into the situation was that a stranger, an animal, had hurt their child. Gary knew this, she was convinced he felt the insult as acutely as she did. She had been so proud of him at the barbecue when he'd turned on that bastard, so proud of his immediate, unquestioning defence of Hugo. And later he had been in complete agreement when she said they must go to the police. Hugo had been inconsolable, she could not get him to sleep, he'd refused to let her go, clutching at her, a hurt, terrified animal. That was why they were doing it, for what that monster had done to their child. Gary had agreed, had been calm, convinced they were taking the right action. That the bastard couldn't get away with it. She had been grateful; for she knew that everything that had occurred in Gary's life had made him distrustful, antagonistic to the police. But all that history hadn't mattered, he'd made the call and she had been proud of him. I don't regret anything we've done, she blurted out, can't you understand we are not responsible, he's the one who has done this to us? It was then that Gary had screamed— literally *screamed*, the whole street must have heard—*No, you did this to us. You fucking caused this. You shouldn't have called the cops.* She refused to bite, tried to brush past him to continue chopping the vegetables for the soup. He would not let her pass. You called the cops. There, she said it. You made me ring them, he hissed at her. She tried to reason with him then. It was a mistake. He was already pissed, way beyond reasoning. It's just a few more weeks, Gary, and then it's all over. It's already over, he yelled back at her, or it should be. It happened, Hugo's forgotten it. He has not, he remembers it. That's only because you keep reminding him of it every bloody day. You're the one who can't forget it. He was pleading now: Let it go, Rosie, just let it go. Her anger resurfaced. How can we let it go? Do you want him to get away with it? Is that the kind of father you are? He grabbed at the wallet and drew the last few notes from it. She tried to snatch them back but he struck her hand away. He was walking down the corridor, he was going to the pub, he was going to stay there all night. She tried to stop him at the door but he had shoved her violently against the wall. *I hate you.* Not yelling, not screaming, just those three words said quietly. He had meant it. Then he was gone and the afternoon seemed filled with silence. She was alone.

No, not alone. Hugo, her Hugo, her lovely child. He had come into bed with her, stroked her face, patted the top of her head as if she were a pet. It's alright, Mummy, it's alright. With Hugo she could cry, she could let the tears fall. Lying together, Hugo curled into her, she was brought back to peace.

She watched him sleep. With his eyes shut, unable to look into the spectral pale-blue eyes that mother and son shared, Rosie could see only Gary in him. He had Gary's chin, his colouring, his large lopsided ears. He was so her husband's child and in recognising her husband in Hugo she could not help but think of her child's grandfathers. She wondered if it was possible to protect Hugo from his ancestry. Increasingly it was said that mental disease, alcoholism, addiction, it was all genetic. How could she protect him from the microscopic particles of his biological destiny? Her own father's alcoholism hadn't been congenital, that sickness had not run in his family. His drinking had a cause, it was an effect. The man had lost his job, his house, his wife, and finally his children. But the sickness *was* in Gary's blood. His father had been a drunk. As had his mother. And his grandparents as well. They were probably drunks all the way back to the first convict ship. She almost laughed. He was an exemplary Australian, her husband. She recalled a conversation during dinner from over a decade ago, when Hector had expounded how Australian drinking differed from all other cultures in its extremity, in its lack of conviviality, in the way it centred on the pub bar and not the dinner table. She had blushed then, as she blushed every time she remembered the occasion. How Hector had been able, without any malice in his tone or distaste in his demeanour, to fill that word, *Australian*, with such derision.

She was shocked the first time she met her future father-in-law. He had only just turned fifty but his skin, his body, his carriage, belonged to that of a dying old man. His liver's fucked, Gary had warned her, but she would have known that at once. His skin was corpse-grey; raw red and purple sores marked his arms. He wheezed when he spoke and every few minutes his body would double over in racked, tortured coughing, resulting in thick, globby phlegm he would spit onto the ground or into a tissue. Even so, a cigarette was always in his hand. Rosie stopped smoking right then. That is what smoking did, what alcohol did. They did indeed kill you, and the body did exact revenge for the poison it had been subjected to. It gave you death with no dignity. Gary's mother, only forty-eight at the time, was grossly overweight. Drink had given her a bulbous nose, criss-crossed with fine red veins. Deep furrows ran from the side of her lips. Gary's sister had been there as well, always with a fag in her hand, a beer in the other.

They had horrified her—the two nights they spent there had seemed endless. The house was tiny, a commission unit at the edge of Sydney's western suburbs, not really urban, but not country either. There had been nowhere to go, nothing to see, only the local pub down the road. They had gone there both nights for dinner and for the first time she had seen Gary really drink, compulsively, to the point of oblivion. Lying next to him in bed both nights she could not sleep for the snoring and farting and heavy wheezing. It had terrified her, and on returning to Melbourne, for the first time, she questioned whether she should marry this man.

It had been the proverbial whirlwind romance. He had proposed, and she had accepted, within the first month of their meeting. One of her treasures that Hugo would inherit was Gary's self-portrait on a small, stretched canvas, no bigger than a photograph, with the words, Will You Marry Me? stenciled in black ink across his face.

She had not long been back from London when they had first met. Like so many other Australians, she had wasted eight years of her life there on temp jobs, partying, riding the crest of the house, techno and rave wave, falling stupidly, conventionally in love with a married older man. She referred to it as love but her feelings towards Eric had never been passionate. She had certainly never truly felt joy with him, certainly never experienced anguish. They had both been aware of the reasons they stayed together, why he was prepared to be adulterous, why she was content to remain a mistress. Eric had a beautiful young girl to fuck; she got to stay in the apartment he rented for them, that great flat with the view of Westminster. He bought her beautiful clothes, paid for the marijuana, the ecstasy and the cocaine. They looked remarkable together, fashionable and sophisticated; Eric knew how to wear a suit. He was a good lover, prepared to indulge every fantasy, she liked his maturity, was happy to surrender to it: Daddy, can I fuck you? He took her to the opening of David Hare's *Racing Demon* and had scored prime seats for Madonna's Girlie Show at Wembley. And most importantly, to give him his due, he had never once offered to leave his wife for her, had never made that ignoble promise. There was another reason why she had stayed with Eric for so long: because it would piss off her mum. But in the end she was sure that she would have returned back home, returned to her friends, even if Eddie had not made the call. Rosie, I'm sorry, Dad's dead. He hanged himself.

She had cried on leaving Eric but they both knew the tears were not for the relationship, that they had both been playing parts in a late-twentieth-century soap opera that needed to come to an end. They were bored with each other. Always the gentleman, he organised her ticket, helped her to pack up the flat, drove her to the airport, and with his final kiss slipped a valium in her palm for the interminable flight home.

The funeral had been organised for the day after her arrival in Perth. Her mother did not attend, and to spite her, Rosie stayed with Eddie for a week, putting up with the scattered pizza boxes, the filthy toilet, the mould-caked bath. She then hired a car to drive across to Melbourne. She wanted to feel Australia again, to immerse herself in the enormous open canvas of the sky and the desert and the soil. She drove in ten-hour stretches, seeing nothing but the burnt scrub and the infinite blue firmament, parking the car in isolated service stations and braving the freezing cold of that emptiness while she willed herself to sleep. By the time she arrived in Port Augusta, avoiding the deadened stares of the Aborigines as she sat in a cheap café to eat hamburgers made with stale bread, she felt that she had washed Europe off her, that the eight years had disappeared.

In Melbourne she first stayed with Aisha and Hector, learned to change nappies on Melissa who had just been born, got work as a receptionist for a boutique clothing company in Fitzroy, and found a flat in Collingwood. Two months later she met Gary at an art opening in Richmond. He was the only one with balls enough to denounce the hopelessly outdated postmodern bricolage of the artist's work. Back then he wore an industrial grey wool suit, a thin black tie, and pale crimson button-braces that he'd found in an op-shop in Footscray. She had noticed him at once, even before he began to insult the artist, because he was the only man in that crowd who dressed as well as Eric. But unlike Eric, Gary was not born to elegance. Gary's flair was instinctive, his style his own. He was not handsome like Eric, but that didn't matter. His features were distinctive, extravagant, the sharp chin, the steep cheekbones, the intense eyes. Honesty was his God. She thought him thrilling, dangerous. She'd had none of that with Eric: for charm, like that her father possessed, and politeness, like that of her mother, were evasive qualities that concealed the truth.

She had gone straight up to Gary and objected that he was being unfair to the artist, that an opening was meant for celebration, not criticism. He'd scoffed at that—was that the first time he had accused her of being *bourgeois*?—but they had both been smiling. He asked for her number and called her the next day. They went to dinner that Friday night and he had thrilled her with a conversation that encompassed music and film and art and the challenge of evolutionary psychology on the dogmas of feminism. She loved that he read widely but had never been a student, that he had left high school at sixteen, took on carpentry as a trade and left that as well to move to the Cross in Sydney and transform himself into a bohemian who would finally remove all traces of his previous life. He kept nothing from her. He had been a rent-boy, had pimped a girlfriend, wasted three years on heroin, had fled Sydney owing thousands. She hardly said anything all night, dazzled by his skill with narrative, his assuredness, by the seductive power he already had over her. She wanted to fuck him that night, but she did not invite him in. He rang again next day and they spent Sunday afternoon on the banks of the Yarra. That night he stayed, and the next morning, after he had left, as she was getting ready for work, she rang Aish. I'm in love.

From the beginning Gary was defensive around her friends. He thought Aisha cold, Anouk arrogant and, most of all, detested Hector's attempts at fake mateship. He thought them all stuck-up and, overcompensating, Rosie found that she fell into a gush of talk when they were together, dominating conversation so that no conflict could emerge. They are so fucking middle-class, so dull, Gary would holler when they returned home to her flat, how the fuck can you stand them? She defended her friends but secretly, surprisingly, she found that she was elated by his resentment of them. Her friends no longer seemed so successful, so assured, so *perfect*, when viewed through Gary's eyes. When she had returned from visting his family in Sydney she said little to Aisha about them. She said nothing about her doubts. She was going to marry him. She loved him. Fuck them, fuck all of them and their disapproval. In the end her friends were loyal. Anouk was there at the wedding, and Aisha and Hector had been their witnesses.

She softly kissed her child on his cheek. He smelled of caramel, of childhood. Hugo stirred, whimpered, then turned over. She knew that it was an awful thought to have, but she was glad that both his grandfathers were dead. One quickly, by his own hand, the other slowly, by grog. His grandmothers might as well be dead—one was a drunk and the other refused to love. It was her and Gary and Hugo. And her friends. That was all that mattered. That was family. Everything will be alright, sweetheart, she whispered, everything will turn out fine.

Next morning, when she found Gary passed out on the back lawn, neither of them mentioned the argument. She cooked an omelette for Gary and herself, made toasted sandwiches for Hugo, and they watched *Finding Nemo* together, Gary making his son laugh, mouthing all of Dory's lines.

The weeks stretched out endlessly to the hearing, but the days seemed to fly by. There wasn't a minute in which the thought of the upcoming trial did not loom. Her keenest desire was to shield Hugo from what was happening. She gave herself over to the house, an enormous spring clean, scouring the oven, attacking the cobwebs in every corner of every room, rearranging the kitchen shelves. She planned menus for the week, shopping at the market, walking with Hugo to the shops on Smith Street every second day. She was attuned to Gary's mood. If he arrived home brooding from work she remained silent until his first beer, allowing him to relax. She badgered Margaret on the phone until she was given another appointment at Legal Aid; and even though there was nothing the lawyer could tell her except to remain calm, she was heartened by it. Margaret reiterated that Rosie and Gary were doing the right thing, that an assault against a child could not go unpunished. Rosie wished Gary was not so suspicious of the young woman. He thought her immature, anti-male. But they were getting her services for free, and Rosie thought they should be thankful.

She was grateful for the assistance of Connie and Richie over those weeks. They looked after Hugo together, or took turns minding him, while she allowed herself the opportunity to go to the pool for a swim, to do yoga, to give herself over to fantasies. Though Margaret had explained the unexciting, bureaucratic workings of the hearing process, Rosie allowed herself the luxury of daydreams. She imagined herself in the dock, passionately, convincingly detailing the crime that monster had committed against her child. She swam fifty laps a time lost in those thoughts.

Shamira too proved herself a true friend, calling every day, bringing her kids over to play with Hugo on the days she wasn't working at the video shop. One afternoon Shamira invited her to a park in Northcote where a group of mothers whose children attended the same school as Ibby would often meet to watch their children play. Rosie appreciated her friend's efforts to keep her occupied but she found the afternoon tiresome. The other women were all Muslim and, apart from Shamira, were all born to Arab or Turkish parents. They were welcoming, polite, but Rosie was aware of a subtle distance between herself and these women. It was not the religion itself that created the barrier. Only a handful of the women were scarfed. But their easy camaraderie, their teasing of each other and their parents as 'mussies', as 'wogs', their disinterest in her life, her marriage, her world, pissed her off. She wondered if Shamira too felt some of this estrangement—would she always be 'that Aussie girl' to these confident, loud wog chicks? Would she always be an outsider no matter how many times a day she prayed? Rosie watched Hugo try to join in a game of soccer with the other boys and he seemed so fair, so *white*. She fell into silence, watching her child. He'd given up on the soccer game and was climbing on the adventure playground on his own. Shamira, noticing, called out sharply to Ibby to let Hugo into the game.

Don't do that, thought Rosie bitterly. Don't shame my son. She rose to her feet, smiling. 'It's been lovely to meet you all but we've got to get home.'

Shamira started to rise but Rosie stopped her. 'It's alright. It will be a nice walk home.'

The truth was that she missed Aisha with an almost blinding, childish indignation. This was the time that her friend should be by her side. This was the moment in her life when she most needed her friend's support. She knew that she was being unfair. Aisha—and Anouk—had supported her through her parent's divorce, the loss of the house, had looked after her the first time she moved to Melbourne. They were there when she returned from London, when her father killed himself. Aisha had come to the funeral. Yes, it was unfair but that was how she felt. Shamira was kind but they did not share a history. Connie was generous, supportive, but she was only a teenager. I'm lonely, thought Rosie, holding her son's hand as they crossed Heidelberg Road. Since having Hugo her life had contracted to her family and a few friends. It must have been over a year since she'd seen the girls she used to work with. You're my life, Hugo. She did not want to give voice to this thought, and he definitely did not need to hear it. But it was true. He was her life, her whole life.

So she felt joy and relief when they got home to a message from Aisha. Rosie, how are you? Do you want to meet Anouk and me for a drink on Thursday evening? Give me a call. We're both thinking of you. Love you.

It felt like going on a date. She had been wanting to visit her hairdresser before the hearing and after ringing Aish back she called Antony and made an appointment. It was exactly what a girl needed. Antony made a fuss of her as soon as she walked through the door, shoving her into a chair and complaining loudly that she had let herself go. She giggled at the banter. He asked about Hugo and she told him that the hearing was in a week.

'Fuck the hearing, fuck messing about with lawyers. Why don't I get my cousin Vincent to deal with the prick? He'll cut off his balls.'

Antony turned to his assistant. 'Do you know that this prick just went up to Rosie's child and slapped him? Just like that.'

The assistant, open-mouthed, was obviously horrified.

Antony nodded in grim assent. 'That's right, we should kill the cunt. Mind my language. But we should kill him.'

She was doing the right thing. She was definitely doing the right thing.

She arrived early at the bar and, on an impulse, ordered a bottle of champagne. Knowing that Anouk would want to smoke she took a seat at a table on the footpath. As she sat down she glanced quickly at her reflection. Antony had, as always, cut her hair short, leaving a heavy fringe across her right cheek. She liked it, it had a hint of flapper style. She was wearing an old white dress shirt of Gary's and over it a blue velvet vest that she had got sometime back in the nineties. The skirt, expensive, short, black, chic, she'd bought from David Jones before she had Hugo. She was delighted to find that it still fitted her. She sat down feeling pleased. No one could accuse her of looking like a hippie today.

Anouk arrived a few minutes later, dressed in a man's suit. She was growing out her hair and the thick black locks, streaked with grey, fell to her shoulders. The two women looked at each other, grinned in mutual admiration.

Anouk pecked her on the cheek.

'You look gorgeous.'

'So do you. You look delicious.' Anouk whipped out a cigarette and lit it. She nodded appreciatively to the young waiter who had unobtrusively placed another champagne glass on their table and was now filling it. 'You didn't come with Aish?'

'You know what her work is like.' Rosie raised her glass. 'I took the tram and she can give me a lift back.'

'Good.' Anouk looked down Fitzroy Street to the grey-green water of the bay, gleaming in the fading afternoon sun. 'It's beautiful, isn't it? Beats the concrete and clay on your end of town.'

Rosie said nothing to this. Though she had now lived long enough in this city to understand its divisions and mythologies, she remained uninterested in their pettiness. It was a treat coming to St Kilda, certainly, she'd enjoyed reading *Vanity Fair* on the long tram ride, had enjoyed dressing up, going out. But the bay could not compare to the ocean of her youth. She certainly never swam in it. It felt dirty the few times she had done so; she had felt like a layer of grease was coating her skin.

'How's the book going?'

Anouk groaned.

'That good?'

'I'm enough of a Jewish princess, sweetheart, to feel the intense shame of having to confess to mediocrity. I'm just trying to write the fucker at the moment, get the story down, but I re-read an earlier chapter this morning and I felt like shit afterwards.' Anouk took a deep breath. 'It was so damn *womanly*. All oogie-boogie, feely-feely.' Her face broke out into a cheeky leer. 'I told Rhys that the next one is going to be porn. Poofter porn. No feelings, no emotions, no girly stuff. Just hardcore sex.'

'When do I get to read it?'

'The poofter porn?'

'No. What you're writing.'

'When I get the courage to show you. When I don't think it's shit.'

'It won't be shit.' Rosie was confident. Anouk had always belittled her talents. Arrogant, tough, unafraid when it came to living her life, she lacked confidence when it came to her art. She and Aisha had always seen Anouk's escape into television writing, into soap operas, as running away. She had made lots of money but it wasn't what she was destined to do. Even as young women, Aisha and Rosie were convinced that their friend was going to be famous, had teased her about which one of them she would choose to escort her to the Oscars. They had both been ecstatic when Anouk announced that she was giving up the soapies to write a book. It would do well, she would be acclaimed, there was nothing to worry about. Anouk had always had *promise*.

'How's Rhys?'

'He's working on a student film and he's over the moon. There's no money but it's a good part.'

Rosie took a sip from her champagne. Anouk wasn't going to ask about Gary, or Hugo. She knew her friend well enough to understand there was nothing deliberate in this omission. She just wasn't interested. It helped when Aisha was with them; somehow the conversation flowed much more easily. She set down her glass, about to recount something from the magazine she had been reading on the tram. But Anouk spoke first.

'I'm glad Aish is running late. There's something I want to say to you.' Anouk glared across at her. 'You have to promise you won't say anything, you won't tell Aish that I've said anything.'

'Cross my heart.'

'I mean it. Fucking promise.'

'I fucking promise.'

'She had a big fight with Hector on the weekend. She wanted to come with you on Tuesday. She's been feeling like crap that she can't be with you.'

Rosie remained silent.

Anouk looked nervous. 'Are you okay?'

Okay? She was bloody gleeful. It was what she needed to hear. Not that she was delighting in her friend's marital conflict, but she needed to know that Aisha was looking out for her, that she understood exactly what this moment meant for her. She didn't have to be physically there because she was there already. Had been all this time.

'I'm glad you told me.'

Anouk took another deep breath. 'Rosie, I'll come with you if you want me to.'

She almost burst out laughing. The last thing she would need that day would be trying to make sure Gary and Anouk didn't scratch each other's eyes out. She grabbed her friend's hand.

'Baby, thank you, but you don't have to.' She winked. 'I'd be too scared that you would make a good witness for the defence.' She saw her friend baulk at this and this time Rosie did laugh. 'I'm joking. Thank you. And thank you for telling me about Aish. I know she can't be there. Shamira's coming with us.'

She realised Anouk was uncomfortable with the physical intimacy; she withdrew her hand.

'How're she and Terry, I mean, Bilal?' Anouk shook her head

dismissively. 'What the fuck is that about, that stupid name change? Can't a Muslim be called Terry?'

In her heart, Rosie agreed. Why couldn't Shamira remain Sammi, Bilal remain Terry? The taking on of new names had always struck her as something affected in their conversion, as if they knew that they were never real Muslims. She recalled the Lebo and Turkish women in the park the other day. One of them had called herself Tina, another Mary. They didn't have to prove their religion. Like you, Rosie looked across at her friend. You're born Jewish. That's what's real, you're just born into it. Nevertheless, she thought she had to defend her friends.

'I guess it's like baptism, proof of accepting the new religion. It's making it public to the world.'

'I don't think the world really cares.'

'I think it took a lot of courage for Terry to become Bilal.'

'Because he's Aboriginal?'

'Yes.'

Anouk lit another cigarette. 'I'm not sure it takes any more courage for an Aborigine to become a Muslim than a white guy.'

Rosie shrugged. 'I think in this world now it takes courage for anyone to call themselves Muslim.'

'And Shamira? I guess she became a Muslim to marry Bilal.'

'No. That's not it. She had already converted. They met at a mosque.'

'Really?' Anouk looked astonished. 'What the fuck makes a yobbo chick like her become a Mussie?'

'She heard the call.'

'The what?'

Rosie felt inadequate for this explanation. She had asked Shamira, early on, the very same question, possibly with an equivalent lack of comprehension. Shamira's answer had been so simple, and so lovely in its simplicity, that Rosie knew she would do it no justice in telling it to her cynical atheist friend. Sammi had been working in the video shop, the same shop she still worked in on High Street, when a man and his young son had come in to look for a video to take home. Sammi was listening to triple J on the store stereo when she became conscious of a song that was falling from the young boy's lips. It was a chant, and it made her switch off the radio. I felt light, Rosie, she'd said. I felt a light and I felt a peace. She had asked them what the boy was singing when they came up to the counter and the tall African man laughed and said it was not a song but a verse from the Qur'an that his son was learning. Shamira seemed to remember every detail about that day: the vermillion skull-cap the father was wearing, the boy's chipped front tooth, the copy of *The Lion King* they'd taken up to the counter. And Rosie, Shamira confided, that night I went back to the flat and Mum and Kirsty were there, ready to go out, and they offered me a beer and a bong and for the first time in my life I said no. I've been smoking bongs and on the piss since I was twelve. But I said no. I just wanted to lie in bed and think about that chant. Really, that was it. That was the beginning. Sure, there was a lot of shit. I had to work hard to get people to believe I wanted to learn about Islam. The Lebo girls at school thought I was crazy. And so did Mum. Kirsty still doesn't get it. But I heard God, I heard him speak.

Rosie poured Anouk another glass of champagne. 'I don't know what made her convert. Ask her yourself one day. What makes anyone religious?'

'Fear of death. Ignorance. Lack of imagination. Take your pick.'

You're hard. You're hard, Anouk. At that moment they heard an insistent honking and they turned around. Aisha was in her car, waving at them, indicating she was trying to find a park. Anouk pointed towards the esplanade. The cars behind Aish started to beep their horns. Aisha nodded and drove off. Rosie caught the waiter's eye and asked for another glass.

Aisha looked flustered when she walked in. 'I've just met the devil and she is a seventeen-year-old drug-fucked bogan from Preston.'

Anouk chuckled. 'Satan sounds like he downsized.'

Aisha, taking her seat, laughed as well. She raised her glass. 'I need this.'

'What happened?'

Aisha looked across at her friends, a scowl on her face. 'Look at you two. I feel so frumpy and middle-aged.'

Anouk scoffed. 'Shut up, you look gorgeous.'

'I don't feel gorgeous. I didn't have a chance to get home and change. I'm scared I smell of dog piss and cat's blood.'

Anouk laughed again. 'That's alright. You always do.'

Rosie smiled at her friend. Aisha's olive top was plain, her navy pants simple and functional, but she would always look beautiful, no matter what she wore. Even in her forties, she had the slim body, the high, elegant neck, the sculptured, lean feline face of a fashion model. And that almost uncanny porcelain skin. She was the most splendid woman Rosie knew. 'You look great. Now tell us what happened.'

'It was my last consult, this doped-up young girl and her kitten. She just needed a vaccination, nothing serious. Anyway, one of our clients rushes in with their dog bleeding all over their arms and in the waiting room. It's been hit by a car, Tracey runs into the consult room to tell me and I turn to this girl and say, Excuse me, I'm just going to have to attend to this emergency.' Aisha's tone was urgent, but as she spoke she began to calm down. 'So I'm trying to revive this dog and we suddenly hear shouting from the front. This little bitch is screaming that she had an appointment, that we should see her first and attend to the dog later. Tracey goes out to calm her and she starts yelling even louder. I'm trying to save this dog, his owner is crying next to me and we have this little shit screaming down the clinic. Anyway, the dog dies on the table, I'm feeling like crap but I go in to finish the consult with this girl who is telling me she's going to lodge a complaint about us. Then she has the gall to complain to Tracey because we don't have discounts for concession-card holders.' Aisha looked from Rosie to Anouk, a look of incredulity on her face. 'I wanted to kill her. How do these people exist? What makes them think they have the right to act like that?'

Anouk crossed her arms, sat back in her chair. 'Don't start me, Aish, don't even start/me. These kids, they're unbelievable. It's like the world owes them everything. They've been spoilt by their parents and by their teachers and by the fucking media to believe that they have all these rights but no responsibilities so they have no decency, no moral values whatsoever. They're selfish, ignorant little shits. I can't stand them.' Anouk's outrage was so vehement it was almost comical. 'You know what you should have said, you should have said that if you can't afford a vet visit maybe you shouldn't have a cat in the first place. Losers. I'm sorry, there's no other word for it. What the hell makes them think any of us owe them a living? How can they be that way?'

Aisha nodded. 'Tell me about it.'

Rosie couldn't speak. It was a terrible story, of course, the selfishness of this young girl, not understanding the imperative for saving the dog's life, but she was hurt by the crudity of her friends' responses. Sometimes you just don't have money, sometimes you just want a discount and you get so embarrassed about asking that you come across as nasty or belligerent. The girl did sound selfish. But not everyone without money was like that.

'She doesn't sound quite normal.'

Aisha swung around to Rosie. 'Oh don't worry, she was out of it on something. Of course she was. She had no money, she was on the dole, she was on drugs, the perfect victim. Just perfect. And of course she was going to report us to the vet board. Of course. She has *rights*.' The force Aisha put into that final word was like a blow.

Rosie twisted her fingers together. I'm not going to say anything. I shouldn't say anything.

Anouk waved the waiter over and ordered another bottle of champagne. 'It's our world,' she said flatly. 'Can you imagine what the future is going to be like when these kids rule this country?

Expecting everything on their plate and having to do nothing for it. It's going to be hellish.'

Aisha nodded in approval.

Rosie thought, when is a girl like that ever going to rule the world?

Aisha looked ruefully at the waiter as he settled a new bottle on the table. 'We better eat or I won't be able to drive home.' She wrapped her arms tight around herself. Dusk was falling into night. 'And can we go inside?' She poked her tongue out at Anouk. 'It's too cold to indulge you smokers.'

'Well, you better not ask for one after dinner, then.' Anouk lowered her voice. 'I'm not sure about the food here.' She mentioned the name of an Italian restaurant around the corner. Rosie stiffened. She'd heard Aish mention it. It was supposed to be expensive. Unaffordable, out of this world expensive.

Aisha nodded. 'Sounds good.' Rosie felt her friend's hand squeeze her own under the table. 'Our shout,' she said quickly, looking across at Anouk who nodded.

'Thank you,' answered Rosie, weakly.

It was a fabulous dinner. That was the word for it—the kind of word she could not use around Gary who would snort in derision at it. She hadn't eaten like that for years: an osso bucco that fell gently off the bone, freshly baked herb bread, a delicious tiramisu that Hugo would have loved.

Afterwards they drove Anouk home and Rosie was glad that Aisha declined the offer to go upstairs for a coffee. Hugo would be missing her; he was unlikely to have fallen asleep without her there. On the drive down Punt Road, crossing the Yarra, Aisha, for the first time that night, spoke about the upcoming trial.

'You know I want to be there.'

'You are there.'

'I hope they make that bastard Harry squirm.'

Rosie, you've got the best friend in all the world, she thought to herself. The best friend in the whole world.

On Tuesday morning she awoke before dawn. Her first thought was that she was sick, as an intense nausea seemed to emanate from the centre of her abdomen. She thought it must be cramps, then remembered that her period had come last week. She carefully slid out of bed, Hugo and Gary both fast asleep, and rushed to the toilet. She forced herself to retch but nothing came up. She sat on the seat and intoned a yoga mantra. It's just nerves, she repeated softly, by the end of this day it will all be over.

Rosie made herself a peppermint tea, wrapped her dressing gown tightly around herself and walked out into the garden. There was no wind but it was bitterly cold, a true Melbourne late winter morning, where the night denied the world any hint of the coming spring. She forced herself to sit on the old, rusting kitchen chair, to wait for the sun to rise. She couldn't bear the thought of standing still but this was exactly what she knew she had to do, stay still, remain calm, fight against the nausea which was only fear, only cowardice.

She had finished her tea when she heard Gary stumble into the kitchen. She went inside and they sat quietly and drank a coffee together. When she asked for a cigarette he rolled her one without comment. She woke Hugo, who took it upon himself to start wailing because he would not be allowed to come with them. But, darling, she said to him, Connie is coming especially to spend the day with you. Thank God for that girl. Connie was taking a day off school to babysit, a day she could ill-afford to lose so close to exams, but she had been adamant. Rosie, I want to do this for you and Hugo. For once she allowed Gary to deal with Hugo's tantrum and she began getting ready. She was not going to give him a feed this morning. There was no time. And she had to be more firm about weaning him off her breast. It was time.

She had chosen her outfit months ago, a conservative fawn business suit she had worn to interviews when she first arrived home from London. By the time she finished applying her make-up Gary had somehow managed to calm Hugo. She made toast for her son while Gary showered and got dressed. He asked Rosie for assistance in doing up his tie; she noticed that his hands were shaking. She clasped them tight, kissed his fingers, which tasted of cigarettes and soap. He kissed her back, on the mouth, with a force that was almost erotic. It will all work out fine, he whispered. Shamira, who had picked up Connie on the way, arrived just after eight. Rosie almost cried when she saw her friend. Shamira was dressed in a thin black wool sweater, with a matching long black skirt. She had let her hair out. She still wore a headscarf but it was a simple cobalt silk shawl that coiled loosely across her head and shoulders, allowing the bulk of her hair to fall as a blonde wave down the back of her jumper. *She had let her hair out.* Can't take any chances, she joked as Rosie hugged her, just in case the judge has it in for us Mussies. Gary didn't seem able to speak. He too hugged Shamira tightly. See, Shamira laughed, wiping a tear from her eye, I told you I'm really just a white-trash scrubber underneath all this.

She drove them to the courthouse in Heidelberg. It was not yet nine o'clock when they parked but already the steps leading up to the building were full of people, all of them seeming to suck on endless cigarettes. Two bored-looking policemen were speaking quietly in front of the court's glass entrance. As they approached the steps, the mixture of people waiting seemed to Rosie to represent the whole world. They were white, Aborigine, Asian, Mediterranean, Islander, Slav, African and Arab. They all seemed nervous, uncomfortable in their cheap, synthetic suits and dresses. It was obvious who the lawyers were. Their suits were finely woven, well-fitting.

Gary was frowning. 'Where the fuck is our lawyer?'

'She'll be here.'

'When?' Gary started to roll a cigarette and a young man wearing a pale blue shirt a size too small for him peeled away from the crowd and walked over.

'Mate, can I scab a rollie?'

Silently Gary passed him the pouch. The young man rolled a cigarette and with a cheeky grin handed the pouch back to Gary.

'What are you here for?'

'Assault.'

'Ma-ate,' the boy called out, making the word into a chant, 'me too.' He winked again. 'Course, we didn't do it, did we?' With a grin he fell back into the crowd, standing next to an old woman who looked spent. Rosie smiled at her and received a sad, fatigued, frightened grimace in return.

Sad, fatigued, frightened. That pretty much summed up the faces of everyone around her. She quickly glanced over at her husband. He wore another face, a face that could also be glimpsed on some of the other men in the crowd. Tight, arrogant, tense, as if the day was a challenge they were preparing to take on. Like her husband, these men scowled as soon as anyone looked towards them. A small number of these men had forsaken suits and ties and cheap department-store shirts for their track-pants, hip-hop hoods and leather jackets. She knew that Gary would admire them, respect their refusal to participate in the charade. She could read his thoughts clearly. She bit her lip. But this wasn't about him or her. This was about Hugo.

The courthouse doors were opened and the crowd started to move inside. Gary smoked another cigarette before Margaret finally arrived, breathless, apologetic, complaining about the traffic. Gary fixed her with a vicious glare that stopped her mid-sentence. She ignored him and turned to Rosie, who introduced her to Shamira.

'Should we go in?'

'Yeah,' Gary replied sullenly. 'I guess we should fucking go in.'

The courthouse was only a few years old, a grey steel monument to the new century's economic boom that had already started to develop the forlorn, dissolute air that seemed to attach itself to any government institution. It smelt of cleaning agents and abandoned hopes to Rosie—there was no colour anywhere and the little there was, in the bad landscapes and still lifes on the walls, seemed to be draining away, as if to conform with a monochrome future. Margaret led them down the corridor to an enormous waiting room where a small screen sat high above everyone's head. There was no sound and the television chef looked ridiculous as he silently instructed the audience how to cook a Thai curry. They found seats and Margaret left them to look at the schedule affixed on the courtroom's door.

'It's a busy day,' she announced on returning, scanning the crowd, not catching their eyes. 'But we're not far down the list. Fingers crossed we might get called before noon.'

Gary cocked his eye up at her. 'Who's the judge?'

'Emmett. She's alright.' Margaret was still not looking at him.

'What do you mean by alright?'

Rosie placed a warning hand on her husband's knee. Don't antagonise her. She's on our side.

'She's good.' Margaret was about to add something further when she suddenly stopped. They all turned around at once.

She hadn't seen him since that awful day he'd come over with Hector to apologise. Not that he had meant it. It was obvious he hadn't meant it. She could never forget that sneer. He wasn't sorry; he had come over to look down at them. He had not once taken that sneer off his face. There was a trace of it now, as he looked around the waiting room. He had not yet noticed them. But everyone had noticed *them*. Rosie's heart sank. He and his wife stood out from this crowd, stood high above this crowd, not because of any elegance or sophistication or style. There was none of that in the new suit, new dress, new shoes, new handbag, new haircuts. All they were, all they screamed of was money. Dirty, filthy money. But that was enough to raise them up above everyone else in the room. Rosie watched as their lawyer, inhumanly tall, like some mutant insect trapped in a suit, led them towards a seat. It was then that Rosie caught his eye. That sneer, that up-himself arrogant cunt, that sneer was still on his face. But that was not what made her gasp, made her body tighten, as a shock of naked, electric fury ran through her. Walking behind them, escorting them there, was Manolis, Hector's father.

She went straight for him. Gary leapt up to restrain her but she shook his hand away. The monster went to say something to her but she refused to look at him, refused to acknowledge him or his trophy wife. She went up to Hector's father and when she spoke her voice did not tremble but there was no mistaking her fury. You shouldn't be here. Aren't you ashamed? You shouldn't be here. Her spittle landed on his shirt. She didn't give a fuck. Their lawyer went to say something to her but she was already turned on her heels and walking back to her husband and her friend. She was trembling as she sat down but she had achieved what she wanted. She had shamed him, she'd seen it in the old man's eyes. She had humiliated him. Good. That was exactly what he deserved. Aisha was the one who should be here, Aisha should be here by her side, but she'd had the human decency to do right by her family. But family was not only blood. She and Aisha were like sisters and Manolis knew this. He and his wife Koula had been there at Hugo's naming ceremony, and how many wog Christmases and wog Easters and namedays and birthdays had they shared with Manolis and Koula, how often had they been guests in their home? Too many to count. She was glad that she felt no urge to cry. He was in the wrong. She would never forgive him.

When they finally entered the courtroom she had to stifle her disappointment at how unimpressive it was. A lone Australian coat of arms sat above the judge's seat and already a stain of weak, lemon-coloured damp was rising in the corner of the hall. They took seats near the front and waited for their case to be heard.

The pettiness of people's lives, the mundane sadness of what people did, mostly for money, sometimes for love or out of boredom, but mostly for the desperate need for money, is what Rosie took away from that day. Young men—just boys really, but already with long, tedious prior convictions read out by equally young, bored coppers in hesitant monotonous tones—faced the dock for stealing toys, stealing radios, stealing iPods, stealing televisions, stealing handbags, stealing work tools, stealing food, stealing liquor. There were young mothers ripping off the dole, young girls shoplifting trinkets and mascara and DVDs and CDs and Barbie dolls for their kids. There were contrite men charged with drunk-driving offences or for having beaten up some stranger who looked the wrong way at them outside a pub. The police would read out the charges, a lawyer—they must have all been from Legal Aid, all young, anxious, weary—would make a stab at a defence and then the terse judge would make her ruling. She seemed burdened by her work, handing out fines, suspended sentences, a short stint in prison for a young bloke who was up for his fourth burglary charge.

After a while Rosie stopped listening. Every so often Gary would get up to go out for another cigarette and she would not look at him. She knew what he was thinking because she had begun to think it as well. What are we doing here? She must not think this way. Their charge was not petty. The crowded, unadorned, windowless room was far too hot, the atmosphere was constricting, claustrophobic. Rosie knew that this was the world Gary had been born into and which he had wanted to escape. It dawned on her that losing money was not equivalent to never having had money. That was why Gary had been so frightened of coming, why he had been so resistant, so angry. He did not want her exposed to this world.

Rosie held tight to Shamira's hand. It would soon be over. She was aware that the monster and his wife were sitting at the other end of the crowded courtroom. Manolis was sitting beside them. She did not glance their way once. She concentrated on the weary face of the judge. It was obvious the woman wanted to be kind, that she was not eager to send these young men and women to prison. But it was equally clear that she had long given up any interest in or passion for the process. Her words, her pronouncements, her explanations of protocol, her summations were all intoned in the same tired, disengaged manner.

Dear God, she prayed silently, grant me victory, please grant me victory.

* * *

Afterwards she realised they never had a chance. The policeman who stood up to read out the charge was the same man who had come to their house the night Hugo was slapped. Then he had seemed mature, direct; he'd been encouraging and seemed to share their outrage. On the stand, he now seemed red-faced, sullen, unconfident. He stumbled over the language of his report. The charge was assault with intention to do grievous harm to a child. The young policeman haltingly read out the details of the incident the previous summer, then Margaret rose and repeated the charges, coldly stating the ugliness of a man hitting a small child of three years of age. In this day and age, Margaret finished, nothing can excuse such behaviour. And then the giant lawyer rose and went in for the kill.

Though outside the courtroom he had seemed ludicrous, a ridiculous caricature, inside he was good, he was very good. What he did, what Margaret had not done, was tell a story. Her earnestness could not compete with this gift. He made a tale of that day and had everyone convinced of its truth. Rosie had been there at the barbecue, had seen that monster hit her child, but for the first time she was forced to see it through Harry's eyes. Yes, it was true, Hugo had raised the cricket bat. Yes, it was possible that Hugo could have hit the defendant's child. Yes, it had all happened so quickly, in an instant, it was over in a second. Yes, it was regrettable, all too human, all too understandable. Yes, it was true, a parent's first instinct is to protect their child. All of it true, but Rosie wanted to rise, stand up and shout, scream it out to the crowded courtroom: that's not what happened. That man, that man standing looking innocent up there, that man hit a child and I saw the look on that man's face. He wanted to hurt Hugo, he enjoyed it. I saw his face, he wanted to do it. He didn't do it to protect his child, he did it to hurt Hugo. That was the truth, she knew it, she could never forget his sneer. The lawyer was everything she had fantasised about. He was *Law and Order* and *Boston Legal*, Susan Dey in *LA Law*, Paul Newman in *The Verdict*. He was what money could buy. But he was wrong, he was a liar. She had seen the look of triumph in the man's eye when he hit her child. Rosie felt squashed, hopeless. The lawyer finished speaking and was now looking expectantly across at the judge. She heard Gary next to her let out a long, slow breath. Shamira was squeezing her hand. She did not need to look at her husband. They both knew it was over. But still, but still, she leaned forward, hoped for a miracle.

The judge's pronouncement was precise, intelligent, compassionate and crushing. For the first time that morning it seemed that she was genuinely interested in the nature of the case, as if she knew it did not belong to this overheated, crammed, ugly courthouse. First she reprimanded the police. It is possible, she began, her voice stinging, contemptuous, that you might have been a little too rash in pursuing a charge of assault. The young cop was staring straight ahead, straight into the faces of a crowd he knew hated him. The judge then looked down at the man standing before her. Rosie leaned forward to try to see his face. There was not a trace of arrogance there, no sneer; he looked ashamed and afraid. He's acting, she was sure of it. The bastard was acting. Violence was never a proper response to any situation, the judge scolded him, and especially never when a child was involved. The monster was nodding respectfully, in full agreement. Fucking liar, fucking wog cunt liar. But, the judge continued, she realised that the circumstances of this particular case were exceptional and that lacking further evidence she had to give him the benefit of the doubt. He was a hardworking businessman, a good citizen, a good husband and parent. His only previous dealing with the law was an adolescent misdemeanour from years ago. She could see no good coming from a conviction. She apologised. She actually apologised for the waste of his time. Then, coldly, the judge looked out to the room. Case dismissed.

Beside her, Shamira was crying but Rosie had no tears. She looked at her husband. He was staring straight ahead, refusing to catch her eye. The next case was about to be called and he suddenly sprang to his feet and marched out of the courtroom. Rosie and Shamira struggled to their feet.

They almost had to run to catch up with him as he headed for the carpark. They heard her name, then Gary's name called, and it was only then that he stopped and turned around.

Margaret was slowly walking up to them. 'I'm so sorry.'

Gary gave a harsh laugh. 'You're a cunt.'

Margaret looked as though she had been slapped—by the word, by his hatred.

'You know why you're a cunt?' Gary continued. 'It's not because of what happened in there. They obviously paid good money for their lawyer and he was worth every cent. You're not a cunt because you're free, you're not a cunt because you didn't do your work. You're a cunt because you didn't stop her, you're a cunt because you let her go ahead with it.' And for the first time in what felt like hours Gary looked directly at Rosie. A look of spite, of contempt, of utter derision.

He thinks it's my fault. Rosie was shocked. He thinks it's all my fault.

Margaret had crossed her arms. A small smile was on her lips. 'I'm sorry it didn't go your way. There wasn't much I could do about the charge.' Her tone, her smile, were glacial as she looked at Gary. 'You're the ones who went to the police.'

Gary's body suddenly sagged. Rosie wanted to go to him and put her arms around him but she was petrified of what he would do.

He was nodding, slowly, shamefaced. 'You're right. I'm sorry. I'm sorry for what I called you.' He turned and headed towards Shamira's car. 'I'm the cunt.'

He did not say a word all the way home. Rosie too was largely silent, occasionally offering muted assent to Shamira's rage over the judge's decision. She was only half-listening. Her thoughts were only for Hugo. What could she possibly tell him? That what happened was alright? That someone had the right to hit you, hurt you, even if you are defenceless? There was only one victim in this whole mess and the victim was her son. He must not be allowed to think that he was to blame.

Even before Shamira had finished parking outside their house, Rosie flung open the door and scrambled out onto the street. She ran to the front door, hearing Gary's rapid footsteps behind her. She must get to Hugo first. She turned the key, threw open the front door and rushed down the corridor. Connie and Hugo were in the kitchen, a sprawl of butcher's paper, pencils and Textas covering the tabletop. The girl's eyes flashed expectantly.

Rosie could hear her husband pounding down the hall. She gathered Hugo into her arms and kissed him. 'It's all over with, honey,' she whispered, kissing him again. 'That awful man who hit you has been punished. He got into such big trouble. He's never going to do such a thing again. He's going to jail.'

She swung around. Gary was standing there, his mouth hanging open, staring at her.

'Isn't that right, Daddy?' she prompted. 'The bad man has been punished, hasn't he?' Oh, he must understand. He must understand that she was doing this for her son.

Gary took a step forward and she cowered, thinking he was going to strike her. Instead he collapsed into a chair and slowly nodded his head. 'That's right, Huges. The bad man has been punished.' There was only heaviness, surrender in his voice.

She just wanted to be with her son. She didn't want to have to explain anything to Connie, didn't want any more of Shamira's consolation, didn't want her husband's accusation or defeat. All she wanted was to be with her son. She took Hugo out into the backyard and lay back on the overgrown lawn. She told him the story that she had been waiting so long to tell him. She described to him how the nice policeman who had come to their house that night—did Hugo remember him, how kind he had been—well, he explained to the court what had happened. You should have heard it. The court was full of people and they were all shocked, they couldn't believe it, they were horrified. She then told him how the judge, she was a lady judge, Hugo, stood up and pointed to the horrible man who had hurt him. Do you think you know what she said to him? Hugo nodded, he looked up at her, smiling. No one can ever hit a child? That's right, baby, that's exactly what she said. And he's going to go to jail? Yes, the bad man is going to jail. Hugo grabbed tufts of grass and pulled them out of the dry, hard soil. He looked up at her again. Will Adam be mad at me cause I made his uncle go to jail? Darling, no, no, of course he won't be mad. No one is mad at you. No one. Hugo touched her breasts. Can I have boobie? She hesitated. Hugo, she said firmly, next year you are going to be in kinder. You know you can't have boobie when you go to kinder. The boy nodded, then brightening, he touched her chest again. Can I have boobie now? Yes, she laughed, kissing him, she felt like she couldn't stop kissing him. They lay on the grass, Hugo sprawled across her breasts and belly. She heard the screen door slam. Gary was standing above them.

'Shamira's taken Connie home.'

She nodded. She did not feel like talking.

'I'm going to the pub.'

Of course you are.

She closed her eyes. She could feel the sun on her, the tantalising pull on her nipple as Hugo suckled. She heard the front door slam and let out a sigh of relief.

He had not returned by dinner time. She'd taken the phone off the hook, put her mobile on silent. She thought she would go mad from all the calls during the afternoon. Shamira had left a message, then Aish, then Anouk, then Shamira again. Connie too had called. At one point in the afternoon, while she was watching and rewatching the Wiggles video with Hugo, they had heard a knock at the door. She had put her finger to her lips. Shh, she had whispered, let's pretend we're not home. He had imitated her action, putting his own finger to his mouth. Shhh, he hissed. Then suddenly he'd jerked forward on the couch.

'What if it's Richie?'

'Richie's in school. It's not Richie.'

'Can we ring Richie? Can we tell him the bad man is in jail?'

'We'll call him tomorrow.'

He wanted a brother, he needed a sibling. It was time to have the conversation again. She and Gary had been procrastinating for too long. No, that was being unfair on herself. All she had been able to think about the last few months was the bloody court case. Well, it was over, she had to move on, she couldn't let herself get depressed. Next year she would be turning forty, getting too old. She was ready for another child, she would love to be pregnant again. They couldn't talk about it tonight, he'd be too drunk. They'd talk it through on the weekend, talk about schools for Hugo, maybe she could bring up the subject of buying a house. And fuck him, if he said no she'd just put a hole in the condom. He wouldn't know. Couldn't he see how desperate his son was for a sibling, how he hungered to play with other kids, how he needed a brother?

By ten o'clock Gary was still not home. She was on her third glass of white wine and had taken half of an old valium she'd found in the bathroom cabinet. But she could not sleep. He never stayed out till late on a weeknight. He had left his mobile behind so there was no way to contact him. She tried to fall asleep next to Hugo but it was impossible. She could not stop thinking that he might do something terrible to himself. She couldn't sit still, kept pacing around the kitchen staring up at the clock. At ten-thirty she made up her mind. Her fingers shook as she punched in the number. Shamira answered on the third ring.

'Rosie, what's wrong?'

She was inarticulate, a mess, all she could let out of her were loud, bestial sobs. She had gone to ring Aisha, but then the thought of getting Hector on the other end overwhelmed her. She became aware of Shamira's panicked questions, could hear Bilal on the other end asking what was wrong.

She took deep breaths, found words. 'I don't know where Gary is. I'm so scared.'

'Do you want to come over?' She could hear Bilal raise an objection and then Shamira quickly hushing him. 'Come over. Come over now.'

Hugo whimpered as she carried him out to the car but he fell back to sleep as soon as she strapped him in the child seat. She hardly knew how she managed to drive to her friend's house, she felt drunk, high, could hardly see through her tears.

Shamira took Hugo from her and put him into bed next to Ibby.

Bilal was dressed in a hoodie and track-pants, and was drinking tea when Rosie arrived.

'I'm frightened he's going to do something terrible to himself.'

'Do you know where he is?'

Rosie shook her head. 'He said he was going to the pub.'

'Which pub?'

Bilal's questions were clipped, harsh. She couldn't answer him, she looked down at her feet. She needed new slippers. The seams were fraying, they were falling apart. She had no clue which pub her husband was at, she didn't know which pubs he went to. That was his life, it was separate from hers and Hugo's. She didn't want to know the places he went to, the people he saw, the things he did when he was drunk.

'I don't know.'

Bilal gulped the last of his tea. 'I'll go and find him.'

Rosie noticed the exchange of looks between husband and wife. Shamira's eyes offered sheer, unadorned gratitude.

Struggling, wobbly, she got to her feet. 'I'm coming with you.'

'No.'

She struggled free of Shamira and followed Bilal down the hallway.

'Bilal will find him,' her friend called out to her.

'No, I'm going with him.' He's my husband. I have to go.

First they went to the Clifton, close to her house, but it was already closed. They tried the Terminus and the Irish pub on Queens Parade before heading into Collingwood. They found him in a pub in Johnston Street, he was sitting in the back, at a table with three other men. As they approached she saw that two of the other men were Aborigines. She was glad that Bilal was with her. He would know what to say, how to act, what to do. He could protect her.

Gary was so pissed he had to squint, to focus his eyes before he recognised them. He started to snort with laughter. He turned to one of the men, an enormous man, all heaving belly, taut arm muscles but lumpy fat everywhere else, his round moon face and shaved bald head the colour of dark ale. His skin leathery, battered. One of his eyes was half-closed, a vicious purple bruise spreading around it. Gary was pointing up at Bilal.

'That's him,' he slurred. 'That's the one of your mob I was telling you about.'

Gary looked proud of himself, as if he had conjured Bilal up at will.

The large man extended his hand. Rosie could see his nose had been broken a few times, that his arm was full of spidery, faded tattoos.

'How are you, cuz?'

Bilal shook hands with the two Aboriginal men at the table. The other white man, a young weedy fellow with a greasy Magpies baseball cap backwards on his head was tapping his finger compulsively on the table. Bilal ignored him.

'Have a beer, cuz.'

'I don't drink.'

The large man started to laugh. The rolls of fat on him bounced, a shimmering dance down the length of his body.

'Just one drink. Come on.'

Bilal's refusal was almost imperceptible. Just a slight shake of his head. He pointed to Gary. 'I've come to take this man home. He's got responsibilities. He's got a young 'un.'

'We'll have a drink and then you can take him home. No problem.' The large man winked at Rosie. 'You want a drink, love, don't ya?'

Bilal didn't let her speak. He tapped Gary's shoulder.

Gary shrank away from him. 'Fuck off. I want a drink. Buy me a drink or fuck off.'

The other men at the table started to laugh. Gary looked surprised, then pleased, grinning at the men around the table.

The large man put up his hand in warning to Bilal. 'It looks like your mate wants to stay here, cuz. Don't worry, we'll take care of him.' He was directing the words to her.

Rosie was conscious that everyone in the pub was now looking at them, that the publican was leaning over the bar. She begged her husband. 'Gary, please, come home.'

Gary shook his head, violently, adamant, like a child. He looked like Hugo. 'I don't want to go home. I don't want anything to do with home.'

It happened suddenly. Bilal grabbed Gary by his shirt collar and hoisted him off his seat. She heard the fabric tear and in that moment she let out a scream. She was terrified. Bilal had become Terry again, the young man who liked to drink, who liked to pick a fight, the young man who terrified her. She was scared he was going to hit her husband. With the scream the publican had come rushing over to the table.

The large man struggled to his feet but the publican placed a warning hand on his shoulder. 'I'll deal with this, mate.'

Bilal was still holding on to Gary, who looked shocked, afraid, again like a little boy.

The publican was short, but he was fit, barrel-chested; he fixed Bilal with a fierce stare. 'You leave now or I call the cops.'

For a moment she thought Bilal was going to strike him. Instead, he let go of Gary's shirt, turned and walked out of the pub. The other white man at Gary's table hooted with derision. 'You're no Anthony Mundine, are ya?' The two Aboriginal men were silent, stone-faced.

'Gary, please come home.'

'Fuck off.'

She had no idea what she should do.

Gary sighed and looked at her with pity. 'Rosie, just go home. I'm not going to do anything stupid. I just want to get pissed, don't you get it?' His eyes were pleading with her. 'I just want to get so drunk that I forget that you or Hugo even exist.'

Bilal was waiting for her in the car. He started the engine as soon as he saw her. She got in and pulled the seatbelt across her.

'I'm sorry.'

Bilal pointed to a man who had come out of the pub, following her. He had lit a cigarette and was looking towards the car.

'Do you know what he's doing?'

She looked over. She had no idea who the man was. She shook her head.

'He's being kind to strangers,' Bilal said quietly, starting to drive away. 'He's making sure I don't do anything to you. He's letting me know he's clocked my licence plate. He's wondering what a nice white woman like you is doing with a boong like me.' With that Bilal started to laugh, his body rocking back and forth, it was that hilarious, his body bashing again and again into his car seat.

He drove her and Hugo home, he wouldn't let her drive. You're drunk, he said. She put her child to bed and came out into the kitchen. Bilal was smoking a cigarette. A charge swept through her body. She could smell the night on him, the adrenaline, the sweat, harsh, intoxicating. He filled her kitchen, his face, his rough skin, his shining black eyes, so handsome and so ugly at the same time. What if I got on my knees for you? She suddenly thought. What if I sucked your cock? Would you like me better if I sucked your cock? Flashes of audio from Gary's porn videos: Do you like black cock? Do you want to suck my big black cock?

Bilal indicated a chair and Rosie sat down opposite him. He pointed to his cigarette packet and Rosie, trembling, took one. He lit it for her.

'I'm going to say something and I want you to let me finish before interrupting. Do you understand?'

She nodded. She felt ridiculously shy.

'That was the first time I have gone in a pub for years, for a long time now.' His voice sounded curious, as if his own words had surprised him. 'I don't know why I ever liked those places. They're foul.' His eyes narrowed.

She must not look away, she must not be scared of him.

'I don't want you or your husband or your son in my life. You remind me of a life I don't ever want to go back to. I don't want you to talk to my wife, I don't want you to be her friend. I just want to be good, I just want to protect my family. I don't think you're any good, Rosie. Sorry, it's just your mob. You've got bad blood. We've escaped your lot, me and my Sammi. Do you get it? Will you promise me that you won't ring or see my wife? I just want you to promise me that, that you'll leave my family alone.'

She felt nothing. No, that was not quite true. She felt relief. She was right: he had always distrusted her. He knew everything she was.

'Yes,' she answered. 'I promise.'

'Good. I'll drive your car back here in the morning. I'll leave the keys in the letterbox.' Bilal stubbed out his cigarette, picked up his own keys, and left her house without a word. For a long time she did not move. Then she walked over to the fridge, took out the bottle and poured herself another wine.

She was a slut. That was what she had become when her father left, when they lost the house. She was sixteen. The girls at school had stopped talking to her—not all at once, not even deliberately; they just stopped inviting her over, and not one friend from school came to visit the new flat. They said it was too far away, that it might as well be a thousand miles from their beach. It was then that she learned about money, how money meant everything.

She got back at them by sleeping with their boyfriends, with their brothers. She fucked their fathers. She continued doing it at the new school, the state school, full of boys to fuck. She had fucked and fucked, one night allowing herself to be fucked by seven of them, each taking turns. She had bled, her cunt had torn. Everyone at the new school knew what she was. The new girl was a slut.

Only Aisha had protected her. How she wished Aish had married Eddie—but, of course, Aish was too good for Eddie. Aish protected her, introduced her to Anouk. She had looked up to the older girls, they had offered her a vision of a life beyond Perth, beyond the desert and the ocean, they had encouraged her to escape. With them she never let on what she was. She hid her real self from them. Then they both left, went east to Melbourne and she was alone. She met Qui. He was only thirty-five, but that made him close to an old man back then. He was her older man, her lover, her businessman paramour from Hong Kong. Qui had looked after her, he was the first to buy her things. She had stopped fucking other boys. She was only a slut for Qui. Then he left. Without a word. She didn't have a number, an address, she didn't even know his surname. He just disappeared, bored with her. Qui knew what she was—he could see through her. The people she loved had no idea who she was, what she had been. Aisha didn't know, Gary didn't know, Anouk didn't. Hugo would never find out. She was what Bilal inferred. He had always seen through her, like her mother had. You're dirty, Rosalind. You're just trash, Rosalind, just rubbish. You're a slut.

No. She was a mother. It seemed to take an eternity to get out of the chair. But she had to. She staggered down the corridor, pushed open her bedroom door and collapsed next to Hugo, who had awoken in tears. She cuddled him tight, so tight into her that they became one, were one. It's alright, Hugo, the bad man has gone, the bad man won't harm us. Repeating it, over and over, she and her child fell asleep.

The next morning she found her husband passed out on the lounge-room floor. His stench made her retch; he had shat in his pants. She got him up, struggled with him to the bathroom where she stripped him of his soiled clothes, bathed him, put him into bed. She fed Hugo, rang Gary's boss, told him that Gary was too sick to come into work. She took Hugo to the park and played with him on the swings. When they returned her car was parked outside their house, the keys were indeed in the letterbox. In the afternoon she rang Aisha on the mobile and when her friend started to console her, Rosie burst into tears. He got away with it, Aish, he fucking got away with it.

Gary, repentant, guilty, did not have a drink till Friday evening. On Saturday night she cooked a baked snapper and made french fries for Hugo. They were in the middle of *Willy Wonka and the Chocolate Factory* when Aisha called to tell her that Shamira and Bilal had bid on the house in Thomastown. They got it, it was theirs.

'I'm so glad,' Rosie gushed loudly on the phone, and even though Aisha could not see her, she made sure she had a wide, brilliant smile on her face. 'I'm so glad for them,' she kept repeating, 'so glad.'

MANOLIS

It's a terrible thing, just terrible, he thought to himself, glancing at the black and white portrait, to die so young. He adjusted his glasses, squinted, and refocused his eyes. The boy was only thirty-two. There was a short obituary. Stephanos Chaklis, thirty-two years of age, loving son of Pantelis and Evangeliki Chaklis. Our precious loving son. The funeral service was to take place in Our Lady's Church of the Way, Balwyn. No wife, no children. No indication of what had caused the young man's death. Manolis scrutinised the photograph again. The young man was smiling lazily at the camera, his hair neat, short, like a soldier's. It must have been taken at a wedding or a baptism. The boy looked uncomfortable in the high collar and tight squeeze of his shirt and tie. Such a good-looking lad, gone before he could father a child. It is a terrible thing to die young.

Manolis peered over his glasses this time and looked up at the sky, to where they said the heavens resided. If there is a God, You're a fool. There is no logic or fairness in this world You have created; how can You be a Supreme Being? He immediately and silently apologised to the Virgin for his blasphemous thought, but he felt no compulsion to take it back, or be ashamed of thinking it. Now sixty-nine years of age, still blessedly fit except for the occasional pain of rheumatism, Manolis felt himself further removed from religion and the Church than at any other point in his life. As a young man he had not dared risk God's wrath by questioning His purpose. Now he did not give a damn. Fuck it. There was no Paradise and there was no

Hell and if there was a God, He was worse than inscrutable. What did exist was the cold, cruel truth of a young man, dead—from cancer or a car accident or suicide or God knows what—at the obscene age of thirty-two. Manolis shivered—a ghost had walked across his spine—and he folded the paper to read the rest of the death notices. The young man's face haunted him. He wanted to forget it.

Anna Paximidis, seventy-eight. That was more like it. Anastasios Christoforous, sixty-three. Not a grand age, but he looked fat and unhealthy in the photograph. Too much of the good life, Anastasios, Manolis admonished the photo. Dimitrios Kafentsis, seventy-two. Fine, fine—that was a decent age, enough to experience something of old age, but not too old to have the body fall apart into useless dependency. That was his greatest fear.

His wife's voice suddenly screeched and he dropped the paper. 'Manoli!' she called out in a shout loud enough to frighten the dead souls trapped in the newsprint. 'Do you want coffee?'

'Yes,' he grunted.

Another screech. 'What?'

'Yes,' he called out this time. He went back to the paper.

Thimios Karamantzis. There was no photograph. Just the age at death. Seventy-one years old. The funeral was to be held in Doncaster. He was mourned by his wife, Paraskevi, his children, Stella and John, and his grandchildren, Athena, Samuel and Timothy. Manolis laid down the paper again and made some quick mental calculations. The age seemed right; Thimios would only have been a couple of years older than he was. As for Doncaster, who the hell knew where people had ended up? They had all scattered to the far ends of this too-huge city. But of course it must be Thimios. The same family name, a wife called Paraskevi. Of course it was him. How long had it been since he had last seen him? Manolis cursed his slowing mind. Think, he berated himself. Was it Elisavet's baptism? My God, my God, over forty years ago.

His wife brought out the coffee and sat on the old kitchen chair that had been banished to the verandah when the children still lived at home. The vinyl back and seat had been ripped to shreds by generations of cats, the legs appeared almost gold from the rust, but he and Koula could never bring themselves to get rid of it. It had been with them since their first house in North Melbourne. She picked up the front page of *Neos Kosmos* and started reading it while softly blowing across the surface of her coffee. She could never bring herself to drink it hot.

'What are the papers telling us, husband?'

He grunted. 'I was just looking through the death notices.'

'Read them out to me.'

Manolis began to read, slowly, one eye cocked towards his wife.

She clucked sadly on hearing about the death of the thirty-two-year-old lad. Unlike Manolis she did not curse God, but proceeded to lament the inequity of fate. He read out Thimios's name and at first her face registered nothing. He began to read out another notice when he suddenly heard her gasp. He stopped, and peered at his wife over the rim of his spectacles.

'*Manoli mou*, do you think that could be Thimio from Ipeiros?'

'I think it could be.'

'The poor bastard.'

They sat in silence, each drifting off into separate memories. Manolis and Thimios had worked together at the Ford plant, had sacrificed their youth to that job. The man was a hard worker but, much more than that, he had been a good friend. The best parties, the best nights, were always to be had at Thimios's house, for he was a generous and exuberant host. His wife, Paraskevi, a ravishing, Slavic-looking brunette, was also full of life and she too loved to entertain. Their house always seemed full of music. Thimios played guitar and would often drag Koula up with him to sing. Manolis had never had much time for that peasant crap that Thimios and Koula enjoyed, all that wailing nonsense about eagles and shepherds and godforsaken clumps of rock, but his wife had had a thrilling voice when she was young. It was at Thimios's house that he had first met Koula. He had not taken much notice of her at first—she was pretty enough, a little too short perhaps, not unlike so many of the young village girls who had come out to Australia back then, ship after ship after ship-load of them. He had paid her scant attention until he heard her sing. She smiled like happiness itself when she was lost in a song, and her voice was clear and galvanising: like pure mountain water dancing downstream, like the first warm rays of the summer sun.

That following Monday on the assembly line, he had asked Thimios about her.

'She's a good girl. And she's pretty.'

They had to yell to hear each other above the ferocious clamour of the machines.

'She's a little short.'

'What the fuck are you looking for, Manoli, a German? Koula's pretty, and a real homemaker. Paraskevi knew her family back in Greece. She's good stock.'

The following weekend, Paraskevi and Thimios had organised another party. Manolis hardly spoke to Koula, but he watched her closely. She was fine looking, no Sophia Loren, but she was delightful when she smiled. She also had spirit, courage; it was obvious in her singing, as it was in the way she dared to contradict and argue with the men. At work the following week, Manolis had interrogated Thimios about her family.

'What can I tell you? From what I hear they are a decent, good family, from a village outside Yiannina, just like Paraskevi. No money there, but that's no different to any of us. She's got no one out here except a first cousin, a good man, a damned right-winger but not one of those crazy ones. You can argue with him. Koula lives with him and his wife in Richmond.' Thimios had then grinned slyly. 'Are you going to take her?'

Had he answered his friend straight away, had he answered then and there that morning in the factory? Age was the most damnable thing. There were some incidents from the distant past that he could recall with precision and clarity, that stood out more vividly than events that had occurred only a week ago. He could clearly see Koula singing, Thimios playing the guitar, he could remember the high ornate Victorian ceiling of his friend's house. But he could not recall what his answer had been to his friend that day. Had he made up his mind by then to propose to Koula? Had it been a few days after that conversation or had it been weeks? Months? It was no good, his memory was incapable of taking him back there. It didn't matter; sometime after that conversation, he and Thimios had walked to her cousin's house and Manolis had asked permission to marry Koula.

She had been lost in similar memories as well. 'We met at Thimio and Paraskevi's house.'

Manolis nodded and looked across at her. Her plump cheeks were lowered, there were tears slowly falling onto the paper. He leaned over and folded her hand in his. She smiled at him, called herself a foolish old woman, but she did not let go of his hand. Getting old was a chore, a misery indeed, but it did have its concessions. Manolis doubted that there had been a day in his forties and most of his fifties that did not pass without him regretting ever marrying, without him cursing the terrible burden of having a wife and family. But age did silence dreams, did mellow desires, even the most ferocious lusts and fantasies. It was clear to him now that Koula was a good spouse. She was steadfast. How many men could say that of their wives?

'We must go to the funeral.'

Koula nodded emphatically. Her coffee was now cool enough for her to sip. 'You could always have a good laugh with him, couldn't you?'

Manolis grinned. 'He was a joker.'

'It would be lovely to see Paraskevi.'

'Yes, you two were like sisters.'

Koula snorted loudly. Her face tightened into a sneer. 'Closer than sisters. My sisters have forgotten me.'

Manolis ignored her. He was in no mood to listen to such rubbish. Of course her family had not forgotten her. But they were all too far away, they had all passed through a thousand lifetimes, of marriage, work, children, grandchildren, death and loss, which they had been unable to share with her. Oceans, a half a world separated them. This was fate. No one was to blame.

'Not one of them can be bothered to pick up the phone.'

'Maria rang on Adam's nameday.'

Koula snorted again. 'Don't talk to me about that one. She rang me to tell me all about her holiday in Turkey and Bulgaria. She just wanted to show off, tell me how European and cultured she now was.' Koula drained the last of her coffee and banged down the cup into the saucer. 'They can all go to hell.'

'Maybe it's time we went back for a visit.'

'Again? Husband, you're crazy. They can visit us for once. I've been in this godforsaken country for over forty years and not one of those bastards has bothered to come to see me. Not one of them bothered to come to bury their brother here. Why should we go? Why should we bother?' Koula shook her head vigorously. 'No, Manoli, I'm staying put. Who's going to look after the grand-children?'

He felt his irritation rising. He looked over to the garden. It was time to plant the broad beans. Thinking of soil and nature calmed his mind.

But Koula was too intoxicated by her wounded pride and self-righteousness to let the topic go. 'Who's going to look after the little ones?' she repeated.

'Their parents.' His tone was gruff, angry, and he was glad when the phone suddenly rang. He was in no mood for an argument. Koula rushed to answer and Manolis grabbed the opportunity to work in the garden. He groaned as he rose from his seat. You damn legs, he swore, you are betraying me. He bent over with difficulty and started digging to make a bed for the beans.

Before long Koula reappeared, standing in the doorway. 'It's too early to plant them.'

Manolis kept digging away at the earth, sinking in handfuls of dry broad beans into the earth.

'That was Ecttora. I told him about Thimio. He says he can't remember him.'

'Of course not.' Manolis gritted his teeth and slowly straightened his back. He banged his hands together, flicking off the soil and grit. 'Hector was five, six, when we left North Melbourne.'

'I suppose you're right. But remember how Thimio would always play with him, swing him up to the ceiling so Ecttora could bang it with his fist? He loved that.'

'What did he want?'

'He's bringing the kids over tonight for a meal. The Indian has to work late again.'

His son had been married to Aisha for nearly fifteen years and still Koula could rarely bring herself to utter her daughter-in-law's name.

'That woman cares more about her work than she does her family.'

And you're a jealous sow. 'What do you want her to do? She has responsibilities, she's a professional. She has her business.'

'It's Hector's business as well.'

Manolis turned away from her and a jolt of pain rushed up his left leg. He grimaced and swore. 'It isn't Hector's business—it's hers. Our son is a public servant, his wife is the business woman. They're both good workers. They are both fortunate. Stop your complaining.'

Koula's mouth tightened. Manolis walked past her. At the verandah he took off his gardening slippers and banged them against the concrete. Specks of earth and stone flew into the air.

'She's refusing to go to Harry's party.'

Manolis sat on the edge of the verandah and rubbed his foot. He looked up at the sky. Dark oppressive clouds were slowly rolling in from the north. It was weeks since they had had rain. God willing, there would be some soon.

'She's an idiot,' Koula announced. 'An ungrateful idiot. Why does she have to shame us, why does she have to shame poor Ecttora?'

He did not answer her. He looked around for the cat. He had kept some fishheads from last night's meal for her. He started calling out for her. 'Penelope, Penelope, *Pssh pssh*.'

Koula raised her voice. 'Why couldn't he have married a Greek girl?'

It was not a question. It was a lamentation that he knew he was cursed to hear till the end of his days on earth. He'd ignore her, he would not be dragged into an argument. But he glanced up and Koula's petulant face disgusted him. Sometimes, sometimes a woman's foolishness was just too much to bear.

'Marrying a Greek did nothing for our daughter, did it? Marrying a Greek messed up our daughter's life.'

'Go to hell.' Koula, vexed, raised a contemptuous fist to him before stepping back inside the house. 'You're always defending the Indian,' she cursed him, before slamming the door shut.

Blessed peace. A couple of doves cooed, and he heard a scramble across the back fence. Penelope jumped into the garden and then rushed straight to him. She purred as he rubbed her back.

'How's my pretty girl,' he whispered. 'Don't listen to that idiot inside. She's gone crazy.'

The cat purred. Ignoring the clutch of pain as he rose, Manolis walked into the kitchen. Koula was banging plates together, preparing lunch.

'Where did you put the fishheads?'

No answer.

'Koula, where did you put the fish from last night?'

'I threw them out.'

'For God's sake, wife, I told you I wanted to feed them to the cat.'

'I'm sick of that cat. I want to get rid of her. The kids keep touching her. They'll get a disease.'

'That cat's cleaner than they are.'

'Aren't you ashamed of yourself? You think more of that cat than you do about your grandchildren.' Koula shook her head in disbelief, chopping at a cucumber with fury. 'You are not a man. I'll say it till the day I die. You are not a man.'

You'll never die. You're a witch who will live forever. Manolis searched through the fridge and found the fishheads rolled up in aluminium foil. He took a deep breath and kicked shut the fridge door.

'Koula,' he started calmly. 'You know that I don't defend her over this stupid trouble with Harry and Sandi. I want her to go to Harry's party.'

'Then talk to her. She listens to you, God knows why.' Koula was not yet ready to make peace.

The Devil take you. 'Make me a coffee.'

'I'm getting lunch ready.'

'I want another coffee.'

'Are you going to talk to her?'

Manolis looked around the kitchen. Koula had studded the walls with pictures of the grandchildren. Adam, just born, Melissa at the zoo, Sava and Angeliki at the village in Greece, school photos, Christmas photos, the kids all sitting on Father Christmas's knee. Why couldn't they remain children? They grew up and they became selfish. It happened to all of them, without an exception. He was weary; man lived too long but clung desperately, foolishly, onto life. If he was a dog someone would have taken him out already and put a bullet in his head.

'Are you going to talk to her?'

Again. This was going to be a battle.

'Make me a damn coffee.' Manolis rubbed at his calf.

'Are you in pain?'

'A little.'

'When are you going to talk to her?'

The unpleasant harsh odour of fish. Thimios had taught him how to fish. On Sunday mornings they would rise at dawn, throw their gear into the back of the station wagon and head straight to Port Melbourne. They were young then, the country was new, and the laws were different. They'd drive with a bottle of beer between their legs, smoking cigarettes, no seatbelts, free men, singing, arguing, telling dirty stories.

'I'm going to my friend's funeral,' he announced, walking out to the verandah. 'My friend has died. Hector, Aisha, Harry, Sandi, the whole damn lot of them can wait. I'll bury my friend and then I'll talk to her. And make me a damn coffee.'

Penelope was clawing at his trouser leg. He smiled down at her and dropped the fishheads on the concrete. He sat back in the old armchair and watched the cat eat.

His initial thought was that they'd made a mistake in attending the funeral. He was unfamiliar with the church and they had got lost in the backstreets of Doncaster. He was driving and Koula was navigating and at one point, fed up with his shouting, she had slammed the Melways shut and refused to answer him. It was a mild winter's morning, chilly, frost on the lawn, but the sun peeked out intermittently from the bank of dark grey cloud and he was hot in his suit. It was years since he'd worn it and it no longer fitted him, he had to clutch in his stomach to slide into the pants. This had made Manolis smile. You are never going to lose this fat now, friend, he'd whispered into the bathroom mirror. He was sweating as they climbed the steps into the church.

The service had begun and he and Koula crossed themselves, kissed the icons and moved into the back of the congregation. The church was full, mostly old people like themselves. A woman, clothed in heavy, shapeless black, was weeping quietly in the front pew, supported by a straight-backed young woman also dressed in black. That must be Paraskevi and her daughter. He craned his neck to look at them but he could not see clearly past the rows of people. He looked around, trying to see if he could recognise a face. His memory seemed to fail him. There was a bent-over old man, his hair completely white, who seemed familiar. But he was not sure. He realised that Koula had begun a quiet, dignified sobbing. Manolis reminded himself that he was here to bury a friend, and a good man at that, and he lowered his head. He closed his eyes and pushed back into his memory until he recalled the smiling face of his friend, the laughter they'd shared. When he opened his eyes again the tears fell effortlessly.

He was shivering by the time the service approached its end. Before the altar sat the heavy wooden casket that contained his old friend's body. It was open; he would have to look at Thimios. The congregation shuffled slowly towards the altar. Manolis was worried that he might faint. He slipped off his jacket and carried it over his arm. He looked up at the forbidding saints painted on the walls. You pricks, he thought to himself, you liars, there is no Heaven, there is only this earth, this one unjust earth. Ahead of him a woman lifted up a young boy to look down into the coffin. The boy was clearly terrified. What madness, what foolishness these rituals were. The bereaved family had formed a line and begun to accept people's commiserations. He tried to see Paraskevi's face but it was shrouded by a black veil. Her body seemed tiny, thin. The woman with the child stepped away from the casket. Manolis took a deep breath and looked down into the coffin.

He did not recognise the impassive dead face. Thimios had gone bald, fat, an old man in a shiny brown polyester suit. Manolis felt nothing looking down at this stranger. He made the appropriate sounds, shed a tear, and then walked to where the immediate family were lined up along the altar. He was anxious about having to speak, to possibly have to introduce himself. Would they wonder who he was, why he was there? He waited for Koula to reach him. His wife came up next to him and he looked up at the line. At that moment, the widow turned and looked at them.

And Paraskevi struggled to her feet and fell into their arms. Through the fine mesh lace of the veil, Manolis could see that her eyes were the same as he remembered. She was old, she looked as though her back could no longer support her, her hair had thinned, her face was a mass of wrinkles, but her eyes were the same. She clutched Manolis's arm tight and though she was unable to say a word, the ferocious desperation of her grip said all that needed to be said. My sister, my sister, she managed to whisper in Koula's ear and then fell into long, anguished moans. He could see members of the family along the line looking at them, wondering who these strangers were to have such an effect on their mother, their grand-mother. Manolis, crying like a child now, choked out a strangled 'I'm sorry' and Paraskevi released her hold on him.

'Please come to the house.'

He nodded. As he moved along the line, the young people shook his hand firmly. They did not know him but understood that it was important he was here. All his doubts melted away. He was glad they had come.

The sun was still shining when he stepped off the back steps of the church into the carpark. An old man in a jacket but with no tie was smoking a cigarette. The man's face was as wrinkled as an acorn, and his neck was scarred a deep raw pink. A worker's face and a worker's neck. His grey hair was cut very short—Manolis guessed that it was the number one on the barber's clippers—and he had the good fortune to not have gone bald. The man looked across at him and smiled sadly. Then, with a quizzical squint in his eyes, he walked over, breaking out into a grin.

'*Re*, Manoli?'

'Yes.'

'You damned cocksucker.' The grin had now spread across his whole face. 'You don't remember me?'

Manolis desperately tried to recall who this might be. Panicked flashes of names and faces entered his mind. But nothing concrete, nothing to hold on to. Koula had come up beside him, wiping her eyes.

'And this must be my Koula.'

His wife offered the stranger a nervous cold nod of her head, but suddenly she dropped her handkerchief and squealed. 'Arthur!'

The old man hugged her. He winked at Manolis as he peered over her shoulder. 'My gorgeous, gorgeous Koula. Why did you marry that loser instead of me?'

Manolis slowly crouched and picked up his wife's handkerchief. As he touched the wet cotton he remembered the man. It came to him immediately, cleanly; sweaty nights dancing at the clubs in Swan Street. Thanassis—Arthur—his shirt would always be drenched at the end of the night. Manolis tried to recall if there was a family connection between Thanassis and Thimios. Second cousins? That did not really matter. What mattered was the friendship they had shared.

Manolis shook the man's hand, he could not let it go. Thanassis finally pulled it away. 'You're going to rip it off, friend.'

Koula smiled up at him, and then looked around at the people milling around the carpark. 'Where's Eleni?'

'Who knows?' Thanassis laughed at Koula's bewilderment. 'We divorced years ago. I think she's in Greece now.'

Manolis could not think of anything to say. Koula cleared her throat. The last of the congregation was leaving and the pallbearers were preparing to carry the casket. Thanassis stepped on his cigarette butt.

'Are you going to the burial?'

Manolis shrugged and looked at his wife. They had not decided on what they would do after the service. But they had to go to the house. They had promised Paraskevi that they would go to the house.

Koula answered for him. 'No. Let them bury Thimio in peace. But we are going to the house afterwards.'

Thanassis nodded sadly. 'Good. I'm doing the same.' He dropped his arms across Koula and Manolis. 'Come on, I'll shout you a coffee.'

He took them to a small café in the middle of brick-veneer suburbia. The place was run by a Persian family; thick woollen rugs adorned the walls, photographs of 1950s Tehran and Qum were hung between the gaps. Thanassis led them through the dark interior, out behind the kitchen to a small courtyard. Three weather-beaten, cheap aluminium circular tables were propped up tight next to each other; the seating consisted of rickety unbalanced benches, the paint peeled back to reveal the dark hard wood underneath. The café sat on a crest of a small hill and the city loomed in the distance behind the low palings of the fence. Stretched out between them and the city skyline there was an ocean of red-tiled roofs, the soaring spindly foliage of gum trees and elms, little islands of green now and then puncturing that crimson sea.

The coffee was excellent, strong and bitter. Thanassis smoked and talked openly of his life. Manolis was reminded that the man had always been a braggart. One of his sons, Thanassis explained, was a lawyer. The other son—Manolis could not remember if he was the eldest—ran a restaurant in Brighton. Thanassis's wife had had a breakdown. Slowly her mind had become diseased to the point where she could not leave the house, all she wanted to do was stay in bed. Koula made appropriately distressed ejaculations, but Thanassis raised his hand to dismiss them.

'Don't waste your pity on her.' He then suddenly banged his fist on the table, upsetting Koula's coffee. Thanassis, apologising, called out to the kitchen. 'Zaita, bring us a cloth.'

He continued with his story. 'I paid for the best doctors, I had her in the best hospital in this city. The money I spent on that bitch. But nothing could cure her. She came back from the hospital unchanged. She just lay around the house all day, doing nothing. I'd come back from work, after working like a damned heathen slave all day in the factory, and she would not have lifted a finger. The house was dirty, the bed unmade, nothing cooking on the stove. The house stank. It stank, I tell you. What man can live like that?' His gaze moved between Manolis and Koula, as if daring them to contradict him. 'What can you do with a woman like that?'

They were interrupted by the young waitress who silently wiped the table clean. She was petite, dark, Oh God, oh God, she was luscious thought Manolis. If only he were still a young man.

Koula ignored her, she was smiling sadly at Thanassis. 'A woman who cannot look after her own house is not good for anything,' she declared. She patted Thanassis's hand. 'We've become spoilt, Thanassis, we don't know how good we have it.'

Manolis stifled a laugh. They were flirting with each other. Thanassis had always been a *manga*, the most hopeless adulterer Manolis had ever met. As a youth the man had been cocky and his burly frame, sly grin and lazy, roguish eyes had always turned women's heads. Manolis experienced a pang of ancient jealousy, then it quickly disappeared. The waitress brought Koula another coffee and Manolis thanked her. The girl smiled, a smile sweet and indulgent. I'm just a grandfather to you, aren't I? Just an old *papouli*. Age, bitter, invincible age. What a monster it was.

'So I sent her packing.'

Koula was obviously shocked by the rude, dismissive contempt in Thanassis's voice. Manolis felt a surge of fury. Eleni had been a decent woman, demure, a bit of a coward. She should never have been given to a man as worldly as Thanassis. The marriage had been a mistake. She was not perfect; her worst fault was that she had a spiteful tongue. She had been a gossip, even when they were young. But she was obviously sick, suffering. He didn't believe Thanassis's talk of the best doctors and the best hospitals. The bastard had always been tight with his money.

'What about the children?'

Thanassis cocked an eyebrow at him. 'What about the children? I took them.'

Koula gasped, then quickly looked away. Thanassis laughed and lit another cigarette.

'Come on, people, of course I took the children. She was crazy, mad, I tell you. I locked her out of the house. I wasn't going to allow that animal to poison my children with her lies.'

Koula's brow was set in fierce censure. Manolis could not meet the other man's gaze.

'Listen,' Thanassis sensed their disapproval, 'I let her see them. Of course I do. I'm not an evil man. They see her all the time, they're always back and forth to Greece. But I couldn't leave them with her. No, that was inconceivable. I did the only thing I could do in the circumstances. I raised them myself.' His eyes flashed, his face hard. 'What do you think I should have done? Been a martyr, sacrificed my happiness, stayed with the cow?' Thanassis sneered. 'Fuck that. There was only one Jesus Christ and he suffered for all of us. I'm no martyr, I love life too much, and unlike the fucking Christ, this is the only life I know I will have. There's no Heaven, there's no Hell. This is it. The maggots and the worms have already started on Thimio and we're not far off from that fate ourselves. I'm not apologising for what I did.'

You did it, Manolis thought to himself, you took the plunge, you dared the opprobrium, the scandal. He looked across at Thanassis and they exchanged a wry smile.

Koula realised that something was being communicated between them that excluded her. When she spoke her voice was smug, cold. 'Of course, you did what you needed to do. But you can't deny it, the children always suffer when it comes to divorce.' Her lips were pursed, tight, she had straightened her back: a vision of propriety, of piety and moral rectitude. Manolis asked himself yet again how he could break her unrelenting sense of conviction. Had she forgotten the long, poisonous years in between youth and age, the years of argument and spite and disillusion and despair?

Thanassis answered for him. 'Shit happens.'

The cocky English phrase of their children made them all laugh. Koula bit her lip, and blushed. She hadn't forgotten.

She touched Thanassis's hand again. 'Arthur, you smoke too much.' Thanassis winked at Manolis. 'Friend, that's another thing I like about being a single man again.' He grinned mischievously at Koula. 'No bloody women telling you what you should and shouldn't do.'

Koula raised her hands angrily in frustration. 'Come on, Arthur, you know I'm right. Give it up. Enjoy the time you have left. Enjoy your grandchildren.'

Thanassis's answer was tender. 'I should have married you, Koula, you would have made me happy. I'm sorry that cocksucking prick got to you first.' He slipped his hand away from hers and he knocked a fist hard against his chest. 'Black death will take me, I know, and it will begin here.' He blew out a long, exultant spiral of smoke. 'What can we do? Black death takes us all.'

Thimios's house was crowded when they finally arrived, the guests all sitting quietly in the lounge room. A young girl answered the door and led them into the house. It was a comfortable brick home, the walls not long ago painted a fresh coat of white, bearing photographs of grandchildren, weddings, baptisms, a few mementos of Greece: a raised bronze engraving of the Parthenon, a small print of a black and white shorthair cat reclining on a white wall terrace above the sapphire sparkle of the Aegean, an outlandish *koumboloi*, a set of worry beads, each pinkish bauble the size of a plump apricot. The interior was like dozens of Greek homes that Manolis had been in, but nothing about the house reminded him of Thimios, the friend from long ago. The house was full of plush, oversized, intricately upholstered furniture; all the photographs were in heavy, ornate gilded frames. Thimios's tastes had always been simple, sparse. What did you expect, he scolded himself, the unadorned apartment of a bachelor? This is a grandfather's home. The young girl took them into the lounge room.

Paraskevi was sitting in the middle of a long, tall-backed rococo couch, her sisters either side of her. When she saw Koula and Manolis she jumped to her feet.

'Come on,' she ordered Koula. 'Come sit with me.' One of the sisters obediently moved along to make space. Manolis and Thanassis stood awkwardly in front of the television.

'Athena,' ordered Paraskevi. 'Get some chairs for your uncles.'

Manolis went to assist the teenager but she dismissed him with a simple wave of her hand. 'I'm okay.'

Papouli, he thought, I'm just an old man. She came back from the kitchen, a chair under each arm. Gratefully, Manolis and Thanassis took a seat. The girl sat on the floor.

'This is my granddaughter, Athena.'

He could see Thimios in her face. She had her grandfather's high brow, his sharp cheekbones, his small, round mouth.

Koula also appraised the girl. 'Are you Stella's daughter or John's daughter?'

'I'm Stella's child,' Athena answered, then she blushed. Her Greek was awkward.

'We were all great friends,' Paraskevi explained, holding tightly to Koula's hand. 'We were the best of friends.'

She turned to Manolis. 'What happened? How did we drift apart?'

Those questions were asked countless times that afternoon. As more of the mourners arrived at the house, Manolis felt as if he had entered the Underworld and was lost among the Shades. Except that he too was one of them. What happened? Where have you been? Where do you live? Are your children married? How many grand-children? There was Yanni Korkoulos, who had owned the milk bar in Errol Street. There was Irini and Sotiris Volougos. Koula had worked with Irini in a textile factory in Collingwood and he had worked with Sotiris at Ford. Along with Thimios, he and Sotiris had got drunk the night the junta fell, and went to the brothel in Victoria Street. Emmanuel Tsikidis was sitting in an armchair across from Manolis. His wife Penelope had died two years ago, he told Manolis, from the 'evil disease', cancer. First her stomach, then her lungs. They chopped so much out of her she died a skeleton. Next to Emmanuel there was Stavros Mavrogiannis, a still refined countenance, but gone to fat. His hair was thick, jet black. He must be dyeing it. His Australian wife Sandra had gone completely grey and, unlike the other women in the room, did not bother to hide it. She was still a fine-looking woman. They had seemed like goddesses, the Australian women, when they had first seen them as young men: tall, slim, blonde and Amazonian. What had happened to the Australian girls? Now they were all fat, bovine. Sandra was still graceful, straight-backed. She had surprised them all in the seventies by learning word-perfect Greek.

At first conversation was stilted, everyone conscious of Paraskevi's grief. They asked after each other's children and grandchildren and then they were unsure what else to talk about. The past loomed enormous, insurmountable. Paraskevi's children, her nephews and nieces, had come in to greet each new arrival. They were polite, sad, of course, but they drifted back into the kitchen, sitting around the polished blackwood table, involved in their own conversations. They were still young men and women, far removed from death, and so soon they could not help laughing, telling their jokes. The grandchildren were outside, the youngest playing hide and seek, the older ones playing footy. Athena and Stella would come in from time to time with fresh coffee, tea, drinks, cashews and pistachios to nibble. Manolis wanted a beer but he knew it would be improper to ask for such a celebratory drink. Instead, he took a whisky off the tray. From the kitchen, in English, they could hear the kids discussing travel. One of Paraskevi's nephews had just returned with his family from Vietnam.

Katina, Paraskevi's eldest sister, shook her head. 'I told them they were crazy,' she said in a low voice, 'I thought they were out of their mind taking the children there.' She tapped quickly on her breast, then crossed herself. 'The disease, the poverty. They had no right to take my grandchildren.'

Thanassis made a loud rude noise. 'Nonsense. It's a beautiful country. I went last year.'

Sotiris Volougos leaned back in his chair, a suspicious look in his eyes. 'You're playing with us.'

'No I'm not. I went. Great food, good people.'

Katina chuckled. 'Did you eat dog?'

Thanassis shook his head, then laughed. 'Katina, I had dog in Athens during the Occupation. I don't mind dog.'

The women all shrieked in horror. 'Did you really have to eat dog during the war?'

Thanassis nodded his head slowly at Athena. 'And not only dog.' He made a retching sound that shocked them all. 'I still sometimes wake up with that vile taste of snake on my tongue.' He turned to the women on the sofa. 'Vietnam is a great country. Beautiful. I lived like a king there for ten days. Everything is cheap. Of course there is poverty, of course. But they're a proud race. I went down those holes where they hid from the Americans. They were living like rats. And you can still see where the bloody Americans bombed them, where they destroyed whole villages and towns. They really fucked them up the arse.'

Paraskevi grunted. 'And who haven't the Americans destroyed? Look what they are doing in the Middle East. It's the same thing.'

'Sure, sure,' answered Thanassis. 'But the Vietnamese defeated them because they were united. Unlike the idiotic Arabs—the English set them amongst each other a hundred years ago and they're too pig-ignorant to see it. If they were united they could conquer the world.'

'Bullshit.' Sotiris used the English expletive and then continued in Greek. 'America is not going to let anyone conquer the world except themselves. They'll blow all of us up before letting anyone else get the upper hand.'

'I blame that cocksucker, Gorbachev.' Thanassis leaned in, excited. He took a cigarette from his shirt pocket.

Paraskevi raised her hand. 'Outside.'

'In a minute.' Thanassis rolled the cigarette through his fingers. 'If that animal hadn't dissolved the Soviet Union we'd have someone standing up to the Yanks.'

Emmanuel laughed. 'Come off it Thanassi, that's ancient history, that's like Homer and Troy. No, let it go, the Americans rule everything.'

'They destroy everything.' Paraskevi undid the clasp from her veil, swung her head and let her hair fall around her shoulders. 'No one dares to do anything to them.'

Emmanuel shook his head. 'That's not true, that lad, that Arab, he managed to bomb New York.'

'And good on him.'

Katina frowned. 'Paraskevi, you've just lost a husband. Think of all the widows who grieved in New York.'

Paraskevi made a loud squishing sound with her lips. It sounded like a fart. 'Katina, are you serious? With all the suffering in this world you want me to care about the damn Americans?' They all burst into merriment at the joke of it.

As the afternoon wore on, they fell into argument, and the stiffness, the forced politeness all fell away. Athena fetched more drinks and Manolis drank more whisky. Koula clucked her tongue loudly and tried to catch his eye but he ignored her. The conversation moved from politics back to their own lives, but this time with a frankness that had not been there before. The wine and the spirits had loosened tongues, but so had something else, a stepping back into the past: they were reminded of a camaraderie that was so exquisite, so cherished that only drawn together in grief over their friend's death could they admit how much they had missed it, how intense their longing for it had been. Conversation returned to the children and the grandchildren, as it always does, conceded Manolis, amongst people as old as us, but this time the men admitted to disappointment, to failure. Tales of divorce emerged, as did curses over a child's laziness or his selfishness or her stupidity. Wrong choices in partners, jobs, in life. Disrespect was a consistent theme, as were drugs, alcohol. The women fell silent listening to the men, their faces closed, concerned. At first they refused to admit to any doubts about their offspring, saying nothing except an occasional warning to their husbands. Shut up, Sotiri, it's not Panayioti's fault he married that sow. There is nothing wrong with Sammy, he just hasn't met the right girl yet. Not another word, Manoli, Elisavet did not bring it on herself. It was Sandra—of course, it would have to be the Australian—who came over, stood up next to Thanassis, and joined in the conversation with the men. She did not, however, speak of disappointment with her children. She stated plainly that sometimes it was hard with Alexandra, sometimes it was hard having a child who was schizophrenic.

No Greek woman would admit to this, Manolis told himself, looking fondly at Sandra. Greek women are tigers when their children are successes, but they fall apart with failures. The room fell to silence. Stavros was looking down at the carpet. Was the man humiliated? To everyone's surprise, Sandra let out a loud, honking laugh.

'You don't have to pity me. She's fine, I'm proud of my Alexandra. It was difficult, for years, in and out of hospital. But she takes her medication now, we bought her a small flat in Elwood. She's fine. Alexandra is happy. She paints now.'

'That's right.' Stavros was smiling affectionately at his wife, nodding his head fiercely, boldly, a wide smile on his face. 'You should see the icons she paints. They're beautiful.'

Tasia Maroudis, who had been quiet all afternoon, sighed deeply. 'We all have our burdens.' Her voice had not changed in all these years. Soft, almost inaudible, the call of a tiny, frightened bird.

Sandra's mouth set in a redoubtable iron grimace. 'I tell you, she's no burden.'

'What are her paintings like?'

They all turned to Athena. The girl blushed.

Sandra answered her in English. 'They are big canvases. She paints women, all different kinds of women—old women, young girls, fat women, thin women, but all painted in the style of old Orthodox icons. The colours are so rich, so strong, completely fantastical.' Sandra smiled down at the girl. 'Do you like art?'

'I want to be a painter.'

Paraskevi massaged her granddaughter's shoulder. 'Don't let your father hear you.' She turned to her friends. 'He says there is no money in art.'

'There isn't.' Sandra shrugged. 'But that's not why Alexandra paints.'

'Athena, go get that painting you did of your grandfather, the one hanging up in our room. Show it to everyone.'

The girl scrambled to her feet, walked shyly across the room. She returned with a small canvas. She hesitated, then smiling shyly, she handed it to Manolis.

He could not recognise his friend in the bushy white hair, the dark wrinkled skin of the portrait. Manolis knew nothing about art and was no judge of the painting. He felt nothing. He passed it to Thanassis.

'It's very good,' Manolis told her.

Athena blushed again. 'It's alright.'

The painting was passed around the circle of old people, each of them making appropriately admiring remarks over it. It finally landed in Paraskevi's hands. She wiped away her tears.

'Thimio was so proud of Athena.'

'Why not?' Koula was smiling at the young girl. 'She's a wonderful young woman, of course he was proud of her.'

Silently the girl took the portrait from her grandmother's hands and left the room.

Tasia leaned forward. 'Did you hear about Vicky Annastiadis's oldest boy?'

Here we go, thought Manolis, more gossip. He recoiled from the sound of her breathless voice. She was timid, but she'd always been a bitch. He remembered now, how she'd gloat over misfortune. He turned to Thanassis to begin another conversation but his old friend had a quizzical look on his face.

'What about him?'

Tasia's eyes were glinting as she turned to Thanassis. 'He's in prison.'

'What for?'

Tasia shrugged her shoulders. 'He's a thief. How and what and where I don't know. But he was always trouble.'

Thanassis snorted in anger. 'You're talking crap. Kosta was a good kid. He was tough. You could rely on him.'

Tasia pursed her lips. 'That may be, Arthur, but he's still a thief.'

Koula tapped her fingers on the coffee table. 'Touch wood that our kids are alright.'

'That you know of.'

She swung around furiously. 'What do you mean by that, Thanassi?'

The old man laughed. 'Nothing, my little doll, nothing. I just mean what do we really know about our children's lives? What they tell us. But how much do they tell us?'

Tasia started to speak and then quickly stopped herself. The words had been a muttered jumble, Manolis could not be sure he had heard any of them, but her malice was obvious, it suddenly lay heavy in the room. Manolis had not heard the words but he knew exactly what had remained unspoken. *That's why your wife left.* It suddenly struck him that it had not been Thanassis who had been brave and walked away. It was Eleni who'd left, who'd had the balls to walk. Had she really left the children with him? Or had he promised to break her neck if she defied him? He would probably never know the whole story; Thanassis was too full of shame and bluster—the story would always be shaped to reflect honour on himself, no, not honour exactly. Manolis looked at his old friend, the thickening waistline, the shaking liver-spotted, wrinkled hands with the nicotine-stained fingers, the folds of fat at the back of his neck. Thanassis was an old man who wanted to believe that he was still a bull. Those days were gone. Lost in his thoughts, Manolis did not hear what his friend replied to Tasia but he saw the reaction: Athena's shocked gasp, a thrilled grin at the edge of his own wife's mouth. Koula had never liked Tasia.

'You're a blasphemer, Thanassi.' Tasia crossed her arms and primly turned her knees away from the men.

'Tasia,' Thanassis roared with laughter, 'you're exactly like my wife. You and she are the kind who walk with God. Which is all I need to know about religion.'

Tasia could not help herself. 'Atheist,' she spat out.

Thanassis clapped his hands, a ferocious sound that silenced the conversation of the younger people in the kitchen.

'Bravo, Tasia, bravo. I am an atheist and bloody proud of it. It's this one life we have, my little gossip, this one life. Then we become dirt, we become flesh for the maggots to feed on. That's it.' He suddenly drew back, his face crumpled, he looked fearful, confused. He took a cigarette from his shirt pocket and, without looking at her, mumbled an apology to Paraskevi.

The old woman grinned. Her eyes were still moist. 'Thimio used to say the same thing. Don't worry about offending me, Thanassi. I don't know what awaits us after death—all I know is I will never see my Thimio again.'

Thanassis rose, chucked the cigarette to his lip. 'I'm going for a smoke.'

Manolis followed him, and, flashing a guilty look at his wife, so did Sotiris.

The back verandah was as big as a room, with a fence of thick slats that rose chest-high. The sun had long set. The little children had played in the backyard all afternoon but with the coming of evening they had crowded into one of the spare bedrooms to watch a DVD.

Thanassis lit his cigarette. Sotiris asked him for one.

'You still smoke?'

'Once or twice a year. Irini will nag at me all night.'

'You're lucky. You've got someone to look after you.'

Thanassis inhaled deeply, he was looking out to the vegetable garden in the darkness. In the centre of the yard was a fine, sturdy lemon tree, now barren. But there would be plenty of fruit in spring. It was clearly a strong tree. Manolis followed his gaze. Thimios had always been good with the earth. He'd planted tomato vines when they lived together, and every year the tomatoes would be plentiful and plump.

Manolis looked at the two old men, smoking silently on the verandah. Was it possible that the last time they had been together was at that filthy brothel in Victoria Street, so damn drunk that he remembered he could not get it up? He had ended up sucking on the whore's tits, pulling his shameful half-erect cock to a pathetic small splatter of a climax. There had undoubtedly been dances, weddings, baptisms afterwards when they had met up, but it was that night that claimed any stake in his memory. He smiled to himself. They had been studs then, confident, virile, strong. They had been lads, *palikaria*. Now they were all dying. Maybe not ill yet, but death had begun, had started tightening its inexorable grip.

'So, what's it like being a bachelor, Arthur? You recommend it?'

At first they thought Thanassis wouldn't answer. He was still peering out into the darkness of the yard. But he turned, his back against the fence, and smiled ruefully at Sotiris. 'Lonely. It's lonely.' He sucked on his cigarette. 'But I've got myself a Filipina girl. Antoinetta. She's a nice girl.'

Manolis was shocked. And jealous. You're cruel, God, you're cruel. I am destined to always be envious of this man.

'How old is she?' Sotiris looked dubious.

'Forty-eight.' Thanassis laughed out loud, delighting in his friend's surprise and discomfort. 'I don't live with her, of course, my children would put me in a mental asylum.' His voice was suddenly bitter. 'Not because they care about my mental health—because they'd be worried she'd get some of my money.' He scrubbed the end of his cigarette against the wood and threw it, high, with determined aim; it landed over the neighbour's fence. 'They don't have to worry. She's not in the will.'

'How long have you known her?' Manolis's voice was a whisper.

'Ten years. She's a good woman, I tell you. She has two children herself. The boy is a man now. The girl turns eighteen this year. They're good kids. Normal people, not fucking doctors or lawyers or cocksuckers like our spoilt children. Just normal, hard-working, good people. To tell you the truth, they're the ones who deserve my money.'

Sotiris put a warning hand on Thanassis's shoulder. 'Arthur, listen to me, you can't deny your children your money. They're your blood.'

Thanassis pushed the old man's hand away. 'Do you think I don't fucking know that?' He groped for another cigarette from his pocket and lit it. He blew out the first puff of smoke and continued. 'I've opened up an account for Antoinetta, I put money in there from time to time. My kids don't know. No reason to find out when I go. Anyway, they'll have my savings, they'll have my house. They're fine. Like all our kids, they'll be fine. They haven't had to work for any of it but they'll be fine.'

What can I say, thought Manolis? He screwed up his nose. The whiff of cigarette smoke was vile. What can I say? He's right, isn't he?

Sotiris had finished his cigarette and was leaning over the verandah. He turned around and looked at them. 'Arthur, you're probably the only one of us left who still gets the opportunity to fuck. I wouldn't complain if I were you.'

The men broke out into laughter.

Thanassis seemed suddenly sober. 'How long has it been since I've been with you, you damn cocksuckers, you fucking pair of demons? How long? Why? Why did we drift apart?'

'Life is like that.'

'Why is life like that, Sotiri?'

'It just is.'

'That's no answer.'

'We just got lazy. We just got too comfortable and too lazy. That's what happened.'

Sotiris grinned. 'That's right, eh, Thanassi. Manoli was always the philosopher. He had a theory for everything.'

Thanassis was smiling. 'You're right, Manoli. We got fat and lazy.' He put his arm around his old friend. Manolis felt its weight, its solidity. Thanassis had not weakened yet. Soon, but not yet.

'You were the philosopher. You and Dimitri Portokaliou. We couldn't get you to shut up.'

Thanassis's arms felt tight around his neck. Manolis shrugged off his grip. His head felt thick. How could he forget Dimitri? How could memory play such a foul trick on him? There had been Thanassis, Sotiris and Thimios. There had also been Dimitri. At the coffee house, at the dances, at the weddings, the baptisms. At the brothel. There had been five of them that night. Of course there had been five. Dimitri and Manolis had come across the world on the same ship and had moved in together when they first arrived in Melbourne. Was it 1961, the bedroom they shared in Scotchmer Street, the middle-aged, widowed Polish landlady, not good-looking, buck-toothed, but a great body, blonde, a real blonde, they had both fucked her. Dimitri, short, funny Dimitri with two years of high school education, his smattering of French, his pencil-thin moustache that he groomed every morning and every evening. He ended up a mechanic; he'd been too slight for factory work, hadn't a machine nearly crushed him at GMH? It had terrified all of them.

Where the fuck was Dimitri tonight? The shiver passed through his body. He gripped onto the verandah. Black death had just passed through him.

'Where is Dimitri? And Georgia? Where are they?'

Sotiris and Thanassis looked at one another.

Death was tightening its grip on them all. One by one, they were like rabbits trying to evade the hunter's rifle. There was no dignity in being human. Not at the end.

But Dimitri and Georgia Portokaliou were not dead. Thanassis answered him. 'No one sees them anymore. You haven't heard what happened to Yianni?'

Manolis tried to remember. The son, the one child. It had been feared that Georgia would die in childbirth. She had lost so much blood. Was that right? Koula would remember. And could she not have children again?

'No, what happened?'

'He was shot. Ten years ago. In the middle of broad fucking daylight. Outside his own home in Box Hill. A bullet in the head and the young man was dead.'

Manolis could not stop himself. He crossed himself three times. 'Why?'

Thanassis said nothing.

'Drugs,' answered Sotiris.

'We don't know that.'

'What else could it be, Thanassi?'

'Money. Sex. It could be anything.'

Sotiris shook his head. 'No. It was mafia, gangsters. It was organised.' He looked at Manolis. 'You didn't hear about it? It was in the papers.'

'Maybe I was away. Maybe I was in Greece.'

'Fuck it.' Thanassis took another good aim and propelled another butt across the fence. 'Whatever the damned reason, it's a tragedy and one that no one deserves.'

Lost in their thoughts, the men wandered back into the house. All that Manolis could remember of Dimitri's Yianni—Little Johnny, didn't they all call him that?—was that he seemed always to have a smudge of dirt on his cheeks and hands; that boy loved to climb, he had been fast and agile. Hadn't Ecttora once kicked a footy with such force that it had landed on the Italian's roof? Hadn't Little Johnny scrambled up the side of the house, swung himself over the eaves and climbed fearlessly up the steep, sloping tiles to grab the football which had miraculously come to rest on the one flat stretch of roof on the old house? Signora Uccello had come out screaming, first in fury, then in terror that Yianni might impale himself on her roof. Hadn't that set off a cacophany of wails as more mothers came out to see what was happening? His own heart had stopped too. And wasn't his own son open-mouthed, breathless, as he watched his friend reach the ball? The boy had grabbed the ball triumphantly in one hand and beamed down to his mate below. Hector! I got it. Hadn't Ecttora then let out a desperate breath? Hadn't he done the same? Hadn't Signora Uccello started to swear at Yianni in Italian as he slid off the roof? Hadn't Georgia come running up to her son, hadn't she held him tight and then released him to bring her hand sharply across his face? The shocked boy had stared at his mother, his lip had started to bleed, and then he had dropped the footy and begun to howl. Manolis remembered Ecttora running behind him, cowering in fear. Don't be scared, my boy, he had told him, you're not in trouble. It had been an extraordinary feeling, his young son gripping tight to his trouser leg, finding sanctuary in his height and solidity and strength, protection from the hysterical wrath of the terrified women. So long ago, when he towered over his son. So long ago, little Johnny Portokaliou with smudges of dirt on his cheeks and a triumphant grin on his face. Now dead, long eaten by the slugs and maggots. That was evidence of God's incomprehensible, monstrous cruelty. That he, Manolis, was alive, and that Little Johnny was dead.

'Uncle?'

How long had he been staring at Athena's face, but looking through her into the past? How long had she been waiting for an answer from him? He came to, realised that the whole room had stopped talking, that everyone was looking at him. He was sitting in the chair, next to Thanassis as before.

'For God's sake, answer the girl,' his wife said impatiently. 'Where were you?'

'Forgive me,' he said quietly to the girl, pulling at his collar. He savagely loosened his tie and breathed in deeply. Still confused, flustered, he looked at the girl. 'What did you ask me?'

'Would you like a drink, Uncle?'

'Another whisky.'

'Manoli?' Koula's voice was a warning. He ignored it. He really craved a beer. Stupid useless rituals, all for the benefit of their malicious God.

Thanassis wrapped an arm around his friend's shoulder. 'We all get old, my Manoli, but don't you dare go dotty on me.'

He was drunk by the time Koula rose, clutching her handbag, her face determined, brooking no argument.

'Paraskevi, we have to go.'

The old woman shook her head furiously. 'Stay—you can't go.' Paraskevi looked over to Manolis who was reminiscing with the men, laughing at an old joke from Stellio. 'Mano, tell Koula that you have to stay.'

Manolis took one look at his wife and shook his head. She could not be convinced. Koula did not like to drive; she particularly did not like to drive at night. He would certainly not be forgiven for his drunkeness if he forced her to stay.

He rose from his chair. 'We have to go.'

The farewell was a blur of hugs and kisses, of shaking hands, of promising to phone, to see one another. Athena showed them to the front door. In kissing the young girl's cheek—the rejuvenating perfume of a young beautiful girl, this was intoxication, this was paradise, this was the only God worth knowing—he also remembered the occasion. Thimios was dead. He offered his condolences once more, but the words came out an incoherent jumble, from both the drink and his emotions. Athena waved them goodbye as Paraskevi walked them down the driveway. She was holding Koula's hand.

'We can't lose one another again.'

'I promise, we won't.'

Paraskevi would not let go. 'Koula, he was my everything, my sun in the day, my moon at night. I fear I will go crazy without him. I need you. I need you.' Her last imploring words were lost in a sudden torrent of tears. Manolis watched the two women, now both crying, holding tight to each other. Slowly, reluctantly the old woman pulled herself away from Koula. She kissed Manolis on the cheek, wetting him with her tears.

'Thimio loved you.'

I know. And I loved him. He knew that.

'You must visit.'

'We will.'

With a great effort, a stab of pain tearing through his knee, he climbed into the passenger seat of the car. Koula adjusted the mirrors, made her prayer, turned on the ignition. The car hesitantly reversed in the drive and turned into the street. With effort Manolis turned his head back to see Paraskevi receding, her hand still waving, looking old, weary, spent, out in the cold, in her funeral black.

The following morning he awoke from a dream of profound tranquility. He opened his eyes to the material world, a childlike smile on his face, his limbs, his bones feeling rested, youthful. He attempted to clutch onto the dream, force it into consciousness, but it eluded him. Thimios had come to him in his slumber; the night had been full of his old friend's musical laughter. Paraskevi too had been in the dream, as had his wife. Koula had been young again, as they all had been. Her skin velvety, her body and breasts firm, as she had been when he first met her, when she had caused his eyes and his heart and his loins to tremble. Manolis stripped the sheet off himself. He was wearing flannel pyjamas, and he had been sweating. He released a shocked blasphemy: fuck Jesus. His cock was hard, upright, was poking through the slot in his pyjama bottoms. You old bastard, Thimio, are you reminding me of youth for the last time?

Koula was in the shower. Manolis shuffled down the hall and into the kitchen. Although they had found peace in the night, his old bones had not miraculously revived.

He grimaced as he bent down to find the *briki*; gently, he bent his knees, grabbed it, and then, clenching his teeth, forced himself quickly to stand upright. He released his breath and started to brew the coffee. He watched the thick lumps of chocolate coffee slowly dissolve into the water to form a thick black syrup. The warm peace of the dream had not yet deserted him. He had not forgotten that he'd buried a friend yesterday, that pain had not been displaced by the dream. But in being reminded of their shared past, and also of the inexorable finality of life, he found a renewal of his pleasure in the raw, coarse reality of being alive. Maybe that was why his cock had fought for one last stand. This vulgarity, this blood and flesh was life. Thimios had died; he too would soon be dead, God willing, as would Koula, as would Paraskevi, as would all of them. The suffering and the pain and the arguments and the mistakes of the past did not matter. In the end, they did not matter. Was that what the dream had shown him? Manolis was glad that there was no outstanding hatred, resentment or feud that he would take to the grave with him. He doubted Thimios had either, he was not that kind of man. Regrets, of course, only an imbecile did not have regrets. Regrets, some shame, a little guilt. But they had all done the best they could, they had raised their children well, educated them, housed them, made them safe and secure. They had all been good people. Death was never welcome but He always came. It was only to be truly lamented when He took the young, those neither prepared nor deserving of it. Then death was cruel. Manolis watched the foam rise in the *briki* and he turned off the flame.

Koula walked into the kitchen as he was pouring the coffee into the small cups. Surprised, but pleased, she tightened her bathrobe around her and sat down.

'How's your head?' she smiled at him.

'Perfect,' he answered, also with a smile. 'I'm still tough, don't worry. A few whiskies won't incapacitate me.'

It did not, however, take them long to start bickering. He couldn't believe how much their perceptions of the previous evening differed. Coming home, they had been too exhausted to talk. They'd eaten a small salad, some feta with bread, and gone to bed and fallen fast asleep.

'Aren't we lucky, husband?' Koula's eyes now shone. 'Our children are doing so well. We have nothing to be ashamed of.'

That glint in her eyes—yes, it was smugness. Was it also spite? He felt his calm deserting him. Koula didn't notice. She continued her excited chatter.

'Of course, one can't blame Sandra and Stavros for their child being diseased in the brain.' Koula touched wood and her lips drooped. Then she immediatley cheered up again. 'But their son sounds like he's hopeless, has no idea of what he wants to do. I'd be tearing my hair out if I was Sandra. But maybe she doesn't care. She is Australian.'

'Sandra is gold,' he growled. 'Always has been.'

'As for Thanassi, a good man, but he's become a degenerate.'

Manolis closed his eyes. He had thought in the joyful rediscovery of his past yesterday that all the petty envies and inanities of the middle years could be thrown aside. He believed he had glimpsed a truth, a possibility: equanimity, acceptance, a certain peace—in old age, all men were equal. Not in work, not in God, not in politics, only in age. But it was not so. He tried to drown out his wife's chatter. He wanted a few more minutes in a world where hierarchy and snobbery and vindictiveness did not hold sway.

'And poor Emmanuel. Two sons and neither of them married. He must be so ashamed.'

'What the devil has Emmanuel got to be ashamed of?'

Koula rolled her eyes. 'The sun hasn't risen yet. Have you already lost your temper?'

She was right. He should say nothing, keep the peace. He sipped his coffee and let her talk.

'And poor Tasia.'

'What about Tasia?'

He had never paid any attention to Tasia. He wasn't going to begin now.

'Her oldest is still unemployed. It's a disgrace.'

He fought the rise of his glee. It served the old gossip right. Then he reprimanded himself. He was not going to get caught up in this. He didn't know the lad. The poor cocksucker had enough to deal with if Tasia was his mother.

'Have we got any *loukoumia* left?'

Koula frowned at him. 'You're not meant to have much sugar.'

'Just one *loukoumi*.'

Koula leaned over her seat, and opened the cupboard. She brought out the box of Turkish Delight. 'And her youngest, Christina, she's divorced.'

'Our Elisavet is divorced.'

Koula was outraged. 'It's not the same thing. Christina was always loose, our daughter worked hard in her marriage. It was not her fault that she married an animal.'

They glared at each other. Manolis lowered his gaze.

Not for the first time, he sighed inwardly at the innate conservatism of women. It was as if being a mother, the agony of birth, rooted them eternally to the world, made them complicit in the foibles and errors and rank stupidity of men. Women were incapable of camaraderie, their own children would always come first. Not that his own children did not come first with him, not that he would not sacrifice for them. He was here, in this house, with this woman, in this particular life: he had sacrificed for them. But he was not blinded to who and what his children were. Of course, there were men who thought as women did, men whose children made them insensible to the worth of others. But they were weak men, not men who belonged in the world. And sure, of course, there were also strong women, women of fire and spirit, women who led revolutions, women who chose martyrdom. But they were rare. Women were mothers, and as mothers they were selfish, uninterested, unmoved by the world.

His wife was still talking, her lips moved, he heard the rush of sounds, but he blocked her out. He read her face instead. There it was: self-righteousness, the flash of mockery, the pleasure in another's misfortune. Had she forgotten the day he had found her banging her fist against the kitchen floor like a madwoman, flecks of blood spattered over the linoleum, her grief and fury at her daughter's divorce impossible to stem? How she had not been able to face going to the factory, to the shops, to leaving the very house when Hector told them he and Aisha were not going to marry in a church? Had she forgotten her grief, had she so excised it from her mind, that she could now gloat over another woman's equal misfortune? Women gave birth to men and hence gave birth to greed.

He finished his coffee and his hand dropped to his lap. He blushed. He was still hard. He looked over to his wife and tried, but failed, to resurrect the girl from the dream. It was years since they had been intimate. It was years since he had been carnal at all, a brothel in Collingwood where a young stoned girl had bitterly, un-enthusiastically tried to arouse him. He had just wanted her to sit on his lap, for him to stroke her long hair and tell her stories. It was laughable. His body failed him when needed and now it was taunting him without mercy. What would Koula do if he stood and asked her to go to bed with him? What possible words were left between them to describe his desire?

I want to fuck you, wife.

She would laugh. She would laugh, she would be cruel, as cruel as his mother had been all those years ago in that other world, in the village, when she stripped the quilt off him one morning and found his cock had slipped through a hole in his trousers. She had pointed at it, cackling, What can you do with that poor little thing? His mother's laughter had awoken his brothers who also began to tease him. They stripped him of his clothes, and he, outraged, had run out crying in to the snow. He had sheltered in the cellar, folding himself among the warmth of the goats. He had wanted to die. He had wanted them all dead, most of all his mother. His poor, hungry, beloved mother.

Well, now she was long dead, as was that life. As was that world. Manolis ordered his cock into a retreat. Damn you, you're no use to me now. He and Koula would never be husband and wife, not in that sense, not in that way, ever again.

Age was cruel, age was an invincible enemy. Age was cruel, like a woman. Like a mother.

At eight o'clock, Elisavet arrived with Sava and Angeliki. The children stormed into the house, Sava cursorily hugging his grand-parents before tearing into the lounge room, turning on the television and slotting a disk into the DVD player. He and Koula never used it. They had bought it for the grandchildren. Angeliki was in a temper. She sat on her grandmother's knee and burst into tears.

'What happened, my little doll?'

'Sava hit me.'

Wearily, Elisavet leaned over and kissed her father on the cheek. Manolis returned the kiss. They were both stiff in their greeting. It had been this way ever since she had ceased to be a child. She was reserved around him and he was the same. Defensiveness had become a habit between them. Neither wanted to be the first to start an argument. Once they started arguing it would always escalate.

'Sava did not hit you. I told you not to play with his DVD.'

Angeliki's contorted face was almost demonic in its fury. 'He did smack me.'

Her temper was like her mother's. Deep, resentful, nursed till the final ebbing of its force. Manolis received no comfort in realising the patterns would be repeated. They circled around each other, uncomfortable and, yes, a little cautious, but he did love his daughter. He was sure of her love for him.

He made a comical monstrous face at Angeliki and she couldn't help herself—she laughed.

'How's my little angel? Are you glad to be spending the day with *Giagia* and *Pappou?*'

Her face went back to its scowl. She was not letting go yet. Elisavet shrugged and sat down next to her father. Her hair was long, greasy, streaked with grey. Manolis knew his wife would want to say something about this, tell her that she should take more care of herself, make herself look younger. She was looking like an old maid—how did she expect to find a man looking like that? Sure, she was still good looking but she was a divorcee with two children. She couldn't afford to be picky, she couldn't afford to let herself go. All those things that she must not say. All those things that could infuriate Elisavet.

'Where are you going today?'

'I told you,' Elisavet shot out, in English. 'To a conference.'

Conference. Both his children seemed to be always attending conferences. He had no idea what they meant by the word. A meeting? Why couldn't it occur at work?

Elisavet spoke more gently. 'It's a teacher's conference, Dad. I helped organise it. It's about literacy.' Manolis did not understand this word.

His daughter struggled to explain it. 'To help children who find it hard to learn to read and write.'

'If they work hard, then they learn.'

'Mama, it's not always that easy. Sometimes they haven't got the opportunity. I've told you, many of the kids I teach come from families with no money, or the parents are not around . . .'

'Where are the parents?'

He watched his daughter inhale abruptly. 'Prison, hospital, dead. Lots of reasons.'

Koula shook her head at the insanity and selfishness of the modern world.

'They pay you?'

'I get time off in lieu.'

Koula snorted. 'They should pay you.'

Elisavet laughed. 'Yeah, well they should.' She reached for a Turkish Delight and popped it in her mouth.

'You have time for a coffee?'

'Yeah, thanks, Mama.'

Koula handed Angeliki over to Manolis. The little girl looked over her grandfather's shoulder, into the lounge room where Sava was sprawled on the floor watching his movie.

'Why don't you join your brother?'

She started to wail again. 'He doesn't want me.'

'Oh for God's sake, Kiki.' Elisavet swallowed the sweet, a shower of icing sugar falling from her fingers. 'I can't take this anymore. Go into the lounge.'

The little girl's sobs increased.

Manolis stroked her face. 'Why don't we go chase the next-door-neighbour's cat?'

'I don't want to.'

'She can come in here,' Sava called out from the lounge. Her tears abruptly finished with, Angeliki rushed into the next room.

Elisavet turned to her father. 'Thanks for looking after them.'

'Don't be an idiot. We're their grandparents, you don't have to thank us for that.'

'I'll pick them up around eight. That okay?'

He nodded. He would be exhausted by the end of the day. He'd have to entertain them, Koula would have to feed them, scold them. He'd take them for a walk in the afternoon. Sleep would be welcome at the end of the night.

'Do you want to leave them with us tonight?'

'No, Mum, their father is picking them up in the morning from my place.'

Koula's face hardened. 'How's that *ilithio*, that worthless piece of shit? Still screwing around?'

'Mum!' Elisavet motioned towards the other room. 'They can hear you.'

'Good. They should know what an animal their father is.'

Manolis intervened. 'Koula, shut up.'

Elisavet looked over to him gratefully. The coffee brewed and Koula brought it over to the table. 'You have them next weekend, don't you?'

'Yes, I do.'

'Good. It's your cousin's birthday. Rocco can't wait to see Sava. Sandi told me over the phone.'

The boy called out over the scream of the television. 'Is Adam going to be there?'

'Of course, my little man.'

Angeliki piped up. 'And Lissie?'

Sava's answer was scornful. 'Of course she's going to be there. If Adam's going to be there, she'll be there.'

Koula dropped her voice to a whisper. 'Have you talked to your brother?'

Elisavet's brow creased. 'Last week.'

'Did you ask him about the party?'

Elisavet's tone was evasive, cold. 'He's coming.'

'And that Indian woman?'

'She's got a name, Mama.'

'Is she coming?'

'No.'

Koula banged the table. 'She was sent to this earth to torture me. Every day I ask the Blessed Mother why my poor son had to be snared by that Indian Devil. Why?'

Manolis shook his head. Aisha had been a wonderful wife to Hector, smart, capable, attractive. They were lucky. Couldn't she see it?

'She's not coming, Mum.'

'Because of that stupid *Australeza* friend of hers? That one's also a cow.'

'Harry shouldn't have hit that child.'

Sava called out loudly from the lounge room. 'Yeah, he should have.'

Koula beamed in triumph. 'See. Your son is smarter than you. Harry should have belted that little Devil. What kind of child is that? He's a monster.'

'That's not the point.'

Koula raised her hands in disbelief. 'Then what is the point?'

'He hit a child.'

'He was going to hit Rocco.'

'But he didn't.'

'No, because your cousin had the sense to stop him.'

'Well, she's not coming. Hector told me.'

Koula looked over at Manolis, who shrugged. He could not understand it either. He was surprised that Aisha would be so petty. Harry had been a fool to hit a child, but the little brat had deserved it and it had not been anything, just a slap. That was all it was. All the money wasted on lawyers, the courts, all that rubbish. They were mad, his children's generation. Was it that they had so much money they didn't know what to do with it? Was it his generation's fault for spoiling them? Had they spoiled them?

Koula voiced his thoughts. 'And to go to the police. What a disgusting low act.' She shook her head slowly.

'Why not? He hit a small boy.'

Manolis tightened his mouth. He should not speak. But what foolishness was his daughter talking? *The fucking police*, the fucking pigs? Over a slap.

Koula tapped the table. 'I've hit Sava.' She crossed her arms, daring her daughter. 'Are you going to call the police on me?'

'You shouldn't hit him.'

'Not when he swears at me, not when he hits his sister?'

'That's different.'

'You've hit him.'

Elisavet's eyes darted from her mother to her father. 'I'm not going to talk about it. Aish is right. No one has the right to hit a child. No one.'

'Not even when they're misbehaving?'

Elisavet hesitated. 'No.'

Koula threw back her chair in disgust, rose and walked over to the sink. 'And you're paying someone thousands of dollars today to tell you why children don't read, why they don't write. You should give me the money. I'll sort it out for you.'

Elisavet swore under her breath. 'So it's alright to bash a child, is it?' she hissed in English. 'Bashing a child is fine, eh?'

Manolis had enough.

'For God's sake, no one bashed anyone. He gave him a slap, one fucking slap. That's all. And now Aisha won't talk to Harry and that stupid Australian whore calls the cops and what's the result? Her child is probably still causing trouble everywhere he goes. It's nonsense.'

'How would you feel if a stranger slapped Sava in front of you?' Elisavet was yelling as well.

'I'd be furious. But if Sava was going to hit his child I'd understand. I'd take an apology and that would be it. Finished. Maybe I'd punch him a few times. We'd deal with it like men, not like animals the way those filthy Australian degenerates did.' Manolis was shaking.

He remembered the crowded formality of the courtroom, Sandi's fear, Harry's shame.

He rose. 'I've had enough of this. I'm going to talk to Aisha. She's coming to the party.'

Elisavet rolled her eyes. 'Good luck.'

Koula shook her head in disgust. 'You should be supporting your brother, you should be helping to fix this madness. But you support her. I'm ashamed of you.'

'Aisha is in the right.'

Koula pointed to the door. 'Go. I've had enough.'

Elisavet picked up her handbag, went into the lounge to kiss the children goodbye. She came in and kissed the top of Manolis's head.

'You'll see. She'll come, she will listen to me.'

'Dad, she won't.'

He wouldn't answer her. Aisha would listen to him. He'd be calm, reasonable. His reasons were sound. She respected him, she loved him. She would listen to him.

Elisavet leaned over to kiss her mother. Koula turned her head, offered a cold, disdainful cheek.

'Thanks for looking after the kids, Mama.'

Koula made no answer.

'I'll see you at eight.'

Koula had got to Elisavet. Her farewell was melancholic, resigned. They both waited till they heard the slam of the car door and the engine start up.

Koula put her hands over her head. 'They're mad, husband, they're all mad.'

He got up, rubbing his knee. Koula looked up eagerly as he picked up the phone.

'Are you going to speak to her?'

He nodded. Excitedly she rushed into the lounge room. 'Sava, Kiki, turn down the television. Your *pappou* is on the phone.'

Sava groaned. 'Do we have to?'

Koula wagged a stern finger. 'Now. Or I'll spank your bottom a hundred times.'

The boy scrambled for the remote and turned down the volume.

Aisha was running late. Manolis did not mind. High Street was busy with people doing their Friday night shopping, and others out walking, taking advantage of the mild spring evening, the lengthening of the day. He did not know the coffee shop that Aisha had chosen and when he first arrived there had been a moment of embarrassing social confusion. A young couple were heading for the door, just as his hand had reached the handle, and he had assumed—had not doubted it at all—that they would make room for him to pass. However, the man, who was in front, did not yield and he and Manolis had bumped into one another. Neither had been hurt, but they had looked at each other in momentary bewilderment. The young man had stepped back, and crashed into his partner. The young woman had then frowned at Manolis, and the old man had blushed. Manolis, rattled, stood there expecting an apology but the young man did nothing, did not move, did not say a thing. He just looked confused. 'Excuse me,' the woman had finally said sharply—an order, not an apology—and Manolis stood aside to let them pass. Out in the street, the young man had turned back to look at Manolis once again. His face still wore a baffled expression.

Manolis took a seat at the back of the busy café and ordered a cappuccino. It would be too milky for him but it was the one English coffee he liked to drink. It arrived promptly. He thought back to the incident at the door. Manolis was almost certain that the young man had wanted to apologise to him, that he was even forming the words when his girlfriend rudely swept him aside. If Koula had been with him, she would still be complaining about their rudeness and selfishness. He too had thought this for a long time, that the abandonment of respect for the aged was an indication of moral emptiness and materialism. He was not so sure now. He wondered if the youth had a father. Did the woman? When there was no father one did not learn respect. Often on the tram or the train he would be taken aback by some clear lack of civility in a young man and then realise that the boy had no notion of how crude his behaviour appeared, how dishonourable. As for the girls, they seemed distrustful of any adult. It used to anger him, it used to want to make him grab hold of their ears and punish them. He no longer felt that way. Now he felt pity for them. They had no fathers and they had not learned the meaning of honour, of respect. The mother was everything, of course, everyone knew that: women gave life and sustained life. But women were too selfish to teach honour. He felt sorry for the young couple, felt compassion for them.

That's no good, he mused to himself, no good at all. Something is wrong in the world when the old pity the young.

'You're deep in thought.'

He kissed his daughter-in-law twice on the cheek. She smelled scrubbed, he could detect the clean antiseptic odour of soap on her. She looked beautiful and, as always, her clothes were simple and elegant. He was proud of her. As a child Manolis had grown up knowing little if anything about the manners and sophistication that came from money. The first film he had ever seen was in Patra when he was on leave from the army, a French comedy set in some distant past. A man with a moustache had kissed a woman's hand and the gesture had made the young Manolis burst out laughing. What the Devil, he'd said to his army comrade next to him, does the idiot think she's a Priest? But when Ecttora had first introduced him to the Indian he'd recalled the film and wanted to lean over and kiss her hand.

'How was work?'

'Friday is always busy.' Aisha placed her jacket over the chair and took a seat. She looked around for a waiter and ordered. 'Hector said that you went to a funeral yesterday. I'm sorry. Were you close?'

He sometimes thought her deep-set eyes were too big for her face.

'An old friend. What is there to say? We all have to die.'

'Was it cancer?'

He nodded.

'Hector hardly remembers him. But he did say that when he was born you and Koula and your friend all lived together. Is that right?'

'Yes, that's right.'

'I am sorry,' she repeated.

The coffee arrived and they sat drinking in silence. They had never been alone in such a way before, and he felt awkward. She must be feeling it too. But he could not bring himself to speak. He realised that he'd given the conversation no thought at all. From the beginning, he and this woman—why, she was still a girl when Ecttora first brought her home—had seemed to fall into an easy friendship. They never did have to talk much, Aisha knew no Greek and he, even after all his time, could not always make his meaning clear in English. But that did not matter. Their immediate trust was something that both of them had been thankful for, allowed them to distance themselves from Koula's anger and Ecttora's stubbornness. Manolis had simply wanted to talk to Aisha and convince her to come to the party. He had no doubt of her love for him. She would agree. But now, watching her sip her coffee, noticing the quizzical look in her eyes, he felt uncertain of his hold on her. He did not know what to say.

'Manoli, why did you want to meet with me?'

Her eyes gave nothing away. However, they seemed to penetrate right into him. She knew, of course. She knew.

'Aisha, I want you to go to Harry and Sandi's house for his birthday.'

She placed her coffee cup on the table.

'Please,' he added suddenly.

'I thought it was going to be about this.' She shook her head. 'No, I'm not going.'

He tried to read her eyes, those dark, alluring cat-eyes. They were unfathomable. Did she pity him? Was she angry with him?

'What he did was bad, terrible, very terrible, but it was a mistake. He is very sorry. Please, Aisha, it is no good for Adam and Melissa. They want to visit Rocco, they are cousins—'

'They can see their cousins whenever they like,' she shot out, crossing her arms. 'I'm not stopping them.'

'It makes problems for Hector.'

'Hector understands my reasons.'

He was getting confused. What were her reasons, how could she maintain such a rage? It creates a problem for me, he should answer, how about the problems you are creating for me?

'Harry and Hector are close, very close. Like brothers.'

She was unimpressed with his play on family loyalty. Her eyes flashed and this time he detected her anger. 'This is not hard for Hector. You don't have to worry about him. Isn't the real issue that this is a problem for Koula?'

This was dangerous ground. His damned knee started to ache, and he lowered his hand under the table to massage it. He was frustrated with Aisha. This was another battle between the women, another petty crusade. He refused to discuss his wife.

'Harry is very sorry.'

'He's not sorry at all.'

She would not budge. Why the fuck should Harry be sorry? Though that idiotic fool deserved a hiding for hitting that boy. Though it was not good to speak ill of the dead, he was exactly like his cursed father, no self-control.

'He is very very sorry. He told me again and again. He is very sad that you are angry with him.'

'You went to the courthouse with him, Rosie told me. She was very hurt.'

This took him by surprise. Of course he'd gone with Harry to the court. What did these crazy Australian women expect? The boy's parents were dead, he was obliged to be there supporting his wife's nephew. If he hadn't been there his wife would not have forgiven him for not standing next to her brother's child. Surely Aisha understood that. She wasn't a bloody barbarian. Did he have to remind her of loyalty and honour?

'I was disappointed myself, Manoli. You shouldn't have gone.'

There were too many people in the damn café! The heating was intolerable and he could not concentrate. He became aware that he was sitting across from his daughter-in-law with his mouth wide open, like some imbecile. Foolish old man. He quickly closed his mouth. Did he understand her correctly? He was unsure of that perplexing English word: disappointed. Was she angry because he had made it difficult between herself and her stupid friend, that mad *Australeza*, Rosie? All this was ridiculous. It had happened, forget it. Too much time and too many tears had already been wasted on this silliness.

'Aisha, you are family.'

She laughed, a short, scornful burst, her eyes not moving from his face. They were the black of a winter night. 'I have known Rosie much longer than I have known your family.'

He forgot the pain in his knee, the incessant rumble of noise in the café. He straightened his back. He must have looked fierce because instantly she perceived her mistake and she recoiled from him. He wanted to grab her hair, pull her face to the table, beat her as if she was a little girl.

'This is not about our family,' she said quickly. 'It's about my friendship with Rosie. Harry humiliated me in my own home. And he did something unforgivable to my friend and her son.'

That *poutana*, and that *moulkio* of a child. He remembered the Australian's words to him in that crowded hallway outside the courtroom. You should not be here. Shame on you. He had been embarrassed, rendered mute by her unforgiving self-righteousness. The sense of shame still stung, but he now knew exactly what he should have said to her. He should have grabbed the *poutana* by the hair, and shouted at her, You created this, you dragged all of us into this. You are a bad mother. He saw the waitress hovering near the table and he drummed his fingers loudly.

'Another coffee?'

Aisha shook her head.

'I'm fine.'

'Harry was wrong. He make mistake. He is very sorry.' He held up his hand to stop her from interrupting him. 'But your friend was also very wrong. Why she not look after her child?'

'Rosie loves Hugo.'

'Why she no stop her son when he was very bad?'

'Hugo is only a child. He doesn't know better.'

Exactly. Exactly the damned problem. He doesn't know better because he has not been taught to know better.

'She is terrible, a terrible mother.' He didn't care anymore, he was no longer interested in conjoling Aisha, in being gentle. He marvelled at her blindness. She was defending the indefensible. This mad woman Rosie should have disciplined the boy herself. And if not her, that fool alcoholic of a husband. Harry was no saint, they all knew that, far from it, but for the first time since the incident had occurred Manolis understood, felt, believed, that his nephew was innocent.

Aisha would not look at him.

'You are going to the party next week.'

She turned to look at him in disbelief. There was a glimmer of an astonished, respectful smile. 'I'm not.'

'Yes, you are.'

'No.'

'Yes.' He wanted to insist until she agreed. He was right. He had never been more right in his life. This time he could read the flashing fire in her eyes.

'You are not my father.'

He wished he could slap her. So it all meant nothing, all those years of shared jokes, of affection, of defending her, of caring for her children, of assisting her and Hector with money and with time. Love and family meant nothing to her? Nothing mattered to her at this moment but her pride. Did she think she was being brave in disobeying him? She, Hector, the whole mad lot of them, they knew nothing of courage. Everything had been given to them, everything had been assumed as rightfully theirs. She even believed her defence of her friend was a matter of honour. One war, one bomb, one misfortune and she would fall apart. He meant nothing to her because like all of them she was truly selfish. She had no idea of the world and so believed her drama to be significant. The idiotic mad Muslims were right. Throw a bloody bomb in this café and disintegrate the whole lot of them. Her beauty, her sophistication, her education, none of it meant anything. She had no humility and no generosity. Monsters, they had bred monsters.

He threw a ten-dollar bill on the table, slurped back his coffee and stood. 'Let's go.'

She rushed to her feet. 'Where are we going?'

'Koula is at your house.'

He walked ahead of her, ordering his weak leg to outdistance her. He heard her rapid steps coming up behind him. She called out to him and he turned. She was standing by her car on High Street, the keys in her hand.

'Tell Koula I go shopping.' He could not bear to be with the women. He could not bear his wife's scorn once she realised he had not succeeded. Old, old fool, to believe they cared for him, respected him, would listen to him.

'I think you should come home with me.'

Go fuck yourself.

'I go shopping.'

She beeped open the car.

'Manoli, I am sorry.'

He turned his back to her and walked away. The words dropped easily from her lips but they meant nothing. Australians used the word like a chant. Sorry sorry sorry. She was not sorry. He thought she loved him, respected him. He'd nursed this hope for years. He wanted to strike himself for his vanity and foolishness. He had never asked anything of her before and she must know that he would never ask a thing of her again. *Sorry*. He spat out the word as if it were poison.

He thought she loved him. He was just a silly old man.

You're lucky, Thimio, he whispered to the wind, to the shade of his friend, how much longer must I wait till death comes for me?

In the end he avoided the plaza, the shops in High Street. He was in no mood for gazing at things; his stomach turned in disgust at the thought of the senseless temptation of so many objects. He also wanted to avoid the faces of his neighbours, the groups of old Greek men and women who congregated at the mall as they once did as youths around the village square. He had left his damn village a life-time ago, sailed across the globe to escape it, but the village had come with him. He turned off High Street and zigzagged the side streets to Merri Station. A young Mohammedan girl, her hair veiled, was standing outside the vestibule on the platform. She was still a child, a high school student. Her quick eyes were darting back and forth; she seemed nervous. He smiled at her. She should not be on the platform alone, this was not a time of good men. She dropped her eyes at his smile. She too had brought the village with her, wherever the Devil she was from. He passed her and glanced inside the vestibule. An older girl, also veiled, was locked in an embrace with a thin youth, his hair a shocking orange. She noticed his glance and drew apart from the boy, who looked up and stared, at first fearfully, then angrily at Manolis.

'What the fuck do you want?'

The girl beside him giggled and leaned back into the embrace. The boy seemed so young, his freckled white face was smooth, had not quite shed the last vestige of infancy.

Manolis shook his head and walked away. They spoke to him with the language of evil. It was not their fault. This was not a time of good men.

The smaller girl watched him walk away and he just caught her hiss. 'You shouldn't swear at him. He's no one, just an old man.'

She was right. He was no one, just an old man. Not a parent to avoid, an uncle to fear, an older brother to escape from. He grinned to himself. That boy had nearly pissed himself, he must have thought that Manolis was the girl's father. He sat on the empty bench at the end of the platform. He could smell nicotine, the kids in the vestibule were smoking. He himself had not smoked for over twenty years but these were the only moments when he missed the habit. Waiting always made him feel like a cigarette.

He got off the train at North Richmond. He had no plan, all he knew was that he did not wish to be at home. He walked down Victoria Street. Every shopfront seemed to be an Asian restaurant, they owned this strip of Richmond. Once it had been the Greeks. He walked the narrow street but he was not seeing the young Asian teenagers, the Vietnamese women with their market trollies. He was in another time. He was walking past the butcher shop run by the guy from Samos, the fish and chip shop that belonged to the couple from Agrinnion, the coffee place where he and Thimios and Thanassis had spent so much of their young adult life. He sighed fondly. He was remembering the evening he'd gambled away all of his paypacket. When he got home, Koula had chased him out of the house and all the way to Bridge Road, calling him the foulest of men, an animal, a donkey, the most miserable of faggots. The neighbours had rushed out of their houses at the commotion and had stood at their gates cheering them on, the men supporting Manolis, the women encouraging Koula.

He stopped at a traffic light and a young Australian woman, a ring through her nose, wheeling a pram, was looking at him oddly, disconcerted. He nodded to her and she tentatively smiled back. He turned into a small street. There was the factory he once worked in, now an apartment block. There was the house in which Ecttora and Elisavet attended Greek school as children. It now had a Vote Green sticker plastered on its front door. He turned into Kent Street.

He stopped in front of Dimitri's house. The homes around it had all been renovated, their facades looked clean, they looked unlived in, like houses in the movies. Dimitri and Georgia's front garden was crowded with the tender stalks of young broad beans, the first thick leaves of spinach and silverbeet. It smelled of the approaching spring. Two torn plastic bags were tied around a thin stick to scare away the birds. A fig tree towered as high as the house. Manolis hesitated. Was his mind playing tricks on him? Surely this house, this garden, belonged to the past? If he were to push open the gate, would it be real in his hands? Would the door disappear as soon as he began knocking on it? It was impossible that they still lived here. They too must have joined the exodus out of the city, pushed far out to the ends of Melbourne's seemingly endless arteries. He did push open the gate. The rusty iron frame scraped across the concrete. The squeal it made was real. He knocked on the door.

'Who is it?' An old woman's voice, accented.

He called out his name, loudly, almost shouting. There was a pause and then the door flew open. It was Georgia. She was dressed in bereavement black, and her hair, cut short, was silver. But it was her. She stood there, blinking at him. He saw surprise flush in her eyes; she had recognised him. They were sharing the same thought, he was sure of it. Oh, how we have aged.

The kiss she offered was polite but warm. 'Come in, my Manoli, come in.'

He had indeed stepped back in time. The house smelt of food, of the solid earth, of flesh and bodies. The dark, narrow hallway was cluttered with small cabinets and bureaus, and he had to squeeze up close to the wall to make it to the end. On the small hall table was an old-fashioned red dial-up phone.

A gruff voice called out from the bedroom at the end of the hall. Who is it? It was followed by a fit of pained coughing.

'Dimitri, it's Manoli. Our Manoli has come to visit us.' Georgia pushed open the bedroom door.

He had not stepped back in time. Cruel time was joking with him. Dimitri, his pyjama top unbuttoned to the navel, was lying in bed. He was skeletal, the ribs pushing ruthlessly through the loose folds of the skin on his chest.

'You haven't forgotten Manoli, have you, my Dimitri?'

The old man in the bed seemed stunned by the intrusion. A plastic mask hung over the bedpost, attached to a thin gas bottle on the floor. The man started to cough again, his body seemed too frail for the spasms racking him. Georgia pushed past Manolis, took the mask and placed it over her husband's nostrils and mouth.

Manolis walked over to the other side of the bed and took the man's limp, cold hand. 'Mitsio,' he croaked, unable to stop his tears flooding. 'Mitsio.' He repeated his friend's old nickname, unable to say more.

Georgia lifted the mask off Dimitri. His fear had vanished. He managed a small, weak laugh. 'Friend,' he whispered. 'I hope you've come to finish me off.'

Georgia slapped his arm. 'Don't talk such foolishness.'

'Why? Who would want this life? What good am I to anyone?' His breaths were short, laboured, puncturing his sentences with staccato gasps.

Manolis looked across to Georgia. Her expression was determined, calm.

'It's the evil disease,' she said softly. 'It is in his lungs.' She slowly bent down and pulled a folded-up wheelchair from under the bed. Expertly, rapidly, she assembled it. Very slowly, with his arms around Manolis's neck, with his wife taking his legs, they moved Dimitri off the bed and onto the chair. Georgia hung the mask around her husband's neck, and pointed to the oxygen bottle. Manolis lifted it into his arms. It was surprisingly light. He followed Georgia as she wheeled Dimitri out of the room. She led him through the lounge and kitchen and into a small, cluttered sunroom that overlooked the backyard. An icon of the Virgin and Child was in a corner, a lit wick floating in a saucer of oil before it. The tiny flame managed to throw a flicker of warm yellow light around the room. Georgia hitched the chair to rest, and indicated a sofa for Manolis to sit on.

'I'll make us a coffee,' she announced, and walked back into the kitchen. Manolis, afraid that any words would be wrong, looked down at his shoes. He had not even brought them a gift, an offering, he had come to their house empty-handed. What an uncivilised animal he must seem. He was surprised by Dimitri's hoarse, rasping laugh.

'Come on,' his eyes were twinkling, 'stop with that fucking long, miserable face. I'm not dead yet.'

'Of course you're not, my Dimitri.'

'What made you look us up?'

The question did not seem to contain any element of threat or resentment. Still, Manolis felt ashamed. 'I went to Thimio Karamantzis's funeral yesterday.'

Dimitri stared out ahead, to the cold grey garden outside. 'I wanted to go.' He took a long breath. 'But, of course, how can I go anywhere?'

'Of course, of course.' Manolis struggled to find words. 'I saw so many people from the past, and it made me ashamed of how long it had been since we had seen each other. Forgive me, forgive me, Dimitri.' Sweet Jesus Christ, Sweet Saviour, Sweet Lord, Sweet Eternal Mother, do not let me cry.

Dimitri turned back to him, smiling. He placed his hand on Manolis's knee. 'You sound like a woman. What the fuck do you want my forgiveness for?' He was wincing as he forced the words out, struggling for air. 'I should ask your forgiveness for not coming to visit you and Koula. There, we're even.' With obvious effort, he stopped the beginning of a ragged cough. He banged his thin weak chest in fury at his pain. 'Life went too fast and fucking death goes too slow.' He smiled again. 'But you look good, you look healthy. You were always an ox.'

'I'm so sorry about Yianni, I only heard about him at the funeral.' The words rushed out of him, almost incoherently. He just wanted them out, he just wanted them out of his body.

Dimitri's smile waned. His face fell, his body slumped. Manolis wondered if he had ever seen anyone so exhausted.

'God is a cocksucker.'

'What are you saying?' Georgia stepped into the room, balancing a tray. Manolis rushed to assist her but she motioned him back to his seat.

'You know what I said.'

Georgia ignored him. She offered Manolis a coffee, and placed one in her husband's hands. They began to shake and she steadied them.

'God did not kill our son. It was those gangsters who did it.'

'Then maybe God is also a gangster.'

Manolis was mortified. There was nothing—certainly not words— he could offer his friends. He sipped his coffee, choosing to remain silent. He was conscious that Georgia was looking at him and he looked up. She was nodding her head sympathetically.

'We understand, Manoli, what is there to say? Fate chose us for misfortune. Fate blackened our hearts.' She looked at her husband. 'Fate has sickened him.' Her words fell out of her mouth with astonishing lack of emotion, as if she was reciting a story memorised by heart, one she had tired of telling. She told him how Yianni had become involved with bad people, bad people who sold drugs. How they had led her son into that life. How they had shot him in the head outside his home, how his young children had found the body. She spoke about drugs, narcotics, gangsters, used the English word 'dealers', and they all sounded ridiculous coming from this old woman's mouth. 'He got in over his head,' she finished, using someone else's words. 'He was destroyed by evil men.'

Dimitri grunted, coffee dribbled from the edge of his mouth and Georgia went to wipe it. He slapped her hand away and wiped his own mouth and chin.

'He was a fool. He wanted the big house, the villa, the swimming pool, the new Mercedes Benz, the best televisions and the best furniture. He wanted his kids in private schools, he wanted his wife in jewels, he wanted it all. He got it all and it killed him.'

Georgia started to cry. Of course, of course, such pain would never go away.

'Stop it, Georgia.'

The old woman brusquely rubbed her eyes and attempted a smile. 'How's Koula? How's Ecttora and Elisavet?'

He could speak now, he knew the words for this conversation. They tumbled out in relief. He spoke about his children, his grandchildren, their successes, and yes, even their failures. Georgia squeezed his hand as she listened to the story of Elisavet's divorce. Her eyes shone as he described Adam, Melissa, Sava and Angeliki.

'You should see our grandchildren. Yianni's children are angels.' She rose and took framed photographs from a bureau at the back of the room. 'This is Kostantino. He's at university.' There was awe in her voice.

Manolis took the photograph and examined it. He did look a fine lad, about eighteen, in a shirt and tie, a real gentleman, and smiling cheekily in the camera.

'A handsome lad.'

'A good lad.' Dimitri gripped the arms of his wheelchair and breathed deeply. He snorted, and continued. 'He's cleverer than his father. I'm proud of him.' Manolis handed the photograph back to Georgia.

'We've done alright.' Dimitri coughed, gripped the chair again. His spasm subsided. 'We did alright, didn't we, my Manoli?'

He looked at his dying friend. Was there a question in the man's eyes? No, it was a fact, not a question.

'We did. We survived.'

'A cognac?'

Manolis looked out to the garden. Darkness was creeping over the yard.

'Why not?'

After the drink, he helped settle Dimitri back in bed. He leaned in to kiss him, twice in the Mediterranean manner, and smelled the man's foetid breath. He was being eaten from the inside.

At the door, he turned to Georgia, 'He should be in hospital. He needs doctors, nurses to look after him.'

'A nurse comes twice a week. I can look after him.' Georgia shrugged her shoulders. 'It's fate, Manoli, I can't fight it. Do I want a stranger washing him, cleaning up after him? No. I'm his wife, he's my responsibility.'

'I'm going to come again. Soon. And I'll bring Koula.'

'Please. I'll make a dinner. It will be good for Dimitri. He misses his friends.'

Are we friends? 'You don't have to make dinner. A coffee, something to drink. That's all we need.'

'Of course I'll make dinner. What do you think, that you'll come to my house and I won't feed you?'

His head was beginning to ache. They were losing each other again, trapped in damned politeness and etiquette. Let's just talk, let's just spend time together, let's make up for losing ourselves in the petty distractions and foolish pride that occupied so many decades of our lives. The rituals of being Greek; sometimes he hated it. Sometimes he wished he could be an Aussie.

'Have you got a pen?'

She squeezed through the corridor and arrived back with a pen. He took his travelcard from his shirt pocket. 'The phone number?'

'Nine-four-two-eight.' She stopped, hesitated. 'I'm an idiot. It's been so long since I've had to remember it.' She rushed through the final four digits and Manolis scrawled them across the ticket.

* * *

The clear night sky had brought a chill to the air. He walked home quickly from the train station, disobeying the objections from his knee.

When he walked through the door, Koula was standing in the hallway, her hands on her hips.

'Where the devil were you?'

He pushed her aside, walked to the cabinet and poured himself a cognac.

'Are you drunk?'

'No.'

'Ecttora rang. He's furious with you. You've upset the Indian. What did you say to her?'

'That she should go to Harry's party.'

'Good. What did she say?'

'She's not going.' Manolis drank the spirit in one shot. It tasted disgusting, then sweet, and feeling began to return to his limbs. He took off his jacket.

Koula bashed her palms over her head. 'Why does she want to humiliate us?'

'She's young.'

Koula stared at him in astonishment. 'Are you going to defend her?'

'No.' He poured another drink.

Koula eyed the glass warily. 'Elisavet has rung as well. She's angry at you too.'

'What for?'

'For making that bitch cry.'

He closed his eyes. A fine, cheeky lad in a shirt and tie. Surely there was a limit to misfortune, surely the fates had dealt enough blows to Dimitri and Georgia, surely the next generation would be spared. There must still be some good in God.

Aisha had cried? She had *cried*

'I'll ring Ecttora tomorrow. I'll deal with it.'

He'd apologise. He'd say the word sorry. He would not mean it but she would latch on to it, appreciate it, forgive him. What the hell? It was one lousy little word.

'Ring them now. He's really upset.'

'Fuck it, Koula, I'm ringing all of them tomorrow. They can be upset for one night. If they think this is trouble, they don't know how lucky they are. Fuck them. We've looked after them, we've educated them, we've done everything for them. And I'm glad to have done it, to have given them a good life. But for one night I want to act as if I never had children. For one night I want to forget them.'

Koula crossed herself. She looked at him with contempt. 'What rubbish are you speaking? You should be ashamed.' She knocked on the frame of the door. 'Touch wood, may God forgive you.'

'I visited Dimitri and Georgia.'

The disdain was replaced by a look of pure pity. 'How are the poor things?'

'Dimitri has the evil disease. He's dying.'

Koula sank heavily onto the couch. It was ridiculous how lavish, how grand the objects in their house were. Koula looked like a doll on it.

'Why do we need such a big couch?'

Koula snorted dismissively and nodded towards the drink cabinet. Manolis poured her a cognac, handed it to her and sat on the arm-chair opposite.

His wife looked down at her glass. 'There is no justice in this world, is there, Manoli?'

He swirled the golden spirit around in the glass. He breathed in the harsh, pungent fumes.

'No.'

The phone rang and they both jumped, shocked out of their reveries.

'That will be one of them.'

'Probably,' he answered.

'They'll want to know whether you've come home. They'll want to speak to you.'

'Probably,' he said again.

She smiled and sipped at her drink. 'Why don't we just let it ring out?' Her grin was mischievous, she was a young woman again.

'Yes,' he smiled at her, 'why don't we?'

The phone seemed to ring for minutes, inexhaustible. When the noise finally ceased he realised he'd been holding in his breath. He exhaled.

Koula stood up. 'I'll heat your dinner.'

He nodded.

From the kitchen he heard the sound of the buzzer lighting the oven, the clink of cutlery. Koula began to sing, and he leaned forward to hear better. It was an old popular song, a classic; he'd first heard it as a conscript getting drunk in Athens, drinking cheap ouzo with the workers and the soldiers in the square at Kaiseriani.

'We'll learn to say that what is done is done
And maybe in the future a bright day for us may come'

He mouthed the words, then clasping his hand over his knee, winced, and lifted himself to his feet. He downed the cognac and placed the glass on the coffee table. He walked into the kitchen, and helped his wife set the table.

AISHA

She glanced down at her watch again, took a deep breath, and made her calculations. Hector's plane would have departed from Melbourne an hour ago. Her own plane could possibly be delayed for another two hours, which meant he'd have to wait for her for at least three hours in the airport in Denpasar. He'd be in a bad mood. Should she leave him a message at the airport, send him a text, tell him to meet her at the hotel in Ubud? It was best to not panic—not yet anyway. The idiots should have some information for them all soon. Around her bored, frustrated tourists, most of them young men and women dressed in grimy singlets and shorts, were mutinously watching the information desk, ready to spring into action at an announcement. Aisha got up from her seat and slung her bag over her shoulder. She wanted to escape the whining and the stink of beer and perspiration. She walked back from the gate to the blaze of neon lights and dizzying movement at the end of the corridor. Bangkok airport never closed. She might as well shop.

Not that she needed anything; but that was not, she mused, the purpose of duty-free shopping. Need was banished to outside the walls of Bangkok International Airport. Pure gratuitous desire was what was celebrated here. She walked into a small fashion boutique and a young Thai woman rushed towards her. Aisha bowed but raised her hand and firmly waved her away. The young girl quickly scampered back behind the counter and started to whisper and giggle with the other shopgirl. After a week in Thailand, Aisha was aware that the women here seemed to be giggling and whispering all the time, and that no disrespect or rudeness was meant by it. But she found it bloody irritating. It always seemed that they were laughing at her.

She pulled a skirt off the rack and examined it. The fabric felt fine, soft and pleasing to her touch, but the pattern was a bizarre swirl of clashing rainbow colours. Christ, it was garish. She did prefer India, preferred the cheerful but resentful and sometimes downright obstructive demeanour of the Indian hawkers to the smiling, deferential giddiness of the Thais. Aisha looked down the aisle. The second salesgirl was coming towards her. She turned and walked quickly out of the shop. And the fabrics were certainly much better in India.

The steady stream of bland, bloodless oriental music from the loudspeakers was interrupted by a loud crackle and a burst of Thai. An effeminate, almost vixenish male voice then translated the announcement into English, asking the travellers on the next United Airlines flight to San Francisco to proceed immediately to their gate for a further security check. The announcement finished with an apologetic giggle. Aisha smiled to herself. Was he simply being Thai, or had there been a gloating pleasure detectable in the request? Around her groups of grim-faced but accepting Americans gripped their hand-luggage and proceeded wearily towards their security check.

'It has rather dulled the pleasure of air travel.'

Art had said that to her, at their first dinner in Bangkok. One of the Italian veterinarians had been complaining about the indignity of today's constant airport security. One of the Americans had replied combatively that if it stopped one terrorist then she was more than happy for the inconvenience of having to wait hours in queues to have her bags searched. The Italian had muttered a response in his own language, something about the Americans interfering in the world, and a rude Neopolitan exclamation that was the equivalent of 'just desserts'. Unfortunately, a Danish veterinarian, whose Italian was faultless, was also sitting at the table and he denounced the Italian vet's 'moral idiocy'. Which only made the Italian more incensed; he looked up and down the table and asked in clear, unaccented English, 'Is it any wonder that Danish women flock south to the Mediterranean every summer searching for a real man?' The ensuing outcry was only tempered by the loud guffaws of a Chinese delegate who'd just had the furious exchange translated for him.

Art had been sitting next to Aisha and it was at this point that he had leaned towards her and made his whispered observation. He had then glanced at the feuding veterinarians and in a breathless little boy's voice asked, 'Gee whiz, how do the United Nations ever get anything done?' Aisha had laughed out loud, a laugh so genuine and clear that it had even stopped the insults flying between the Italian and the Dane. But only for a moment.

'I know,' Aisha whispered to Art. 'We're just the International Veterinary Association and we can't get along. I don't think there's a future for this world.' He had also laughed then, and in doing so, had lifted his hand and placed his arm across the back of her chair. It had seemed totally unconscious, an innocent gesture. But its intimacy seemed daring. And exciting.

She had noticed him immediately. She assumed every woman at the conference had, for he was almost ridiculously handsome, Eurasian, with a delicate snub nose, a gym-trim body and the most pale-white skin she'd ever seen. At first she had thought he might be Spanish, but the surname on his name tag was unmistakably Chinese, Xing. Art Xing. It sounded like the name of one of the bands that Hector enjoyed listening to.

At the first dinner, after their shared laugh, she had asked him where he was from.

'I'm Canadian.'

'Obviously,' she snapped amiably, rolling her eyes and pointing to the red and white maple-leaf insignia at the end of his tag. 'But what's your ethnic background?'

'I used to think that was a very Canadian question. But I'm discovering you Australians are exactly like us.' He was smirking, his eyes teasing her. She found she had to force herself to look straight back at him. Her impulse was to look down at her empty plate. She felt absurd, but his beauty did make her swoon. Oh grow up, Aisha scolded herself, you're not some teenage twit at a Beatles concert, you're a forty-something mother of two.

'My father is third-generation Chinese from Toronto. My mother is Czech.'

'Goodness.' She had been embarrassed by the inanity of her response, but his explanation had sounded so incongruous.

'Yes,' he smiled. 'They met in Prague where my father was a diplomat. It was, as you can imagine back then, a bureaucratic nightmare to get both governments' consent to the union, but true love did win out. By which I mean that Dad secreted my mother illegally on a diplomatic flight to Paris for which the service kicked him out on his arse. From that day on he was free to succeed outrageously in business and conform to the demands of being Number One Chinese Son.'

'That was before the Prague Spring?' It was a deplorable gambit but she was suddenly overwhelmed by the fear—Why should she be fearful? she angrily demanded of herself—that he was much younger than her.

He chuckled. 'Certainly, well before. I'm flattered. I'm forty-two.' He looked pointedly at her. 'And you?'

'What?' She was disconcerted. Did he expect her to blurt out her age at the table?

'What's your ethnic background?' He deliberately extended the vowels in that phrase, teasing her.

'My father was born in Lahore. His family fled to Bangalore after partition. My mother's family was Anglo-Indian.'

'You're Hindu?'

'Originally. I am an atheist.' She smiled cheekily. 'If you are allowed to say that these days?'

'Shh,' he whispered. 'Don't tell our American cousins.'

After that first dinner they sat together every day of the conference. It somehow became assumed that it would be the case—every morning she found herself waiting for him in the ostentatious cavern of the Hilton's breakfast room. Of course, they were never alone. Yvonne was a curt, no-nonsense French veterinarian in her late forties and she and Aisha developed a quick, early rapport. Their table also included two Germans, Oskar and Sophie, both younger than Aisha, trained veterinarians who now worked for one of the large pharmaceutical companies. Art was courteous and charming to everyone but Aisha was aware that his eyes always strayed towards her. She herself deliberately avoided his gaze, but she could feel it. In part, she avoided it because she realised that the flirtation, though enjoyable, was also dangerously provocative and intense. His knowing smile, his dancing eyes, his gentle attentions, made her feel light-headed and girlish, an altogether astonishing sensation she had never expected to feel again. She could not stop thinking about him.

It was that first morning at breakfast that she had noticed his hands, long fingers and broad, soft palms. His wedding ring was a simple curved band of pure gold. It was almost exactly like hers.

Aisha bought the latest airmail editions of *Vanity Fair* and *Marie Claire* and a crime novel from an English writer she had enjoyed reading in the past, and walked back to the gate. The seats were still packed with the expectant passengers but their frustration and rage had turned into exhausted, resigned collapse. The young Thai woman behind the counter beamed at her, and gushed, 'The plane departs in one hour and thirty minutes, thank you very much.' Aisha stared, incredulous, at the girl. Why was the little fool smiling? She was tempted to make a scene but fought against the impulse. It would only alarm the girl, and— the thought made her smile—just confirm whatever prejudice she had towards Indians. Without acknowledging her, Aisha turned and walked away.

She had noticed a café with internet connection and headed straight for it. She ordered a white wine, extravagantly priced but she didn't give a damn at that moment, took it to a carousel and logged onto her server. Hector had sent her a short email confirming his flight to Bali. Adam and Melissa had also sent her messages, simple, lively and full of news about school. She missed them. She had looked forward to the trip, to time away from the obligations of her work and marriage, and, yes, time off from the demands of her children. The conference had provided a perfect excuse and opportunity. She had been able to step away from the role of mother for a week and it had indeed been a pleasure, had made her feel young again. She thought of Art. It had made her feel desirable as well. But looking at the clumsy, clipped sentences from her children, Aisha felt an overwhelming desire to step back into her real world, to be back home. She wished she hadn't agreed to the extra week in Bali; all she wanted was to be sitting down to dinner with her children and with Hector. She wanted to cook, to be in her own house, to sleep in her own bed. But she'd said yes to a week away with Hector—she knew it was a good idea. She and her husband had not had a holiday alone for years, not since Melissa was born.

She clicked open her husband's email again. He had signed off with a kiss. Did he still love her? Did she love him? The holiday was indeed a good idea, was necessary, but she was now dreading the coming intimacy she would be sharing with Hector. It was so long since she and Hector had spent any decent time together, she was now childishly shy at the thought of being alone with him. She hoped that there were no expectations of thorough analytical talk about their lives and their relationship, their marriage and their family. She didn't think she'd know what to say. They had been together so long that this life was the only one she knew.

The conference itself had met all her expectations, which was to say that it had proved to be only moderately interesting. There were only two sessions she attended in which she felt she had learned anything new at all. The first had been on the opening day and the second on the last day: in between, spokespeople for pharmaceutical companies had spruiked and sold their wares. She could not begrudge them their efforts for she was aware that they were paying for her fine hotel room, for her breakfasts, lunches and dinners. The lecturer who had impressed her on the first day was a Swiss researcher in immunology who had presented a well-articulated report on immunisation and domestic cats, arguing that there appeared to be a demonstrable link between feline renal failure and what the researcher referred to as 'over-immunisation'. Aisha had listened intently to the woman's talk and felt it confirmed observations she herself had come to after years of practice. The immunologist had proposed that instead of annual vaccinations for adult cats, a booster shot be administered every two or three years. The representatives from the pharmaceutical companies had obviously opposed much of the findings, arguing vehemently for further studies on the long-term range of the vaccinations. Like most of the vets there, Aisha knew that the companies must have already begun conducting such longitudinal studies. It was also clear that if the immunologist had been allowed to deliver her lecture above what must surely have been strenuous complaints from the pharmaceutical representatives on the conference board, then her findings were solid. Aisha scrawled a quick reminder on her conference notebook. She would talk to Brendan as soon as she got home about their introducing a new vaccination regime.

On the final day of the conference, in a session just before the plenary, a Thai veterinarian and academic had presented a straight-forward clinical study on the bird-flu epidemic in his native country. The information was chilling, in particular the data on contagion and spread. Aisha, who was not a specialist in avian medicine, found the talk both frightening and stimulating. Because of the economics of food production and distribution, it was inevitable that such epidemics would reach even a relatively isolated continent like Australia. When the academic finished his talk, and humbly bowed to the audience, the applause was prolonged, genuine and effusive. Clapping firmly himself, Art had leaned across to her and whispered close to her ear, his breath warm on her neck, 'We're fucked.' The obscenity had sounded delicious.

She had been in her hotel bathroom, getting ready for the final conference dinner, when her phone rang. It was Art.

'Can I come to your room?'

She was flustered, she should say no, she should seem offended and tell him that it was inappropriate.

He laughed at her silence.

'I'll be there in half an hour.'

She rushed back to the bathroom. The evening before she had sneaked out of a lecture early in order to catch the Skytrain to Gaysorn Plaza. Yvonne had assured her it was the best place in the city for lingerie. Straight after shopping she had gone to her appointment with the hotel hairdresser, and got a leg and bikini wax. All in preparation for Bali, she had told herself. Aisha slipped into her lingerie, then looked into the mirror, at her long brown limbs, their dark glow a startling contrast to the pure white of her new silk bra and pants. She pulled back her hair and arched her neck. Hector always teased her that her neck was that of a swan goddess. She stared at her reflection in the mirror, refusing to hide from herself. She was making herself beautiful for Art. But as aware as she was of the implications of her actions, she was not yet convinced that their flirting, their dance around each other, would be consummated. They were not adolescents, no matter how foolishly they were behaving. She was forty-one, for God's sake, married, a parent, as was he. She let her hair drop down to her shoulders and began to apply mascara. God, it was so much fun to flirt.

His calling her room shocked her—the audacity of it. For the first time that week the possibility of her sleeping with another man seemed more real than at any time since her marriage. It was now a decision she would have to make.

She hadn't touched the bar fridge in her room but after she had finished getting dressed, she fixed herself a gin and tonic.

The knock on the door made her jump. She checked herself in the mirror, twisting to catch her image from behind. She was wearing her favourite dress; it was short-sleeved and fell just above her knees, a faint lemon-coloured silk with a motif of blood-red rose petals. The lightness of the silk, both the fabric and the colour, suited her skin, and the floral pattern added a hint of feminine chasteness. She looked good. She straightened her back. There was a second knock.

Art was wearing a smoky grey, light cotton suit that fitted him perfectly. He was clean shaven, and she caught the hint of peppery spice in the fragrance. He stood back from the door, looking her up and down.

'Lady, you look amazing.'

She kissed him on the cheek. 'Don't be silly.' She stood aside and let him in.

'I'm not being silly. It's a fact. You're the best-looking woman at the conference.'

She ignored the compliment, such as it was. 'You want a drink?'

He eyed the gin and tonic on the coffee table. 'You hitting the mini bar?'

For the first time she minded the accent. There was something too ordinary, too familiar in the North American drawl. This was not real, this was a fantasy. She wished his parents had never left Eastern Europe and that he could speak like a suave, handsome criminal in a James Bond film. He asked for a beer and she handed him one.

He looked around the room, eyeing the bed. Oh God, she thought, don't let him sit on the bed. But instead he took the sofa.

'Cheers.'

'Cheers. To a very successful conference.'

She sat on the desk chair across from him. 'Yes, it wasn't bad, was it? It was so much better than I thought it would be.'

She twirled her glass in her hand. Christ, Aish, she thought, could you sound any more insipid?

He was smiling impudently at her.

'I take it back, what I said about you being the most beautiful woman at the conference. I think you are the most beautiful woman in all Bangkok.'

She laughed. 'I don't think you've conducted a proper scientific survey.' But she was blushing. The foolish, cliched compliment made her feel terrific. She glanced at her watch. 'What time is dinner?'

Was he smirking at her? She deserved it. Dinner was at eight o'clock. They had been reminded of this every hour on the hour at the conference earlier that day.

'Relax, we've got time. We'll head off in twenty minutes.' He finished his beer and looked expectantly at her. She went over to the fridge and poured herself another drink. He was smirking, she was sure of it. The arrogant bastard, he probably did this all the time. A girl in every conference port. With that thought she slammed the fridge door.

Art looked up, startled. 'You okay?'

'It's been a long week. I'm just tired.' She looked at him evenly and smiled coolly. 'Maybe I'll have an early night tonight.'

Art laughed and shook his head. He fumbled in the inside pocket of his jacket and threw a small packet on the table.

'What are they?'

'Diet pills. For when we go dancing.'

'Are we going out dancing, are we?'

'Sure we are. There's no early night for you.'

She picked up the box from the table and read the side of it. The information was printed in Thai and badly worded English. She laughed and chucked the box back on the table. 'I don't think so. It's been a long long time since I've touched speed and I have no interest in doing it again.'

Art's face expressed mock outrage. 'These are no gutter drugs, lady. These are legal and above board.' Art narrowed his eyes. 'So, you have dabbled with speed? I'm not surprised. I knew you were a woman with a past.'

'Exactly. And that's where taking drugs belongs. In the past.'

He shook his head vigorously. 'I disagree. And you disappoint me. There's nothing to worry about. As I said they're perfectly legal. I picked them up from a pharmacist this afternoon.' He winked at her. 'Don't you just love Thailand?'

'I don't know what I think of Thailand. I haven't seen very much apart from hotels, conference centres, Khao San Road and shopping malls.'

'Exactly. That's why we must go dancing. We must.' He looked at her eagerly.

'We'll see.'

They did go dancing. Of course they did. Aisha allowed herself two champagnes at dinner, just enough to feel light-headed but not to lose control. She and Art shared a mango brûlée and then he slipped her two pills under the table. She rubbed them along her fingertips, then, furtively, she slipped them into her mouth, took a quick sip of champagne, and looked nervously down the table.

No one was looking at her, they were too drunk to notice anything.

Art's arm was resting on her chair. She leaned back against it.

After dinner everyone moved to the hotel bar for a spirit. She found herself squeezed between one of the Americans and a Dutch veterinarian whom she'd hardly spoken to during the conference. He was exceedingly tall, fair, in his late forties, but with a cherubic innocence that made him seem much younger. He was eloquent and witty and it was clear that he thought Aisha attractive. Wondering if it was the first flush of the drugs, she found herself striking a pose, wanting to appear beguiling, flirting with him. She knew that Art's eyes were following her every movement.

It was midnight when, as a crowd, they scrambled through the hotel's revolving doors into the sticky humid heat of the tropical night. Taxi drivers tooted loudly for their attention. Art called two of the cabs over. The Dutch man got into the back seat of the first cab and Aisha went to follow. Coolly, but firmly, Art gripped her arm and pulled her aside. Along with Yvonne and Oskar, they took the second cab.

In the back seat, Aisha experienced a delicious wave of euphoria as the vehicle seemed to glide over the twinkling lights of the city. The taxis sped down the freeway that formed an enormous arc over the sprawling metropolis below. Aisha was aware of sweat: hers, Art's, Oskar's, the driver. The moist, dank air seemed to have weight, to be sinking down from the sky into the very earth itself, into the thick sludge from which the city had emerged, the jungle earth to which assuredly the city must one day return. The flickering frantic neon lights were a valiant refusal, a defiant protest against this very inevitability. The cab veered off the freeway and it seemed to Aisha they were all plummeting with it down to the fervid world below.

A million souls in the street. Bands of youth standing, smoking, outside nightclubs; women sitting on the footpaths chatting, their babies sleeping on their laps; stalls on every corner emanating the smell of meat and fish and lemongrass and ginger. Aisha had not been to Asia since her children were born but she remembered the liberation that could be experienced in this chaos of dirt and heat and noise. Australia would seem sterile and antiseptic for the first few days of her return. Art, who had sat in the front with the driver, turned and looked at her. She returned him a smile full of rapture and delight.

The cab pulled up in a small, dusty street filled with bars and cafés. Bored Thai waiters and stoned white tourists were sitting at outdoor tables watching the ubiquitous television screens. Aisha stared at the largest screen. It was playing the new Brad Pitt movie. His voice was drowned out by the mechanical, ferocious pulse of the music coming from the clubs. Usually Aisha couldn't abide doof-doof but now she found herself swaying and tapping, enjoying the music's frenzied single-minded dedication to movement and to dance. Art led them up a narrow stairway, into the music, and she moved straight to the dance floor, unable to resist the compelling, thumping beat. The dance floor was filled with youngsters, drunk European backpackers, but she did not mind. She closed her eyes and found a space of her own amid the jerking bodies. A screeching female vocal called out through the throng: *My love, my love, my love.*

Art had slid in next to her. She sensed it even before she opened her eyes. Art was dancing with her, Yvonne was dancing with her, Oskar and the Dutchman. They were all dancing with her and she was the centre of the dance. She closed her eyes again. *My love, my love, my love.* The drugs had not led to a loss of control; if anything they seemed to have brought her lucidity. She was aware of the whole world around her, the light, sound, sensation. It was years since she'd danced and she found that her body was moving confidently to the music, unselfconsciously, her movements smooth, unexaggerated. Art, she was pleased to see, was also a good dancer. She must take Hector out dancing in Bali. It had always been a point of pride for her, his skills and his ease as a dancer. Hector loved music and in his dancing he proclaimed it to the world. Art was good but he was not as good as Hector. She closed her eyes again. *My love, my love, my love.*

The DJ's drop into the next track was clumsy, the rhythms clashed and the resulting noise was ugly and discordant. But the crowd was cheerful, forgiving. Aisha almost let out a squeal of delight as she recognised the hypnotic whiplash of the song—Beyonce's *Crazy in Love.* Melissa had adored the song as a toddler. Aisha and Hector would fall about laughing watching their naked daughter wiggle her bum in rapt imitation of the singer's movements on the video. The dance floor was full, she was surrounded by flesh, by joy. They were all singing. She was complete in her body, her mind and body were one, and the one was the dance. All that mattered was the dance. It came to an end too soon, the frantic rhythms faded into the dull, unvarying thud of a track she did not recognise. Aisha walked away from the dance floor.

The toilets were disgusting, crowded: the suffocating stench of excrement, the floor flooded. Aisha splashed water on her face, careful to not get any in her mouth, and she slipped through the mob of girls into the corridor outside. Art was standing there, his tie loosened. A lanky Thai lady-boy, heavily made up and wearing a shimmering gold lamé dress, was chatting him up. Aisha walked over and put her arm around Art.

'She your girlfriend?'

Art cocked his eyes sheepishly. Aisha winked at him and turned to the drag queen, nodding. At that moment Art turned to her and kissed her full on the lips. The drag queen squealed.

'You are one lucky lady.'

Art's mouth tasted salty, of spices, chilli, lemongrass. Gently he broke away from her. He was looking into her eyes. 'I'm one lucky man.'

Hector and Aisha had been together for nineteen years. In all that time she had never been unfaithful. She had been with other men before him, but only a few. She silently counted them as the lift sped to Art's floor. Eddie, tall, good-natured, what the girls back then referred to as a 'hornbag'. Their courtship began on the beaches of Scarborough. He was older, she was gratified that someone so popular, so attractive, had made a play for her. But she quickly became bored with him and dumped him as soon as she started uni. The only good thing to come out of being with Eddie was her friendship with his sister Rosie. After Eddie there was a boy she had met at a party in Northbridge, a half-Croatian guitarist with the beginnings of a heroin problem. Michael was tall, just like Eddie, but that was the only similarity. Michael was certainly not dull. Instead, he was moody, unkempt, unshaven and noncommittal, and he might just have broken her heart if she had let him. She did not let him. It was not just his drug addiction. At that time what pissed her off more was his inability to return messages or keep to appointments. She did not find his masculine evasiveness endearing or masochistically romantic and when he took a week to return a call, she asked her mother to say she'd call back. She never did. After Michael there was Mr Sam De Costa, her tutor in anatomy. Sam was thirty, also tall, married, stylish and always well-dressed, passionate about European cinema and early rock and roll. Their affair lasted the whole of her second year of veterinary science. That had definitely been love and Sam had definitely broken her heart. Soon after the breakup she had a drunken one-night stand with an inexperienced young science student. She'd ended up in his dorm and he had passed out before coming. She had stumbled out of his room and gone back downstairs to the party where she followed another inexperienced young science student back to his room. She had fucked both of them in order to feel desired again. Sam's abandonment of her had made her feel so gutted that she believed she could never be whole again. It had broken her, led her to step into the shadows of annihilation, but she had not succumbed. The closest she came was scraping the edge of a knife against her wrists and acting like a silly self-loathing whore with those two science undergraduates. After that she transferred her studies to Melbourne. Soon after she met Peter, a carpenter, the brother of another vet student, and they had dated for six months. He was only a few years older than her, and she had felt very little for him. But he was very attractive, virile and confident. They also looked good together and she found that this was important to her. The sex with him was the best she had ever had. Peter, however, had fallen in love with her and in order to make him hate her, she slept with his best friend, Ryan. And then she met Hector.

Eddie, Michael, Sam, the two undergraduates, Peter, Ryan and Hector. Eight men, the only thing they had in common was that they were tall and good-looking. As was Art. It was not much of a pattern.

She could hear Art pissing in the bathroom. She fell onto the bed, her head was spinning and her mouth felt dry. His room was identical to hers, watercolours of Buddhist temples on the wall, an unadorned desk and chair, a thick cushioned armchair, generic hotel floor-to-ceiling windows overlooking the neon and lights of Bangkok below. The sound of his urinating was faintly repellent to her. Eight men and now Art would be her ninth. She was hardly a slut. She heard the toilet flush. She was married, she was a mother, she was about to sleep with another man, a stranger really. She *was* a slut. She would have sex with Art, that would be it, a one-night affair, she would file it away, far from her life, far from her family and marriage. It would not count. It would not be part of her life.

Art was standing at the foot of the bed. He had taken off his tie and slowly he began to unbutton his shirt. There was nothing effeminate about his actions; he was being deliberately slow, he seemed firm and confident. He flung off his shirt and she looked at his chest, smooth, almost hairless except for the few long, fine black strands around his nipples. His trousers bunched clumsily around his crotch. She could tell he had an erection.

'What's your wife like?'

He stopped. Aisha knew that she was stalling, that she had not fully committed to what was about to happen. She had thought the decision made—in the cab, at the dance club, back at the hotel, in the lift—but she could stop it all now. She could make it not happen. Art stretched out next to her on the bed. She was overwhelmed by the pugnacity of his smell, sweaty and masculine, like Hector but not

Hector. His hand was slipping over her thigh. He was lifting her dress and she was aroused.

'My wife is beautiful. And smart. She works in public television. Her family is French-speaking and apart from her perfect English she also speaks Spanish, Catalan, Russian and passable Arabic.'

'What does she do in television?'

'She produces documentaries.'

'She sounds brilliant.'

He drew his hand away from her and rolled over onto his back.

'Aisha, I want to make love to you. At this moment I don't want to think about my wife or about my life back in Montreal. I don't want you to think about your husband or your life in Australia. I think you are possibly the most desirable woman I have ever met. I am not just saying that to seduce you further, it is the truth.' He rolled back on his side and looked down at her. 'I'm not interested in the morality of what we are doing, the right or wrong of it. I want to fuck you—that's all that matters, all I care about at this moment. But I won't if you don't want me to or are too scared to. If we don't fuck, it will be a regret of mine till my dying day.'

He grinned and suddenly, without warning, he gently kissed her lips. 'Don't you want to fuck me?' he asked.

His purpose, his determination, his assurance convinced her. She had felt this once about Hector, the visceral swooning lust a woman could experience in a man. She took Art's hand and slid it under the crotch of her new silk panties, and as she did that, she arched her neck, raised her face to his, and kissed him.

An announcement came over the airport public address system asking for travellers on the next Garuda flight to Denpasar and Jakarta to proceed to their gate. The confirmation acted as a balm on the exhausted travellers around Aisha, and they began to talk excitedly to one another. Across the seat from her sat a young American couple, students, she presumed. The girl seemed agitated, as if the message from the loudspeaker had upset her in some way. Aisha's practised medical eye took in the situation. The girl was under the influence of some drug; her pupils were dilated, her skin unnaturally flushed and she was sweating profusely, even in the artificial air-conditioned chill of the airport. The woman was overheating. It was stupid to be in such a state in Bangkok airport. She hoped the fool didn't have any drugs on her. The girl began to cry.

Aisha sighed, rolled up her magazine and forced it into her handbag. 'Is there anything I can do to help?'

The boy's face was grim. He too had probably taken some form of narcotic but his body was metabolising the drug much more effectively. 'We're okay. She's a bit scared of flying.'

The girl shook her head violently. 'I'm not fucking scared of flying. I'm scared of bombs. I'm scared of getting blown up in the middle of the air.' Her tone was not yet hysterical, but it could get there.

Aisha looked across to the counter where a stewardess, still smiling, was clearly observing them. The girl seemed paranoid. That too could be the drugs.

Aisha knelt before the girl. 'We are perfectly safe. Thailand is very safe.'

'There's been bombings in Thailand.' The girl had stopped crying, but wore a petulant scowl. It reminded Aisha of Melissa after a tantrum. The face was daring Aisha to argue with her.

And, yes, she felt like saying, there have been bombings here, that is true. She herself had felt flutters of fear on entering the airport, joining the queue for the security check; she had even experienced a moment of senseless panic on seeing two Saudi men in the queue. Grow up, she wanted to say to the girl—you want to travel, deal with it. This is the world.

She took the girl's hand. 'I'm a medical practitioner. I think part of the problem is that you might need some food and water.' She looked up at the man. 'We've got plenty of time before the flight leaves. I'd get some food.'

The boy looked grateful for her intervention.

The girl scowled again. 'I'm not hungry.'

Aisha rose to her feet. There was nothing more she could so. She sat back in her seat and took out her magazine.

An elderly woman, heavily made up, was sitting next to her clutching a stuffed overnight bag. 'That was very kind of you,' she whispered. She was also American. They watched the boy lead the girl down the corridor.

'My husband was exactly like that. He was terrified of planes.'

Aisha nodded, curtly, flicking the pages of the magazine. She stopped at a perfume advertisement, two naked bodies, one black, one white, entwined such that their gender was a blur.

'Where are you from?'

Aisha faked a gracious smile and turned to the woman. 'I'm Australian.'

'I'm going there, I'm going there.' The woman was almost absurdly eager. 'It looks so beautiful, and I just think Australians are wonderful.' She beamed at Aisha. 'You're exactly like us.'

Aisha resisted laughing. Art had said that too. What reassurance were the North Americans seeking?

'Everyone loves Australians,' the old woman continued, but was now sounding glum. 'We just love you.'

Aisha turned back to the magazine, and turned the page over. But the photograph remained vivid in her mind. Two bodies entwined, one black, one white, impossible to tell where one began and where the other ended.

Art's whiteness had surprised her. His face, neck and arms were tanned from the unrelenting Asian heat, but the rest of his body was the hue of Arcadian marble. Her body had seemed almost obscenely dark next to his. She had allowed him to lead their lovemaking, had submitted to the sureness of his desire. At first, she was afraid that the amphetamines in her body would make her detached from the experience. Her own pleasure seemed muted, she could not give herself over to the rush of lust. Art's body felt strange, foreign; she could not help comparing him to her husband. Hector was a better kisser. Art's litheness, so attractive when he was dressed in his suit or his expertly chosen shirts and jackets, seemed almost too slight for her. She did not know how to hold him, where to put her hands. The smoothness of his body was distracting, so different from the carnality of Hector's hirsute flesh. She closed her eyes and gave in, dropping her hands to her side. She allowed Art to explore her body. And then, as his hand moved between her legs, her body jolted, and she pressed herself against him. She was now part of the sex, not outside it, no longer remote but aroused by the unfamiliarity of him, his body, his smell, his cock, his breath, his hands, his skin. She opened her eyes and pushed him off her. His eyes expressed a momentary confusion until she straddled him and began to kiss his chest, his nipples, his neck, his chest again, tracing her tongue down his navel to his crotch. She took his penis into her mouth, heard his moan of pleasure. It felt slutty, dangerous. His salty masculine taste was in her mouth, on her face, she was enveloped in it.

She lifted her head. 'Have you got a condom?'

'In my pocket,' he whispered. Still teasing him with her tongue, she felt for his trousers which were around his ankles. She found the condom and then pulled his trousers and underwear off him. Not moving her eyes from his, she tore open the packet and slipped the thin rubber over his cock.

He pulled her towards him, lifted her dress over her head and then expertly unhooked her bra. 'Let me look at you.'

She put her hands behind her head, stretched back on the bed. He touched her face, her lips, her nipples, her cunt.

'*Magnifique.*' His eyes wandered over her whole body. He repeated the word, his voice dazed, almost breaking from his desire.

He was a better fuck than Hector. At first, as he pushed himself inside, it had seemed strange. Hector's cock was larger, thicker;

sometimes, if she was not ready or aroused, it hurt. Once intercourse had been initiated, Hector could not control his passion. His thrustings were almost violent and over time she had allowed herself to slip into fantasies of assault to accommodate his zeal. In the beginning, Art's slow, gentle fucking of her seemed timid, disconcerting. But very soon she began to respond to his rhythm and she pushed her body hard into him to meet his thrusts, until all that remained was the glint in Art's adoring eyes as he watched her, the feel of his mouth against hers when they kissed, his cock filling her cunt as they fucked. There came a moment when his body began to buck, to resist the urge for release. She felt him tense and falter. She gripped his thighs and whispered an appeal in his ear: come. He pushed into her, held her body against his, his hips spasming. He groaned, orgasmed, let out a cry and pushed his face into her neck. Then abruptly he was kissing her. Spread your legs, he ordered, and she obeyed. He was kissing her again, his fingers furiously working, filling her. Their mouths could not let each other go. A rush of delirious pleasure flooded through her. Slowly, very slowly, the world came back in.

The brevity of the flight, as always, came as a surprise. It took at least six hours to fly across the length of Australia but in less than half that time they had begun their descent into Denpasar. After the metropolitan sprawl of the airport in Bangkok, Bali's international airport seemed provincial, easily navigable and not at all daunting. She paid her arrival tax and confidently followed the bilingual signs to the baggage carousel. Customs proved efficient. She was glad for the abrasive manners and countenance of the mainly Javanese security staff. She smiled to herself. It was a welcome to allow herself to be brisk, methodical, straightforward, after the suffocating politeness of the Thais. She had heard enough to know that she would expect similar courtesy from the Balinese. But at least, till she cleared customs, entered the street, she could be herself.

Hector was sitting on a bench, arms outstretched, waiting for her. He was dressed casually but she noted the good taste of his new short-sleeved shirt, the fine cut of his loose cotton trousers. She was glad he was in long pants, a stylish contrast to the unshaven, long-haired backpackers swarming around her. He had just had a haircut, as she knew he would have. He broke into a wide grin as she approached and embraced her warmly. He smelt of her life, of her home and of her kids, and she slipped happily, relieved, into his strong arms. Art had been too thin. With that thought the decision was made. Art disappeared out of her life.

She kissed her husband and asked about Adam and Melissa.

'They're fine. They miss you but *Giagia* and *Pappou* are going to spoil them rotten. And they know it. They've been looking forward to it all week.'

'Have you been waiting ages?' she asked apologetically.

'A few hours.' He shrugged good-naturedly. 'What you gonna do? I've been taking in the local colour.'

She could not smell nicotine on him. He said he had not smoked for three or four months, but she thought he'd probably sneaked a few when he was out drinking with Dedj or his cousin. Secretly she hoped he would smoke during the holiday; he could be a moody shit otherwise. He did not smell of tobacco and he seemed relaxed and happy, even after what must have been a tedious, fretful wait for her. A group of young Australian women passed by, wheeling ridiculously enormous luggage, all sheafed in rolls of shrink-wrap. Aisha noticed that two of them had glanced back at Hector. Smiling, she linked arms with her husband.

'Well, I hope you haven't been flirting with the local colour while you were waiting for me.'

Hector winked. 'The locals aren't interested in my pasty white arse. And the tourists all seem to be cashed-up bogans with plenty of money and no bloody taste or brains.' He indicated the doors. 'You ready to brave getting a driver?'

The pleasant, sterile chill of the long hours she had spent in the sealed air-conditioned world of airports and aeroplanes was immediately shattered once they stepped through the doors into the moist, viscid air of Asia. She let Hector guide her through the mob of tourists haggling diffidently and inexpertly with the beaming Balinese drivers who formed shouting, gesticulating circles around them. Hector bowled through the crowd, ignoring both the tourists and the Balinese and he led her to a bench where two old men were smoking. They sat down. One of the old men went to say something but Hector rudely held up his hand and silenced him. He put his arm around her and though it was almost unbearably hot, even with the intensity of the noise and the smells and the light, she was glad for the weight of him, the warmth and wetness of his skin against hers.

'What are we waiting for?'

'Just let the madness die down for a moment.' He massaged her neck. 'It's an old smoker's trick. You go off to a corner, have a cigarette, wait for the non-smokers to deal with the riff-raff.' He beamed at her. 'Except I'm no longer a smoker.'

The strategy seemed to work. Anytime someone approached them, Hector would start whispering in her ear and the hawkers would wander off. An old man, with close-cropped white hair, his skin tough, lined with savage deep wrinkles, sat down beside them, his back straight, dignified. He nodded, smiled, and took a cigarette from his shirt pocket.

'You go Kuta?'

Hector shook his head. 'We're going to Ubud.'

The old man slapped his chest. 'I go Ubud. I take you. I am very cheap.' He smiled an almost toothless grin.

She let Hector negotiate a price. He was more generous than she would have been, but she didn't care. She had enjoyed her week of independence, but she preferred the security of coupledom, the knowledge that there was someone there to share responsibility, someone there all the time. The week in Thailand, Art and her infidelity, all that was evaporating.

She had seen nothing of the countryside in Thailand and she was intoxicated by the lush colours and smells of the jungle as the car drove away from the congested city and up into the central mountains. Not that there was any stretch of land free from the presence of human settlement. Stalls lined both sides of the road selling a dizzying array of jewellery, ceramics, Hindu and Buddhist idols, trinkets and clothes. Dogs, hens and roosters darted out across the street and every few minutes their driver would furiously beep the horn to avoid hitting them. The air-conditioning was on full blast in the car but Aisha had wound down her window and was breathing in the rich, foetid aroma of the world outside. Hector and the driver were discussing Ubud but she was only half-paying attention. She was aware that the driver had started some harangue about Muslims. She caught his eye looking at her in the rear-view mirror.

'You Christian?'

Hector answered before she had time to formulate a response. 'I'm a Christian. My wife is Hindu.'

Flinching, she moved away from Hector. She knew the island was largely Hindu, it was obvious in the overwhelming number of domestic and public shrines. But just as obviously she did not belong to that world. She was tempted to clarify Hector's comment, to announce her atheism, but she knew that would be rude. The driver's eye was on her again, it seemed he was about to speak, but he remained silent. Hector, unaware of his faux pas, grabbed her hand. She fought the urge to pull it away from him.

When the driver did speak again it was not of religion. 'You go beach?'

Hector shook his head. 'We're not interested in seeing Kuta at all.'

'Why?'

'Too many Australians.'

The driver laughed out loud. Then he turned and patted Hector on the arm. 'Australians very good people. Balinese like Australians very much. Only stupid Muslim pigs not like Australians.'

Aisha wondered if he would begin another tirade.

'You go north for swimming. You go Amed. Amed is beautiful and quiet.' He sighed. 'No good since bombing. Bad for people in Amed.' His voice brightened and he turned back round to face them. Watch the road, Aisha wanted to scream at him.

'This week is full moon, very special the full moon in Amed. Very beautiful. Very good beaches. Very good fishing.'

'Are you from there?'

'No. My wife from Amed.'

Aisha leaned forward. 'Is she very beautiful as well?'

The old man chuckled. 'She grandmother. She old.'

For the rest of the drive he and Hector discussed children and family while she sunk back in her seat, stared out the window and was engulfed by the breath of Asia.

The first thing she did after they were shown to their room was to ask Hector to fuck her. Hector responded to the urgency of her request; he kissed her roughly, biting her lip, exactly what she wanted from him. Moaning, she turned around and lay on her stomach on the bed. He pulled her underpants off, forced her legs apart, she heard him unzip, the tearing open of a condom packet, and then his cock was entering her. She gritted her teeth, choked back a cry as he pushed hard inside her, the pain slicing her, the sensation exactly what she wanted, needed, what she deserved. She took one, two, three, four shallow gulps of air, winced, and then she was above the pain. Hector was now a jackhammer, slamming into her, she was full of him, as much in her belly as in her cunt, she buried her face into the coverlet, her outstretched hands were clutching at the sheets, the fabric coiled around her fingers: she wanted him to fill her completely. He was smashing into her, tearing her apart, destroying her and putting her back together. She was crying from the pain and from the relief. She was still nowhere near arousal when he climaxed—he came with a roar, not touching her—but she let out a loud, grateful moan. He fell on top of her and she savoured the heaviness of his wet body over hers. He had made her his again.

Hector rolled off her, flicked off the condom and chucked it on the floor. His shorts dangled from his left foot, his shirt was open to his midriff and he rubbed the moist thick hair on his chest. He hadn't taken off his sandals. She raised herself on her elbow and took his red, still half-erect cock in her palm. Droplets of watery semen oozed out of the top of his foreskin.

He shuddered, pushed her hand away. 'It's too tender,' he complained. She wiped her hand across the bedding. He softly kissed her on the lips.

'Do you want to come?' he asked.

She shook her head and returned his kiss. 'No,' she whispered, 'I don't need to. I'm happy.'

Over the next few days she fell in love with Ubud. The town itself consisted of a cluster of villages and she and Hector immediately fell into a routine that consisted of having a tropical breakfast served on the balcony of their room, then taking a long walk through the forests or the villages, before coming back at noon for a swim in the art deco pool at the hotel. The water was fresh and clean, and Aisha loved standing underneath the tall battered stone statue of a laughing, reclining Buddha which poured water into the pool. After their swim they would have a drink by the pool, read, and then stroll into town for lunch. After lunch there would be more exploration of the countryside, or the crowded market where freshly slaughtered meat and plump fruit and vegetables were sold to the villagers while the tourists strolled through the walkways above, bartering for fake designer watches, rolls of cheap fabrics, and small faux silver and bronze icons. In the late afternoon they would return to their hotel, have another swim to refresh themselves, and then wander the main street for a place to eat. The stroll returning home in the afternoon became her favourite time of day. They would take a zigzag path, follow the tiny alleys that took them past courtyards where, in the cooling shade of evening, young women would light incense and proffer offerings to the shrines of their ancestors. In the back streets they were not bothered by touts, or the surly desperate drivers. They would be largely ignored except for a shy smile from the young women, a polite grin from workmen and the pealing laughter of the old women and children. *Hello, hello*, the children would call out to them in their sing-song English, *Where you from?* They would fall about laughing when told they were Australian and a boy would invariably call out a mangled, *Goodday*, while another would mime the hops of a kangaroo.

The outrageous poverty of the island, the all-too-obvious reliance on a faltering tourist trade was something she and Hector had discussed on their first night, and from them on he refused to barter, simply handing over the amount of *Rupiah* first requested by a hawker or a stall owner. She had to stand away from him when he went to buy something, a shirt, presents for the children and his family, because she was embarrassed that the Balinese mistook his extravagance for him being a dupe. She had to stop herself reprimanding him, You could have got it for half the price, because she knew he would answer, I'm not going to haggle for something worth less than a coffee back home. She could not bring herself to be like him. She was her father's daughter and believed that negotiation and bartering were integral to trade. But in Ubud, uncharacteristically, she favoured the seller in bargaining, and she tipped generously.

The leisurely pace of village life was attractive to both of them, but Aisha was also conscious that everyone, man, woman and child, worked hard. It was obvious in the bowed bodies of the old women in the rice paddies, in the weathered, leathery hands of the workmen rebuilding the bridge over the river, or the drenched skin of the young stonemasons they passed on the way back from the Monkey Forest. The calm, dutiful morning and evening offerings to the ancestors, the gentle smiles, the intense organic smells of the tropics, the submission to work and family, the sharp light and constant shine of the Asian sun, the cheer and fearlessness of the children who ran and roamed the streets freely—an abandonment lost to her children; Aisha fell in love with Ubud.

The peace was shattered on their third night with their first argument. The day had begun badly. Hector had woken her before breakfast with a silly, lascivious grin on his face and his fat erection poking in her thigh. She had submitted to his lovemaking—penance for her adultery, the thought wickedly and shamefully crossing her mind as her husband mounted her—but she resisted his roughness. She could see his puzzlement: delighted by her animal hunger on that first day, he had no doubt assumed that she was willing to indulge what she found the most prurient of his appetites—to dominate her, to get off on the aggression in sex. But she felt unable to be reckless and realised that she resented his assumption. She felt like a whore; after Art Hector was now fucking her like a whore. With her consent, yes, even with her encouragement. But as he slobbered over her while she attempted to bring herself fully into consciousness, all she felt was a repulsion for the absurd theatrics of his lust. They were not newlyweds, adolescents embarking on a new affair. They were husband and wife, parents. She rolled out from underneath him as soon as he had climaxed and left him lying naked on the bed, embarrassed and resentful while she went into the openair bathroom, splashed water on her face and looked into the mirror. She felt lousy. And her period was coming.

Hector had been snarly all through breakfast, and snappy and uncommunicative on their walk. She was happy with the slowness of the pace in Ubud and happy to remain in the mountains for the duration of the week. Hector, she knew, would prefer to spend a few days at the beach, his argument being that it was not a real holiday unless it involved lying on the sand somewhere by the sea. Aisha, who had been raised on the edge of the nurturing solitude of the Indian Ocean, did not agree. Western Australia probably had the best beaches in the world. She had been to the Mediterranean, and indeed, the azure waters were breathtaking, the joy of life on the Greek islands was intoxicating, but she had detested sharing a beach with scores of other humans. Her upbringing had spoiled her. She felt no need to visit Balinese tourist beaches.

They returned to the hotel tired, sweating, and Hector wordlessly headed to the pool, dumped his bag on a fold-out chair, stripped to his underpants and hurled himself into the water.

When he emerged he was smiling. 'Come in,' he called out. 'It's refreshing.'

'I'll go change.'

'No need. Strip to your panties.'

'Don't be silly.'

He came to the pool's edge. She realised he was pulling at his cock under the water. 'There's no one around.'

'There's the staff.'

He laughed. 'They won't mind. We're just decadent Westerners. I'm sure they expect it.'

She shook her head. 'I'm not a decadent Westerner. I'll go get into my bathers.'

'Suit your fucking self.'

His mood had darkened again and he dived back under the water. She cursed him as she walked back to the room. He was a child. He was a child every time he did not get his own way. He wanted her to agree to the beach, he obviously wanted a cigarette, he wanted everything to go his way. She did not look at him as she dived into the pool. The water was indeed lovely, another world away from the thick, humid wall of heat. She swam laps and then floated on her back, staring at the white wisps of cloud in the startling sky above.

Hector's mood continued to sour all afternoon and by dinner time he was spoiling for a fight. She had suggested going to La Luna for dinner. It was expensive, for Bali at least, but the food was excellent and she loved that the balcony looked over the hothouse lushness of the river.

Hector groaned at the suggestion. 'Again. We've already been there for dinner and once for lunch. I want to do something different.'

'Fine.' She was sitting at the vanity table, putting in new earrings she had bought that afternoon from a stall in town. She jiggled her ears. They looked good. 'There's heaps of places. We'll find somewhere else.'

'I'm bored.' He sat on the bed scowling at her. She looked at him in the mirror. His hair was plastered back against his scalp. He had just finished showering and his towel was loosely folded across his lap. In two days his skin had tanned dark. She turned away from his reflection and concentrated on her earrings. She had been startled again by how handsome her husband was. Even with the sprinkle of grey in his hair and unshaven face, he looked much younger than his years. It seemed an apt irony that she, who prided herself on her cool, rational logic, was still locked into a love for this man that sprang completely from desire. Sometimes she didn't know if she even liked Hector—he could be such a lout. He was still scowling heavily at her, she could sense it behind her back, like Adam in a temper, waiting for her to make things right. But Adam was a child and Hector was middle-aged. She might not like her husband but she still thought him the most beautiful man in the world. Beside her, together, they looked a great couple. They inspired envy. She was startled by his shout.

'I'm bored,' he called out, clownishly falling back on the bed, his legs in the air, the wet towel slipping to the floor. 'I'm fucking bored with fucking Ubud.' He rolled back to his feet. 'Let's go tomorrow. It will be full-moon Thursday. Let's go and see the full moon in Amed.'

He was such a child.

'I'm sure every driver on the island claims that the full moon looks best from their village. I like Ubud. I don't see any reason to leave.'

'I want to swim.'

'That's why we booked a place with a pool.'

'I want to swim in the sea.'

Adam was exactly like Hector. What would she say to Adam? 'If you want to go to Amed, you organise it. You organise the travel, the hotel, the drive back to the airport. If you take care of it all I'm happy to go wherever.'

He eyed her suspiciously. 'You sure?'

'I'm sure.'

'Nah.' He sniffed dismissively. 'You'll hold it against me.'

She swung the chair around. 'I will not.'

'You won't like the room I book, you'll find something to complain about.'

She turned back to the mirror. 'Fuck you, Hector. I'm not your mum.'

It was a good shot, she had wounded him. He went silent. She finished applying her make-up and looked around for her shoes.

'Sandi's pregnant.'

She didn't respond, wary of the dangerous terrain they were entering.

'She's past the first trimester.' A pause. 'Harry told me just before I left for here.'

She was certain he purposefully had missed a beat between sentences. The bastard was toying with her. 'That's good news for Sandi.' She managed a smile, and headed towards the bathroom. 'I'm very happy for her.'

She heard his mutter. He said it low, under his breath, but it was clear and distinct. *Bet you aren't so happy for Harry, are you?*

Why did those words sting so much? Why did she feel so ludicrously jealous? She *was* jealous. She wanted him to choose between her and his cousin. It seemed so simple. She wanted his loyalty. She would not think about Art: she deserved her husband's loyalty. Harry was a violent, cruel man.

She sat on the toilet seat and looked up at the sky. She didn't know what she was doing in the bathroom. The clouds had disappeared and the emerging constellations beamed down at her. She could smell the nutty sour spices of Indonesian food.

He knocked on the door. 'I need to get dressed.'

He was still in a temper. She rose and flushed the toilet. She walked past him without speaking.

She wished she could go back to the beginning of the day and change everything. Wake before Hector, suggest a lazy morning by the pool rather than a long, hot walk. But the day had begun as it had, and it seemed determined to follow its own course. Every step seemed to escalate their animosity so that by the time they sat down to dinner they could not complete a sentence without wanting to kill each other. He had suggested they have a drink and then dinner at a posh-looking restaurant set in the grounds of a Hindu temple. A moat covered in gigantic luxuriant lily pads surrounded the tables. She wanted to eat there but she was still pissed off with him for refusing to return to La Luna and so she just replied shortly, No, let's not go there. It's too expensive. He didn't answer. Instead he walked ahead at an infuriating rate, so that she had to almost run to keep up with him. An anxious-looking young man stepped out to offer them a car and Hector spat out the words, Fuck off, in his face. The man recoiled, as if Hector was a viper in his path, as if he was the very devil himself. Aisha was convinced that Hector's temper was due to his not smoking. She was going to buy him a packet of cigarettes. She'd bloody well force them down his throat. Let him die early. She wanted him to die early. She raced after her husband, slipping on the uneven broken footpath and nearly twisting an ankle. Hector didn't even bother to stop. It was not just the smoking, there was something about a holiday that accentuated every irritation and annoyance she felt about her husband. What they had together over the last three days was uninterrupted time and that was something that had not been theirs for years. Again she wondered, Do I really like this man?

Hector abruptly turned into an over-lit touristy cabana. A four-piece band was glumly picking and hitting their gamelan instruments, playing traditional Indonesian music as if it was muzak in a mall. The place was terrible and she knew Hector knew it and had veered inside deliberately.

'Will this do?'

She wanted to hit him.

Instead, she nodded.

The young Balinese waitress rushed over to them and they were seated. The nervous young girl, in hesitant English, offered them menus. Hector ordered beers for both of them. The waitress inquired about what they would like to eat and Hector slapped the menu on the table. Give us a bloody moment. The girl, shocked, embarrassed, stared at him, and then hung her head and bowed. Aisha could not bring herself to look at her.

'That was a terrible thing to do,' she chided him as the girl walked away. Hector ignored her, but he was blushing. Good, he was ashamed. When the girl returned with the drinks, he apologised to her. This seemed to alarm her even further. He ended up repeating *Terima Kasih, Terima Kasih,* until she smiled and he could smile back. Aisha wanted to laugh, suddenly he seemed goofy and lovable again, but in his present mood he was liable to interpret laughter only in a thousand negative ways. She would not speak until he spoke. Her stomach felt tight, her head was throbbing. She doubted she could eat. The beer was refreshingly cold and she drank it greedily.

'I think you should ring Sandi and congratulate her.'

'I'll send a card.'

'*I'll send a card.*' He made his voice hideous, whiney, jeering her. He turned away from her, shaking his head. 'You're fucking incredible.'

'What?' She meant it. What had she done? What did he want from her?

'I don't want you to send a card. I want you to ring her. I want you to go over and see her.'

'I have no problem with seeing Sandi, you know that.'

'You just have a problem with my cousin.'

My cousin, *my* mate, *my* man Harry. 'Yes, I do have a problem with your cousin.'

'Can't you just forgive him?'

'For assaulting my best friend's child? And for doing it at my home? No, I'm not going to forgive him.'

'That child deserved it.'

'Hugo is a child. Your cousin is meant to be a grown man.'

'*Your cousin is meant to be a grown man.*' That same ugly jeer. Aisha watched two couples walk hesitantly up the steps and into the restaurant. One of the women held a baby and one of the men was holding a toddler's hand. Another waitress emerged from the shadows at the back of the restaurant. For the first time Aisha was aware of the world just a few metres away from her. She could see bodies moving around in a kitchen, the flicker of a television set. She knew her husband's eyes were looking straight at her but she ignored him. Reaching for her beer she caught Hector's eye and he pounced.

'He's a terrible child.'

'He's just turned four. How can a four-year-old be terrible?'

'By not having been disciplined, by not being taught to respect other people. He's a terrible child now and he'll turn out to be a cunt of an adult when he grows up.'

She would not take the bait. He was using the word *cunt* in exactly the way she hated it to be used, as a vileness, as an insult to her. He was doing so deliberately. The two couples were French and she was conscious that the young waitress had switched easily to speaking the language.

'Harry at least had the decency to go and apologise to them.' Hector was shaking his head in disbelief. He leaned across the table, furious. 'It should have been Rosie crawling on her hands and knees asking his forgiveness.'

She felt her reserve break, split apart. That sounded exactly like his mum. Exactly Koula's words, her expression, her sentiment.

'What did Rosie do except protect her son?'

'What Rosie has done is use Hugo as an excuse not to deal with the failures of her relationship with Gary. And just like she indulges Gary and refuses to deal with the reality of his situation . . . like his being a fucking alco, like his being the world's greatest artist in his own head but unfortunately he doesn't have any bloody talent . . . like the fact he never wanted the kid in the first place.' Hector breathed deeply. When he spoke again his tone was quieter, more measured. 'I don't doubt that Rosie loves her child. Jesus, Aish, I don't doubt Gary's love for him. But they are complete fuck-ups as parents. He's a little monster. No one likes him. Our kids can't bear being with him. What does that tell you?'

She kept silent. She felt overwhelming pity and despair for Hugo. She saw him interact with such puzzlement and hurt when confronted with the world. He was shocked that he was not the centre of the world when he stepped away from Rosie. But he'd learn. Of course he'd learn. That was also the way of the world, that was what happened with kids. They met other kids.

'He'll change when he goes to school.'

'Yeah,' Hector was laughing. 'Yeah, sweetheart, he'll change and you know why he will change? Because the other kids are going to bash the living shit out of him. Have you asked our kids what they thought of Harry slapping him?'

She could not believe he'd had this conversation with their children. She leaned across the table.

'What have you been saying about this to Adam and Melissa?'

He gauged her temper and sat back. 'Nothing.'

'So how do you know?'

He didn't answer her.

'How do you know?'

He crossed his arms defensively.

She suddenly guessed. She let out a hollow laugh. 'Your bloody mother. Of course.'

'Harry's family, Aish. Rocco is their cousin. They know what's going on.'

'You mean they get *told* what's going on.'

He spoke calmly. 'They were there. I think they made up their own minds about it.'

She experienced a moment of panic, almost vertigo. It had to do with her children. They belonged to Hector in a way they could not belong to her. Her husband and her children were connected through family, through that network of kin that was not available to her. It would not have mattered if her mother lived in Melbourne with them. Her mother would not be able to bear a life revolving only around her children and grandchildren. She had her practice, her friends and her own life; her family were part of that life, not all of it. Aisha thought that was wise—how life should be. She could live a continent apart from her family. Hector could not. She knew this when she had married him. In agreeing to be with him, she had to agree to be with all of him. But she had never stopped resenting that fact, and knew that her children would never be able to understand that resentment. She wished Raf lived in the same city with her. They loved her brother as much as she did. But she couldn't share their love for their *giagia* and *pappou*, for their uncles and aunts. Of course, she had affection for Manolis, sure, a solid friendship with her sister-in-law, Elizabeth. But her real family in Melbourne was Rosie and Anouk. And her children did not love them.

She looked at her husband with something approaching hatred. You've bound me to your life, she thought bitterly. How had it happened?

One of the women called out in French to the toddler who was walking over to the bandstand. She half-rose to grab him but the band leader raised his arm, called out *D'accord, D'accord*, and lifted the child onto his lap. Delighted, the little boy began to shyly tap on the xylophone, drawing excited laughter from the musicians.

Aisha nodded towards the bandstand. 'Isn't that lovely?'

Hector turned around and looked at the little boy now happily bashing the xylophone's keys. He smiled widely and turned back to Aisha. 'He's having the time of his life.'

'So's his mother.' The French woman was holding a beer and laughing with her friends. The child's laughter, garrulous, ecstatic, suddenly seemed to have banished all the bitterness and resentment of the day.

Aisha touched her husband's hand and he folded his fingers around hers.

'I loved seeing the children in Bangkok,' she said wistfully. 'I'd see them every morning, on my daily walk, and they'd all be dressed neat as could be in their school uniforms, boys and girls, laughing and swinging their bags high in the air. They looked like they owned the streets. Not at all in a threatening way, not like when you see packs of kids back home. They just looked safe and happy and completely at home.'

She glanced back at the toddler who was now sucking greedily on a slice of mango that the band leader had offered him.

She turned back to Hector. 'Greece and Sicily were like that, do you remember?' she urged. 'The kids owned the streets there as well.' She sipped her beer and was lost in a reminiscence of their time in the Mediterranean. It was so long ago, before their marriage—their first overseas trip together. They had been so young. They had fought then as well, a terrible, destructive argument in Santorini.

Back in Athens, Hector's cousin, Pericles, had told them that everyone fought on Santorini. The *brakolaka*, the vampire spirits, caused arguments because they could not bear to see a couple happy in love.

'Greece must have changed so much. We must take the children soon. We must.'

It was then that Hector started crying. Not quiet, discreet tears, but a sudden explosion of painful sobbing. His body shuddered, rocked, and heavy tears streamed down his face and onto his shirt. Aisha was shocked, could not speak. Hector never cried. His grip on her fingers tightened, and it felt as if he could, with just one further squeeze, break her hand. The waitress had been on her way over to them, but she stopped, confused, scared, looking at Hector in openmouthed wonder. The French couples had fallen silent; the women were looking down at their menus, the men lit cigarettes and were looking deliberately over the bannister to the street below.

The embarrassment spurred Aisha to action. She jerked her hand away from her husband. 'Hector, what's wrong, what's happening?'

He could not speak. His sobs had become louder, deep, racking cries. His breathing was jagged, his face and nose and eyes red and contorted. She grabbed a napkin and wiped under his nose. Ice water was in her veins—for the first time in her life she understood the metaphor, experienced it as real: she was feeling nothing but chilling detachment. She had never seen her husband cry. She would never have imagined this, the shedding of dignity so publicly, in such an agony of grief. She had never seen a man cry like this; or maybe only once before, long ago, an elusive but distinct memory of her father. He too had been howling, sitting on her parents' bed, in his underpants and singlet. Her mother had slammed the door on her and Ravi's terrified faces. Yes, only that once had she seen a man cry and her father too had been howling, like a wolf, like a maddened animal. There was nothing weak or submissive about her husband's crying. He was a man broken, a man vulnerable, inconsolable in despair, but yet, for all that, still a man. Lost, but still a man. She had seen many women lose their control and weep, submit to the raw intensity of grief. She had done it herself. And every time it happened, she had encouraged the woman or the girl—or herself—to cry, to let their emotions play out their complete and necessary symphony. This was not the same. Every sob took Hector further away from her. She wanted it to stop. Her body, her heart, her mind, her soul, her hands, her lips, every part of her felt brittle. Ice water flowed through her veins. She knew why she had recalled her father's inexplicable anguished outburst, an incident that had never been referred to by her parents again. Just like she had been then, she was scared. She was so scared that she couldn't even form rational thoughts. All she felt was fear, the terror that after this moment, everything would be changed. After this, things could never be the same.

Until she had got Hector back to their hotel room, time ceased to be what she knew it as; it became impossible to comprehend. Time was both compressed and infinite, impossible to follow. She must have paid the bill, she must have somehow convinced her husband to get to his feet, must have struggled with him along Monkey Forest Road, or had she led him along the path by hand, as if he were a child? Later, much later, she would awake from nightmares that she knew were memories of that night. All she knew was that there was the street, the struggle to be home, the confused faces of the touts, the hawkers, the drivers, the tourists, and then they were in their room, he was sitting on the bed and she was kneeling before him and he had placed his arms around her, still distraught, still weeping, holding her tighter than he had ever held her before, his breath hot on her face, spittle, tears, saliva dripping around her neck and shoulders. Slowly, very slowly, time began to fall back into itself, to become recognisable again. Hector stopped howling. His sobs now came intermittently, with deep, shuddering breaths. She was conscious that her right calf was cramping, could hear the ticking of her watch, a Western pop tune playing from somewhere in the back of the hotel. She sat on the floor and rubbed her leg. Hector blew his nose and threw the sodden handkerchief to the floor. He rubbed his eyes. His voice, when he spoke, surprised her. It was firm, controlled.

'I'm alright now.' He roughly brushed his hand across his mouth. 'Last Wednesday I went to fetch Melissa from Aftercare. Dad couldn't go—St Vinnie's had rung and he had finally gotten an appointment to see a specialist about his gout. Mum wanted to go with him and I said that was fine. I had an RDO due and so I took that. I pottered around the house, got some stuff ready for this trip and then at three-thirty I got in the car to pick up Melissa.'

She let him talk but she was confused. Why was he telling her this now? Then she realised that, just before his outburst they had been talking about children; she was describing how happy she had been watching the school children in Bangkok.

'There were cars stretched along Clarendon Street for what seemed like miles, just all these cars waiting to get to the school gates so parents could pick up their children. It was like a traffic jam. We were hardly moving, I was stuck behind this big black shiny new four-wheel drive and I started to panic. I thought I was going to stop breathing. I really believed I was going to die, stuck behind that bloody four-wheel drive, that the last thing I would see in life would be one of those fucking Baby on Board stickers.'

His voice had started to shake. Fearful that he might start crying again, she sat beside him on the bed. She made sure her voice was measured and reassuring.

'It happens somedays. It can be a shit, it's like all the parents have descended on the school at exactly the same time. It's awful when that happens. How long did you have to wait?'

He didn't answer. She stroked his hair.

'I didn't wait. I just honked till the bitch in front of me made some room and I did a U ey and got the hell out of there.'

'What happened to Melissa?' Her voice was now sharp, panicked.

He started to laugh. She wanted to hit him.

'What happened to Melissa?' She was not far from screaming at him.

Through hysterical whoops of laughter, he spluttered out his story.

'I took the car home.' Laughter. 'I walked back to the school.' Howl. 'The black four-wheel drive had still not reached the gate.' More hilarity. 'I found Melissa and we walked back home.'

He was now on his back on the bed, screaming with laughter. She would wait it out. She caught her reflection in the mirror on the dresser. She was smart and attractive and good. She did not deserve this. This was not what she deserved at all. The body next to her on the bed was now still.

'I'm sorry, Aish.' Hector's voice was low, quiet. She did not yet turn around. She was still drawn to the reflection of the assured, attractive woman in the mirror.

'I'm sorry,' his tone now firm again, insistent. 'I can't continue to live like this.'

She froze. He was going to leave her. She stared back at her reflection. She was good looking, yes, she was intelligent, with her own business. She was forty-one. She did not want to live alone. When she spoke it seemed to her that her voice came from somewhere outside of herself, from the woman in the mirror. 'Do you want a divorce?' The word sounded heavy, a deadening load. At the same time, expressing it made her feel light, weightless.

'No.' Hector's response was again resolute, there was no doubt in his voice. Aisha breathed out, experiencing a moment of blessed relief; and, for an instant that flashed by so quickly she barely registered it, she also felt a pang of regret.

Like the morning after an abortion, is how she would later describe it to Anouk, who would nod her head and say, yes, I understand. What couldn't be, what you didn't ever want to be, but in which you could not also help wondering what could have been.

Hector looked straight at her. 'I don't know anything at the moment except that I want to be with you, that I love you and that you are the only thing I am sure of in my life. I've been so stupid. I don't know what the fuck is happening to me but I do know that I don't want to lose you.'

The ordeal of weeping had exhausted him. His face was puffy and red. He looked his age.

She kissed his wet brow. 'I'm going down the street and I'm going to get us some food. You take a shower and when I get back we'll talk, alright? We'll talk about whatever you want, we'll talk about whatever you need.'

He nodded. 'Hold me tight before you go,' he whispered.

She held him, his grip desperate. He would not let her go. She gently disentangled herself from him. 'I won't be long.'

It was a relief to be back in the muggy Ubud streets, away from Hector, away from his need for her. She ordered nasi goreng from a small, crowded café and sat outside on a crate looking across at the rice fields over the road. It would be a full moon the night after next and every stalk of grass, every tree, leaf and branch, every silhouette of a house or a temple was clearly etched in the radiant silver light. An American voice said something loud, sharply, from inside the café, and she gave herself over to fantasising. She was with Art, she had come to Montreal. He fell into her arms. He would divorce his wife and she would divorce Hector. She would learn French, they would open a practice in the city and both work only half-time. They would have long weekends in New York City. Then she thought of her children and brushed the sweet, impossible fantasy aside. She picked up her order and walked back to the hotel.

They talked for hours, lying next to each other on the bed. Hector had ripped through his meal, ravenous, and then he had begun to talk. He talked first about Hugo, about how he did not hate the little boy. It is impossible to hate a child, he said, and she agreed. He did talk about his anger at Rosie and Gary. He was sceptical about their professed commitment to active parenting, to the supposed enlightened and child-focused philosophies that underpinned Rosie's approach to motherhood. Hugo is lonely, Hector argued, and what he really needs is a brother or a sister, cousins, kids to put him in his place. He spends too much time around fucking adults. But Gary's too selfish to have another child. Aisha agreed.

She let him talk. She was unsure why it was Rosie and Hugo he was talking about, but the incident involving the child had greatly disturbed him. He talked of loving the responsibility of being a father but hated the fear he felt for his children, detested the notion of status that had become part of their social world, their friends, their family, when it came to raising children. I want my kids to walk home from school, I want them to play in the streets, I don't want them to be so protected that they are made to be scared of the world. The world has changed, she argued, it's dangerous. No, he contested, the world hasn't changed—it is we who have changed. He made it clear that he would not consider private schools for their children. This had been a source of disagreement between them for years and at first she thought it would replay itself as it had done every other time, with each side fought for and no decision made. But that night he was resolute and convincing. He explained that he loved his children but he thought private schools elitist and he wanted nothing to do with them. He could not trust what his children would become at such schools. It was not a matter of money—he was happy to spend twice what they would spend on fees to take Adam and Melissa to Greece and India, all over the world. He was only too happy to do that for his children. But he did not like the cold, selfish new world and, even if his allegiances were nostalgic, no longer relevant to that world, he wanted to hold tight to some vestige of morality and political belief. Otherwise he feared he would drown. That's your choice, she tried to point out, but your children shouldn't suffer for those beliefs. He groaned at that. They're not suffering—they are very lucky kids. He took her hand. They are going to do alright. You knew when you married me that this was the way I felt. I'm not going to change. I can't be a man who sends his children to private schools. I can't be that man because I'm not that man. She saw that she could not move him, and though she felt it impossible to understand because she had grown up in a family in which wealth was a virtue and politics were unspoken, she realised that she would have to acquiesce to him. So she negotiated. If Adam, or Melissa, she added quickly, are not doing well at their high school, are you prepared to move to another area with better state schools? A suburb away from your folks, a suburb in the east? Yes, he had answered, and lying there, husband and wife had negotiated, had come to an agreement.

He then confessed that he had been unfaithful to her, with a young university student, a nineteen-year-old social sciences undergraduate called Angela who had joined his unit on a placement. He had thought himself in love; there had even been moments at the height of his obsession when he had thought of leaving Aisha, his children, his work, his life, to run away with the girl. And then he had realised that she was, indeed, only a girl. He was struck by how close to calamity he had come. Abandoning Aisha would have been death. The girl was sweet, intelligent, she would be a good woman, a great woman, but she had only been a cipher for him: what he wanted from her, he realised, had been her youth. He desired her in order to believe that he was still young. But she had shown him that he was an ageing man and that one day he would die. She had meant nothing to him—he was disgusted now by what he had done, the risks he had taken. I promise you, he told Aisha, I promise you that we were only together twice and neither time did we have intercourse. He was so ashamed. Since he had told the girl that it had to end, he'd been waking up every morning at 3.14, without fail. Every morning his eyes would flick open, alert, and the red numerals on his electric alarm clock would read 3.14. Not wanting to wake Aisha, he would get up and go naked into their garden, where he would shake and start to weep. He was convinced that he was going to die—the beat of his heart seemed so tenuous, so irregular, his breath short, strained. He was going to die and what would his life have been worth? With that question he began to sob again. I'm scared, Aish, he shuddered, I'm so fucking scared.

She had listened to his monologue without anger or jealousy or scorn, feeling nothing. She watched her husband cry and put out her hand to stroke his shoulder. She felt nothing at all. She watched him as though from afar and tried to examine her own reaction. *A nineteen-year-old?* The girl's age had first sounded shocking to her, but now the ridiculousness of it was all she could think about. She did not even feel jealousy. Men were ridiculous. She had not even experienced relief at his confession, that his affair might somehow cancel or nullify her own infidelity. She had suspected for years that her husband fucked around. That gutter expression aptly summed up how she conceived of his affairs. He was lustful, had an enormous sexual appetite that had intimidated her from the start. She knew that in allowing the subject of monogamy to remain unspoken she had given tacit agreement to his anonymous or casual encounters with whores, one-night stands, with God only knows. As he poured out his confession, she had asked herself the question: Why are you telling me about this? In any other circumstances his choosing to tell her would have aroused her suspicions, that this woman meant something to him. But she was convinced this was not the case. He was terrified, a little boy confronting the immensity and indifference of the universe. You've had a long adolescence, Hector, she thought to herself as she stroked her husband's heaving back, a long adolescence. It is time to grow up. She did not mean this cruelly, she was not angry. She felt nothing. It was a fact. Just a fact.

She took his hand, kissed his knuckles, and she told him about Art. Not the truth, only the things that mattered. She did not tell

Hector about their lovemaking, but she did describe the intimacy and excitement of being attracted to another man. It was possible—she thought of this later, back home—that she had hoped to hurt him by revealing the details of her near betrayal. He listened intently to her every word and did not attempt to interrupt her. He listened to her describe Art's beauty, his erudition and charm. From time to time he would get up from the bed to refill their glasses from the duty-free Johnny Walker Black. She continued to talk, a relentless surge of words, except that her voice was steady and her meanings clear-headed. She hardly stumbled as she spoke. The sips of whisky assisted her monologue, steadied her. She drank constantly but did not feel drunk. She told Hector that Art had made her see possibilities, that she had come close to an affair not through fear but through curiosity. Anyway, she added, almost an aside, women feared the deaths of others, the deaths of their children, lovers, family, not the disappearance of self. Even as she glibly produced this statement she thought of Anouk, and, as if reading her mind, Hector asked, How about Anouk? Maybe women without children are different, Aisha conceded. Though they often start a charity or take up a cause; they go off to Africa to save young souls. It is possible the world is divided into three genders—there are men, there are women and then there are women who choose to have nothing to do with children. How about men without children, he answered quickly, aren't they also different from fathers? She shook her head firmly, daring him to contradict her: no, all men are the same.

She told him that she had been thinking about divorce, that she had been thinking of it long before Art. Once that word had fallen from her lips it was clear that there was a form of release for both of them in its utterance. She spoke the word and looked down at her husband. She was resting on a pillow, her back against the headboard of the bed and Hector was lying at her feet, his head propped on his elbow. She said the word and he smiled weakly at her and, hesitantly, she smiled back. They occupied a strange twilight world now in which their hotel room in Ubud had been somehow set adrift from the real world. There was a humming in her ear that was, she was sure of it, the sound of the universe spinning around and around, ready to fling both of them off into an orbit, one in which they either surrendered finally to each other or were forever flung apart. They both discussed their longing for freedom, for a life without a spouse, a life not dictated to by the whims, joys, petty angers and obsessions of another. Hector laughed and said he wanted to have nights where he could come home, strip to his undies, smoke a joint and watch porn, falling asleep on the couch. What she spoke of was something so much simpler, just to have the bed to herself for one night.

I just wonder what it is like being single sometimes, Hector said, it's been so long. I could never marry again if we divorced, he insisted, this is the only marriage that could mean anything to me. She kept silent. She was thinking of Art. Hector continued. I'm not going to have other children. This marriage is you and Melissa and Adam, he told her. As he spoke the words he sat up and looked straight at her. I'm not giving this up, I don't want a divorce. With his mention of the children her thoughts of freedom were banished. They were an adolescent fantasy. She knew he was awaiting an answer and she gave it to him. Neither do I. He crawled along the bed and kissed her. The dawn light was beginning to flutter through the bamboo blinds; a babel of birdsong suddenly rang out, all of it unfamiliar except for the coarse gloating call of the roosters. They were both too exhausted, too stripped to make love. They rang reception to cancel breakfast, swallowed a Temazepam each with their final gulp of whisky, and lying next to each other, barely touching, their shoulders just kissing, they fell asleep. She awoke at the height of midday, sweating, her mouth dry and foul-tasting. She turned her head and Hector's eyes were on her.

'I want to go to Amed,' she announced.

It took three hours to drive through the mountains to Amed on the east coast of the island. They had booked an apartment that had looked reasonable and well-serviced in the photographs on the internet and when they arrived they were glad to find that it was indeed clean, luxurious, cheap and very close to the beach. There were very few tourists in Amed, no ATMs, and every time they sauntered down the main street or walked along the beach they were accosted by good-natured young men asking them if they were hungry, did they want to snorkel, would they like a trip out to sea on one of the boats? But for all the haggling and desperate bartering, for all the half-finished construction, the paucity of technology, she liked Amed. She liked the still, warm waters of the sea, the smells of fish frying in the early evening, the sight of elderly cloaked women walking their goats and pigs on the eroded hills that fell down to the sea. On their first night they did little more than eat a hurried meal at a small restaurant on the beach. And the moon was not quite full but it still looked holy and magnificent perched over the choppy night waters.

On awakening that first morning there, Aisha found that she had begun once again to feel. Her eyes opened, alert, just before dawn. She could hear Hector snoring lightly and she was suddenly gripped by an unforgiving jealousy: she was enraged. She crept out of bed, put on a T-shirt and sat out on the balcony. She waited for the sun to rise, all the time thinking of her husband with another woman. Slowly, thankfully, the sun began its ascent, splintering the sea into a million blue-silver shards. Dozens of kayaks and boats were dotted on the horizon, the fishermen like small insects as they dragged in their nets. When Hector finally rose he was playful and flirtatious, wanting sex, flashing her his erection from under the sheet. It repulsed her and she snapped at him, Don't be so childish. In minutes they were squabbling. They ate a rushed breakfast, reading yesterday's edition of the *Indonesian Times*, occasionally glaring at each other over the top of their newspapers. An elderly New Zealand couple tried to be friendly with them but Aisha was in no mood and gave monosyllabic answers while Hector was overly friendly, insincerely polite, deliberately chivalrous. His falsity sickened her.

She abruptly rose from the table without a word to the couple or her husband. She grabbed her bag and walked confidently to the beach. She did not turn back, knowing he would follow. He did, red-faced and furious. She threw her towel on the sand, put on her sunglasses and began to read her book. Hector ran into the water.

She could not concentrate on one word on the page. She was in a rage. *A fucking nineteen-year-old?* He had been with a child! The bastard had no idea how that made her feel. She looked down at her long-limbed body. She could tell herself that she was attractive, but it would not matter. She did not believe it. Her skin was still smooth, the cellulite hardly visible, her tits had not yet started to sag. None of that mattered. He should not have told her the girl's bloody age. She turned onto her stomach and looked up the beach. Near a cluster of boats moored on the sand, two young Balinese men were smoking. They had been looking at her. The oldest had fine oriental features, long, greasy black hair and a short, sleek goatee. The other boy had a broad, almost Semitic tanned face. He wore a grease-stained white singlet that fitted tightly around his dark, muscular chest. Unlike the older boy, who wore long cream cotton pants, he was wearing denim shorts that fell to above his knees and revealed equally well-muscled calves. He suddenly winked at her and the confident rudeness of the wink reminded her of Hector's cousin, of Harry. She turned her face away from them, ignoring their breezy laughter. He was probably nineteen. She clutched a fistful of sand, squeezing it tight, watching it trickle through her grip. He was a child, just a fucking child.

A sprinkle of cold water splashed on her back. Hector was above her, drying himself. He was grinning. 'You should come in. It's fantastic.'

She turned onto her back, ready to snap at him. He was silhou-etted against the clear, open sky and she had to shield her eyes with her hand to see him properly. His smile was wide, the hair on his chest and torso was wet and flattened. There was hardly any fat on him, and that which was there, small bumps around his hips, his slightly chunky thighs, was masculine, comforting. She stifled her complaint. There was a photo of her husband from when she'd first taken Hector to Perth. Whose photo was it? Rosie's? Ravi's? They had all gone south to Margaret River for five days of camping and joints and reading and bushwalking. And swimming of course, lots of swimming. Hector had seen dolphins and his childlike wonderment had made all of them shriek with laughter. Someone took a photo of him from below, a young boy in his early twenties framed against an almost domed bright blue summer sky. He was the most handsome man she had ever seen and he was still the most handsome man she had ever seen. Of course a nineteen-year-old girl would fuck him, of course a nineteen-year-old girl would swoon to be wanted by him. All those years and he still had her in his grip.

'Don't you ever betray me again,' she shouted, and suddenly she was in tears. 'You're not allowed to sleep with another woman. Never again. Don't you fucking dare.'

He looked shocked. Two male tourists were walking past. They stopped on hearing her shouts and she turned her face away from them. Hector, forcing a smile to his face, mouthed, We're okay. Both of the men were in their fifties, in ridiculously small and tight matching black speedos, one short, fat and dark, the other one tall, skinny with his body shaven smooth all over. Reluctantly they nodded back at Hector and resumed their stroll. Aisha watched them walk past the Balinese boys. They stopped and talked amongst themselves, then the fat man turned and stooped next to the boys. They spoke for a few moments and then the youths jumped to their feet and followed the men along the beach.

Hector shook his head in disgust. 'Those poor kids.'

She rubbed her eyes, smearing the salty tears across her face. 'They're probably nineteen.'

He turned a sheepish face towards her. He sat next to her on the sand and touched her shoulder. She flinched.

'How could you?'

'It meant absolutely nothing.' His voice was meek.

'Are you going to do it again?'

'I'm not going to see her again.'

'I meant with anyone.'

He didn't answer straight away. A young man walked towards them, brandishing a set of snorkelling gear for rent. She shooed him away.

'Aish, I don't know what I'm going to do tomorrow, let alone for the rest of my life. I do know I will never leave you, that I will never love anyone but you. But I can't promise I won't have sex with another woman again in my life. I don't want to lie to you anymore. I just don't.'

He thought he was being so brave. Fuck you, she wanted to say, lie to me. We've been lying for years. He had given expression to something she'd known since they'd first got together, something she had even joked about with Anouk and Rosie. But in saying it, in giving it voice, making it real, she would forever be wondering as he lay next to her in bed at night, Have you been fucking someone else? She would be straining to smell another woman's perfume or her scent. To hell with your honesty. She couldn't leave him because her love was bound up with his beauty—she loved being next to him, adored being the most attractive couple in the room, couldn't let that go. Together they were more than the sum of their parts. She wanted to say take your fucking honesty and stick it up your arse.

She jumped to her feet and ran into the water, dived into the warm, gently rippling grey-green waves. She swam out as far as she could, she could hear thrashing, loud splashing behind her. He was following her. She took a deep breath, put her head under water and willed herself into one ferocious final effort to pull apart from him. He was too fast, much stronger than her. He caught up with her, then was under her, lifting her straight out of the water. She thought he was going to throw her into the sun. Instead, he held her tight and she felt the ropy thickness of his arms around her, the firm muscles of his chest. She surrendered. It was such bliss to drop away from herself and be held by him halfway between the ocean and the sky. She closed her eyes. She was his.

That night they saw the full moon over Amed. After their swim together, her mood lightened but she had not yet forgiven him. They spent the afternoon apart, Hector reading and swimming, Aisha taking a long walk along the coast road that cut through four or five villages. Everyone was busily preparing for the night's festivities. The women and girls sought shelter from the burning sun under the shared verandah of the village compounds, where they were busy cooking the delicious array of sweets and spiced cakes to be offered to the gods and ancestors; the men and boys were in the temples, sitting in circles, praying, each wearing a brightly coloured tunic and a sharp-cornered triangular headdress. Only the very young children followed Aisha, practising their English on her, a weird amalgam of Australian colloquialisms and American hip-hop slang. At one point, feeling the fierce dry heat, she sat near a well and listened to the conversations of the women and children. She felt peace in watching the preparations for the religious festival, their Hinduism both reassuringly familiar and strangely exotic. Aisha's upbringing had not been religious—both her parents were determined secularists. Their religion was democracy—the labyrinthine devotions of Hinduism were almost an embarrassment to them. But Aisha's paternal grandmother had been devout and as a little girl she had delighted in assisting her *Nani* prepare the daily sweetmeats and rich milk desserts for the gods. Then her *Nani* died and religion went the way of fairytales and dolls, the stuff of childhood to be forgotten. Eavesdropping on the Balinese now she felt neither nostalgia nor loss. She did not even feel that way in a Hindu temple in India itself. She simply enjoyed the serenity of ritual and family. As the sun began to drop in the sky she gathered her bag and walked briskly back to the hotel. Sweat was streaming down her face and as she opened the gate she nearly collided with a young maid coming down the steps to offer fruit and cake to the ancestors. Aisha bowed to the girl, muttered *kasim*, and watched her place the laden banana leaf onto the first step. The girl flicked a match and lit the incense.

Hector was curled naked on the bed, snoring the same way his son did. Aisha knelt on the bed and kissed her husband's shoulder. He awoke and looked straight into her eyes. His were alert, shining, concerned.

'Am I forgiven?'

'Yes.'

He was not forgiven yet, not inside her, but she would forgive him, she knew that. He smelt sour, of sweat and heat. She kissed his shoulder again and then stripped and went for a shower. The sharp bursts of cold water were a soothing delight and she let the water hit her face as she arched her neck and stared straight up to the sky above. As she turned off the tap she was startled to hear what she thought was her husband crying. She stepped out into the bedroom, the towel wrapped around her. Hector had slipped on his shorts and was on the balcony. He was smiling when he turned to face her but she could see that his eyes were red.

'How about a swim before we head out for dinner?'

She had just showered, she didn't feel like a swim. But she feared that if she said she wanted to lie in bed reading he would stay with her. She didn't want to talk. She didn't want any more confessions or apologies or revelations. She didn't want to ask him if he had been crying.

They returned to the same restaurant in the village where they had gone for dinner on their first night in Amed. The owner, a chatty young man called Wayan, had impressed them both with his charm and humour. At first they had both thought him still only an adolescent, but as they were about to leave that first night he'd introduced them to his two young sons. The food that night was excellent, delectable and spicy, cooked by Wayan's wife who'd remained invisible in the kitchen. Seeing them again tonight, Wayan greeted them with delighted laughter and led them onto the beach, sat them at the table closest to the water. This full moon night he'd swapped his denim shorts and fake Mossimo T-shirt for traditional ceremonial dress. Two Italian men seated at the table directly under the shade of a palm tree, nodded to them as they were seated. They were young, heavily tanned, as if they had spent months under the Asian sun. She and Hector ordered beers and she sat back in her chair, watching the last of the sun disappear in the horizon.

It felt like a first date. The events and emotions of the last week had forced Aisha to view her life anew. Her husband, for the first time in so long, appeared mysterious, a stranger. Her rage was gone. The sense of betrayal was still there, she knew it, somewhere underneath, waiting to be released. But now was not the time to give it expression. She wanted her husband to return to her, she did not want him to be the despairing, vulnerable creature he had revealed himself to be. The moon's borrowed light was beginning to cleave a rippled silver path along the darkening surface of the sea. She would keep her anger submerged. She wanted to make peace with her husband so she could pull him back to land. He was too far adrift; if he was to fall apart, her life too would be shattered. She would be patient with him. She had learned patience as a mother. Sacrifice, too. She beamed at her husband, nodded out to the slowly bobbing waters.

'I'm so glad we came here.'

He began to cry. She bit her lip; her impulse was to order him to stop it, to not be a child. Thankfully this time his tears lasted a short moment. The two young Italian men, so vain and distant, had not even noticed. She found herself ignoring Hector, thinking instead of how, in the end, she preferred the North Americans to the Europeans, who too often, like the men at the next table, were snobbish, ungenerous and arrogant. Hector sniffed, wiped at his eyes, and took up his menu. She looked at him, her expression quizzical, unsmiling.

'I'm fine. I don't deserve you.' Oh Christ, don't let him start crying again. 'I'm so ashamed, Aish.'

She too looked down at the menu. She had no idea what would be the right thing to say. She felt bereft, drained of any compassion or sympathy towards him. At the same time she felt him to be completely in her care. It was this distance between her intentions and her desire that was making her so weary. She would have been furious if he had not felt shame. But she did not want to minister to his grief, his self-pity and to his sense of failure. A cruel thought flashed quickly and guiltily in her mind: be a man, deal with your fucking mid-life crisis—it is so boring. She scanned the list of dishes. She would order the whole fish smoked in a banana leaf in nonya spices. She shut her menu.

'I'm going to call Sandi when I get home, congratulate her on being pregnant.' He brightened as soon as she said the words, his eyes widening in relief. She immediately regretted her impulsiveness. I will concede nothing else, she promised herself. Again she experienced a wave of weariness, a numbing heaviness to her neck and shoulders, to her very bones. This, finally, was love. This was its shape and essence, once the lust and ecstasy and danger and adventure had gone. Love, at its core, was negotiation, the surrender of two individuals to the messy, banal, domestic realities of sharing a life together. In this way, in love, she could secure a familiar happiness. She had to forego the risk of an unknown, most likely impossible, most probably unobtainable, alternative happiness. She couldn't take the risk. She was too tired. And anyway, she scolded herself, the moon is hanging low and gigantic and golden over Amed, I am with my handsome husband who loves me and encourages me, who makes me feel safe. I am safe and that's all the world wants, only the young and the deluded would want anything else, believe that there is anything more to love than that.

'It's fantastic she's got pregnant. I know how hard she's been trying.'

'I know, it's terrific, isn't it.' Hector was beaming, thrilled. 'Harry told me at his birthday that if they hadn't got pregnant by the summer they were going to try IVF. That would have been so hard on them.'

'On Sandi, don't you mean?' Harry. He would be the cost of her concession; she and Harry would be forever partners in a strained dance of pretence and evasion. Her voice rose. 'It would have been tough on Sandi. Harry would have been fine. Harry will always be fine.'

Hector caught the scorn in her voice and his happiness ceased, his smile evaporated. She couldn't help it, it was spiteful, but she was glad. He beckoned Wayan over and they ordered.

'People do change, Aish.'

She had been looking out to sea and was at first confused by his words. She laughed cynically when she finally understood his meaning. 'Harry will never change.'

Hector groaned. 'He's apologised for hitting Hugo. They've dragged him through court, they fucked him well and truly. What else do you want from him?'

'I'm not just talking about that. You know what I'm referring to.'

'Jesus, that was over ten years ago . . .'

She snapped. 'He bashed her. The bastard bashed her.' She was glaring at him, coiled and alive and ready to strike.

He did not answer. She knew he was recalling the night as well. She had been pregnant with Adam. They heard the car's brakes screech in their driveway and when Sandi had emerged, the blood thick and black on her shirt and pants, they had thought her drunk. Then they realised that her nose was broken, her lips split, her jaw so dislocated she could not speak. She fell on Hector and two teeth dropped onto the ground. Leave him, Aisha said, almost making it an order. But Sandi had not left him. Hector took her to the hospital on Bell Street and she told them she had fallen down the Fairfield Station steps. She and Aisha had never spoken about it since.

'He's never hit her again.'

'So he says.' Aisha lifted her head and looked her husband straight in the eyes. 'I will visit Sandi, I will be a friend. But I will never forgive your cousin, do you understand? I hate him. I detest that he is in my life.'

Hector was the first to blink, to look away. 'I understand,' he mumbled, and she believed him. She breathed a sigh of relief.

Her anger dived back into the deep, straight under the waves, down to the depths. She smiled serenely. 'It's a heavenly night, isn't it?'

She did not feel normal again until they were home, until she walked out into Melbourne Airport and saw her children. She scooped them both into her arms, smelt them, Adam's bracing, earthy scent, Melissa smelling girly and fresh, of the honey and almond soap that Koula used; they both smelt of garlic and lemon and of her in-law's home. She wanted to take them away, for them all to be together as a family. This was life, this was what mattered, this was what made all the concessions and compromises and defeats worthwhile. She could not let them go, held her daughter's hand in the car, kept sweeping her hand across Adam's hair. They chatted away to her, interrupting, arguing, calling each other names, telling her about school and sports and *Giagia* and *Pappou* and about the cat and about football and about dancing lessons and about *Australian Idol* and their friends and their trip to the cinema and she took it all in and wanted to hear about it again and again. She had missed out on two weeks of their young lives. The moon over Amed, the rich smells and succulent food, the hours lazing in the sun, none of that compared to the two weeks she had missed out of her children's lives. She couldn't help herself squeezing their knees, kissing them, touching them. Melbourne unfolded tediously and grimly as they drove down the freeway towards the city. It looked like a carcass that had been out in the sun for too long, stripped of life, of meat, of texture, of smell. But when Manolis dropped them all off in front of their house she had to stop herself from crying with relief.

Within a few days she was safely back in the warm hearth of

suburban first-world life. Clean streets and fresh air. Bangkok, Bali, all of Asia receded and all that had occurred there began to be forgotten. She found too that being at work excited her again, for the first time in years. She was glad of her assured, practised skill with the animals. The questioning and hesitations that were an inevitable aspect of diagnosis had not changed but they no longer filled her with trepidation. Those fears belonged to a young woman. She was not that. Tracey baked a cake for her first day back and even Connie biked down from school to attend the lunch. She distributed the little gifts and souvenirs she had picked up for them in the stalls and markets of Ubud and Bangkok. Later that day, in a brief moment of respite from the solidly booked afternoon—her regular clients had taken every available consultation with Aisha for her first week back—Brendan came in with pathology and blood results from the lab. Aisha quickly scanned them, noting the client's name. She knew the animal, a goofy, sad-eyed Alsatian called Zeus. The results were quite clear. Brendan had removed two small lumps from its right foreleg and they had returned, malignant. But there were anomalies in the blood results as well. Her hunch was pancreatic cancer. It was Brendan's case but they had both treated Zeus and they had both been concerned about recurring abdominal pain and vomiting, the reason the animal had first come in for a consultation. The owners were good people, Greeks, both on pensions. They loved the dog but in the Mediterranean way, not as part of the family. Zeus's function was to protect them and their house.

'Should I book him in for amputation and maybe get Jack in for an ultrasound?'

He was a good dog, but already a good age for the breed. The owners could be guilt-tripped into more tests but the prognosis was not good.

She handed him back the path reports and shook her head. 'They can't afford it and the costs could skyrocket I think it's time to put him down.'

'I missed you.'

She blushed, surprised. They worked well together but neither of them were demonstrative or affectionate within the workplace.

'I've missed you too,' she answered. 'I've missed this place, I've missed being home.'

And it was true. She hadn't missed anyone individually as such—except her children, and even with them it had not been missing her son or missing her daughter, she had missed *her* children—but she was glad for the familiar textures, rhythms and shapes of her life. Family, work, friends. Brendan was an excellent colleague, smart, capable; she could leave her business confidently under his care for a fortnight. She enjoyed work, she enjoyed swimming eighty laps three times a week at the local pool, she enjoyed the bitchy, honest camaraderie she shared with Anouk, she enjoyed being married to a man who still made women's heads turn, she enjoyed—most days—the quarrels and mischief of her children. She did enjoy her life.

Nevertheless, something had changed. The first Friday back at work something snapped. She returned home drained, a slight pain at her temple; it had been a full schedule of consults with irritable, demanding clients. They happened, days when everyone seemed to be a shit. Hector had left her a message saying he was at the pub near his work in the city and could she pick up the kids from his parents'. She could hear him smooch a kiss to her on the message followed by a guilty, swift, 'I love you, I'll be home in time for dinner.' She was meant to cook it, of course. She clamped her mobile phone shut and cursed. Fucking bastard.

Something had changed for her in Asia and it had been brought back home. That change, she was sure of it, had more to do with her husband than it had to do with her. She had come to take it for granted that marriage was a state of neutrality between herself and Hector, that all the accommodations, negotiations and challenges had been met. Of course, there was accident, illness, tragedy; all that was still possible. But she had no idea that the properties of their very marriage could be altered. She had taken her husband for granted. She wanted what she had, she wanted him to remain a young, charming, attractive man. She wanted him to be content, with her, with the children, with his work. She was disturbed to find that the long nights of tears and confessions in Ubud and Amed had not led to resolution.

A few nights before Hector had scared her by talking about leaving the public service, finding new work, gaining new skills; he wanted to return to study. She had been encouraging but the words that she dared not utter were these: What about the mortgage? Are we never going to move to a bigger house? You've got a great job, security, fantastic pay—are you expecting me to look after us all? She could not say it. He was sleepless, anxious. He rarely joked, made her laugh—he always looked exhausted when he got back from work. And it was true, he no longer was a heavy sleeper. How had she not noticed that before Asia? He barely communicated with Adam. Their exchanges consisted of a series of surly and suspicious grunts. This scared her. What resentments would a teenage Adam act out in the near future?

Her husband hardly listened to music anymore, and of all the changes, this was the most disorientating. Their home had always been filled with music; their study, two walls of the dining room were packed floor to ceiling with the thin spines of CDs. In the past she had resented the amount of money he spent on his passion. But now she wished he would come home with the tell-tale canary-yellow bag from JB Hi-Fi, the thick paper package from Basement Discs or the garish plastic bag from Polyester. Hector rarely switched on the radio anymore. Aisha distrusted his unhappiness, she believed it to be a pose. But she dared not reveal her doubts. Instead, she was tender, tried not to snap at him. Just the other day she had read the music reviews in *The Age*—she never did!—and had slipped out from work to the small music shop in the plaza and bought Hector a CD from a band called Yo La Tengo. She was sure he had earlier records by this band and the reviewer had claimed that the CD would be one of the albums of the year. She had bought it home and he had been grateful, playing it immediately. But just that once. The disc remained in the stereo, the sleeve sat empty, desolate on top of the glass case that protected the turntable. Hector seemed unable to sustain happiness. That was what was unusual, what she had taken for granted. That is what she wanted back in her life. Let her take him for granted, let him do the same with her. This was marriage.

Fucking bastard. She had tears in her eyes as she drove the few short minutes to her in-laws. She could not bear Koula to know she had been crying. She fixed her face in the rearview mirror, breathed slowly and deeply three times. She was ready.

She kissed her mother-in-law on both cheeks. Melissa dragged her over to the kitchen table and they sat together while her daughter, with a conceited cock to her head, proudly showed off her maths homework. She was so much like Hector. Aisha walked into the lounge room. Manolis was asleep in the armchair and Adam was watching some silly reality show on television. She kneeled and lightly brushed her lips on the tips of his hair. He smelled of olive oil, of his grandmother's food; and there was a slight putrid stink, mangy, animal, boyish, that made Aisha wrinkle her nose. Adam neither recoiled nor accepted her kiss. He was becoming something that was not a boy anymore. She felt the world crush down on her. Everything was changing. Manolis let out a sudden harsh gasp and she quickly turned around. He was stretching his arms out, yawning. She kissed him. Manolis smelled the same as always, the comforting odour of the garden, the lemon and garlic and oregano: like her kids he smelled of his wife's cooking. She smiled down at him. His eyes analysed her coolly.

'How are you, darling?'

She felt a pang of guilt. She still had not rung Sandi and it had been over a fortnight since their return. She had promised her husband.

'I'm fine.' She hesitated, then promptly lied. 'I've lost Sandi's number. I really need to ring her . . . and Harry,' she added hastily.

Manolis's eyes were still unsmiling. She helped him rise from the armchair.

'I'll get you the number,' he said.

He wrote the number down on the back of a torn envelope, the numerals shaky, oversized, like a child's writing.

He handed her the envelope.

'Thank you.' This time his smile was genuine, real. She almost broke into tears again. Nothing more must change.

She swiftly cut up the vegetables for a quick, simple curry. Hector arrived, drunk, and she stopped herself from snapping at him. While he was showering and the kids were squabbling over the television, she rang Sandi. She was trying not to think of Rosie. She scrolled down on her phone till she got Sandi's name on the screen—thank God, Manolis did not understand mobiles or he would have seen straight through her lie about Sandi's number. Sandi's name appeared on the screen. Aisha paused, then pressed for the number. The phone began to dial. It did feel like a betrayal. The woman's voice on the other end took her by surprise.

'Hello,' Sandi repeated her greeting. 'Is that you, Aish?'

Caller ID. Aisha composed herself. She would not hang up. She had done it, she had made a choice. Things were not the same, they would not remain the same.

'Yes.' She stumbled through her congratulations, and followed them swiftly with a quick apology, rushing the words. 'I'm so sorry we haven't spoken for so long. The circumstances have been trying.'

She had actually rehearsed that line. It had come to her on the plane back from Bali. It was true but as a statement it did not apportion blame. Sandi's laughter in reply was loud and genuine. I made the right decision, thought Aisha, I think I've done the right thing.

'You're not wrong, babe. It's been a shit of a year but everything's good now. I'm so happy now.'

'I'm glad, I really am.' And she was. 'I know how important this is for you.'

'For both of us.' She was being reminded of Harry. Aisha flinched. That conversation would be much harder. 'Rocco's so excited, as well,' Sandi continued, her voice airy. 'He can't believe he's finally going to have a brother or sister.'

'How is Rocco?'

A chant, a snatch of lyric from a CD Hector played to death in the early nineties was in her head. *This is a new day, this is a beautiful day.*

'He's great. Bring the kids over for a visit.'

Aisha did not answer at once. She called out Melissa's name, pretending to admonish her daughter. She would have preferred to first see Sandi on her own, over coffee, outside their homes, away from their husbands. But Aisha knew that would not be possible. Sandi's voice was friendly, sunny and inviting, but nothing would be forgiven till she stepped into their home and greeted Harry. She would have to shake his hand. She would have to kiss him. He would be unshaven, his cheek would feel coarse, he would tower over her. She realised he scared her. She hated that he scared her.

'Sorry, Sandi,' she lied. 'Melissa was playing with some scissors. What were we talking about?'

'When are you and Hector going to come over with the kids?'

'Soon, we'll be over soon.'

'When?'

This is a new day, this is a beautiful day.

'I'll talk to Hector.'

Sandi laughed again. 'He'll agree to anything.' The laugh ended brusquely. 'So when?'

The tone was steel. *This is a new day, this is a beautiful day.*

'Sunday week,' Aisha suggested cheerfully. 'How's Sunday week?'

How the fuck do you sleep with that monster at night? After what he did to you? *I saw you.* He broke your jaw. How do you forgive that?

'Great. I'll get Harry to fire up the barbecue.'

'Great,' Aisha echoed falsely. 'I'll see you then.' She switched off her phone.

'What should I tell Rosie?'

They were sitting at the front bar of the All Nations waiting for a table to become free in the dining room. Anouk was the centre of the largely male crowd's attention. She was wearing her thigh-high black leather boots and a faded suede cowgirl jacket over an old New Order tour T-shirt that Aisha remembered her friend buying in 1987. It still fitted her perfectly. Anouk's hair had been recently cut radically short into a masculine buzz cut and also dyed a glistening blue-black. Aisha had also dressed up, in a delicate soft cotton burgundy two-piece she bought on impulse, but what had looked cute in the David Jones window suddenly seemed drab and bourgeois and middle-aged next to Anouk. It's because the bitch doesn't have children, she thought spitefully to herself when she'd walked into the pub and seen her friend smoking at the counter. But Anouk's excited, grateful smile on seeing her made Aisha feel terribly guilty for her ungenerous thought. It did not do justice to her friend. Even with kids, even if she had a brood of half-a-dozen, Anouk would still look a knockout.

They had ordered a bottle of sauvignon blanc and Aisha watched the bartender pour them a glass each. He's almost a child, thought Aisha. He was thin and pale, with unkempt swampy hair. His attempt to grow a beard had stalled; the thin straggles of hair on his cheeks could not quite meet their fellow tufts on his chin. He was very attractive and very young. But he was keenly focused on Anouk who pretended to ignore him.

'Cheers.' They clinked glasses. Anouk lit a cigarette and mischievously blew smoke towards Aisha. 'You don't have to tell her.'

Aisha had thought of this option, but she had reluctantly decided that it was not possible. She did not want to be fearful and deceitful towards her oldest friend. At some point Rosie would discover that she had made peace with Hector's cousins and she would feel betrayed. Aisha prided herself on the longevity of her friendships with both Rosie and Anouk. They were just like family except, unlike family, she hid nothing from them.

She gave voice to this. 'I don't want to be in a position where I'd have to lie to Rosie.'

Anouk cocked a disbelieving, sarcastic eyebrow in her direction. 'You've already lied to her. You didn't tell her that your sweet cousin-in-law beats up on his wife.'

'He only did that once.' As soon as the words were out of her mouth she regretted them. They were cowardly, an unconvincing defence. She would never have let Hector get away with them.

Anouk struck. 'Once that you know of.' Aisha turned her face away, distraught. Anouk took her friend's chin and forced Aisha to look directly at her.

'I don't care, sweetheart. You know I don't give a fuck about Rosie and Gary's vendetta. You know I think Hugo deserved all he got.' Aisha was about to protest but decided not to. She would not change Anouk's mind. 'The point I wanted to make is that you have already lied to Rosie. What's one more little lie?'

'I did not lie to her.' She was not being disingenuous; she almost felt indignant at Anouk's casual accusation. 'Sandi would have denied that anything had happened. It would have been no good for her to know about it. She couldn't have used it at the hearing.' Anouk seemed unmoved, her gaze was still sceptical. Aisha shrugged in frustration. 'Anyway, if I had said anything Hector would never have forgiven me.'

'Exactly.' Anouk flicked her cigarette towards the ashtray but she missed and ashes plunged to the floor. Aisha impatiently tapped her foot. This is why Anouk always wanted to meet at a pub rather than a café or restaurant. So she could bloody smoke. Aisha smiled to herself rebelliously. Well, the laws were changing any day now and Anouk would have nowhere to smoke indoors. Maybe she'd bloody well give up.

'Christ, Aish, don't work yourself up about this. Rosie doesn't need to know everything about your business. And don't encourage her to play the victim. You spoil her.'

Anouk was right. Aisha did indulge Rosie. But Anouk was also intolerant.

'She'll find out.'

'Okay, then tell her.' Anouk's firmly stubbed the end of the cigarette into the ashtray. 'But she'll be guilt-tripping you for months. Don't bore me about it if she does.'

Yes, you are intolerant. 'It's still raw for her. She's never going to forgive Harry.'

'So what? What do you care?' Anouk fell silent. The bartender was refilling her glass. It was Aisha who thanked him.

'Rosie and Harry have got nothing to do with each other,' Anouk continued, watching the young man walk away. 'And it's no business of hers what relationship you have with Hector's cousin.' Anouk took a quick sip. 'Are you ever going to forgive Harry?'

No. Never. Aisha finished her drink and placed the wine glass on the counter. I wonder if he's going to fill my glass, she thought sourly. But the bartender did promptly come over and poured her another. He had such lovely soft features, his beard was like down, not yet hair, not bristles. He was not yet a real man. He went back to serving a couple of businessmen at the other end of the bar.

She lowered her voice and shifted closer to Anouk. 'He's young enough to be our son,' she whispered, grinning. 'Isn't it awful?'

'What's awful about it?' Anouk winked. 'He looks about the same age as Rhys.'

'How is Rhys?' She wanted to talk about her friend, hear about her life. She had made up her mind. She would talk to Rosie. She knew she would, she had just wanted to articulate it to Anouk. Once said it would need to be done. But she was shocked by Anouk's response.

'Fuck it, Aish, I need to end it.'

'What's wrong? What's happened?'

Aisha wanted to touch her friend's cheek, to caress her, but she did not dare. Anouk would hate that. She would feel pitied, and thus even more shamed. Sourly, she couldn't help thinking of Hector. If she hadn't had to think about him all the time now she would have known something was wrong in her friend's life.

'He's still a child. That's the whole bloody problem.' The moment of vulnerability had passed, Anouk was once more mocking, sardonic. 'He thinks we can have it all. Children, independence, travel, world peace.'

'You can have a child.'

'What makes you think I want one?'

The two women stared at each other. Is this our unbridgeable difference, Aisha wondered, is this a separateness we cannot overcome? This tension, this stand-off, this dare, did not exist between herself and Rosie. Being a mother was a fact, not a question.

'I don't know if you necessarily want one. I'm just saying that you can have one.'

'Well, I don't bloody want one.' Anouk beckoned the bartender over. 'Is that table free yet?'

He apologised and brought over a bowl of cashews for them, and refilled their glasses. Aisha brought the rim of the glass to her lips and realised she was getting drunk. It was a good thing she hadn't driven. She rolled her shoulders, concentrated on keeping her back straight. The wine didn't seem to have affected Anouk.

'Rhys has a good friend called Jessica. She's a nice kid.' Anouk popped a cashew in her mouth and swallowed. 'She's a lesbian. They're talking about having a baby together.'

Aisha drew in a sharp breath. Choices, so many choices available. She envied how the young manoeuvred so casually through them all.

'Well, I think that's great.' It was mortifying, she was stammering. 'I mean it,' she rushed through her words. 'I think it's fantastic.' She took a pause. She was being ridiculous. Anouk would not judge her. 'It's fantastic for them,' she added. 'But how do you feel about it?'

'It's their decision. I'm not involved.' Aisha was about to interrupt her but Anouk bowled straight through her friend's objection.

'I'm right, it has nothing to do with me. We're not married, we're not like you and Hector. You made a decision together.' Anouk ran her finger along the rim of the glass. 'I'll be happy for Rhys if he has a child with Jessica. I'm happy to play Auntie on weekends and public holidays. But if I want to go off, I will. If I want to spend a month just concentrating on writing my book, I will.' She pushed the glass away. 'I will not be a mother.'

Aisha could find no words to answer the finality of that statement. Something stung about Anouk's casual and easy reference to her relationship with Hector. As if marriage foreclosed adventure, as if in marriage there was no risk.

'I got an email from Art.'

'The Canadian?'

Aisha nodded guiltily, but was unable to suppress a triumphant smile. She had not intended to say a word about the email. It had arrived at work yesterday, a simple two lines: I haven't been able to forget you. Do you feel the same? It was an email that demanded an answer. She had not answered it. She had left it in her inbox but throughout the day and into the evening she had returned to look at the words, thrilled to see them—so explicit, so enticing.

'What did he want?'

Aisha repeated the words in the email.

'Don't answer it.'

Anouk sounded vehement, so sure of the decision she should make. Was she imagining it? Was her friend a little angry with her? Aisha made no answer.

'You're married, Aish. Don't answer him.'

The words were so old-fashioned, the tone so outraged, that she assumed her friend was joking. Aisha laughed out loud.

Anouk swooped on her. 'I mean it. You're married.'

I know I'm fucking married. This was just a fantasy, a game. Art was fun. How dare Anouk assume a moral rectitude?

'Don't lecture me on marriage.' She badly wanted a cigarette. She would not ask for one. As if reading her mind, Anouk lit one and blew the smoke at Aisha.

'I'm not lecturing you on marriage.' Anouk's frown disappeared. 'I wouldn't do that, Aish, you know that. But you've come back from Bali concerned about Hector and his mental health. You keep telling me how worried you are about him.' Anouk leaned on the bar. 'I don't care if you slept with a dozen men in Bangkok. Good for you if you did. But that was a conference fuck, a fantasy, not real. What's real is you and Hector. Do you want to be with Hector?'

Aisha did not answer.

'Do you?'

'Yes.'

I think so.

'You don't sound sure?'

'I am sure.'

I don't fucking know. That's what you people who are not married don't ever understand. When can you ever be sure?

'Then don't answer the email.'

'I won't.'

I might.

They lapsed into silence. Aisha grabbed the cigarette from Anouk and took two quick puffs. She handed it back.

'How's the book going?' No more talk of men. Or at least, no more talk of Art.

Anouk groaned. 'I'm writing words, what seems like millions of fucking words but I don't know if any of them are any good.'

Aisha couldn't imagine that this was the case. Anouk was good, Anouk was smart and talented and funny and sharp and inspired. Of course the book would be good. She couldn't say this to her. Anouk would snap her head off.

'Can I read it now?'

'It's not finished.'

'I'll read what you've got.'

'It's not ready.'

Should she push it? She should push it. 'You'll never be ready. I want to read it.'

The bartender was trying to grab their attention. The two women slipped off their stools and Anouk butted out her cigarette.

'We'll have another bottle,' she barked out to the young man.

'Please,' insisted Aisha.

'Please,' repeated Anouk, her tone fake and sickly sweet. She sculled the last of the wine in her glass and banged it on the counter. 'Okay,' she said sullenly. 'You can fucking read it.'

Hector and the kids were asleep when she got home. Tipsy, she flew through brushing her teeth, combing her hair, getting ready for bed. She slipped under the blankets next to her husband and his arms automatically closed around her. You're cold, he complained. Warm me up, she urged, and pushed her arse hard against him. She groped behind her with her hand and started rubbing his soft cock, playing with the wrinkled folds of his foreskin. He pushed her hand away. I'm asleep, he mumbled. She lay there, listening to him breathe. She had wanted him to fuck her so she could close her eyes and pretend he was Art. She lay there, hoping for sleep. After ten minutes she rose and headed for the bathroom. She took a Temazepam and headed back to bed.

The next morning was a Sunday. Hector had, so rare for him, risen before her. She staggered out of bed and the first thing she did was ring Rosie and arrange to meet for a coffee in Queens Parade. She could not shake off the grogginess from the sleeping pill, even after her shower. Hector had made breakfast for her and the kids and she feasted ravenously on his cheese and tomato sandwiches, enjoying the buttered toast, the thick, gooey, sticky cheese. He made her seconds and she was late getting to the Q Café. Rosie was sitting at the table reading the Sunday paper. She jumped up and rushed over to Aisha, hugging her tight, all the time calling out her name.

'It's so good to see you, it's so good to see you,' Rosie sang in a deliberately high-pitched little girl's voice. Though this was exactly like Rosie, though this was what Rosie did, Aisha wanted her to stop. She pulled away from her friend and sat down.

Rosie looked tired. There were blue-grey bags under both her eyes, almost like bruises against her pale skin. Her friend's hair was unwashed, a long greasy blonde lock refused to rest and arched aloft, an unfinished bridge, above her friend's scalp. Aisha fought the temptation to straighten it, then surrendered. She patted down Rosie's hair. Rosie laughed at her friend's attention, and grabbed hold of Aisha's wrist.

'Forget about my bloody hair. It's just that I'm not showering on weekends. We're teaching Hugo about water restrictions.' She quickly swiped at her unruly hair. 'I want to hear more about Bangkok and Bali. It's been years since I was in Asia. Was it fantastic?'

She was not going to tell her about Art. It felt disloyal, but she knew it was also exactly the appropriate thing to do. By the end of their coffee together, Rosie would be furious, would lash out anyway she could. So she did not speak of Art, only of the conference and the temples in the city. She described Ubud and Amed and brought forth two gifts out of her handbag; an elephant wallet for Hugo and a small, nuggety Buddha statue for Rosie. She also told her friend about Hector's shocking outburst, the crying that had terrified her, appalled her, moved her; his profound, unfathomable unhappiness.

Rosie held her friend's hand. 'What do you think it's all about?'

'I'm not sure.' She wished Rosie would let go of her hand. She did not deserve this tenderness.

'Sandi's pregnant,' she blurted out and at the same time she drew her hand back. Rosie let it slip out of her grasp and Aisha rushed through the next words. 'I'm going to see her next week, next Sunday. At her place. The whole family is going.'

Rosie was staring somewhere beyond her, over her shoulder. Aisha followed her gaze.

Her friend was examining her reflection in the café's window. 'Shit, I look awful.'

'You don't.' And Aisha meant it. Rosie could never look terrible. She was perfect. She always had been, with her elfin face, her bewitching pale blue eyes, her almost translucent skin. Rosie was perfect.

'I fucking do.' Rosie's lips began to quiver but then she sharply drew in a breath. 'I'm not going to fucking cry,' she insisted. 'I'm not going to cry in front of you.'

It was more awful that her friend had withdrawn from her than it would have been to see her fall apart in grief and hurt and disbelief.

'I'm sorry, darling. I have to do this for Hector.'

Rosie was staring at her, her eyes dry, insolent and condemning.

'Do you?'

'Of course.'

'You know what I told Hugo after the trial?' Rosie's fists were clenched. 'I told him that the judge put the bad man who hit him in jail. I told him that the judge said that people who hurt children were the worst kind of scum on the earth.' Rosie had raised her voice. 'The fucking worst.' A plump woman at the next table, all double-chin and headmistress cold eyes, shook her carefully coiffured matron's bob in disapproval. 'How can you bring yourself to talk to that animal?'

Aisha wished she had followed Anouk's advice. She had seen Rosie angry before. It was always the unexpected fire and strike of a cobra. But Rosie had never been angry at *her* before, had never lunged at *her* in this ferocious, unforgiving manner.

She could only repeat herself: it was her only defence. 'I have to do this for Hector.'

'Hector's always been a cunt.'

It was such an ugly, brutal word. The word struck her as hard as a blow. She could not open her mouth to answer.

'He's worse than Harry. He's an arrogant shit. He's boring.' Rosie had started to cry but Aisha was convinced that she was also enjoying part of her outburst. 'He put Shamira and Bilal against us—he puts everyone against us, including you.' Her tears were now streaming down her face and onto the tabletop. Aisha went to touch her friend's hand but Rosie pulled back as if stung.

'I'm sorry, Rosie.' She wanted to defend Hector as well, to answer her friend that her husband did not hate her, did not want anything evil or unjust to befall her and Gary and Hugo. But heat was forming a tight ball in her belly. Was it true? Hector was arrogant, Hector was jealous of her friendship, he always had been. What was she destroying? She tried to reach out once more and hold her friend's hand. This, all this time and memory and history, this she could not lose.

'I am sorry. Believe me.' Rosie did not remove her hand this time. Aisha felt her friend's cold fingers. She squeezed them hard.

'Don't go and see him.' Rosie had softened again, the viciousness had gone from her voice, the fierce hatred had disappeared from her face. 'If you do go to that man's house I will never forgive you.'

The world around her seemed to have receded, only Rosie's insistent face was visible and real. She wished she had not taken the sleeping pill last night. Nothing was clear, everything was a thick, stifling fog.

'I promised Hector.'

Rosie punched Aisha's hand away from her. 'I don't fucking care,' she yelled.

Everyone now turned around. Everyone was looking at them.

Aisha looked down at her near-empty coffee cup. She felt naked, exposed. The flush of humiliation dissipated. She looked up at her friend, whose wrathful eyes were unwavering. Aisha was being asked to make a choice. All she wanted was to comfort her friend, make things return to their rightful places, return to what had always been. She could do it. She could take back her promise to Hector. She knew since Asia that to be with him was to move forward into an uncertain future. Rosie, her friendships, they all represented life and youth, and yes, they were part of her, who she was. She could betray Hector and choose another life. She felt a growing excitement. It would be a new life in a new world, with Art, in a new country, a new city, a new home, with new work. She would make a new body for herself, a new history for herself, a new future for herself. She could construct a new Aisha. It was possible, Rosie had given her the opportunity. All she had to do was say the words. She would say them. Of course, she would.

And from a table she heard a little girl ask her father, a long-limbed, denim-clad man with a salt-and-pepper goatee, a staid unremark-able man reading his *Guardian Weekly*, she heard the little girl ask him, in a hushed, scared voice that reminded her of Melissa, Dad, why is that woman crying?

She means me.

She could not say those words. Rosie was waiting.

'I'm sorry.' Aisha said it flatly, unconvincingly. Then, with passion, 'I am going to visit Sandi. I promised my husband.' Aisha's eyes were pleading with Rosie. 'Sweetheart, let it go, it's over.'

Rosie looked stunned, looked as if she herself had just been slapped. Blinking away fresh tears she stood up from the table, fumbled through her purse and threw a ten-dollar bill on the table. Aisha was about to force the money back when she stopped herself.

'Fuck you,' screamed Rosie. 'Fuck you, fuck your cunt of a hus-band, fuck your children, your whole perfect, middle-class family. I fucking hate you.'

Aisha watched her friend storm off as she wiped Rosie's spray off her cheek with a napkin.

The matronly woman leaned across. 'Are you alright?'

Aisha nodded. 'Thank you.'

She was, in fact, overwhelmed by what she was experiencing. The light from the sun seemed overpoweringly luminous. Queens Parade was drenched in supernatural brilliance. She herself felt punched and pummelled and exhausted. She also felt blessed. She felt intoxicating relief.

Aisha did not go straight home. She drove to work, switched on the office lights and fired up her computer. While waiting for the screen to come up she walked into the kennel room. The cages were spotless, all lined with newspaper and clean towels. The floor too was shining. Connie or Tracey must have buffed it after their Saturday shift. She sat on a stool and looked across at one of the drip machines. This was a game she sometimes played with herself; not only when she was sad or confused. It was a method she had come to, a way of stilling her mind. She would imagine how she would kill herself if there was the need to. She would go to the drug cabinet and fill a sixty-milligram syringe with Lethobarb. She would inject the green liquid anaesthetic into a bag of saline solution and then attach the bag to the drip. She would click the drip rate to maximum. Then she would insert a catheter in her vein, probably her left arm, and she would then connect herself to the drip. An emerald death. She would fall asleep, she would die. She still believed it was the most humane method to euthanase an animal; and what were humans if not animals? She'd seen enough of death, her work dealt in death as well as life, and she had no romance left in her for suffering. She knew that there was always a way out and she felt at peace. She walked out of the dark of the kennel room and into the office.

The computer screen threw a throbbing silver light in the dim room. She clicked on her mailbox and retrieved the email from Art.

She read it, its promise, once again. *I haven't been able to forget you. Do you feel the same?* The song was in her head, the one that she had been humming to herself all week. *This is a new day, this is a beautiful day*. She must ask Hector. He would know it.

She pressed delete. The email, unanswered, disappeared. She erased it from her computer's memory.

Aisha switched off the lights, set the alarm, locked up and drove home.

Hector was in the backyard, mixing mulch and compost into the vegetable patch. The kids were in the lounge room watching a DVD. Aisha walked into her kitchen and closed the door behind her.

RICHIE

Richie, who believed the world was spiralling out of control, that it had dislodged from its axis, that the ether could not expand fast enough to contain the implosion, that it was all leading to a violent, catastrophic and, for the human species if no other, a deservedly sadistic end, was certain of only three things in his life. He had counted them down in the short time his father had left the table to go to the toilet. One, that his mother was the best mother on the planet. Two, that the American television series *Six Feet Under* was an alternative universe, a better universe, and the one in which he wished he existed. And three, that he was in love with his mate, Nick Cercic. These three things were the only certainty. Everything else was just bullshit, fake, a con. Everything else did not matter. Wait. He counted one more certainty. Connie was the best friend a young art-fag boy could have.

He started to panic. Four was an even number. He did not like even numbers, did not trust them. He needed one more certainty. He looked around at the crowded pub, grimaced at the smell of beer, cooking oil and stale smoke, tried to block out the incessant *ching chang ching* of the pokie machines. He needed one more item for his list, one more certainty, and he needed to find it before his father came back from the toilet. Mum, *Six Feet Under*, Nick Cercic, Connie. Just one more. He started tapping furiously on the table. His chest felt tight, he was going to need his ventolin. You fucking idiot, he snarled at himself, stay calm. He tried to block out the congealed fatty mess of his half-eaten chicken schnitzel on the table. He couldn't concentrate. Not with the barrage from the pokies, not with the Delta Goodrem video playing on the plasma screen over the bar. He detested Delta Goodrem. He wished she had died of cancer. Mum, *Six Feet Under*, Nick Cercic, Connie and . . . and . . . His dad was coming back. He had to make a decision now. *Now*. His father was sitting down, looking at him with that bored, sheepish grin that said, I don't want to be here any more than you do.

His father burped. Richie got a whiff of beer and smoke and tomato sauce.

Five. If he ended up anything like his old man he would off himself. Five. Richie breathed out slowly. He wasn't having an asthma attack, he didn't need his ventolin. He slumped back on his chair, crossed his arms. Mum, *Six Feet Under*, Nick Cercic, Connie, and that he'd kill himself if he ended up like Craig Hillis sitting opposite him. They were all the certainties he needed.

'Aren't you hungry?'

Richie shook his head. He pretended to yawn. He knew that would piss his father off.

'Didn't you like it?'

'S'alright.'

'I reckon the grub is fantastic in this place.'

Richie slumped further in his chair and looked up at the ceiling. It was a tacky pokies pub in the middle of nowhere, boganville. Every street looked the same, every house looked the same, everybody looked the same. It was where you came to die. Zombies lived here. He could hear them monotonously tapping away at the machines.

'But you don't like it?'

'I said it was alright.'

His father pointed to the empty glasses on the table. 'You want another beer?'

Richie nodded.

His father almost fell over in his rush to the bar. They were both glad for any excuse to be away from each other. Richie watched his father smiling and chatting away to the big-breasted young girl who was serving. Her tank-top read I ♥ NY but if you looked closer at the ♥ it was made up of tight, red-scrawled letters that read 'Haven't been to'. His father had thought it cool and funny when they had gone up to order. It had made Richie want to take a knife and jam it into his own throat. The woman was now pouring the drinks. His father turned around and winked at Richie who pretended not to notice. His dad always wore jeans that looked like they were two sizes too small for him. It was a bad idea. Like his mum said, Craig Hillis had no arse to speak off.

'Here you go, mate.' His father, with a forced smile, clinked glasses. Richie downed nearly half the glass with a rapid, throaty glug. Why the fuck not? He had no school left, he was in the middle of *Dawn of the Dead* land with his zombie father, and he would be legal age in a matter of weeks. Might as well get drunk as fast as he could.

It was at least eight months since he'd last seen his old man. In terms of their history together, that meant that they were now closer than they had ever been. He had been seven years old before he'd met his father. Back then all he had wanted was to love the man, to have someone he could call Dad. His Nana Hillis had set up the meeting; she had never lost contact with Tracey and Richie and she had finally forced her own son to face up to his responsibilities. Richie found this out much later. As a young boy his mother had told him nothing of her battles through the courts to get child support from Craig. All Richie was told was that his father was a truck driver who lived far away. Then at seven he had met him. Craig had taken him to a football game. Even back then, Richie had a dawning sense that the fact that men loved kicking a leather ball to one another boded ill for the sanity of the human race. Nevertheless, he made an effort to become familiar with the codes and rituals of being a supporter of the Collingwood Football Club, forcing his mum to buy him a black-and-white team singlet, standing in line outside the Northland Toys"R"Us one pre-finals Saturday in order to get his singlet signed by Nathan Buckley. But after a few desultory weekends, Craig simply stopped coming around to see him. Then soon after Richie got a call from Craig, saying that he had married and moved up to Cairns with his new wife. He didn't see him again for six years. In the meantime, he heard through his nan that he had a baby half-brother, and he secretly hoped that one day he would be invited up north to visit Craig's new family. No invitation came, but he had not been entirely forgotten. Every Christmas he would receive a card and a gift voucher for a CD. It seemed every second year his father would remember to ring him on his birthday. He's a bloody selfish prick, Nana Hillis would say to him, I'm glad you take after your mum. When Richie turned fourteen, his father returned to Melbourne. Craig's marriage had ended in divorce and he was back to driving trucks. At fourteen, Richie was not into pretending any love for footy or Formula One racing or the arse-end of the Arnold Schwarzenegger back catalogue. Father and son literally had nothing to say to one another.

'Another?' Richie raised his eyebrow. This was Craig's fifth beer. There was no way he could drive Richie back to Preston tonight. He'd have to ask him for cab money.

'Yeah, why not?'

His mobile phone started to throb. He quickly yanked it out of the pocket of his shorts. Connie had sent him a text. He read it and giggled. *Shld we cum + save u?* He quickly typed a return text. *Safe 4 the mmnt. Zmbies hvnt gt me yt.*

'Who you texting?'

'A friend.'

'I guessed that. Which friend?'

Richie looked across at his old man. He had his legs spread wide apart, showing the faded white material of the groin of his jeans. Richie wished his father would close his bloody legs. He tried to ignore his father's crotch.

'Connie.'

'She's your girlfriend, right?'

Richie sipped at his beer, not answering. He hoped his disgusted expression was answer enough.

'How long have you been together?'

Richie almost spilled his beer, he banged his glass on the table so hard. 'She's not my fucking girlfriend. She's got a boyfriend.'

'Who?'

'Ali.'

'An Arab?'

He was stuck in *Dawn of the Dead* land. Eat me, thought Richie despondently, rip out my guts and heart and stomach. Make me the Undead.

'What's wrong with that?'

'Jesus Fucking Christ, Rick.' His father flinched. In turning round, he had slammed his knee into the table leg. Good, he'd finally shut his legs. 'I didn't mean anything by that. I don't give a fuck if she's rooting some Arab.'

'He's Australian. He was born here.'

'You know what I mean.'

'Yeah.' Richie pointed around the pub, waving his finger like a wand. 'I know exactly what you mean. You don't like Arabs or Asians or black people or fags or anyone except boring white people out here in zombie suburbia.' Richie rocked back and forth in his chair. 'I bet you voted for John Howard.'

'This is a boomtime, mate. There's plenty of money going round.' Craig made the words sound like shotgun fire. 'None of your business who I voted for anyway.'

Richie said nothing. He pulled out his phone and texted to Connie: *The Zmbies R Coming, the Zmbies R Coming*. He looked up.

His father sighed heavily. 'Look, Rick.' His father and Nana Hillis were the only ones who called him by that name. His grandfather's name. 'I know we don't have the best relationship. All my fucking fault, I admit it. But you're old enough to understand things now.' His father stopped, scratched at his hair, smiled hopefully.

Richie put his phone away.

'I had just turned nineteen when your mum got pregnant. A year older than you are now. I wasn't ready. I fucked up and ran away. What do you want me to do?'

His phone was vibrating. He wanted to answer it but, just now, for the first time in years, he didn't want to provoke his father. He sat still, drank fitfully from his beer.

His father had taken out a packet of Winfield Blues and was playing with them on the table. 'You want to come out with me while I have a smoke?'

Richie nodded. 'Can I have one?'

Craig hesitated. 'Does your mother know you smoke?'

'I don't smoke. I like to have an occasional one.'

'Does she let you?'

'Yeah.'

'Does she let you?'

'I said yeah.'

Craig flicked him over a cigarette. 'Come on then.'

The carpark was full of smokers. The night was warm, and as soon as they had walked out into the heat Richie felt himself starting to sweat, moisture damp and squishy in his armpits. He watched his father smoke. They held the cigarette in the same way. Two fingers coiled tight around the base. Was it just him and Craig? Or did everybody smoke that way?

'Did you want to get rid of me?' He startled himself by asking the question out loud.

His father was frowning.

'Did your mother tell you that?'

'No.' For the first time in his life Richie had been thinking of his father as a young guy, nineteen, with a pregnant girlfriend. What did the girls at school do? Either they had the baby or they had an abortion. What would he want to do in that situation? Lose the foetus pronto—that was all you could do. Craig must have been furious at Trace for keeping him. He must have gone fucking ballistic.

His father was sucking hard on the cigarette. Richie realised that his father must be thirty-seven years old. That was pretty young for a father of a kid his age.

'It's okay if you did. I'd want her to have an abortion if I got a girl pregnant.'

Craig laughed. 'I'm glad your mum didn't do it.'

They stood next to each other, smoking, nearly touching. It was uncomfortable, like they should hug or something. But neither of them knew how to do that.

By the end of the night his father had become too drunk to drive him home. Craig, sounding shocked as the words slipped out, asked his son if he wanted to crash at his place for the night. Richie, to his own amazement, accepted. Connie had sent him another text; she and Ali were in the city. He looked at the throbbing steel-blue illuminated screen and quickly punched a message back. *C U 2mro.* Leaving the van in the pub's expansive carpark, they decided to walk the kilometre or so back to Craig's house.

They hardly spoke to each other on the walk. Richie wondered if his father was feeling the same anxiety that he himself was experiencing, a faintly nauseating discomfort at their sudden closeness. Richie had never visited anywhere his father had lived in. Now he was about to stay a night in this near stranger's house.

Flat. It wasn't a house, it was a small red-brick shitbox flat on the first floor. Craig switched on the light and almost shoved Richie through the door. The tiny space stank of the mildew and smoke. Richie took a quick glance around the living area. The walls were bare except for a poster of Tony's gang from *The Sopranos* Blu-Tacked above a sunken snot-green sofa. One of the cushions had fallen onto the rough, chocolate-coloured carpet; the upholstery was faded, stained, Richie could see the exposed coils beneath. Craig pushed the cushion back in place and pointed to the armchair opposite. Richie sat down on the chair and Craig plonked himself on the sagging sofa: his arse nearly hit the floor which made Richie want to laugh. A bong and a half-full ashtray were the only items on the table. Craig struggled forward, perched on the edge of the sofa and grabbed the bong.

'You smoke?'

'Sure.'

After three rounds of the bong, Craig had fallen asleep on the sofa. Richie got up, turned off the Led Zeppelin II CD on the stereo and walked into Craig's bedroom. He switched on the light.

There was a mattress on the floor. The sheets had been cast off, and the pillow was doubled over. Richie slid open the window and looked over the tiled red roof of the brick-veneer house next door. There was a distant hum from traffic on the Maroondah Highway. But otherwise the silence was disconcerting. *The Night of the Living Dead*, thought Richie, this is the land of the zombies. He turned around to examine the room. His father's clothes were all stuffed in a hanging canvas frame. Underwear, T-shirts, socks, singlets, everything was jumbled in together. There was a stack of magazines next to the mattress. Richie squatted and looked through them. An AFL form guide, a few issues of *Drive*, *Ralph*, a *Penthouse* and heaps of porn. He glanced nervously behind him. He could hear his father's slow, even snores. Richie shut the door, stripped to his underwear and pulled the sheets over himself. He grabbed one of the porn mags and began to flick through it. An anatomically ludicrous woman was writhing on a kitchen floor, her shaven cunt shoved to the camera, disinfectants and cleaning agents scattered around her. Richie suppressed a giggle. He dropped the magazine and picked up another. A hairy, olive-skinned man, a Celtic tattoo on his forearm, was fondling a blonde woman's breast. The guy looked like a Muzza, or an Italian or Greek, he looked a bit like a thuggish, more chunky

Hector. That seemed off, a betrayal of Connie. Hector was a prick, a fuckwit, a pervert. He put the magazine back on the pile.

Richie's cock was hard. He looked down at his body. So fucking white, so many freckles, pimples still on his shoulders. His bush looked ridiculously hairy in the harsh light of the naked bulb above him. His cock looked too big, grotesque, on his too-thin body. He jumped up and turned off the light. He got back into bed, breathed heavily, adjusting to the dark. He could just make out Craig's snores. Richie knew he would have to wank before he could fall asleep but he was too stoned to concentrate on an image, on a fantasy. He tried to think of Nick. He was at the pool with Nick, they were showering. A burst of heavy snoring came from the next room. Richie closed his eyes tight and started to vigorously pump his cock. He wouldn't think, he'd just let his mind go, let it take him where it took him. Hector was in a car, his legs outstretched, Richie was sitting beside him. Hector was pulling down his zip, he was forcing Richie down over his cock. Richie was almost punishing himself as he brutally rubbed his dry fist up and down the shaft of his dick. Semen burst over his hand, it oozed, warm, sticky, through his clenched fingers, disgusting him. Fuck, he cursed himself, I'm one perverted fuck. Hector was evil. He had hurt Connie, violated her. He was sick sick sick. Had she enjoyed any of it? She must have kissed him, touched his skin. She must have enjoyed some of it. Richie's cock twitched. *Sick sick sick.* His semen, now cold, clammy, was sliding down his thigh. He groaned and threw the sheets off himself. It would be too wrong and too weird to get any of his cum on Craig's bedding. He pulled off his undies and cleaned himself off. In minutes he was asleep.

It was the middle of the morning when he awoke. He pulled on his jeans and T-shirt and walked into the lounge room. His father had left, his cigarettes weren't on the coffee table. Richie put the kettle on to boil, and munched on a half-eaten bar of chocolate he found in the fridge. There was no bread. He sat on the sofa and looked at his mobile. No messages, everyone was probably still asleep. Should he drink his tea and leave? Did he just close the door behind him? The bag of dope was still on the table. Quickly, Richie pulled out four or five heads and wrapped them in cigarette papers. He stuffed them into his pocket. The kettle started to whistle. Richie made a tea, sat cross-legged on the floor and switched on *Rage*. He drank tea and watched music videos till his father returned with a loaf of bread and some more milk.

'I went to get the van.'

Richie didn't answer. He watched Nelly Furtado mouthing the lyrics to 'Maneater'. It was a shit clip. He muted the volume.

'You want some toast?'

Richie nodded. They munched on vegemite toast, both listlessly watching the silent screen.

He should have gone back home last night, he should have asked Craig for taxi money. He knew he should say something, have some kind of creepy conversation with his father but he couldn't think of anything to say, nothing that didn't sound stupid or suspicious or dangerous or just fucking gay. He couldn't think of anything normal to say.

'You want me to drive you to the station?'

'Yeah.' It was a relief. He'd be getting out of here.

'You want a shower first?'

'I guess.'

'I'll get you a towel.'

In the shower he used his finger to rub the toothpaste across his teeth. He had gone to use Craig's brush but it felt too wrong. He dried himself, tried to smooth his boofy, stupid hair into some decent shape and then gave up. He looked at his soiled underwear lying on the floor; the dry cum had formed a streaky web. He had brought the undies into the bathroom, thinking he would wash them. It was a ridiculous idea, he'd have to carry wet undies on the train. He looked at the toilet. He threw the undies into the bowl and then grabbed the shit-speckled toilet brush lying on its side. He pushed the underwear deep into the drain and then flushed the toilet. The water swirled, gathered force, and began to rise in the bowl. Richie looked at it with horror. The water wasn't subsiding, it was filling the bowl. He'd fucked the drain. Richie shrugged. Let his father deal with it.

Craig dropped him off at Ringwood station. Richie went to fling open the door but Craig reached over, grabbed his shoulder. He seemed agitated.

'I know it's your birthday next month.'

Richie mumbled, fast. 'It's okay if you don't get me anything.'

'Of course I'll fucking get you something.'

Why? You've just sent cards before.

'It's your eighteenth, it's important.' Craig let go of Richie's arm and smiled. 'Your grandma and me are thinking of pitching in and getting you an iPod.' His smile disappeared and he looked concerned. 'You haven't got one, have you?'

'No.' Wow. An iPod. Brilliant. He wanted to ask if he would get one with heaps of gig, that could play video. But that wouldn't be right.

'Thanks,' he mumbled.

'I guess you'll be having a party.'

'I guess.' Did his father want an invitation? No way, he couldn't do it to Tracey. It wasn't going to be a party anyway, just a dinner.

'Or are you just going to go out with your girlfriend?'

She's not my fucking girlfriend. Richie's right leg began to twitch. The air in the car felt old, it stank. Can I just go?

Then Craig did something completely unexpected. He playfully brushed his hand over Richie's hair. The boy automatically shot out his arm to his head but stopped himself in mid-motion.

'I'll call you on your birthday. Maybe I'll take you out for a legal drink.' Craig switched on the ignition. 'See ya then.'

'See ya.' Richie slammed the door shut and ran all the way up to the platform, not looking behind him. He sat on a bench and breathed out slowly. He tapped the ventolin in his pocket. It was okay, he didn't need it. He felt safe now. He took out his phone and checked for messages.

Everyone was waiting for Tuesday, which was when they'd all get their ENTER scores. Richie hadn't thought much about what they meant while he completed the school year but now that high school had finished—had finished forever!—it slowly began to dawn on him that the future was not a straight linear path but a matrix of permutations and possibilities, offshoots from offshoots. The map of the future was three-dimensional—that thought had literally never crossed his mind before. School had made him blind to that truth. The school years were flat, two-dimensional: sleep, school, study, sleep, school, study and some holidays. That world was splintering, and no longer made sense: and that, more than anything, *that* filled him with both a ferocious excitement and an anxious confusion; he could never go back to that other world again.

His hope, of course, was that he would pass. It was unlikely, impossible—surely it must be impossible?—that he would fail. He was an average student, not brilliant, but certainly he was not lazy or an idiot. He had filled out his preferences diligently but without much thought. Mapping and Environmental Studies were kind of what he wanted the future to look like. But just after Christmas he and Nick had taken the tram into the city and smoked a joint in Melbourne Cemetery and then walked across to the university. Nick wanted to do Medicine. That was all he wanted to do, what he'd wanted to do all along. If he didn't do Medicine, his life would fall apart. They had wandered the buildings, mostly empty in the height of summer and Nick had pointed out a tall, ugly concrete edifice on the edge of the university. My uncle helped lay the bricks to this fucker, he told Richie. He says that if I make it to this place I will be the first one in my family. Nick's face had looked ecstatic that day, had looked alive and dangerous. Richie stood next to his friend and looked up at the building. My uncle's hands built this place, Nick uttered again, and then his face tightened into a grimace. I have to come here. He then turned to Richie, elated, excited. And you know what that means, don't you, mate, if we get here? We'll be better than all the private school rich cunts who make it here. We'll have made it because we're the best, because we're smart—we don't just have to pay for it. Richie had nodded, not quite understanding his friend's passion. But on the bus, as they made their way back home, Richie suddenly spied the future, its complicated, mulitfarious possibilities.

He gazed out of the window onto the shimmering asphalt footpaths of the northern suburbs and suddenly, chance, accident, fate, will, they all made sense to him. And they made him scared. Nick would get into uni or Nick would not. He and Nick would be at uni together or they would not. That was only the one strand to the future, the one path out of all those myriad possibilities he cared about. He had looked across at his best friend. Nick Cercic was looking straight ahead. He looked calm. But Richie could see that his own hands were shaking on his knees. The hurt in his chest that was a bullet tearing him apart in slow motion, that hurt, that pain that he hoped would never go away, that was love, wasn't it? It fucking had to be. It was so strong it was like the force of the universe inside him. It could be a Big Bang, it could shatter him into infinite fragments, annihilate him. Richie held his breath and looked out the window. If he could make it to sixty, slowly, not rushing it, not cheating, in real time, if he could hold his breath for sixty seconds, then Nick would get into Medicine, he would get into a diploma of spatial engineering, they would be at the same uni, they would be in the same future. Richie took a huge breath and counted down to sixty.

The Friday night before that crucial Tuesday they went to see *Marie Antoinette* at the Westgarth. Nick had been suspicious about it, thought that it sounded chick-flicky, gay. 'Anyway,' he complained, 'I've got too much on my mind. I can't concentrate on a movie.'

Richie wondered what his friend would do if he didn't get into Medicine. Go fucking apeshit, that's what. He'd want to take himself out and everyone around him.

'It's got Kirsten Dunst in it.'

That did the trick. At the last moment they were joined by Connie, which made Nick even more agitated. They took their seats near the front of the cinema, Connie almost forcing Richie to sit in the middle. As the theatre darkened and the first trailer screened, Richie took a sideways look at Nick. He had already started fidgeting. During the course of the feature he went off to the toilet twice, the second time coming back smelling of smoke. After the film ended they went for an iced chocolate down the road. Nick had nothing to say about the movie at all. Richie had liked the music, the sensuality of it all. Connie had been bored, though she too liked the music. She thought Marie Antoinette was a dick. Nick's eagerness to finish his drink and get out of the café was almost comical in its urgency. The boys walked Connie home. Usually she would kiss and hug Richie on saying goodbye but she never did when he was with Nick. They walked back to Richie's house.

His mother was up, with her friend Adele, sitting in the booth in their tiny kitchen. The boys squeezed in next to them.

'Have you guys eaten yet?'

Richie shook his head.

Tracey pointed to the stove-top. 'I made some stir-fry. There's plenty left over. Heat it up in the microwave.'

Nick suddenly shot up from his seat. 'I've got to go.' It almost sounded like a wail.

'Come on, love. Eat. Then you can go.'

Nick shook his head furiously. 'No,' he squeaked, then made a gesture halfway between a salute and a wave towards Richie and bolted down the hall. They heard the door slam.

Adele laughed rudely. 'What the fuck is up with him?'

Richie scooped two ladles' worth of stir-fry onto a plate and placed it in the microwave. 'He's strung out,' he answered defensively; he never wanted to hear any criticism of Nick. 'We get our results on Tuesday.'

Adele clucked, a strange abrupt sound that seemed to come from deep in her throat. It could have been meant sympathetically or dismissively—you couldn't tell with Adele. She was snappy and curt, looked like she drank and smoked too much—which she did—and she was overweight. She and his mother had been friends before he was born. In a way, he often told himself, she was like an aunt; and like an aunt you never gave her too much thought.

The microwave beeped, a sound he always found infuriating. He sat down and started to attack his food.

'Are you nervous about it?'

What do you think? Our whole freaking future depends on it. His mouth stuffed with food, he nodded at Adele.

'You'll both be alright.'

Richie kept munching at his food, hoping his mother and her friend would not start talking about the future. The future was about to ram itself right into his face in five days' time. The future was about to happen: the exams had been sat, the results were in and now there was nothing to do except wait for the future to call. He wanted to explain all this to Nick; he wished he could *comfort* his friend. He didn't know how to. Just shut up, he silently willed his mother and Adele, just shut up, we don't need to hear any more about it. He took a last mouthful, gulped it down in one swallow and burped loudly.

'Charming.'

He grinned. 'Sorry, Mum. Good grub.'

'What's your first choice?'

He looked across at Adele. He was sure he had already answered this question. She had forgotten, as she would forget again.

'Geomatic Engineering. Geographic Information Systems to be precise.'

He enjoyed the blank look on her face.

'What the fuck is that?'

I don't know, I don't know, I don't know. Computers and maps, one of the treacherous paths in the matrix which is the future.

'He wants to make maps,' his mother answered for him, giving him a sympathetic wink. 'I think it's perfect for him.'

Adele was about to open her mouth.

'Mum,' he interrupted excitedly. 'Craig wants to get me an iPod for my birthday.' He had rushed into changing the conversation without thinking. He caught a brief tremble on his mother's lips, a quick flicker of the eyes, a moment of uncertainty. He wished he could take the moment back, let Adele ask a thousand questions about the future. He thought back to his list of certainties—it was the first one, the most important. His mother was the best mother on the planet. And he'd off himself if he turned out anything like his old man.

'I told him not to get one without talking to you first,' he lied. He peeked up at her. 'You might want to go in it with him.' Fucking stupid stupid stupid thing to say. *Duuhh.*

His mother's lips pressed together. She tapped Adele's cigarette packet. Her friend nodded and his mother pulled out a cigarette. Richie stopped himself from protesting. Smoking made her look old. The kitchen already stank of Adele's tobacco. He looked down at his plate again so she wouldn't see his scowl.

'I've already bought your present.' Tracey lit her cigarette and exhaled. 'I bought it months ago.' She kissed her finger, leaned over and touched his lips with it. 'I'm glad you and your father are getting along.'

He kissed the top of his finger and blew her back a kiss. He got up from the table. 'I'm going to bed.'

'What are you up to tomorrow?'

'I'm babysitting Hugo. Rosie's got a doctor's appointment and Connie's working. I said I'd do it.'

He caught the furtive look that passed between the two women.

'Aren't you working?'

You *know* what time I'm working. He had found a part-time job at the Coles at Northcote Plaza. Lenin had got him the job.

'I don't start till one.'

Adele was wanting to say something. He held in his breath; he'd count to ten. He had his back turned to her.

'Hey,' he heard her call out. 'Tell your dad I'll go in on the iPod. Might as well get you a good one.'

He swung around, a big grin on his face. Adele was exactly like an aunt.

'Really?'

'Really.'

Of course, she had known his father. They were in school together.

'Thanks!'

He kissed the two women goodnight.

As soon as he was in his bed he reached underneath it and pulled out three notebooks and flicked through them. The oldest, its once vibrant indigo vinyl cover now faded to a pale cyan, held his maps and notes for Priam. This was a small island continent, half the size of Australia, that lay far east of Madagascar, in the middle of the Indian Ocean. The second notebook, A3, a present from his mother when he had turned fifteen, a Green Day sticker fading on the black binding, contained all the maps for Al'Anin, an archipelago of four hundred and seventeen islands off the coast of California and Mexico. The third notebook was full, and contained his sketches and designs for the city of New Troy, the capital of Priam and one of the most beautiful and awe-inspiring cities in the whole world. Its deep, natural harbour ate into the lush tropical coast. The harbour city with its ancient temples once dedicated to the old Greek gods stopped at the imposing cliff faces of the Poseidons, a mountain range that had collapsed into the ocean, leaving a sheer escarpment that ran for hundreds of kilometres along the coast. Towering hundreds of metres above the city, on the enormous plateau that stretched to the horizon beyond the cliff face were the dazzling skyscrapers, mosques, churches and temples of New Troy, a shimmering jumble of silicon and marble and concrete and brick—all gold spires and silver minarets and bronze domes shining in the cobalt tropical sky.

Richie opened the first notebook again and began to write. Priam was the place to which a group of the defeated warriors of Troy had escaped. They had discovered this continent, bred with the proud indigenous population that lived there, and named their new world after their last king and ruler. They too established a kind of Rome but unlike the founders of that city, these Trojans of Priam had disappeared from Asian and European history for over a thousand years. He had filled the book with stories of the intermarriage of Trojans and Aborigines, had detailed notes on the unique fauna and food crops of this rich, fertile kingdom.

He had now come to the point where he had to deal with what happened to Priam with the arrival of Christian explorers and settlers. He knew that he did not want the Spaniards to discover it. He guessed he had to make the explorers English, as it was the only language he knew. He had played with the idea of making the first Europeans to land Russian, but that did not accord with any of the history he had read on European colonisation. The Renaissance and the World, his favourite unit in Year Eleven, taught by the profane, impatient Mrs Hadjmichael, who always wore a Collingwood jumper in winter and a Brasillia soccer shirt in spring, had made him hungry to bring the ideals and values of modernity to the closed hierarchical world of the New Trojans—though he knew that the old religion would survive; even in the twenty-first century there would be New Trojans who worshipped Zeus and Athena, Poseidon and Artemis.

Vasili Grigorovich D'Estaing, the legendary French Huguenot admiral who had defected to the court of Queen Elizabeth I, was infamous not only for being the bastard child of Ivan the Terrible, but also for his ribald behaviour: it was said that he had boasted of one hundred mistresses and a dozen or so boy catamites. He was also the Renaissance World's greatest explorer after Columbus and Raleigh, and it is often claimed that he was arguably greater than both of those men. He was certainly more courageous. For years Grigorovich D'Estaing was convinced of the existence of a great southern continent in the Indian Ocean: a land that was part of Egyptian, Nubian and Ethiopian legends. He believed that discovery of this new world would bring riches and power to England. He was driven to open up a universe to his beloved adopted sovereign, to exceed the gifts the conquistadors had brought home to Ferdinand and Isabella. After the English victory over the Spanish Armada, Grigorovich D'Estaing received permission from Queen Elizabeth to head an expedition into the heart of the Indian Ocean. This was to prove momentous for the New Trojans. For centuries, over a millennium, they had deliberately closed themselves off from the world. Their continent had proved abundant in food and ore, and any strangers who by misadventure or chance landed on their island were immediately enslaved. The children of these adventurers and pirates became citizens of the new world. However, the rising population of the continent had been placing a heavier and heavier burden on the kingdom. Increasingly the Emperor was being besieged by his council to open trade with the world. It was into this crisis that Grigorovich D'Estaing sailed his fleet into the harbour of New Troy. His journals communicate some of the wonder his men experienced on looking at the immense splendour of the city, the towering gold statue of Pallas Athena, the Parthenon on the cliff's edge, the roofs of the Summer Palace just visible beyond it. The Emperor's regiments waited by the harbour walls, their swords and lances ready to welcome the Europeans. This confrontation, this meeting, was to shape the history of the whole world.

He stopped writing. He turned back a few pages and looked at his sketch of Grigorovich D'Estaing. He traced the outline of the man's face. The music thundered through his headphones. He turned the volume up even louder and the pen dropped to the floor. His wrist was sore. He had not done too badly with the sketch, especially the shading of D'Estaing's copper breastplate, with its insignia of a dragon fighting a phoenix, which he had copied from a fantasy site he found on the internet. He shut the notebook and lay on his bed, turning the volume to its loudest setting, letting the music bash against his eardrums. When the CD was finished he removed his headphones and opened the third notebook. In the back there was a little plastic pocket he had created and in that pocket were all his precious mementos: a photograph of a drunk Nick at Jenna's party, his arm tight around a smiling Richie's neck; a slim ticket of shots of himself and Connie, piled into the photo booth at Northland Mall, their cheeks touching, her grin, his smile, exaggerated, hysterical; the cards his dad and nan had sent him; his ticket stub to the Pearl Jam concert his mother had taken him to for his thirteenth birthday. And finally, tucked at the end, the photocopy he had made of the photograph he'd stolen from Rosie and Gary's place, the young Hector cast against a clear turquoise sky, his naked torso wet from the sea, his heroic profile calm and unflinching in the sun. This was the model for Grigorovich D'Estaing. The photocopy was creased, torn on one edge. He would have to be more careful with it. Richie gently pulled it out of the folder. He held the photocopy high above him, imagining that it was real, made flesh, that the man in the photograph was about to turn his face away from the sea and the sun and look down at Richie, part his lips. Richie closed his eyes and reached for his cock.

He had asked his mother to wake him at seven and her voice cut into his sleep like nails screeching down a blackboard. He groaned and tried to toss himself back into sleep. He must have succeeded because he was woken again by his mother coming into his room and clapping her hands close to his ear. He shot out of bed. His mother laughed at him cruelly.

'What time is it?'

'A quarter past seven,' his mother called on her way out of the room, 'and if you're not out of the shower and dressed by seven-thirty I'm not driving you to the pool.'

Seven-fifteen. That felt like a school day. Like the old days. He had not woken before ten since school had finished, and most days not before noon. His two shifts at the supermarket were in the afternoon and evening, though Zoran the shift supervisor had intimated that there would be some morning shifts available after the school holidays had finished. Richie loved the liberation of uninterrupted sleep, especially as he realised that it was possibly his last opportunity to indulge in it, that the future would soon grab him and study and work and life would again order his body to a clock. Seven-fifteen. He ran to the shower in his underdaks. As always, he stayed under long enough to quickly wash and brush his teeth. The drought had forced him to change his ways: he used to love spending ages under the shower, ignoring his mother's tirades over his waste of water. He'd clean his teeth, shave if he needed to—still only once a week—and most often wank. Not anymore.

His mother was already waiting for him in the car. In minutes she had turned into the driveway of the YMCA. Thanks, Mum, he called out, slamming the door shut. She hooted and he waved, not bothering to turn back to look at her.

He didn't need to be at Hugo's till nine-thirty, and he was determined to swim for at least forty minutes. Richie had decided at the end of school that he wanted a new body, a fit, strong body. Eventually, like Nick, like Ali, he would join the gym, but he wasn't ready for it yet. He'd never been particularly good at sports or Phys. Ed. He was too scrawny, felt too weak.

Undressing in the change rooms he eagerly anticipated his birthday present. An iPod. Awesome. That would make the gym bearable. He slipped into his trunks and jumped into the pool.

He was determined to get to one hundred laps, that was his goal. Nick had told him that by swimming he would be exercising all the muscles in his body but that he needed to concentrate on speed and endurance if he wanted to build up his strength. So far, in just under two months, Richie had built up to fifty laps. The first twenty were always the killer—he always found them excruciating to complete; they seemed to take ages. Time passed slowly, and he experienced every boring second of it. He detested the monotony of repetition. He had nearly given up swimming in that first week; it was only the embarrassment of seeing his thin, reedy body in the change-room mirrors that forced him back to the water. But he discovered that if he did persevere, if he reached the twentieth lap, and kept on going, he entered what he-tried-not-to-but-ended-up-calling-it-what-the-fucked-up-jocks-at-school-called-it, 'the zone'. The zone was a space of timelessness and disassociation. It was like being stoned, but healthier. In the zone, time was not made up of dull seconds and even more tedious minutes; in the zone, time had no markers, no beginning and no end.

Sometimes, not very often, he and Nick would swim together. But it was uncomfortable, and he found it impossible to enter the zone with Nick swimming next to him. He was too conscious of his friend's body, of the ferocity of his own desire. Not that he ever dared look at Nick when they were changing; they always dressed facing away from each other in the showers. He did take peeks, he couldn't help it. He could describe every part of Nick's anatomy, a composite body he had snatched in illicit glances. The light wave of golden hair underneath Nick's balls, the almost scarlet blotch of the birthmark above his friend's right nipple, the boy's stubby, hooded cock, so much smaller than his own.

Richie swam to eighteen laps, breathing heavily, struggling to reach the magical twenty. He tried not to think of his friend's beautiful cock, of the almost perfect profile of the pool attendant standing bored over the empty kiddie's pool. Nineteen. He wanted to give up, go home, go back to bed. He touched the cold tiles and tumbled into the next lap. Twenty, he had reached it. He was in the zone. When he touched the wall to finish his fiftieth lap, it felt as if no time had passed at all. He sucked deeply from the tepid warm air, then taking a breath, he folded his legs to sink beneath the water. He'd count to thirty. He reached twenty-one and his chest began to hurt. He refused to panic. He got to thirty and broke the top of the water. Grabbing his towel he dashed for the spa.

An old Asian gentleman, his skin a bronze colour, was the only person in the spa. Richie quickly showered, ridding his body of the stench of chlorine, and then slid into the frothing water. The jets pummelled into his back. He quickly turned around, felt the warm punches of water against his stomach. He lifted himself up and let the water throb against his crotch and, turning again, the jets slammed into his arse. It was always a nice feeling, it always felt sleazy and a little pervy. Would a cock up his arse feel like this? Nah, he'd stuck his fingers up himself once and, though kind of hot in a dirty, pornographic way, it had also hurt. A cock would definitely hurt. He turned again and slid into the water, his back against the spa wall, his arms outstretched on the tiled rim. His armpits seemed lewd, gross and hairy, especially compared to the near hairlessness of the Asian man. Richie looked up through the glass. A man, sweaty from a workout, his singlet drenched, was opening a locker.

Richie's back straightened. He stared open-mouthed at the man. It was Hector.

Richie's eyes followed him as he grabbed his bag, shut the locker again and walked down the corridor towards the change rooms. At that moment, as Hector disappeared around the corner, the jets in the spa fell quiet. The water trembled, then became still. It would be a few minutes before they would start again. Usually Richie would then go into the sauna. Usually. But he did not do that. He took his towel and headed for the showers.

They had renovated the men's changing rooms in the spring and instead of open showers there were now six cubicles. Hector was showering in one, his cubicle door left wide open. Richie stood looking at the man's hairy arse, his tall, defined body. Hector looked as if he was about to turn and face him, and Richie quickly ducked into the cubicle next to him. He swiftly turned on the water and let it fall down hard on him, far too cold, but he didn't care. He could hear the man next door turn off the shower. Richie stood beneath the water. He stripped off his trunks. He decided to count to fifteen. Fifteen was a lucky number.

Fifteen. He turned off the shower and walked into the change room.

Hector was standing across from him, naked, a white damp towel draped across his shoulder. Richie, not daring to breathe, looked at the man, then offered a shy, scared grin. Hector, looking confused, smiled back. 'Hello.'

That was exactly how Grigorovich D'Estaing would have sounded, a voice rich and resonant and deep, nothing soft about it at all.

Richie just nodded back, not daring to say a word. He would squeak, sound like a girl, he just knew it. He should ask about Aisha, about his kids—what the fuck were their names? Hector continued to dry himself. Richie took him all in, knowing it could be the only opportunity he would ever get. He looked at the man's neck, his chest, his belly, his thighs, his cock, his balls, his crotch, his knees, elbows, fingers, hands. He would not let himself forget a single thing about him. The dense dark swirls of hair around his nipples, the faint pink scar on his left arm, the fact that his right testicle seemed rounder, larger than the other. Hector was pulling back his foreskin, wiping at it. Richie's cock suddenly went hard; he had no control over it. It jutted out, wobbly, huge, ugly. Drying his shoulders, Hector glanced over at Richie, then looked away immediately, shocked, embarrassed, but not before Richie had caught that look somewhere between distress and disgust in the older man's eyes.

Hector made a sound, a grunt, a mumbled indecipherable obscenity. Cold loathing dripped from that sound. He had turned away from the boy, hiding his body from his gaze. Richie burned red. He wanted to cry. He mustn't cry. Frantically, he pulled on his trunks and rushed out of the change rooms. His cock was still stiff, threatening to slip out of his swimmers, and he held his hands protectively over his crotch as he ran, shaking, pretending to be cold. He almost slid on the tiles as he ran to the pool. He dived in, ignoring the signs forbidding him to do so. He immediately swam, beginning his laps anew, his strokes hard, violent, the water churning around him. Richie was swimming away from what had just happened, trying to race against Hector's contempt, the fact that Hector must think him a pervert, had no clue who he was, had not recognised him. That should have made him glad: there was no chance Hector would say anything to Aisha, which meant neither his mother nor Connie would ever hear anything about it. But it did not make him glad. Hector didn't remember him. He was nothing to Hector—just a fag, a freak, all sick, stupid childish fantasies and dreams. Richie swam and swam, lap after lap, churning through the water, punishing himself into exhaustion. Finally, too knackered for another lap, he placed his brow against the cool tiles of the pool. Sick sick sick.

He walked to Rosie's still cursing himself. He hated his body. It had betrayed him. He shouldn't have run; he should have stayed and confronted Hector. I know what you did. *I know.* He knocked hard on the door. The bell had stopped working and Gary had not got round to fixing it. He knocked so hard he nearly tore his knuckles.

'You're early,' smiled Rosie as she ushered him in.

He mumbled something unintelligible. Hugo was watching a DVD in the lounge room but leapt up as soon as he heard Richie. It wasn't until that moment, the child's arms tight around his neck, that he finally felt some respite, did not feel like tearing himself apart, ridding himself of his useless body, his dirty, sick mind. He cuddled the boy and then carefully disentangled himself from the hug. Richie pulled out the ventolin from his pocket and took two sharp puffs. He could breathe again. He smiled down at the little boy who was looking at him in alarm.

'Don't worry, little man, I'm just a bit short of breath.'

Rosie too looked concerned.

'I'm okay,' he protested. 'I just overdid it at the pool.' He slumped on the sofa. 'Where's Gary?'

'Asleep.' Hugo was giggling. 'He always sleeps in. He says if I wake him up on Saturday morning he's going to cream my arse.' The boy plonked himself next to Richie. 'That means he's going to slap my bottom.'

Rosie was shaking her head. 'You know he doesn't mean it.'

Hugo ignored her. He was looking up adoringly at Richie.

'You want to play soccer in the park?'

'Yes.' Hugo screamed out his glee and began to run circles around the coffee table. 'Kick to kick, kick to kick,' he yelled.

Rosie crushed a ten-dollar bill into Richie's hand.

'He wants an ice cream,' she whispered. 'But only buy him one scoop.' The woman hugged Richie close to her. She smelt nice, of soap and sweet floral woman's smells. She smelt clean. 'And buy one for yourself.'

Richie nodded, not wanting her to drop her arm from around him. But she did. Soccer, kick to kick, an ice cream, a walk. That's all he wanted, to be a boy, to be a child again. He wished Rosie could hold him forever.

'I'll be finished by eleven.'

'It's okay. I like hanging out with Hugo.'

'He likes hanging out with you.'

'That's because he's a monkey.' He tussled the boy's hair. 'That's right, isn't it, buddy? You're a little monkey?'

'I'm not a monkey, I'm not, I'm not,' the boy objected, but the protests were cheerful. Richie waited with Rosie outside on the verandah while Hugo searched for his ball. The sun was naked in the sky, it was already a hot day. He would not think of Hector. Soccer, kick to kick, ice cream. He would not think of Hector at all. He could not allow himself to, because every time he did, humiliation ripped into him so deeply he felt he was being torn in two.

They played in the park for an hour, kicking the ball and occasionally alternating it with some rougher ball play when Hugo got bored. In the physicality of the play, in his alertness to Hugo's moods and sensitivity, Richie found that he could forget the morning, put it aside.

After playing, Richie took Hugo across the park and into Queens Parade for an ice cream. As they were eating, Hugo explaining about the *Lost Boys* and *Pinocchio*, Richie's mobile beeped. It was a text from Lenin asking if he wanted to walk into work with him. Hugo watched Richie text back. Reluctantly the older boy looked at the time on his phone's face. It was just on eleven. He had to get Hugo home.

Hugo shook his head violently at the suggestion. 'No. I want to stay.'

'Sorry, little man. I promised your mum I'd have you home.'

The boy scowled and drew swirls of ice cream with his finger on the tabletop. 'No,' he declared defiantly. 'I'm not going home.'

I don't want to go home either, little man, I want to stay here with you forever. 'How about if I give you a piggyback home?'

Hugo's face brightened. 'All the way?'

Richie hesitated. Hugo was now four. He was getting big. 'Until I fall down.'

The little boy was weighing it all up. 'Falling down' meant until Richie got tired.

Hugo pushed his ice cream aside. 'I finished,' he announced and got off his chair.

Richie knelt and Hugo jumped on his back. 'Shit,' Richie groaned, 'you are getting heavy.'

'You said the "S" word.'

'You're lucky I didn't say the "F" word.'

Hugo scrambled up higher on Richie's back, gripped his arms tight around the older boy's neck. He leaned into Richie's ear and whispered, 'Fuck.'

'Shh,' Richie laughed. He held the boy's hands. 'You ready?'

'Ready.'

Richie made a neighing sound and scampered off, Hugo's jubilant hollers in his ears.

It was at the traffic lights on Gold Street that Hugo spat at the old man. He was one of those elderly gentlemen who would soon become extinct. He looked like he'd stepped out of an old Australian movie, wearing a tie and an ironed white shirt, a jacket, even in the heat, and an old-style brimmed hat on his head. They were standing next to each other, waiting for the light to go green. The old man's back was straight, even though he looked ancient. The old man looked up at Hugo, and smiled.

'I'm bigger than you,' the boy called out.

The old man chuckled. 'I think you have an unfair advantage.'

Richie had laughed politely. It was then he noticed the look of abrupt shock on the man's face. Panicking, he wondered if the old guy was about to have a heart attack. He was ready to order Hugo to the ground when he saw the old man wipe away foam and spit that was sliding down his cheek. The shock had left him, there was only disappointment on his face now, and an unbearable, condemning resignation.

Hugo let out a peal of laughter. 'Got ya,' he taunted.

The old man made no reply.

Richie reached up and gripped the boy's arm. 'Hugo, apologise.'

He turned to the old man. 'I'm so sorry, sir.'

'No.' The boy on his shoulders was still laughing, still thought it a joke.

'Hugo, you apologise now.' He tightened his grip.

'No.' Hugo was trying to tug his arm away.

Richie would not let him; he was twisting his neck, trying to get a view of the boy. Both of them scowled at one another.

'Say you're sorry.'

'I don't have to.'

'Now!'

The boy was wriggling, and Richie let go of his arm and gripped his leg, fearful that he would fall. He saw Hugo's other foot kick out and strike the old man across the shoulder. Again, the old man just stood there. It was a weak kick and would not have hurt, but there was that same shock and puzzlement, the weary, resigned acceptance.

Richie felt judged. He grabbed Hugo's waist and pulled him off onto the ground. He held tight to the boy's hand. Hugo realised he had crossed some kind of line, and was beginning to sniffle, to protest. Richie pulled at Hugo's hand. He wished he could pull it right out of its fucking socket.

'Sir,' Richie said again his voice shaking. 'I'm so sorry.'

The lights had been green but had now turned red again. The old man, confused, dazed, looked down the street and suddenly stepped off the kerb and began crossing the road. Brakes screeched, and a horn sounded violently. Richie wrenched Hugo's hand and they began to cross as well. Richie ignored the outraged honking and yells. The boy was now in tears.

'It hurts,' he whimpered.

'I don't fucking care.' He yanked him forcibly across the road, quickly passing the old man. Hugo was trying to free himself and Richie quickened his pace. He was now dragging the boy along, who was screaming, his face going purple, 'It hurts, It hurts!'

Richie knew the whole world was watching him: the old man behind him, the shoppers on Queens Parade who had looked up at the boy's cries, the drivers and passengers in the cars. He did not care. He was worried that if he stopped moving that he would turn on Hugo and belt the boy into oblivion, bash the little monster's face in for what he had done to the old man. He was impervious to the boy's screams. They passed the pool, crossed North Terrace into the park, the boy stumbling, wailing, trying not to fall. In the shade of the park Richie let go of the boy's hand. He turned around to him, his anger still boiling, to yell at him, I want to kill you, you fucking arsehole. But his words froze. Hugo was stricken, his cries hysterical, his body shaking. The boy's face was scarlet, he looked as though he couldn't breathe. Fear and shame flooded through Richie's body. He knelt and put his arms around the boy.

Hugo clung to him, not letting him go. Richie held onto him, waited for the howls and shaking to subside. Soon Hugo's sobs were intermittent but he had not loosened his hold on the older boy. Richie gently pulled away and began to wipe at Hugo's face. He wished he had a tissue. He squeezed the boy's nose. 'Blow,' he ordered.

The boy obeyed. Richie wiped the snot off his hand onto the grass.

Hugo was looking up at him, still apprehensive. He was massaging his arm.

'Does it hurt?'

Hugo nodded firmly.

'Sorry, buddy. I was so angry at what you did. That was so wrong, you know it, don't you?'

Hugo kept massaging his arm, resentment gathering, then losing its potency, his head dropping in shame. 'Sorry, Richie.'

Richie took Hugo's hand. 'Let's take you home, buddy.'

As soon as Rosie opened the door, Hugo started to cry again. His mother immediately picked him up and kissed him again and again.

'What happened?'

Hugo was groping for her breast.

Richie shrugged, avoiding her, not wanting to see her release her breast.

Gary came to the door, wearing a singlet and his pyjama bottoms. 'What happened?' he demanded.

Hugo grabbed Rosie's nipple from his mouth, then released it. He pointed at Richie. 'He hurt me.'

Richie backed away, onto the verandah. 'I didn't do anything,' he protested, wanting to point at Hugo, needing them to know how unfair all this was. 'Hugo spat at an old man. I told him off. That's what happened.'

The two adults looked stunned. Rosie shook her head. 'I can't believe that.' She stroked Hugos' hair. 'Did the old man scare you?'

Richie's mouth dropped open. Hugo had not answered; his mouth was pulling at Rosie's tit.

Gary stepped out onto the porch. 'Hugo,' he shouted. 'Did you spit at an old man?'

The boy buried himself deeper into his mother's breasts.

'Hugo!' the scream startled all of them. 'What the fuck did you do?'

The boy started to wail and Gary went to grab him out of his wife's arms.

Rosie struggled, evaded him, and started running down the hall, her son still in her arms.

Gary shrugged, turned around to Richie. 'Come on, mate, come and have a beer.'

Gary opened two tinnies and handed one to Richie. Rosie had the kettle on to boil. She had also started singing to herself, as if the incident had not happened.

'Yoga was great,' she turned around and beamed at Richie. She came and sat beside him. Hugo, playing with a tiny toy truck on the other side of the table, suddenly smiled at Richie. His eyes were clear, almost teasing.

'Okay,' his mother sang out. 'Friends again. We're all friends again.'
Hugo rubbed at his arm. 'He hurt me.'

Rosie winked at Richie. 'I'm sure he's sorry. You're sorry aren't you, Richie?'

What about the old man? What about what Hugo did? Rosie's eyes were boring into Richie, forcing an apology out of him. Tears stung his eyes and he blinked them back, confused. Don't cry, you little bitch, he scolded himself, don't you dare cry.

'I'm sorry,' he gulped. He remembered Hector's derision and the old man's wrecked dignity and he closed his eyes as tight as he could as if by shutting out the image he could make it go away, make it not have happened.

It didn't work. The sobs came and he couldn't stop them. He was crying exactly like Hugo had been, crying like a baby.

'Drink your beer.' Richie wiped his eyes and cheeks. He did not dare look at either adult. He obeyed Gary but the alcohol tasted sour, curdled. He took a sip and put it down.

'We know you wouldn't do anything to deliberately hurt Hugo.' Richie finally looked up, grateful for the affection in Gary's voice. 'Just tell us what happened.'

I was mortified that your son spat at an old man, that's what happened. How does that happen? I hurt Hugo, I hurt a small kid, how the fuck does that happen? I am not a bad person. He wanted to close his eyes, he wanted to shut out the memory of that jeering, arrogant, hateful sneer.

'I saw Hector at the pool.' The words tumbled out, a rush of relief. They were out before he could stop them. Richie went cold, realising he was about to change things, enter into unfamiliar and dangerous territory. He nearly shivered. Gary and Hugo and Rosie seemed to diminish, as if he was suddenly looking at them from a long way away. He'd count to fifteen. He'd count to fifteen and hold his breath. Then he'd make a decision. He started to count. Rosie and Gary looked at him, baffled. Hugo was ignoring him, sitting on his mother's lap and scrawling over an old phone bill.

Gary looked at his wife and then back at the teenage boy. 'What the fuck has he got to do with any of this?'

Eight. Nine. Ten.

'Did Hector say something to Hugo?' Gary's voice rose in panic. 'Did Hector do something to Hugo?'

Thirteen, fourteen.

No. To me. *To me.*

Fifteen. The words rushed out. 'It's what he did to Connie. It's what the dirty bastard did to Connie.'

There. The words were said.

'What did Hector do to Connie?' Rosie was rising from the table, coming over to him, her face over his. 'What did he do to Connie?' she ordered. She was shaking him now.

'He did things to her. He made her do things to him.'

He was paralysed. The two adults exchanged glances. For just a moment, Gary looked elated, like a footballer who had just scored a goal. That moment dissolved into a frown.

'That fucking wog cunt,' Gary sneered at his wife. 'Your friends, your rich snob friends. He's a fucking paedophile.' He jumped up from his seat and stormed down the corridor.

The word slapped hard. Richie held his breath. Not that word. That was the ugliest word in the world. Rosie started to cry.

Hugo clambered back onto her lap. 'Mummy, Mummy what's wrong?'

'Nothing, baby, I'm alright.'

Hugo turned to Richie, calm, serious. 'I forgive you, Richie,' he announced solemnly, as if he had been rehearsing the words. 'It didn't hurt very much.'

Gary was in the doorway. 'Let's go.'

Rosie did not move. 'Rosie, we're going to confront that animal now.'

Richie could not bear to look at the woman, she seemed lost, appalled.

Gary tore Hugo off her. '*Now*. You're going to tell Aish all about it. You're going to tell that stuck-up bitch exactly what kind of man her husband is.' He turned to Richie. 'And you're coming with us. You're going to tell them exactly what you said to us.'

No. He couldn't face Hector. No way. He couldn't do it.

'She's at work.' He yelled it out, remembering that his mother had told him she was working with Aisha at the clinic this Saturday. He could face Aisha. He couldn't face Hector, there was no way.

'Fine,' growled Gary. 'Then we'll go to the clinic.' He was smiling, still holding his son. 'Wait till she hears, wait till she finds out the truth.' He put a hand on his wife's shoulder. She shook him off. 'Come on,' his voice softened. 'It should come from you.'

Rosie got to her feet. 'Okay,' she announced, her voice now hard. 'You're right. It should come from me.'

It all seemed to happen in slow motion but also in an instant. Was this what was meant by relativity, quantum physics, all those ideas and calculations that were so hard to get his head around? It all seemed to happen so deliberately, as if their movements were all rehearsed and preordained, that it would be impossible to stop any of it. Getting into their car, buckling Hugo into the child seat, fastening his own belt, driving down High Street, parking, walking into the clinic. The waiting room was full, smelt of dogs and air freshener. His mother was at the counter, she was looking up, surprised, then scared. She rushed to him.

'What are you all doing here?' Her voice rose. 'What's happened?'

'Where's Aish?'

His mother ignored Gary. 'Sweetheart, what's wrong?'

'Where the fuck is Aish?'

One of the clients looked up, distressed. A dog barked.

His mother swung around at Gary. 'This is a waiting room. Behave yourself.'

'We want to see Aish. Now.'

'She's busy. She's in a consult.'

'Fine.' Gary pushed past Tracey, walked through into the office. 'We'll wait.'

'You can't go in there.'

Gary's laugh was mean, jubilant. 'Trace, trust me, I'm fucking happy to say my piece out here in the waiting room but I doubt Aish would want me to.'

His mother and Gary faced each other like warriors in a video game. Slowly she nodded her head. 'I'll tell her you're here.' Her voice was shaking. Aish would be furious. Gary laughed harshly again and walked through, followed by Rosie, hand in hand with Hugo. Richie went to follow but his mother put a warning hand on him.

'What's this about?' she hissed.

He shrugged helplessly.

Thankfully the phone rang at that moment and his mother, hesitating momentarily, had to answer. He escaped into the office.

Hugo was playing with a small statuette of a white horse, one side of its body skinned to reveal the equine anatomy underneath. Rosie was sitting on the chair next to the computer. Gary was standing, arms locked, waiting. He looked as if he would explode from anticipation. The room was tiny, cluttered. Richie sat on the floor. The phone rang again and startled everyone. He could hear his mother answering it in the waiting room. They heard a door slide in the corridor, a dog yelp.

Aisha appeared at the door. She looked stunning. He knew she was older than his mother but she didn't look it. Her skin was clear, didn't have any of his mother's wrinkles and lines. She was wearing a white medical coat. His mother appeared beside her.

'Aish, I'm sorry, they forced—'

Aisha cut her off. 'Trace, please put the phones off the hook.' His mother nodded. 'And please apologise to the people waiting. Tell them it is an emergency and I'll be with them as soon as I can.' She walked into the room and closed the door. She did not take a seat. Gary was staring at her but Aisha ignored him. She nodded to Richie and his cheeks burned. He smiled weakly.

Aisha kissed Hugo on the cheek. 'How are you, Huges?'

'Good,' the boy replied, then quickly looked at his father.

Aisha turned to Rosie, still ignoring Gary. 'What's all this about?'

'It's about that animal you're married to.' The words were brutal, but suddenly, in front of the calm, serene Aisha, Gary no longer seemed threatening or confident.

He hates her, realised Richie, he really hates her.

'Gary,' Aisha laughed, finally acknowledging him. 'Don't be an idiot.'

'Of course.' Gary was trembling. 'Hector's shit doesn't stink, does it?'

Aisha put out her hand, interrupting him. 'This is my work, my business. Please keep your voice down.'

'Did you know that your husband was fucking Connie?'

The ugly words tumbled out. Richie wanted to be sick. His mother had just walked back into the room, had heard the words. Her mouth fell open.

Aisha shuddered; for one moment she seemed uncertain, to lose her composure, and reached out a hand to the back of a chair to steady herself.

She straightened and looked directly at Rosie. 'I don't believe that for a moment.'

Gary gestured to Richie. 'Tell her.'

Aisha swung around to him. He wished he could disappear. He looked down at the vile green carpet he was sitting on and wanted to drop through it. He could not bring himself to hold the woman's gaze.

'What do you have to tell me, Richard?'

He wished she had not used his real name. He knew what she was doing, she was making him an adult, making him responsible. He would not look up: he could not face Aisha's penetrating stare, his mother's confusion.

'Tell her.' Gary was insistent.

Shut up. Shut up.

They heard footsteps down the corridor, a dog barking again, the creak of the office door knob turning. His mother called out, petrified, 'Don't come in.' As soon as the words were uttered the door opened. Connie was standing there, her work uniform in one hand. At first puzzled, then alarmed, she looked at everyone in the room. Her eyes rested on Richie. He looked at her, open-mouthed, amazed. He had no idea of religion, had never learned a thing about it, but it was as if she was a messenger from the heavens. Connie would make it right, somehow she would make it all right. The girl bent down to Hugo, who leapt up to embrace her. Connie looking around at the adults, her face fearful, her eyes suspicious.

'What's wrong?'

Aisha's voice cut through the silence, firm, steady. 'Richie seems to think that Hector has done something to you, Connie?' Aisha's voice suddenly broke, she made a choking sound. 'That's he's done something terrible. Is it true?'

Richie held his breath. This was big, this was too big. He'd have to count to sixty, to ninety, hold his breath to ninety. This would be the only way to make it right. He'd count to ninety, he'd start now. One, two . . .

But he couldn't block out the world. Connie's voice sliced through.

'Aish, I swear, I swear, I don't know what he's talking about. I don't have a clue.' He'd never heard her sound like this, so scared, almost delirious. He could feel her shaking next to him. Her voice became a wail. She was screaming at him. 'What the fuck is this about, Richie? What did you say? What the fuck did you say?'

He could not speak. He could not breathe. Where was his ventolin? He began to search frantically through his pocket.

It was Gary who answered her. 'He implied that Hector molested you.' His voice was a whisper, ravaged. Richie pumped the ventolin into his lungs, his eyes firmly on the dirty carpet. He would not dare look up, could not dare face Connie.

'It's not true.' He could hear the sobs in his friend's voice. 'Aish, I promise it's not true.'

Aisha quickly came over to the girl, put her arm around her. 'I know, darling. I believe you.'

Connie's next words lacerated him. 'He's obsessed with Hector,' she spluttered. 'He's fucking sick. He's making it all up. He took your photo.' She must have turned to Rosie; Richie was concentrating on a half-submerged staple hidden in the carpet. His breath was coming back. 'Just look in your photo albums at home. He's stolen your photos of Hector. He's sick, he's sick, he's a real sick fuck,' she screamed again. She kicked him hard on his leg. He didn't call out, he did not cry.

'Why would you do this? What fucked game are you playing?'

He could hear Hugo beginning to cry.

'Rosie, please take Hugo home. He shouldn't have to listen to this.' Aisha's tone was hard, cruel. He heard another sob. Rosie? Connie?

His mother.

He could not look up, he dare not look up.

Rosie was trying to say something, the words could not come out, they were gibberish.

Aisha, for the first time, exploded. 'Just fucking go. Get out of my life.'

They went. They had left. He went to pick at the staple, remove it. It suddenly seemed crucial it not be there. Someone could step on it. Not someone, a dog.

'Get up.'

He shook his head. He would not get up, he would not listen to his mother.

'Rick, get up!'

He obeyed. Aisha was still hugging Connie. Neither of them could look at him. He would not look at his mother.

'Is this all true? You told all those lies because of some . . . some . . . some sick obsession with Hector?' He could not look at her. His mother's voice was scornful.

They must loathe me. All he could do was shrug. 'Yes,' he mumbled. Even to his ears it sounded weak, inadequate.

'I am so ashamed of you.'

He faced his mother. It felt like the first time. He thought she would be crying, but she wasn't. Her eyes were dry, furious. She raised her hand. He closed his eyes.

When the slap came it struck him like fire, made him stumble back onto the desk. It stung. But it was just. He heard Connie cry out.

It didn't really hurt, the actual violence was nothing. What hurt was his mother's words. They would never go away. She was ashamed of him. He deserved it. He fucking fucking deserved it. That's when he began to run, his feet air as he ran through the waiting room, past the startled animals and clients, out of the door, into the street, out into the world.

He ran and ran. He was in his street, he was at his house, he was through the door. He was in the bathroom, searching through the cabinet, jars smashing on the floor. He found a bottle of pills, did not bother to read the label, poured them all out in his hand. He took them all, gulped them down, flushed water from the tap into his mouth, down his throat. He sat on the edge of the cold bathtub and that's when he found he could stop. He stopped. He let it go, he was in the zone. He'd wait for death now that he was in the zone.

There were three things that made him not want to die:

The *dipt-dipt* of drops of water falling from the tap onto the porcelain of the wash basin;

The yellow ray of sunlight refracted into crimson and gold through the stubbled glass of the skylight above;

The thought that he did not want his mother to be alone without him.

Richie pulled his mobile from his pocket. He started to dial. 0—0—0. He heard the front door slam open.

'Mum,' he cried out. 'Mum.' His mother's footsteps thundered down their narrow corridor. She burst into the bathroom. He held out his arms, the empty jar in one hand, his mobile phone in the other.

She made him vomit, bent him over the tub, her fingers forced down his throat. He resisted, gagged, then chucked, thin bile running down his chin and his mother's fingers. His body convulsed and lumps of half-digested toast, pills, more bile flew onto the enamel, splattering across the bathtub. He was grateful for his mother's calm. Now that he knew that he did not want to die, he feared the poison he had taken. She drove fast, but she drove carefully, all the way to Epping Hospital, cursing every red light, cursing the politicians who had sold the old hospital he had been born into, the one that had been just around the corner from their house. She stroked his head from time to time, asking him to describe exactly how he was feeling, what he was experiencing, whether he had begun to feel any numbness or pain. What he did feel was an astonishing peace, an awareness of the complex structure of light and of sound. His mother weaved and overtook the traffic on Spring Street.

'Honey,' she said to him, as the car turned onto the long stretch of the highway. 'I am so sorry I slapped you. I will never do that again.'

'It's alright.' And it was.

'I've never hit you before, have I?'

'Just once or twice.'

'No.' She was sure, vehement. 'I smacked you a few times, when you were a young pup.' He nodded, he realised this was important to her. 'I smacked you once when you were about to put your hand into a candle flame. I remember once smacking your bottom when you were rude to your nan. But I never hit you. I never did that.'

It was true. It was important to her and that made it true. He grimaced. He could taste the foul residue of bile on his tongue. He placed his hand over his stomach.

'We're nearly there,' his mother counselled, her eyes straight ahead on the road. 'Nearly there.'

'I'm so sorry, Mum.' He was. He really was.

'Rich, I love you. I am so proud of who you are.' Her voice was cracking, her stained yellow fingers gripping the wheel, her pink nail polish chipped. She blew her nose. 'But what you did to Hector and what you did to Aisha and to Connie, that's fucked, mate.' She glanced over at him. 'You know that?'

'Yes.'

'Hector's a married man, baby. He loves Aisha. He can never love you.'

No. He released his hand from over his stomach. There was no pain, not yet. He'd be fine. He'd be alright.

'Hector doesn't even know who I am.' He closed his eyes, the wind was pushing hard against his face. Warm; no, hot. It was comforting. 'I think I'm in love with Nick.'

There. He'd said it.

His mother took his hand and squeezed tight. Her hand was wet, oily with sweat.

'Oh, baby,' she whispered, lifting his hand and kissing it. 'Oh, my sweet baby boy.' The car screeched into the entrance to emergency. 'You'll fall in love with other men and many men will fall in love with you.'

She dropped his hand and the car came to a sudden stop. She had illegally parked and a young nurse, smoking a cigarette, tried to wave them away. His mother ignored the woman.

The last thing he said to her before they pumped his stomach was, 'Mum, I wish you wouldn't smoke.'

He awoke to a too-bright white room. The light hurt; he had to close his eyes, and it seemed to take an eternity to open them again. He did, carefully, taking in the room, the world around him. He felt woozy, and dropped his head to the side. His mother was sitting on a chair, reading *New Idea*. Someone took hold of his hand. With effort he forced his head to turn to the other side. Connie was standing beside his bed.

'Hi.' His mouth was dry, tasting awful, of metal and chemicals, and could not seem to make the right movements to allow the sound to escape. The word, when it finally reached his ears, sounded like nonsense, one of the words those weird Christians made up when they were speaking in tongues. But it was a sound. His mother rushed to the bed.

It took a few minutes but he gradually broke through the punishing, sluggish after-effects of the anaesthetic. He gratefully slurped at the glass of water his mother offered him, not minding the liquid sliding down his lips and chin. He took in the room again, this time aware that across from him was an elderly man watching the TV screen above his bed, that there was another bed next to him but whoever was in it had chosen to draw the curtain. He asked his mother if he could be alone with Connie.

'I'll go grab myself a coffee. Do you want anything?'

Connie shook her head. He just wanted water. He doubted he would ever feel like eating again.

'Does it hurt?'

It must hurt, for there was a numbness that seemed to affect the whole of his abdomen, as if his body had been separated in two; like one of those old-fashioned cartoons, where those bumbling coyotes or cats had their torsos flattened to a sheet by a falling boulder or because they had been wrung through a mangle. He winced and nodded.

Connie pulled back the sheet, kicked off her runners and got in next to him in the bed. He realised that he was wearing a white smock, that he was naked underneath it. Connie pulled the sheet back. The old man across from them looked shocked, then, grinning, turned his head back to the TV. Richie's memory returned, a sudden flood. He thought of Hector and of Rosie and Gary, of Aisha and his mother, the nightmare in the office and he winced again, this hurting much more than any physical pain.

'I'm so sorry I said anything to Rosie. I shouldn't have.'

'He didn't rape me.' Connie was whispering, her chin nearly to her chest, contrite. 'That's not what happened.'

'Okay.' He rolled his tongue on his cracked bottom lip, wanting moisture. But his tongue too was dry.

'I'm sorry I lied.'

He struggled for recollection. Which lie was she referring to? The truth seemed indecipherable. Maybe one day she would tell him the truth but that was not what mattered. He shifted in his bed, a pain shot through his back. He wanted her to forgive him for betraying her to the adults.

'How's Aisha?'

'She's so cool.' Connie's voice was full of admiration. 'She's so fucking cool. She's not angry at you at all. She's furious at Gary and Rosie. Particularly Rosie.' Connie's tone hardened. 'And so am I.'

'It's not their fault.'

'Yes it is.' She was unforgiving. 'They didn't give a fuck about me, did they? If they did they would have come to me first. They just wanted to hurt Aish. They're fucked,' she spat out. 'Fucked.'

But what about Hugo? He didn't want Hugo to think that any of this had anything to do with him. That would be what Hugo would be thinking. Richie was sure of it. He was sure of it because Hugo was a lot like him.

'How's Hector?' He said it in a tiny, scared voice. *Does he hate me?*

Connie smiled at him, tickled him under his nipple where he was sensitive, raising a laugh.

'Your boyfriend?'

'Shut up.'

'He doesn't know.'

'Oh.' His body seemed to sink back into the bed, finally released, finally free.

'Aish isn't going to say a word to him. She doesn't think he needs to know.' Connie looked dazed, a little perplexed. 'You know, I don't think she would have believed it was true even if I wasn't there. I don't think it would have mattered what you said.' His friend's eyes widened, they looked enormous. 'She just loves him. She just knows he wouldn't do those awful things.' Her bottom lip quivered. 'And she trusts me. She wouldn't believe it of me.'

Lucky, lucky, Hector. Richie thought with sadness, and with relief. Some people walked away clean. That was a lesson he was learning. He was exhausted, confused. So what was the truth of what happened between Hector and Connie? Truth was this supposedly sacred thing, this thing that everyone—teachers, his mum, everyone—seemed to believe was important, that must be respected above all else. But the truth did not seem to matter here, not to Connie. Maybe not to anyone. Certainly, at this moment, not to himself.

'I'm tired,' he whispered. *Let's not talk, let's just lay here together.*

Connie wriggled and dug out something from her back jean pocket. It was a small envelope. She handed it to Richie, who opened it. A ticket to the Big Day Out slipped out.

'It's from me and Ali. It's an early birthday present.'

'Wow.'

'Wow,' mimicked Connie. 'Wow.'

'Get out of that bed!'

A fat, mean-looking nurse, her arms full of bedding, had popped her head through the door. Connie obediently jumped straight off the bed. The nurse shook her head and walked back down the corridor.

The two teenagers started giggling, which turned into laughter. Richie had to force himself to stop. It hurt too much to laugh.

He had to see the hospital psychologist before he could be discharged. The man, in his early forties with a thick Ned Kelly beard, had sparkling eyes that reminded Richie of Nate in *Six Feet Under*. The man was forthright. He wanted to know why Richie had wanted to kill himself. The boy struggled to find words. It all seemed too hard to explain. Maybe this was what Connie understood, that the truth did not always have words. What was important was that feeling that had been so potent straight after he had taken the pills. He had not wanted to die. That was important, maybe the only thing that mattered. The man was waiting expectantly. He was sincere, warm, a nice guy. Richie didn't want to disappoint him. He told him that he had wanted to die because he was having trouble coming to terms with his sexuality. It wasn't true but it was exactly the right thing to say. The man eagerly leaned forward and began to talk about the rich diversity of sexuality, how being gay was normal, that human culture was a broad church. Richie nodded, trying to look interested. He was a nice guy. He talked exactly like one of the good teachers. A little too earnestly. The man wrote down a few numbers for him, the emergency counselling number at the hospital, the number for the gay and lesbian switchboard. Richie pocketed the numbers, thanking the guy, and meaning it. He was only trying to help. But Richie was glad when the session was over. The psychologist signed a form and Richie joined his mother in the waiting room. He was free to go home.

* * *

On Tuesday afternoon they all got their results. His ENTER score was 75.3. He was not going to Melbourne Uni. He could probably get into Deakin, maybe RMIT, on second-round offers. Connie got 98.7. She'd get into Vet Science. Nick got 93.2. It was a brilliant score but not good enough for Medicine. Richie had rung his mum with the news, who had cried, said she was proud of him, and then he had walked around with his results to Nick. His friend's parents had both left their jobs to come home and celebrate with their son. Mr Cercic had poured his son and Richie a whisky, shouting out repeatedly that Nick was the first Cercic to get to university. But Nick was morose, disappointed with himself.

'I'll probably do Science at Melbourne,' he said glumly. Then he brightened. 'I'll work really hard, get a good score and apply to transfer into Medicine the year after.'

Nick looked across at him expectantly.

'Sure,' said Richie, 'of course you will.'

Nick's face fell again. 'I'll be in debt forever.'

Richie shrugged his shoulders. 'What do you care? The world's going to end before we have to pay it back.'

They got a little tipsy with Mr Cercic and then the boys took the train into town. They met Connie and Ali, Lenin and Jenna and Tina at the Irish pub. No one was asking for ID that afternoon, they all got in. Ali had got 57.8. That was enough for the mechanical engineering course he wanted to do at TAFE. Jenna wasn't sure what she was going to do. She and Tina had just scraped through, as had Lenin. That was all he wanted. For years he had wanted to be a cabinet-maker and had a promise of an apprenticeship from a Yugo who ran a small workshop in Reservoir. The man had demanded that Lenin get his VCE before he would take him on. Lenin seemed the happiest of them all. Richie was glad he had passed but he realised that everything was about to change. He and Nick would not be seeing each other every day. Jenna received an upset call from Tara who had failed. The others went quiet as they listened to the girl's despair on the phone. The girls decided to go and look after her, and Ali, Lenin, Nick and Richie got sodden drunk. In the taxi home, squeezed in between Lenin and Nick, he fell asleep for a moment, jerking awake at Lenin's laugh: he had fallen asleep on the boy's shoulder. Lenin had a musty locker-room stink, of underarms and football, acrid but arousing; the deodorant could not mask it. He raised himself groggily, and apologised.

'S'alright,' said Lenin, winking.

That night, as he tumbled fully clothed into bed, Richie fell asleep wanting to hold on to that smell, to not let it go.

On the morning of the Big Day Out he was so excited that he got out of bed before the alarm. He spent an hour deciding what to wear, putting on and taking off every single item of clothing he owned. He decided against a button-up shirt because all of his looked too daggy. But every single one of his T-shirts seemed wrong. Finally, he asked his mother for her old Pink Floyd top. It was ripped at the left shoulder, long-sleeved, a little tight around his chest—maybe the swimming was finally paying off—and the cartoonish logo of an elongated screaming man was faded to a ghostly impression; but he liked the look of it on him, and it was cool without being too cool. Richie protested when his mother entered the bathroom and pushed two twenty-dollar notes into his back pocket.

'Oh, go on,' she complained, backing away from him, 'just go and enjoy yourself.'

'Thanks.' He tousled his hair, wanting it to look nonchalantly unkempt but not to lose any of its sculptured form; he leered into the mirror, inspecting his teeth for any goobies or cereal caught between them.

His mother was watching him. 'You look good.' She sat on the rim of the bath. She kept opening and closing her mouth, as if she couldn't get words out. She cleared her throat and suddenly barked out, 'Are you going to take drugs?'

He looked at her reflection in the mirror. She looked small, a little afraid. Slowly, he nodded.

'What kind?'

'Weed, I guess.'

'What else?'

He shrugged. 'Stuff.'

'What stuff?'

'Speed. Maybe an E.'

'Oh, baby.' She began to reach out to him then abruptly withdrew her hand. 'I guess you're all grown up.'

He eyed her reflection warily. Was she pissed off with him?

She stood up and kissed him quickly on the cheek. 'Just be careful.' She stopped at the door. 'I heard on the radio there's going to be sniffer dogs. Better put your gear up your arse.'

Up his arse? Yuck. Disgusting.

He heard her chortling in the hallway. 'You'll be alright. They're not going to be busting anyone for one or two pills.'

Fine, fine, fine. Just shut up. Enough.

He took one last look in the mirror, flattened a mutinous, stubborn lock of hair that kept flopping over his left eye, and switched off the bathroom light. He was ready. He was ready for the day.

He glanced at his phone. He had an hour before he was due at Connie's. On impulse he took the tram into Clifton Hill. He wanted to see Hugo. He thought about the boy's parents and cringed at the wretched memory of the last time he'd seen them all. It was enough to make him turn back. But he didn't—he wanted to see Hugo. He decided against ringing the house first. Rosie and Gary might well choose to ignore the phone and he would feel pathetic leaving a message on the machine, knowing that they could be listening to him. He couldn't do it. He was shaking with nerves as he pushed past their gate. He walked up to the front porch. He took a breath and began counting to fifteen, just to fifteen, and then knocked. He heard Hugo running up the corridor.

The boy opened the door and stared up at Richie. His face broke out into an enormous grin.

'Richie,' he screamed. Hugo hugged tight around his legs, so tight that the older boy thought he would fall over. Richie steadied himself against the door and then picked up the excited child. He was still standing outside, on the porch. He ignored Hugo's animated babble and looked down the dark corridor. Rows of cardboard boxes were neatly stacked against one wall; and then Rosie appeared, in the kitchen doorway, half-shrouded in the darkness.

Richie swallowed, lowered the boy, and attempted a smile. 'Hey,' he mumbled, shit-scared.

The woman emerged into the light, started running, fell on him and wrapped her arms around him. She gripped hold of him so tightly, with such desperate force, that he thought she would squeeze the very life out of him.

They were leaving. A workmate of Gary's had started a job on a project at Hepburn Springs, the renovation of the spa complex, and had managed to score some work for Gary as well. They had rented a house in Daylesford for a year, Rosie explained, her excitable chatter so similar to Hugo's, and she was looking forward to leaving the city, to starting Hugo in a country school, to Gary doing more painting. As she was talking, Gary walked into the kitchen. He lit a cigarette, sat down, nodding at Richie but saying nothing. Hugo was sitting on the boy's lap, occasionally interrupting his mother's monologue. Richie listened but he had to struggle to concentrate on the meaning of Rosie's words. There was a buzzing in his head. He kept glancing up to the film poster on their kitchen wall. The man in the poster looked like a better-looking Gary and the woman like a less-beautiful Rosie. He was conscious of the unsmiling man sitting across from him. He couldn't meet Gary's eyes. He felt scrutinised, spotlit. He quickly gulped down his tea. 'I have to go.'

Rosie's face fell in disappointment, but quickly brightened. 'You'll have to come and stay.' Hugo was nodding wildly. 'You will, won't you?'

Richie peeked quickly over at Gary. The man's lean face seemed severe and unforgiving.

It was Hugo, however, who answered for him. 'You have to come. You have to.'

'Of course I will, buddy.'

Rosie kissed him goodbye. Hugo seemed to not want to let him go, holding fiercely onto his hand all the way to the front door. Gary, still silent, followed behind them. Richie was about to wave goodbye when the man gruffly spoke.

'You've got our numbers, haven't you, mate?'

Richie nodded. Gary extended his hand. There was, Richie was convinced, both forgiveness and apology in their handshake.

It was not exactly happiness that he felt as he walked to Connie's house. There was still sadness, still shame, and a humbling, keen emotion that Richie imagined might have been regret. He did not feel happy, exactly. But he did feel a lightness, was glad he had seen them.

It was one of the best days of his life. Ali had scored the speed from his brother, Musta, and for the first time in his life, Richie shot up drugs. Ali had the syringes prepared in his pockets and he took Connie and Richie into the bathroom. Connie's aunt Tasha was making them lunch in the kitchen. Richie panicked, wondered if he was going to die as Ali wiped his forearm with a swab of alcohol, ordered him to flex his muscle, tapped the thick blue vein rising on Richie's arm. Richie held his breath as the needle slipped under his skin and watched as a slithering scarlet thread of his blood entered the chamber. Then the drug flowed through the needle and into his vein. 'Let go,' Ali hissed, and Richie released his wet grip on the belt around his forearm. He was sweating, the world buzzed. Then, his hair seemed to be tingling, an electric current was flowing through his whole body, and he was thrust into a new world: light seemed to dance all around him, brighter than he had ever known, sound rushed through him, he could *feel* sound. His body was singing, his mind alert, his heart racing, his mood joyous, ecstatic. He watched as Ali carefully, lovingly, shot the magic into Connie's vein, and when he was finished the three of them looked at each other in stoned wonder. They broke out into such delirious laughter that Tasha knocked on the door. Ali quickly pocketed the syringes, the swabs. Still laughing, they fell around Tasha. She looked at each of them, shook her head resignedly and herded them into the kitchen.

This is what Richie remembers of that day: meeting up with Jenna and Lenin at the bus stop on Victoria Street, the boy wearing a black T-shirt with the Australian flag across his chest except that the Union Jack had been replaced by the Aboriginal flag, Jenna in a baby-doll dress and Goth make-up; Jenna dealing out the pills at the back of the bus, Richie watching the placid face of a veiled Ethiopian woman sitting in front of him as he slipped thirty dollars to Jenna in exchange for the ecstasy; the incessant laughter and talk talk talk on the bus; the crowds of youth walking to the gates of Princes Park, music thumping all around them, the sun bright and burning in the sky; a German Shepherd dog, held tight on its leash by a young blond stud of a cop, the dog's eyes seeming to follow Richie, making the boy panic, making him raise a sweat, until Richie saw that the dog had turned to look at other humans and that he was forgotten; handing his pass over to a young Indian-looking guy at the turnstile who had dyed his hair albino-white; wandering around the park, peeking into the Boiler Room, listening to music, watching the crowd; Connie holding his hand; rushing to see Lily Allen, he and Connie and Jenna shouting out the words to 'LDN'; Ali sneaking them vodka and cola in a Pepsi bottle, the five of them sitting in a circle, laughing, drinking, smoking; pushing through the thick crowd to get to the front of the Peaches gig, going demented at the end, all in one voice, everyone jumping in one body, chanting the chorus to *Fuck the pain away*; taking the pill straight after, swarming through to the bright daylight outside the tent, sucking on it like a lolly, scabbing a mouthful of water from Jenna's bottle to wash it down, sitting on the grass, listening to My Chemical Romance; Ali and Lenin and Connie in the cage, waiting to enter the mosh pit, he and Jenna sharing a cigarette; trying to get in to see The Killers but the cage is full, the light screaming red; he and Connie wandering to the edge of the crowd, lying on their backs on the lawn, holding hands, the first chords of 'When You Were Young' seeming to rip through into his body as he and Connie belt out the words; the first wave of the drug kicking in, starting to shiver, freezing, thinking he might be sick but then concentrating on the blue sky above, the music all around him but seeming to be coming from so far away, the cold and the fear deserting him and he suddenly submitting to the warm, lush seduction of the chemical; his arms around Lenin and Ali, the boys walking off to see The Streets, the girls going to Hot Chip, trying to walk normally, without stumbling, knowing that everyone could tell he was on drugs, grateful for Lenin's firm arm around him; standing at the entrance of the Boiler Room, listening to the band, the hard beats of the music entering his body through the soles of his feet, suddenly drunk on the beats, rushing to the front of the stage, Lenin right behind him, pushing past bodies, the crowd parting for them, everyone all smiles, no anger, no hate, all smiles, and then they were there, right in front, the music exploding around them, he and Lenin in a new world, dancing, jumping, thrashing; closing his eyes as The Streets break out into 'Blinded By the Lights', hearing Lenin's voice, distinct, clear, rising above the song, above the crowd, above the music, *Lights are blinding my eyes, people pushing by, they're walking off into the night*, and as the rap reached its climax the crowd, as one, dropping to its haunches, and then the tent is drenched in light, the beats break into a ferocious, frenzied crescendo and him leaping up into the air, weightless, beyond gravity, beyond his body, it is his soul dancing, at one with his body, *lights are blinding my eyes, people pushing by, they're walking off into the night*, and Lenin dancing there with him, their arms around each other, the boy has taken off his shirt and his pale chest, studded with thick black curls is wet, shiny, how had he never seen how sexy his friend was; Ali finding them and the three boys now a circle, their hands punching the air, going spastic to the music and when it finally stops they stand cheering, Richie thinking he will lose his voice, and then they are walking, shivering, back out into the park, Ali screaming in his ear, What did you think of that, and him screaming back, That was fucking amazing, Lenin laughing, uncontrollable, delighted laughing; night falling, watching the stars, seeing half of Tool, not enjoying it, the drug beginning its slow reversal; going with Connie into the mosh pit to see Muse, his arms outstretched, bringing the night into himself, the stars, the moon, the boys and the girls, the music and the band, all of it through him and with him and about him; dancing to the close of the night, dancing to anything, not caring, just wanting the movement to never stop, dancing with Connie, their eyes never leaving each other, feeling her body next to his, leaning over to kiss her, her kissing him back, then apart again, dancing, Ali there, Lenin there, Jenna, but what is most important is that kiss, a kiss that feels like an apology and also like forgiveness; and then the night is over.

It is one of the best days of his life.

They ended up back at Ali's house, sore from the dancing and the long walk to Royal Park station. His parents had a bungalow at the back, where Ali lived. It had its own kitchenette and shower. Mrs Faisal was up, waiting for them. She had prepared them a meal of roasted vegetables, a whole chicken floating in a rich almond sauce, a spicy potato salad. Richie had not thought of food all night, but as soon as he sat at the table he began to attack the food voraciously. Mrs Faisal watched him eat, laughed, and said something in Arabic to her son.

'Mum says you should come over more often. She'll fatten you up.'

'Sure,' Richie beamed. 'Any time.' He grabbed the last drumstick, and then, realising his rudeness guiltily put it back. Mrs Faisal placed it back on his plate. 'Eat, eat,' she commanded.

'*Shokrun*,' he mumbled and attacked the meat.

At the end of the meal Mrs Faisal kissed them all goodnight, waved them out to the bungalow and got them to promise that they would keep the noise down. Richie sat on the bungalow step. He wanted to ring Nick. Nick should have been there.

'How was it?'

'Fantastic.'

'Who was the best?'

'The Streets.'

'Yeah?'

'Yeah.'

Richie touched the sharp needle of a cactus. 'We're in Coburg, at Ali's. You want to come over?'

'Nah, mate. I'm off to bed.'

'Sweet.'

'I'll catch up with you this week.'

'Sure.'

Richie stayed sitting on the cold concrete of the step, looking out over the Faisals' garden. There were tomato plants struggling to survive the drought, zucchini flowers running across the vegetable patch. He heard the door open, smelt the marijuana. Lenin sat beside him and offered him the joint. Richie was conscious of the boy's salty, sweaty tang. Lenin's leg was twitching, pressed hard against Richie's, the space tight, constricted on the small step. Richie did not move. Warmth spread from his stomach, seemed to descend into his crotch. He moved his leg away from Lenin.

'It was fucking awesome, wasn't it?'

'Yeah,' Richie's mouth was dry.

Richie turned to look at his friend. Lenin was staring straight ahead, sucking on the joint. Richie wanted a drink. He was about to take the joint when, there, in the dark, Lenin kissed him. It was quick, it lasted a moment, a fleeting touch of lips, but for Richie it tasted of all the longing and fear and desire he was feeling. Richie took the joint. The boys moved away from each other, embarrassed.

'I'm not working Tuesday,' Lenin mumbled, his voice a little shaky. 'How about you?'

'No.' He was going to count to ten, hold his breath. The muted stars in the suburban night sky seemed to tease him, the faint hum of the traffic on the Hume Highway was the only sound in the world. They were both holding their breaths.

'Do you want to come around? Hang out, watch a DVD?' Lenin's voice nearly broke. 'Only if you want to.'

'Sure.' Richie's voice did squeak.

A shadow fell over them. Ali was standing in the doorway, his arms crossed. 'You going to share that joint?'

They went inside.

Jenna had put on Snow Patrol. The five of them were on Ali's bed. Connie and Richie were next to each other, she curled up against him as he stroked her hair. Jenna, next to Connie, had her eyes closed and was singing along to 'Chasing Cars' which she was playing for the third time. Lenin and Ali were talking at the end of the bed.

'She's thinking of Jordan.' Connie's whisper was low, almost inaudible.

Richie listened to the girl singing. Jenna had a good voice.

'I think I've got a date,' he whispered back.

'Who with?'

'Shh.' He nodded towards Lenin. He and Ali were still involved in their animated, stoned conversation.

Connie curled up closer to her friend. 'He's nice.'

'Yeah, he is.'

Jenna's voice sang out, broken, sad, pretty.

They watched dawn spread slowly over Coburg. They had taken a blanket from Ali's bed and spread it on the lawn. Soon after day arrived Mrs Faisal woke up. She shook her head in disapproval to find them all awake. She made them coffee and tea, cooked them breakfast, and ordered each of them to ring their parents so that they knew they were all safe. After his shower, Mr Faisal drove them all home before he headed off to work.

Richie's mother had left him a note. It was simple, two lines: I hope you had a great night. I love you. He kicked off his runners and jumped into bed. He couldn't even be bothered taking off his clothes, brushing his teeth; his limbs weren't capable of anything, he just wanted to sink into unconsciousness. He wondered if he would, if the drugs were not still wickedly working their magic inside him.

As he closed his eyes he ran through the only certainties in his life. There really were only two that mattered. Two. That was an alright number. That his mother was the best mum in the world, and that he and Connie would be friends forever.

Soon, unexpectedly, like the future that had begun to creep up on him, sleep did come.

ACKNOWLEDGEMENTS

Thank you to Jessica Migotto, Jeana Vithoulkas, Spiro Economopoulos and Angela Savage for first pushing me in the right direction.

Thank you to Shane Laing, Alan 'Sol' Sultan and Victoria Triantafyllou for the feedback on earlier drafts.

Thanks to all my colleagues at the veterinary clinic for being so flexible and understanding.

Thanks to Fiona Inglis, Michael Lynch and Sol (again) for keeping me solvent.

And to Jane Palfreyman and Wayne van der Stelt, your faith, encouragment and honesty is so very greatly appreciated. *Havla. Bedanki. Euharisto.*